"My responsibilities are primarily in research, gentlemen. I have to justify the theories of my associates. In this case, the initial clue was so obvious they didn't need me. No American has ever been invited to Vladivostok since President Ford ten years ago. As a matter of fact, since then we aren't sure when the last one was there. He probably went unwillingly. It's headquarters for their Pacific Fleet and has been off limits to just about everyone but Russians themselves. So, when any American is invited there, not to mention the U.S. Seventh Fleet this coming New Year, the Russians have to have something up their sleeve."

Charter Books by Charles D. Taylor

FIRST SALVO
SHOW OF FORCE
THE SUNSET PATRIOTS

THE SUNSET PATRIOTS

CHARLES D. TAYLOR

CHARTER BOOKS, NEW YORK

THE SUNSET PATRIOTS

A Charter Book / published by arrangement with
the author

PRINTING HISTORY
Charter Original / June 1982
Second printing / May 1983
Third printing / February 1985

ISBN: 0-441-79116-6

Charter Books are published by The Berkley Publishing Group,
200 Madison Avenue, New York, New York 10016.
PRINTED IN THE UNITED STATES OF AMERICA

This book is dedicated with love to my wife,

Georgeanne

ACKNOWLEDGEMENTS

Much more than an author is necessary to complete a book.

This one would have been difficult without Candy Bergquist's typewriter and patience, technical assistance from Commander Stephen H. Crane, U.S. Navy, personal glimpses of China from Emile Coulon and Arch and Jeannie McGill, Russian translation and insights from Peggy Coleman, and assistance in opening the closed port of Vladivostok from Lynn H. Loomis, the Map Room of Widener Library at Harvard University, and Captain W. M. McDonald, USN (ret.).

I am bothered by books that take place in faraway places with exotic names, yet fail to show me visually where the author is taking me. Alice W. I. Loomis was kind enough to prepare the map in the front of this book—even pinpointing Petaiho, which only the Chinese know of.

Equally appreciated is the willingness of friends who allowed me to borrow their names: Bob Miller became a character in this one from his help with my first book; twenty years ago, as young naval officers, Ted Magnuson and I exchanged tales of the Atlantic and Pacific and today he is the author of one of my favorite adventure novels, A SMALL GUST OF WIND; and Tom Loomis, the last of the true tilters at windmills, is a much softer and more loving person than the character in this book.

Every word of TRIPLE MURDER that appears in chapter twelve was written by Jack Darby after his release from a Japanese prisoner of war camp in Burma—"taking a shot" at becoming a writer as he put it to me. He never achieved that goal but it was one of the few he missed. As a real life adventurer and world traveler until his last days, he fancied being a character in this book. Jack died on September 14, 1981 in Auckland, New Zealand, before he could ever see himself in print. He was a fine and good friend and I think he would have liked the fictional rogue, Jack Darby.

The PROCEEDINGS of the United States Naval Institute continue to be an invaluable source for all my work.

And, it meant a great deal to me that Dan Mundy and Dominick Abel had no qualms about casting a critical eye my way.

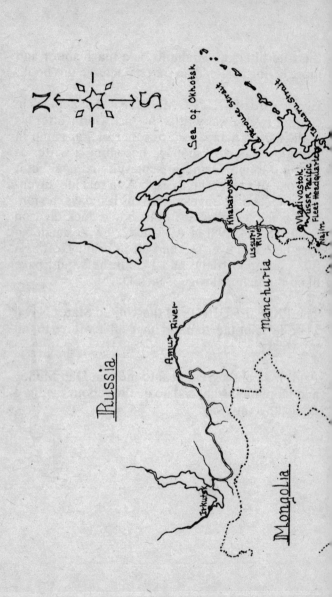

"We should lure the enemy to penetrate deeply into our territory . . . For victory, we must not hesitate to surrender some parts of territory . . . all this so the Red Army can hold the initiative . . . "

"It is possible to live on nothing but a furious hope."

"Power grows out of the barrel of a gun."

Chairman Mao, 1893–1976

"Freedom costs, and it costs more than money. I paid four years of my life . . . and I never had a better bargain."

Herman Wouk

DECEMBER 1984

PROLOGUE

At first, it appeared as a fleeting shadow on the ocean surface, perhaps a cloud. The Chinese pilot, his anti-submarine patrol plane in a gentle descent, circled lazily over the newly constructed oil platforms, the pride of the People's Republic of China (PRC). On the second pass, the cloud assumed a shape, cigar-like. Cloud shadows were larger. Then he realized there were no clouds in that perfect, brilliant sky. Something ruffled the placid surface.

At almost the same instant, his radar operator reported a contact . . . one sweep . . . two sweeps . . . a solid contact right on the pilot's visual bearing, possible snorkel . . . too small for a surface craft.

Contact lost! The pilot saw the shadow, now close off his port wing, disappearing, growing fainter. But there was no doubt about his contact. Submarine! Enemy submarine! No Chinese boats were reported in this area of the South China Sea.

A frantic call to Zhanjiang, South Sea Fleet Headquarters of the People's Liberation Army (PLA) brought an immediate response. A torpedo boat, already nearby, rose gracefully onto its hydrofoils and was vectored to the area. Perhaps intelligence had been correct. Soviet subs had finally penetrated a secure sector. They must be sunk!

The little boat, flitting on top of the calm sea at over fifty knots, occasionally dipped a bit to port or starboard. The crew, at battle stations, held on tightly with one hand, the other shielding their eyes from the sun's radiance, the brilliance merging the horizon of sea and sky.

The oil platforms shimmered ahead like islands, their decks in contact with the surface. Then their legs began to show. In moments, they grew out of the sea like trees.

The captain, dropping her binoculars for just a second to use the radio, tapped the helmsman on the shoulder, pointing just to the left of the bow. The wheel turned ever so slightly. The boat changed course almost unnoticeably, heeling slightly to port.

A sailor next to the captain shouted, pointing almost directly ahead of the bow at a plane lumbering slowly over the water only a few hundred feet in the air. Smoke floats appeared, marking the placement of the sonobuoys in the water. They were spread in a large, uneven circle miles in diameter. Somewhere inside that circle was the invading submarine.

The captain, her expression resolute, reached for

the control lever, pushing it forward slowly, allowing the boat to gently decrease its speed. Retracting its hydrofoils, the hull settled gradually into its natural habitat, bow dipping slightly to the waves. It heeled a bit now as she steered for the center of the circle.

The plane swept out to the flank of the string of sonobuoys, banked sharply, then came in low over the water. The boat captain heard the pilot clearly over the radio. The sonobuoys had the contact located exactly, the magnetic detector on the plane's tail confirming there was a submarine desperately trying to escape. They knew it had to be a conventional boat with diesel engines. A nuclear sub would already have departed the area at high speed.

The plane banked to the outside of the circle, then swept back in again. This time, the boat crew saw an object tumble from the aircraft, immediately followed by another, then a third. Water rose into the air from the depth charges.

The plane turned toward the outside of the circle, running parallel to the invisible line of explosives it had dropped. The boat moved slowly toward the spot the plane had attacked as calm temporarily returned to the surface. The crew knew that a submarine was frantically maneuvering underneath, seeking a new course and speed and depth even before the splash of the depth charges announced the attack.

Then came a deep rumbling from the ocean. The surface lifted perceptibly for a moment, foaming white, then erupted into an immense geyser lifting tons of water hundreds of feet into the sky.

A second followed, then a third, the last bursting forth even as the first began settling. The aircraft turned down the same line again, coming in lower than before, dropping three more depth charges in a position ahead of his first run, anticipating a new location for the undersea craft if the first three charges had not made contact. Again, the placid ocean was warped by mammoth eruptions.

The boat, on command from the pilot, picked up speed slightly, turning toward the roiling waters. This time, the pilot did not make an attack run, instead coming in low to determine the effect of the depth charges.

The boat captain listened carefully to her radio. There was oil on the surface. One of the depth charges must have been close. But there was none of the flotsam that normally surfaced from a sub breaking up. The pilot reported a shadow, vague at first. Then he could identify the long, narrow craft struggling toward the surface. It had to be seriously wounded, its crew terror stricken, desperate to escape a watery grave.

Suddenly, there it was, popping from the water like a cork, out of control. The plane could not complete the job of finishing off the sub as well as the patrol boat could. The pilot ordered the small craft to attack.

Torpedoes were set for just ten feet of depth. The attack was simple. The submarine didn't appear to be moving. From five hundred yards the first fish was fired, and then a second, both at point blank range. The run was short, much less than a minute. The first torpedo hit forward of the sub's sail as some of its crew were tumbling out of the hatch in the conning tower. The explosion lifted the sub's bow into the air, the bullnose completely out of the water for just a second. Then the blast rolled over the craft, shaking men from its sides, enveloping the boat with cascading water. The sound of the explosion followed, cracking across the water, blotting out all sound on the patrol boat.

The second torpedo somehow missed, but it wasn't needed. The sub was already settling bow-first into the ocean, its stern lifting slowly, almost gracefully like a diver. More men scrambled out of a hatch in the after section. The captain gave an order and her boat moved closer to the sinking craft, her machine guns already chattering. No survivors were desired. No pity was felt for the invading sub or its crew. Anger replaced the logic of returning with a prisoner.

A small raft was inflated. The sub's remaining sailors frantically tried to launch it from the side opposite the patrol boat. The captain swung around the sub's stern, now high out of the water, allowing her machine gunners to rake that side. The remaining survivors, desperately scrambling for any safety, were hit again and again, the heavy bullets smashing them into the deck, tossing them in bits and pieces into the water.

Then there was quiet. No human beings were moving. The boat slowed down and the captain and her crew watched the sub slide, slowly at first, then more rapidly as the angle increased, toward the bottom of the South China Sea, the ocean it had no right to have been found in.

The pilot and the captain spoke again briefly on their radios. The plane waggled its wings in salute, then headed just slightly south of west, back to the Zhanjiang headquarters base.

Captain Li Han went from sailor to sailor, saluting each of her crew in turn. This was the first Soviet vessel sunk in Chinese territorial waters, and they had faithfully performed for the People's Liberation Army and the People's Republic of China. This should be a lesson to the Soviet forces increasingly in evidence in the seas surrounding their peaceable country—when the Russians learned that one of their subs was missing.

But, the attack and probable loss of that sub was already known. When the sub floundered to the surface, it managed to radio position and the desperate situation, not knowing if it could hold out. Immediately, the Russian carrier lurking to the south of the island of Hainan launched jet fighters.

The hydrofoils lifted the victorious patrol boat free of the ocean's surface, the engines roaring at full power to carry the heroes back to base, to the welcome they had earned. The sun, now past its zenith, was in her eyes as the captain headed her boat west toward their base. The fifty knot speed would have them home by mid-afternoon.

Li Han was startled by the hand tapping her helmet. Turning, lifting her binoculars in the same motion, it took no time to locate the jet fighters coming in directly astern. They were already in the last stages of their approach, the lead plane close to the surface, the other slightly higher.

Frantically, Captain Li Han grabbed the wheel, yanking it hard to the left, the boat instantly heeling to port to avoid the closing aircraft. But the boat's little weapons were no match for the large rapid-fire guns of the jet, and the boat was bouncing too much to shoot accurately.

The lead jet had no such problem. The pilot saw the splash of his shells, adjusted his stick minutely, and watched the track in the water follow the wake of the boat. The splashes reached the craft. Wood and metal flew as he raked one side of the boat, tearing apart the starboard gun crew as he passed over.

Instantly, the second jet was on them, following the wake of the patrol craft as the captain frantically swung her rudder to starboard for a few seconds, then back to port. Her plan worked, briefly. The high speed jet was approaching too fast and only a small number of shells hit the boat. But those bullets found their mark, hitting the sailor next to Li Han, spinning him off his feet, then over the side. The captain momentarily lost control as the panel disintegrated in front of her, miraculously leaving the steering gear intact.

Now the third plane was upon them, this time firing rockets that clawed jagged chunks out of the deck before destroying the port gun and its crew. There was no longer any method of defense, no matter how meaningless. The captain threw her wheel over again as deadly shards of metal flew in every direction, cutting down her crew. A series of shells from a fourth jet ripped the bow completely off.

A diesel engine coughed and stopped. A second sputtered, then caught on again, only to race out of control as its shaft broke. One engine continued, but it couldn't push the craft through the water at anywhere near the speed the boat needed to remain on its hydrofoils. The slowing of the boat was gradual at first, as was the settling effect. The captain could no longer swing her rudder. The remnants of her crew huddled on the shattered deck of the boat, the terror of impending death reflected in their eyes.

The first Russian plane completed its circle and was making a second run on the patrol boat, machine guns blazing, bullets ripping into boat and bodies with equal ease. The captain's voice ripped from her chest in a loud scream of rage and hatred. She knew in her heart that the aircraft would show no more mercy than she had to the submarine. Without feeling initial pain, she was thrown to the deck by the impact of a heavy caliber bullet tearing into her shoulder. The roar of a jet engine competed with the sound of her command breaking apart as she became aware of her own blood spurting across the deck.

The boat was settling, canting to port as water surged into the hull where the bow once existed.

Captain Li Han rose slowly to her feet, lifting her body with her good arm, the other hanging by shiny tissue from the remainder of her shoulder. There was no movement on deck. She gazed blankly at the torn bodies amidst the wreckage of her proud little boat.

As another jet swooped down, she attempted to turn the rudder, anything to evade the incessant tearing sounds, the exploding of the rockets around her. Something struck her right hip. She lost her footing for a moment then recovered, noting calmly that there was still no pain. Yet the blood on the controls was her own. With her left hand she turned the wheel, but there was no response. Her boat was dead in the water, the cant to port increasingly rapidly.

She was slipping in her own blood, unable to stay on her feet. Another thump on her side spun her around, knocking her torn body into the jagged remains of a torpedo tube. Looking up, she could see the jet bearing down, tracer bullets spurting from its wing guns, ripping into her boat, her command, the first PLA boat to sink an enemy submarine!

Her last thoughts were of the happiest days of her life and of the handsome American who had loved her. Once again, she saw the moon over the beach at Petaiho, the shimmering sea. "I love you, Ben," she whispered.

Through the haze of blood in her eyes, she was aware of the line of bullets bursting up the deck toward her.

Intelligence was correct. They had said it could start at any time. The Soviet pincer was closing.

AUGUST 1984

CHAPTER ONE

Vladivostok is situated at the end of the Muraiev Peninsula on a deep, well protected harbor called Golden Horn Bay. While it is not a beautiful city, the Russians consider it one of the more attractive ones in Siberia. When the Soviets occupied Manchuria, it was the terminus for the Trans-Siberian Railway. At that time they were more concerned about foreigners' opinions of the city. As it is the headquarters for the Soviet Pacific Fleet, it has been a closed city for many years. The last time a capitalist had been invited there was in late 1974, when it was the site for a summit conference between President Ford and Party Secretary Brezhnev.

To Admiral V. P. Maslov, Vladivostok was a comfortable, if not perfect, place to live. He had been Commander of the Pacific Ocean Fleet since the American President's visit in 1974, and he took a great deal of pride in the way both the city and his command had grown since then. Maslov, himself, had not changed. He remained short, stocky, and bald and his eyes were the same color as his bushy, black eyebrows. On the top floor of the building serving as Fleet Headquarters, Admiral Maslov's office looked over the expanse of the naval base, toward units of his mighty fleet currently in the harbor, and out to the Sea of Japan. While Vladivostok was the southernmost Soviet port in eastern Russia, and kept open to the sea much of the year, it was not open to the Pacific Ocean. Across the water, about five hundred miles distant, was Japan. Access to the open ocean was through three straits which could easily be closed: Tsushima to the south, Tsugaru to the north of the main Japanese island, and La Pérouse between the northernmost Japanese island of Hokkaido and the Soviet island of Sakhalin.

It was a warm, lovely August day and Maslov knew it should be taken advantage of, for the cold Siberian winds would begin to blow within three months. He had therefore taken his guest, Colonel Bespalov, on a tour of the base. Because of the weather, he insisted on walking, that he might show his guest that Vladivostok was not nearly as bad as some of his peers in Moscow and Leningrad claimed. Bespalov was Commandant of the Vol'sk Higher Military School of the Rear Services, a fancy title for a supply school as far as the Admiral was concerned, even if it was the most elite in the Soviet Union. The Colonel had been impressed with the town and said so. He had spent most of his life in the interior and had never been aboard a ship in his life. Maslov made sure that the tour included a guided missile cruiser, a new destroyer, the only submarine in port, and a ride on a small Nanuchka guided-missile boat to the outer reaches of the harbor.

Now, they were back in Admiral Maslov's office. The view from his huge bay window, the only large one in the building, was impressive. It had been installed at his request in 1976 and he now stood before it pointing out the ships they had been aboard earlier.

"If every ship to be assigned to the Pacific Fleet over the next few months were in this port right now, Colonel, there would be over one hundred and fifty of them. You could walk across the harbor without getting your feet wet. And, wherever you might see some open water between them, we could provide a small coastal boat, like the one we rode on today. Luckily, that will never be the case, because even you and your whole school would not solve those logistics problems."

"I'm sure you're quite right, Admiral. I'd hate to even consider that possibility." He turned to the Admiral and continued, "How many are in port right now?"

"Only about twenty-five large ships, I'd say. One of my aides could give you an exact figure if you find it necessary."

"No, no, not at all. I'm just trying to get an idea in my own mind of the magnitude of this command, Admiral. Back in Moscow, Vladivostok seems so far away. We tend to forget the size of your fleet here."

"When we were a small navy, Colonel, even 20

years ago, this was considered the *tiny* Asiatic Fleet, just a coastal defense force. Today, this is the Pacific Fleet," he said with emphasis. "And I think we can match the greatness of any ocean going force that ever existed in the world. Including command of the ships in the Indian Ocean, this is now our country's largest fleet by a good number."

"Please don't misunderstand me, Admiral Maslov. I am aware of the numbers. It's just the individual and combined demands of these ships themselves. I have seen them every day on sheets of paper back in Moscow. We plan so much food, so much fuel, so many spare parts. But when you see it for yourself, like that cruiser we were aboard today, the sheer size and power amaze me. I am what I think you call a paper shuffler. I think in numbers. I solve my problems with computers. But I don't equate those numbers on paper with what really exists. This visit will create better understanding of your problems over the next four or five months."

Maslov nodded with satisfaction. That was exactly what he had hoped would happen with Bespalov. During the earlier meetings that spring with his staff, his supply people had impressed upon him the importance of rear services for an operation of the magnitude they were undertaking. The understanding of the Commandant of the Rear Services School was of the utmost importance if they were to provide logistics for their naval units in the many new locations their ships had never been before.

"I'm sorry I couldn't have taken you to

Petropavlovsk," said the Admiral sincerely, referring to the sub base farther north opening directly
on the Pacific across from the American Aleutian
Islands. "There are more than eighty submarines
that call that little city home. Half of them are nuclear and it is an impressive sight to see so many tied
up together when they are home. Their equipment
and needs are so different from the ships you see
out there, that it would have been worth your time
just to have spent some time aboard one." He
smiled proudly. "Perhaps on one of those that will
be taking a Delta assignment off the U.S. But there
will be many more visits in the next few months.
Perhaps the next time you are back here, we can
journey north."

Their conversation was interrupted by a knock
at the door. "Come," called Maslov.

A Captain First Rank, one of his staff members,
stuck his head through the door. "The staff is as-
sembled, Admiral. You may begin at your conven-
ience."

"Five minutes." Maslov turned to Bespalov.
"You should find this meeting fascinating also,
Colonel. You are concerned with coordinating our
logistics. Now you are going to have the opportunity to hear the concerns of the commanders
who must ensure that all their units arrive in their
assigned areas battle ready and at the right time.
The sub captains' assignments are so different from
their surface counterparts, yet they must depend on
each other so much in a two-pronged operation.
They will accomplish what I ask, but watch the
jockeying for what they feel are the choice assign-

ments. It may appear confusing at first, but mark my words, it is the best method of developing morale I know of." He poked his chest with a stubby thumb. "I already know where each unit should be. Some of them may offer me a better idea, and I will agree to it. But, by the time we are finished, each one will think he has accomplished his own objectives, even though one force remains on this side of the Pacific and the other will lie off the coast of the United States."

The two men passed through the outer office, down a long corridor to a flight of stairs ending at a solid wall, rather than a floor similar to the one they had just left. Maslov pressed a button causing a door to slide into the wall. They entered a large room, obviously built into the core of the building for security purposes. The area on their right was divided into sectioned-off cubicles, each containing electronic equipment. An intelligence area, Bespalov decided. At the far end, to their left, was a long table. The walls on three sides were covered with a variety of charts of the western Pacific and the Asian continent. Seated at the table were a number of senior naval officers, none below Captain First Rank.

Maslov neither smiled nor uttered a word, but simply nodded them back to their seats after he had taken his own. He gestured to Bespalov to take the vacant seat to his left. "Gentlemen, this is Colonel Bespalov, Rear Services. He is the Commandant of the Vol'sk School and assigned to this operation to coordinate logistics. Senior officers in his school will be assisting him with the most advanced logistical software programs possible. To anticipate any of your questions, my decision has been to limit outside involvement in the planning stages. Mouths would become too loose and heavier security than usual would simply create unwanted curiosity. You may fully anticipate that final logistical operations will be in the hands of those directly involved by late fall, at which time the tightest security will be in effect." He had been looking each of his officers in the eye as he spoke, to prepare them for his final words. He nodded toward Krulev, who sat on his right. "Any questions, problems, or requirements for rear services must go via my office or Rear Admiral Krulev's. You have my apologies and I ask your understanding that I want no other fleet or unit command to deal directly with rear services at this stage."

Rear Admiral Krulev was Chief of Political Administration for the Pacific Fleet, the youngest political officer to reach that high position in the history of the Fleet. He had accomplished his goals through a personal, inherent drive and pure dedication to the Party. He coupled this with a remarkable knowledge of the blue water Navy and its methods from his years as political officer on increasingly larger ships. Tactics and strategy were as important in his education as ensuring devotion of his sailors to the Party's goals. Admiral Maslóv was also depending on Krulev for maintenance of security during the initial planning phases. Other staff officers combined respect for Krulev's abilities with fear of his relationships with senior operatives of the KGB and the feared GRU, the intelligence arm of the Soviet military. There was also an aura of toughness about Krulev. Though he was tall and blond and looked very young, his cold, blue eyes over high cheekbones matched his military authority.

Maslov's announcement had been received in silence, a few solicitously nodding their heads in agreement. The Admiral continued, "I have invited the Colonel to attend this particular session that he might have a better understanding of what you will expect from his command over the next few months. I have spent the better part of today with him explaining the Pacific Fleet, our current and increasing operational levels of ships and men, and the basis of our plan." Maslov paused to look at his watch. "As soon as Captain Batov presents a visual review of the scope of the Chinese segment of the operation, Admiral Krulev and I will leave you gentlemen to discuss your individual responsibilities with Colonel Bespalov. As you gather, it's an opportunity to sell yourselves to the Colonel." Maslov smiled, again passing his eyes over each man at the table. As before, there were no questions though he had halted his talk, as was his habit, to allow any.

The Admiral nodded at Batov. "Please," he said, waving his hand toward a chart covering half of the wall behind him.

Captain Batov, staff officer for planning, rose from his chair, wiping his rimless glasses nervously as he did so. He walked to the large chart, overlayed by a clear plastic sheet. He uncapped a grease pencil, then recapped it again as he realized he was not yet ready to utilize it.

Batov began, "This is the first visit to this room for some of you, in addition to Colonel Bespalov, to actually view the strategy of this operation." He put his left index finger on the location of the Pacific Fleet Headquarters. "From Vladivostok to the northern tip of the island of Tsushima," and he bent down to touch Tsushima, just off the South Korean city of Pusan, "is just about five hundred and ninety miles. At twenty-five knots, that's a bit under twenty-four hours at sea for any of our surface units.

"The strait between South Korea and Japan is a hundred fifteen miles wide, with Tsushima providing a natural roadblock to anything trying to pass through. From Pusan across to the northern tip of the island is about twenty-five miles. From the southern tip of the island to the coast of Japan is another fifty miles, but there are other smaller islands to provide additional natural blocks. You can see how few submarines or surface units it would take to prevent passage through there." Captain Batov drew two thick lines with his grease pencil to show the closed straits.

Then he turned his body so that his right index finger pointed at the tip of the southernmost Japanese island. "This next step is a bit more complicated, but here we again have a system of islands aiding us." He bent down to touch the northern tip of Taiwan with his left hand, stretching to keep both places marked. He strained to turn his head and his voice to his audience. "This measures about six hundred fifty-five miles, but there are over eighty major islands in almost a steady chain, the Ryukyus, with Okinawa right here in the middle. The widest body of water, and the only one to present any sort of tactical problem is just south of Okinawa, and that's only a hundred thirty-five miles wide." Again, he used his grease pencil, slashing downward toward Taiwan to show how that segment of the Pacific would be closed.

"The distance from here," touching the southern tip of Taiwan, "to here," placing the other finger on the northern point of Luzon, is only two hundred twenty-five miles, but all these tiny Philippine Islands in between would make it a nightmare for any ship trying to escape. That stretch could be monitored simply with aircraft." His grease pencil discounted the Luzon Strait.

Captain Batov looked momentarily at Admiral Maslov, who was sitting calmly in his chair, his hands pressed together, forefingers pointed upward against his chin. Maslov nodded imperceptibly to him to go on.

"If you're thinking this operation is too easy, then I can assure you there are problems, right here." His hand swept from the island of Luzon westward across the South China Sea to the huge island of Hainan, the southernmost extension of China. "This represents six hundred forty miles of open water. It also represents the most important strategic aspect to us. Right here," and he covered a large section of the ocean area around Hainan with both hands, "are the largest untapped oil fields known to the world today. Perhaps if we were to capture those initially, the remainder of the operation. . . ."

Maslov raised his head, waving one of his hands. "You may go on. We are interested only with the naval strategy today. That's politics, Captain."

"Yes, sir." Batov's grease pencil crossed the South China Sea, more slowly this time as if to emphasize the problem. "This will involve coordination of surface and air units, in addition to a large contingent of submarines. The ships in this area will be homeported in Vietnam at our new bases at Cam Ranh Bay and Da Nang. If we were to undertake this today, those ships would have to rely on their onboard supplies." He smiled at Colonel Bespalov. "This is where your people are going to really be needed, sir. As you can see, we can't bring anything to Vietnam by land. The problems just with fuel, spare parts, and ammunition are immense, not to mention the fact that our sailors don't eat the food the Vietnamese do."

Admiral Maslov heaved himself to his feet. "Good, good. Thank you, Captain Batov. A good start. Concise and excellent. If you would review our plans for the American visit, that will show how we can use their fleet to our advantage." He grinned broadly toward Bespalov. "It's not often that our greatest problem agrees to set up camp on our doorstep."

As Maslov rose and moved toward the door,

Krulev silently joined him, having never spoken a word. Instead, he had studied each of the individuals around the table as Batov presented his review. Krulev was also security chief for the Pacific Fleet and he knew at least one person in the room was on the American payroll.

"Captain Batov, bring the Colonel up to my office when you're finished here." He nodded to Bespalov. "We will have a little social hour before your departure. We're not all business here."

"Well, Pietr, any indications?" asked Admiral Maslov.

"None, none at all. Each man there sat silently, intimidated as usual. If no one will pry into affairs that don't affect them, we'll never have any leads," answered Krulev.

Maslov and his political officer were seated in the former's office. Admiral Krulev was massaging his almost colorless eyebrows with one hand, his eyes closed, apparently deep in thought.

"While I don't want any of them to get the idea there is a traitor in their midst," continued Maslov, "I want to be wary as much as possible for slips like Batov's. The Americans are well aware of those oil fields off Hainan, but it would be a sad mistake to make them a gift of our knowledge."

"Valery," Krulev was the only person to ever use Admiral Maslov's first name, "trapping a thief is much easier than trapping a traitor. The former sometimes wants to be caught, perhaps to be reformed. A spy, especially a turncoat in this case, never accepts the possibility of being revealed or of reform. While part of the game is the game itself, they fear only the torture that would eventually be their due, rather than the violent death. They have a psychological pride in maintaining a cover amidst the opposition, and they have no terror of death as long as it is self induced or occurs in a valorous way. But the fear of being cornered by the enemy and possibly revealing others is the only fear they know, and that is what we must work for."

Maslov leaned over his desk, eyes alert. "You have an interesting way of making the revolting idea of a turncoat attractive."

They knew information was being leaked to the Americans. Who it was and how it was getting out had been a puzzle. Each of their staff was a respected senior officer. Background investigations revealed nothing. None were suspected, yet one of their own was working for the Americans.

Maslov leaned back in his chair, his face hardening as he looked across the desk at Krulev. It had been extremely difficult for him to accept the fact that a Soviet naval officer, one that had earned his trust, was actually making war against him. In Maslov's mind, that was the only way he saw it. Either a man was on his side, or it was war. There was no middle road, no reason that any one of them might have for wavering. He also did not like fighting a war with his mind rather than his might. The current operation involved skill and cunning and mighty forces.

"And the Americans aren't going to make it any easier for us, Valery."

"Oh?" Admiral Maslov's eyes opened wider, his mouth remaining pursed in an "O" as he waited for Krulev to continue.

"This is just something I picked up before our meeting, while you were giving Bespalov his tour. Apparently ONI, the Office of Naval Intelligence in the United States, is making some references to our plans. They did go to the President, with no success at the time."

"And is the President involved now?"

"Not to our knowledge. But I am told that ONI's Admiral Magnuson, who might be similar to the head of our GRU, is making some moves. Again, there is nothing definite, but it seems he may use some outsiders, some non-intelligence people."

"That's ridiculous!" exclaimed Maslov. "What can amateurs possibly do for them?"

"I can't answer that, Valery, and I still have no supportive documentation. My man has said more than once that everyone in their CIA is suspicious of each other. Information of this nature can be pretty sparse, especially if their approach to this is similar to ours."

"I don't doubt what you're saying at all," admitted Maslov reluctantly. "But push anyway. Do anything you have to. I would hate to imagine the problems if they ever got wind of the Delta assignments when their President is working so hard to renew détente."

CHAPTER TWO

Lieutenant Commander James MacIntyre, aide to Admiral Theodore Magnuson, Director of the Office of Naval Intelligence (ONI), knew when to keep his mouth shut. This was one of those moments. Magnuson had started to say something twice, and stopped in mid-sentence each time, shaking his head. Now the Admiral turned slightly to stare out the window, arms folded in thought. Whenever the Admiral's eyes narrowed like that, Jim MacIntyre would wait calmly.

Magnuson retained most of his hair, which was cut short in the style he wore when he entered the Navy in the early 60's. Not yet 50, there was only a bit of gray around the ears. His short sideburns emphasized a thin face that accompanied a slim, athletic body. Piercing blue eyes, along with a square jaw, completed the image one would have of the military man. After taking over as Director of ONI he had developed an affection for simple civilian clothes, as if he were a Washington businessman rather than a military intelligence specialist. But somehow he could never effect the role he thought he could imitate. He would never be mistaken for a businessman, not with the spit shined shoes and the knife-edge press in his slacks.

Magnuson looked back at his aide, a slight smile wrinkling his face. "Did you ever get chewed out by a President before?"

"Can't say that I've ever had the opportunity, sir."

"Well, I was. This morning. He ran up one side of me and down the other." He looked thoughtful for a moment. "And when he was finished, he said he never wanted to see anyone from the military in his office again making statements like I did without having absolute evidence to back themselves up." Magnuson rubbed his chin as if he'd just been hit there. "And he shit all over Benjamin, too."

MacIntyre knew Benjamin, one of the President's aides. He'd made an earlier visit to ONI. Ever since Admiral Magnuson got wind of the Soviet Pacific Fleet's rapid expansion, he'd been postulating how the Russians might take advantage of the U.S. Seventh Fleet's appearance in Vladivostok at the end of the year.

That fleet visit had all been the President's idea. It sprang from the summit meeting with the Soviet Premier the previous winter. They had both agreed it was time to rejuvenate détente. The American President had offered to open the west coast ports to a Soviet goodwill visit the following summer. Soon after the two leaders had returned to their capitals, the Premiere had written suggesting that the American Pacific Fleet should visit the Soviet Union even before that.

The President hadn't bothered consulting the Navy. He had simply committed more ships than were prudent to visit Vladivostok that coming winter and help the Russians ring in the New Year. Christmas wasn't a recognized holiday in the Soviet Union so New Year's Day was their national celebration. The President was an idea man, not a detail man, and the details could be worked out later by the Navy. It was détente he was after, and the Navy would just have to adapt to new administration policies.

Magnuson had contacts everywhere, and Benjamin was the one in the White House. He'd agreed with Magnuson that a message intercepted by ONI seemed to be authentic, and he was the one who'd authorized the Admiral's appointment with the President. They couldn't determine who the addressees were, but the message was ominous:

> MOSCOW CONFIRMS US COOPER-
> ATION IN NEW YEAR OPERA-
> TION. IT IS VIRTUALLY ASSURED
> MANY SEVENTH FLEET UNITS
> WILL BE WITHIN USSR BOUND-
> ARIES. STAFF COORDINATORS
> REPORT VLADIVOSTOK HDQTRS
> 10 JULY STRATEGY SESSION PER
> MASLOV.
>
>   KRULEV

Magnuson was familiar with Admiral Krulev, Chief Political Officer of the Soviet Pacific Fleet, and second only to the famous Pacific Fleet Commander, Admiral V. P. Maslov, and he had to assume the addressees were senior officers from the seabased commands of the Soviet Fleet. He thought it was justification for going to the President.

"Admiral Magnuson," the President had said calmly, handing the message copy back to him, "don't ever request an appointment in this office again, unless you can bring me something substantial to prove any allegations you are about to make. What you have insinuated is an insult to the office of the President, an insult to me personally, and an apparent individual effort to subordinate the spirit of détente. If you ever return to this office with nothing stronger than this I will forget what your seniors have said and have your resignation the same day."

And that had been that.

Magnuson looked across the desk at his patient aide and shook his head sadly. "How the hell do I substantiate something like this out of the blue? I don't have any idea what they're after yet, but Krulev wouldn't do anything like this unless it was big. And so many of the Seventh Fleet ships are scheduled for Vladivostok that we'd be virtually powerless in the western Pacific. Held hostage, for Christ's sake!

"Shit, Jim, I can't just drop a note to one of our agents in Russia and say, 'Hey, find out what this message is all about.' Those guys would have it handed to them if they happened onto anything Krulev was involved with." He shook his head.

"I've got to find out some other way . . . some way that won't have Maslov and his spooky partner onto us."

MacIntyre watched his boss rise from behind the desk. As was his habit, he brushed against his flag, and strode over to his favorite 'thinking place' by the file cabinets. He leaned against them tentatively, staring at the blank wall. "Shit."

"You need someone outside the Navy, Admiral, someone with a perfect cover the Russians aren't familiar with."

"Who?" He'd been grasping at straws himself.

"How about Royal? You've only used him once. He's clean . . . never been associated directly with us."

The Admiral turned to MacIntyre, his eyebrows rising in agreement. "You know, Jim, you've got a point there. The last time we had a couple of drinks together, Royal said he planned to visit Russia sometime." The idea was becoming his own. "Yeah, he said something about some business opportunities over there. If I could get him in touch with Petrov somehow. . ." He moved back behind his desk. "See if you can get hold of Jack for me. And, Jim, while you're at it, call over to State, would you? Get a list of all the American businessmen who've applied for visas to Russia or China lately."

"China?"

Magnuson nodded. "Right. I don't know what it is. Just something in the back of my mind. Let me do a little more thinking on it first." He pointed an index finger at his aide. "I'm going back to that Oval Office sometime. And when I'm finished there, that son-of-a-bitch is going to apologize for what he said today."

Those who were chosen to attend the meeting at ONI later that month listened intently while Admiral Magnuson beamed. "I thought we'd better give this operation a code name to distinguish it. After a bit of thought, *Seagull* came to mind. Nice name, isn't it? Gives you a smell of the sea."

"Is there any special reason for choosing that name?" questioned Benjamin, the man from the White House.

"As a matter of fact, yes," answered the Admiral. "During the OKEAN-75 Soviet naval exercises about ten years ago, that was the code name for their Admiral of the Fleet Gorshkov. While they normally use code for all transmissions, they did experiment with plain language during some of the phases of that exercise, just as they might under combat conditions. We picked that name up, identified it as Gorshkov, and sort of teased them with it a bit over their own circuits—after the exercises were over, of course," he grinned. "We didn't want them to think we were interfering."

"I can't imagine they were very amused."

Magnuson broke into a large smile. "You're absolutely correct. They've no sense of humor when it comes to something like that." Magnuson paused to indicate he was becoming serious again. "There is a method behind our madness. There are one or two of our codes the Russians have access to, and we haven't let on that we're aware of this. We try to accommodate them by making sure they get information we'd like them to have. You may be certain that Operation Seagull will get into their hands through one of those codes—just the name and the fact that it involves them—and they won't know whether or not we're playing with them again."

Magnuson brushed against his flag as he stood up. "My major objective now is to coordinate our intelligence with the CIA's to ensure that Mr. Benjamin's updated, since he's a bit touchy these days." He stared down directly at the young Presidential aide, smiling broadly. "I wouldn't be surprised if you became attached to some of the people in this room in the near future. Our friend from the CIA," he nodded at a man who had been introduced as Staubach, "wouldn't have allowed you to join us today if he didn't know a great deal about you." His glance took in the others around the room. "Mr. Benjamin has only been with the President for the past year but he's one of his closest advisors. It's his job to feel us out just like we, or Mr. Staubach I should say, have already done with him."

"Oh. . . ." Benjamin meant to say more, but was interrupted by the Admiral.

"Mr. Benjamin, like it or not, you're one of the cleanest ones we could find in the White House, by way of being apolitical I mean. The President has explained to Mr. Staubach that you can keep a secret." He smiled at the man he was addressing. "That's our business you know, secrets . . . our secrets and everybody's."

"All right, I'll shut up if you'll just answer one more question for me." With Magnuson's nod, Benjamin continued, "The CIA usually comes to us with these wild reports first. When you made yourself known, my own check with the CIA was a dead one. They claimed no knowledge. How come?"

"Mr. Staubach probably can answer that better than I, but let me say simply that our business is more oriented to the military and theirs is political. At certain points, our lines cross."

"Right," answered Staubach, turning to Benjamin. "We overlap a hell of a lot, but you won't find us hanging around naval installations or checking out ships' movements unless someone asks us to. I believe this all started when the Admiral's people noticed something unusual a month or so ago in Soviet fleet movements, especially in breaking their low priority message traffic. They checked it out with us. I suppose someone junior was assigned to their request, and no more was heard in our section until our man probably went back to ONI and said, 'Hey, you got something there.' I was invited in by the Admiral just about the time I heard about it at the office." He nodded toward Magnuson, who had now settled behind his desk again. "We've worked together before."

A Navy captain, who had said little since the

conference began, at a nod from the Admiral, arose and moved over to a wall chart they could all see. "My responsibilities are primarily in research, gentlemen. I have to justify the theories of my associates. In this case, the initial clue was so obvious they didn't need me. No American has ever been invited to Vladivostok since President Ford ten years ago. As a matter of fact, since then we aren't sure when the last one was there. He probably went unwillingly. It's headquarters for their Pacific Fleet and has been off limits to just about everyone but Russians themselves. So, when any American is invited there, not to mention the U.S. Seventh Fleet this coming New Year, the Russians have to have something up their sleeve."

"Perhaps we're just getting an early warning of a show of force," remarked Benjamin.

"No, I don't think so," said Magnuson. "A show of force is normally an immediate reaction to an international situation. Someone else has to force it, whether a client country is provoked, or you're reacting to a buildup by another power. Call it what you want, coercive diplomacy, crisis management, whatever, it's generally a short term reaction. The plans for Seagull are apparently very definite, security measures have been superb, and we are just recently aware of a massive buildup without knowing the specific purpose."

"Mr. Benjamin, the CIA has a number of operatives in Moscow, as you know," added Staubach. "One of them is assigned full time to this particular operation. We anticipate he will make contact with our Mr. Royal. And I believe the Admiral also has a man in Vladivostok. Isn't that right, Ted?"

"As a matter of fact, he's assigned now to Admiral Maslov's staff," answered Magnuson. "You can't get much closer than that."

"What would you do if you found one of theirs on your staff, Admiral?" asked the man from the White House.

"That's very simple, Mr. Benjamin. Once we had no further use for him he'd disappear. You can be damn sure we'd never make him available to the courts."

Staubach interrupted before Benjamin could speak again. "In this business, as you refer to it, there are very high stakes, sir. Our agencies are formed and paid to develop specific information and influence policy in other countries, not to provide a social welfare program. I know Admiral Magnuson well, and I'm sure he wouldn't have considered a civilian if he didn't think there was a better-than-average chance of accomplishing our goals and then returning to a normal existence again."

"You don't see any moral factors involved, nothing the United States should do to avoid further involvement?" Benjamin inquired sarcastically. "After all, Admiral, it all could backfire and we could be right in the middle."

"Mr. Benjamin, you're absolutely right. I'm just playing with some computer projections we've developed in the last couple of days. You might call them pure speculation or you might call them genius. But, if you tell the President that, I'd say you were a goddamn liar . . . and you know he's not feeling too strongly about either of us right now." Magnuson handed the green-striped printouts to Benjamin.

"I have the greatest loyalty to my President, Admiral Magnuson. You're making a big mistake if you think I might ever support anything that would damage him."

Magnuson raised his hands in a gesture of surrender. "Believe me, we work for the same boss in the long run. There's just a simple matter of him thinking we're all full of shit right now. Mr. Benjamin, the President's a man with a dream, and that dream has him starring as the one who leads us into a generation of peace. Any of us—you, me, Staubach, any of us—insinuating that we could get sucked into a Soviet trap, is like the messenger who brought the bad news. So, we shut up around him and develop something more substantial."

"Some of these ideas are preposterous," remarked Benjamin, looking up from the printouts Magnuson had given him.

"No one's more aware of that than me. We're just playing ball with some of the concepts the computer's thrown back in our faces. And they're pretty sobering." The Admiral stopped, his expression changing to one of thoughtfulness. "I'll tell you what. I'm the first one to admit that the track we're taking right now is just like predicting the weather. Imagine that the computer says a storm's going to hit here. The TV weatherman fifty miles away says exactly the opposite. The old man on the courthouse steps says something entirely different from the first two by looking at the sky and sniffing the air. Who's to say who's right until the weather has passed?"

"But what you're talking about from Staubach's phone call yesterday is like night and day. You think the Soviet plans involve an action against China—not America. You think they might be using us as a screen. You also say we could come out ahead if the two countries bang away at each other, or we might find ourselves in the middle of World War III."

Magnuson's face relaxed and he smiled again. "Just like my views on the weather. What are the chances of rain today?" Then his expression changed again. "There's something else there, too. I can't figure out what the hell it is and there's no way a computer's going to mention it if there's no input in the first place. But look at the submarine preparation up at their northern base at Petropavlovsk. Not only are they preparing their conventional subs for something way out there, but the missile subs, the ones aimed at us, are involved too. Think about that," he added, tapping his teeth with an index finger. "Would the Russians ever do anything of this magnitude . . . draw us right into their lair like that . . . without threatening us? Think about that. There's something else there. . ." he murmured half to himself. "I'm sure of that."

Magnuson leaned forward over his desk. "Timing will likely be the critical factor, whether we should stick with one side or the other, or maintain an ignorant neutrality. There's no moral problem there, Mr. Benjamin. Ask the President yourself if you don't want to believe me. Of all aspects of diplomacy, the most successful is a policy of making the one hopefully correct decision at the proper instant. You are either right or wrong, and that's exciting when the stakes are as high as they appear to be here. The President would love to have the U.S. come out of this smelling like a rose. That's what gets him re-elected, right?"

"It would seem to me, Admiral, that his opportunities for running again would be enhanced by less interference in another country's affairs. As a matter of fact, you're suggesting policy decisions without the President's knowledge." Benjamin was on the edge of his chair now. "Believe me, the President should be the one to make any final decisions on this operation."

"Then we see eye-to-eye, Mr. Benjamin, because that won't happen until the President believes us. And, as of right now, he doesn't believe a word we've told him. As a matter of fact, and correct me if I'm putting words in his mouth, the only reason you're at this meeting right now is because Mr. Staubach convinced him to send you after that chewing out he gave us. And, if I may put words in your mouth, you're beginning to think Operation Seagull is a reality."

Benjamin smiled insincerely. "You may be correct. However, why not think for just a second about what you may be getting us into. This doesn't seem to be a simple border incident. You're talking fleets—not single ship actions! When you start using those terms, you're talking World War III, or at least the possibility we could get involved in something like that. And," Benjamin's voice rose in consternation, "you don't really know the basic who, what or where. You're shooting in the dark, playing some damn foolhardy games, just because you can't admit you don't know what's going to happen."

Magnuson responded. "The Russian fleet is doing all the dirty work. That fleet has become a floating border. That astute definition came from a brilliant, underestimated statesman, Anwar Sadat. He was well aware of that as the President of a Mediterranean country who saw fleets come and go, carrying their borders with them. The same is true for our own Seventh Fleet. It's a floating United States border. If it is held hostage in Vladivostok, then it is no different than holding our President hostage. Mr. Benjamin, we aren't committing America to anything yet. But I'm sure you're as familiar as I am with the fact that foreign diplomats in Moscow figure the chances are three in ten, at least, of a Soviet pre-emptive strike against China. Russia is going to make all the preliminary moves and we're just going to play along with them."

"And your so-called volunteers. . . ?"

"Perhaps that's a bad term. You see, the average person misunderstands who wins wars. It's not the man in the trenches or on the flight deck of the

carrier. Intelligence wins conflicts. People are
merely the means to that goal. A very few men,
who may never carry a weapon or fight the enemy
directly, achieve the final victory. They may not
even know it at the time. But that is how a war is
fought and won. Right here . . . in this room . . . we
are the nexus of victory in Seagull."

"And are your people aware of that?"

"Only one, Royal, is really aware of what we
need. The others will be on an as-needed basis. If
they happen to fall into place, so much the better.
Now," he paused momentarily to collect his
thoughts, "the reason I want to use at least one
civilian in Russia is because the key to Seagull is in
the computer . . . or their computer." His mouth
opened, then shut again as he reformed his words.
"Please accept this as a fact—the confirming information we need is stored in a computer . . . theirs.
You've heard about computer theft before?" His
eyebrows rose as if he were pondering the question.
"In the wink of an eye, if . . . if you can gain access
to that computer, you can get that information on
your own tape. Like that!" He snapped his fingers.
"And it's all based on logistics—the key to moving
military forces. If we can get that logistical plan, we
can prove exactly what they're planning. And, Mr.
Benjamin," he added, turning to the Presidential
aide, "our agents are good, but they're not computer experts. They could steal your pecker without your being any the wiser, but I need someone
who can get that tape for me, and that someone
will be a civilian who can somehow be coerced into

helping his country. And, Mr. Benjamin, there is a
man I know of who can do this . . . and he will be
in Moscow when Royal is."

Admiral Magnuson needed to touch his office
buzzer for only an instant to summon his yeoman,
a second class petty officer. The sailor's summer
white uniform was immaculate, and the shoes
polished to a spit shine as he came to a relaxed
attention in front of the desk.

"These are those ancient service records you
picked up from the Bureau of Personnel earlier today." The Admiral slid a large envelope across his
desk. It contained the old records of officers who
had once been in the Navy. He knew them. Their
names had popped up from the visa list the State
Department had provided at MacIntyre's request.
"You might as well take them home with you tonight and get 'em to Bupers first thing in the morning. Make sure you get a receipt."

"Yes, sir." The yeoman picked up the package
from the desk, nodded to Magnuson, and turned in
a semi-about face, pulling the door behind him as
he left.

Back at his desk, which displayed the nameplate,
Butler, Samuel N., YN2, the sailor checked his
watch. It was almost 1700. He had stayed later
than usual at the Admiral's request. All of Washington, even the military, called it quits by 4:00
p.m. unless there was an emergency. But Butler
had been with Magnuson for a long time. He carried the highest security clearances and he knew,

with the Admiral's help, he would eventually become one of the youngest chief yeomen in the fleet. Before he left, he dialed a number on his phone, let it ring three times, then hung up. He repeated this twice more at intervals of one minute before he left with the package under his arm.

Admiral Magnuson remained in his office well after dark. Much of that time he did nothing. He simply sat at his desk, sometimes twirling a pencil between his fingers, his eyes fixed on an invisible spot on the wall. Finally, his ideas sorted and compartmentalized in his mind, he began to write a letter to his old friend in Beijing. As they had agreed many years before, it was in long hand. Li Zhiang would understand. It would take a long time for the old man to work his way through the English script, and even longer to sort out the message within the letter. What he would learn when he was finished was short and to the point:

> I am sure you are aware of the Soviet fleet buildup in the Pacific. Be assured that we are utilizing all modern facilities to maintain a strategic picture. Our computers indicate USSR movements may be against China. Do not be fooled by planned US Seventh Fleet presence in Vladivostok at the end of this year. US President is purely interested in détente. You will be contacted at a later date concerning the arrival of an American busi-

nessman in Beijing named Bennett H.
Goodrich. Get to know him well. He
may be important to us at a later date.

The Admiral had no idea when he finally sealed the
letter just how Goodrich might be useful to them.
Magnuson had not seen the man in almost twenty
years. As for Goodrich, he had forgotten Ted
Magnuson soon after he'd left the Navy.

YN2 Butler had gone home first to a second rate
walkup apartment in the southeast section of the
city. It was too small for all of them. His wife was
pregnant again and there were three small children.
After dinner, which was one more in a list of in-
numerable casseroles that his wife developed to
feed the family on his small navy salary, he left
with the package under his arm. He was dressed in
civilian clothes.

He took the subway over to 16th Street, and
boarded a northbound bus. Traffic was light at
this time of the evening, and the ride was a short
one. When he got off, he crossed the street and
walked a few blocks west to an old brick home near
the zoo. He was admitted seconds after ringing the
bell.

Inside, he turned over the package to a woman
who nodded only a mumbled greeting to him before she trotted upstairs with the package. Butler
waited in a room on the first floor to the right of
the stairs, one he had been in previously. As before,
he would sit for a time, then get up and thumb ner-

vously through the stacks of books in the cases along one wall.

Perhaps half an hour later, as he was again getting out of his chair to peruse another shelf, he recognized footsteps coming down the stairs. The woman entered, handed him the package containing the service records, and then a small plastic bag. Putting the package on the side table, he opened the bag, sniffed the white dust inside, then, satisfied, placed it in his pocket. Butler left through the front door and retraced his trip exactly.

This time, he felt much better than when he had begun the journey to the house near the zoo. He never used the drug himself, but this final delivery would bring in enough money to add to the kitty he had begun a few months back. Now they could break out of that run-down apartment and buy that home his family needed but could not afford on a military salary.

The following morning, right after dropping the service records at Bupers, Butler was waiting for a bus back to ONI when a car pulled up. A woman called his name as she opened the window. It was the woman from the house near the zoo, offering a ride which he was only too happy to accept.

Even before she responded to his polite small talk, a man rose from the floor behind the seat, placing the point of a long bladed knife at Butler's neck, just below the right ear. He was instructed not to say a word, not to make a move. At the next corner, the car swung in the opposite direction from his destination. He was told that the wrong bag had been given to him the night before. They'd work out a solution when they got away from the traffic. The car worked its way through the traffic, past the Jefferson Memorial and down to East Potomac Park, where the famous cherry trees bloomed each spring across the river from Washington National Airport.

There were no other cars at that hour of the morning. The woman got out of the driver's seat when they stopped by the river, and walked around to the back of the car. As Butler reached for the door handle, the realization suddenly came to him that he would never leave the car alive. He had moved his hand toward the handle when the point of the knife was no longer below his right ear. The blade had moved with lightning speed under his chin to the left side of his throat. The scream that began deep in his chest was cut off by the wooshing sound in his ears as his throat was opened to the warm air and he caught sight of his own blood spraying the dashboard. He had no strength to fight the rising blackness.

The woman came around to the open window next to the dead sailor and sprinkled a bit of the white powder on the front seat and on his uniform to mingle with the blood. It would be classified as a drug related murder. No one would ever suspect what Yeoman Second Class Samuel Butler had done with the four service records the night before.

CHAPTER THREE

The black limousine's speed had been reduced to a crawl through the streets of Beijing. Since the Hongchi was an automobile reserved only for very important people, and one that automatically assumed the right of way, the passenger was disappointed that no one was in the street to impress.

Another of the torrential cloudbursts, so common in mid-August, was pounding on the car with tiny fists, leaving the windshield wipers next to useless. Admiral Chen Liang leaned from the back seat in an effort to see past the driver to locate a familiar city landmark. But there was nothing for him to glimpse even though he was sure they should be near bustling Tian'Anmen Square, the cultural and political center of the city.

The widened highway made the trip from the airport much faster than it used to be, and Admiral Chen had been looking forward to seeing Beijing. Teeming with bicycles and people, the streets of the capital city brought the Admiral's love of his homeland to life.

But he could see nothing through the windows. The torpor of the rainy season of July and August was overwhelming. Today was no different than many other August days, the temperature and humidity both nudging one hundred. Perspiration dripped down into the high, stiff uniform collar as the car inched towards the meeting at Special Security Unit 8341. The administrative organization of the People's Liberation Army (PLA) was similar to the Soviet system, and the Security Unit could be compared to the Russian GRU. It was the center of military intelligence in China.

For a brief moment, the torrent let up and the Admiral saw they were almost at Tian'Anmen Square, where the Chang'An thoroughfare is at its widest. Usually, the square was jammed with people on foot or on bicycles, and the hundreds of flags lining the street provided a festive air. The upturned roofs of the Forbidden City, former home of the emperors, offered a perfect comparison of the old to the new government buildings in the capital city. Today, only a few drenched citizens scurried about their business and the soaked flags hung limply in the still air.

Then the rain dimmed his vision again, and he leaned back in his seat, wiping the perspiration from his face and neck with a handkerchief. The large Hongchi crept along, unseen and unadmired as the driver searched for the turn that would take him down to the PLA Headquarters where 8341 was also located.

Admiral Chen had flown in that day from

Shanghai, where he was the Commander-in-Chief of the East Sea Fleet, by far the greatest responsibility of any of the operational commands. The North Sea Fleet guarded a large ocean area but with a minimum of ships. Chen's East Sea Fleet had more ships and men and it defended a massive surface area all the way to Japan on the northeast, the Ryukyu Islands almost 500 miles to the east, and Taiwan to the south. Most of the country's major combatants, destroyers that had come from Russia when the two countries were still amicable, plus the Chinese-built frigates, were also under his command.

The Admiral had earned his coveted position every step of the way, first as a foot soldier in the PLA, then when he was elected an officer. Later he had requested and received transfer to the coastal forces. That had come after Chiang Kai-shek's Kuomintang were driven from the mainland leaving behind a few old, tired ships. He had worked closely with his Russian advisors during the fifties, often spending as much time in Vladivostok as he did in Shanghai, learning his trade. If a naval leader could be home bred and then designed from the top of his head to the tip of his toes, Admiral Chen was that man, totally involved with, and dedicated to, The People's Republic of China, the Chinese Communist Party, and the People's Liberation Army.

Now, he had been called to PLA headquarters in Beijing for a very special conference. For some reason, he had not been informed of the nature of this meeting either by word of mouth or letter, and he was a bit upset by that fact. Even the slightest hint that an important matter might have been withheld from him was of concern, for an immense ego was part of his personality. Chen was from the north, tall and slightly stooped much as Mao had been, and he beamed when someone would note that he bore a resemblance to the venerable Chairman. The slighter southerners were particularly aware of his ego and often took pains to remind Chen of the vast improvements in the administration of the Navy since the Chairman had passed away and once again the PLA had more independence from the Party. The successful and dedicated Admiral would always smile, to let them know just how far their teasing could go, before his lectures on the Party would begin. He was the acknowledged leader of the Navy, junior only to Admiral Hung in Beijing who was in administrative command. It was known that Chen would be in operational control should an emergency arise. Hung always deferred to him, and the slightly younger Chen accepted the responsibility gracefully, for the Party had elected Hung, instead of himself, to that position.

Nevertheless, Admiral Chen was still bothered that some of the southerners might be aware of the meeting and its purpose before he would be informed. He pulled at his tight, high naval collar, now soaked with perspiration. In this mid-summer weather it was perpetually uncomfortable, and he preferred to remain in Shanghai as much as possible, near the cooler breezes that occasionally blew in from the water. He thought of loosening the collar but rejected that idea instantly. He was proud that only the Navy wore uniforms that differed from the standard PLA issue. There were only 300,000 people, of the almost 5,000,000 active members of the PLA, that wore that coveted naval uniform and he was proud to show it off. He wiped his face with the handkerchief again, in an effort to look cool and comfortable when the car would pull up before the entrance to the PLA headquarters.

He had no idea how the driver located the turn, but Admiral Chen quite suddenly found himself looking out at the engraved wooden doors of PLA Headquarters, dwarfed by the elegantly carved archway hanging just far enough over the steps to allow the single guard some comfort from the elements. The guard recognized Admiral Chen instantly, even through the sheets of rain. The passenger had leaned just a bit forward to ensure he was seen and the guard had immediately turned to push a button at the side of the door.

Two immaculately dressed PLA soldiers materialized by the car door, one opening it and maintaining a salute as the water poured down his face, while the other held an umbrella.

Admiral Chen emerged quickly, drawing himself to full height so that the soldier literally was on his tiptoes to avoid knocking the Admiral's hat off with the umbrella.

As Chen entered the door, he was greeted by a senior PLA naval officer who gave him a sharp salute and then dismissed the two soldiers to change their soaked uniforms.

"Admiral Chen," he began, "we were concerned you would be detained longer by this horrible weather."

The Admiral held up his hand. "No bother at all, Captain Ma. I prefer Shanghai in the summer, if I have a choice. But, the weather means nothing to me when it appears such an important meeting has been called." He smiled and looked quizzically at the other officer, a tall northerner like himself and a former shipmate, and therefore someone with whom he could be forthright.

Captain Ma smiled back understandingly. When they were much younger he had once served with Chen on KUEI YANG, one of the earliest frigates built in China. They could not be considered close friends, for the Admiral maintained no "close" friends in the Navy. But Ma probably knew Chen better than anyone else in the PLA, and he had become Chen's eyes and ears in Beijing. "None of the others are aware of the subject matter either, Admiral." He looked closely at his senior. "I can assure you of that. This session belongs to 8341. As far as I know, only Admiral Hung and I have knowledge of its subject." Captain Ma was Hung's Chief of Staff.

Chen felt a wave of relief, and smiled back at Ma. "Perhaps I am too touchy about these matters."

The Admiral *was* touchy. He knew that. He also knew that there had been purges within the PLA before, by the Party hierarchy, and that one could never be too careful. When one got right down to it, the Party ran the military. Mao had forged that doctrine, and it had been reaffirmed in 1971 when Lin Piao was killed in the Manchurian plane crash. "Politics come first" Mao had said and the only time the PLA had interfered since was to ensure the Gang of Four would not take over. But Admiral Chen's history went back to those cataclysmic early days, and he was still a suspicious man.

Captain Ma held the door for his senior as they entered the conference room on the second floor. It must be a vitally important meeting, Chen noted, as he surveyed the others in the room. In addition to the head of Special Security Group 8341 and Chen's peers from the North and South Sea Fleets, there was the Minister of Defense, two members of the Military Commission, various members of the General Staff, and the heads of the Air Force, the Second Artillery (the Chinese nuclear force), and the Infantry Corps. Even senior militia members of the Local Forces were present. Rarely had Admiral Chen seen so many powerful people in one room, and not since the death of Mao.

General Yeh stood at his position at the head of the table until all were seated. Rather than speak from a standing position, he, too, took his chair. Yeh was an old man, one who had been on the Long March with Mao, and no one would dare fault the necessity of his running a meeting seated. Though he wore the rumpled, high collared uniform of the PLA as Mao had always done, he exuded the dignity of an official from a rich country who might appear in a dark suit, white shirt and conservative tie.

Yeh adjusted his round glasses, drew his shoulders back, and began to speak in a slow, metered cadence. "Each of you have likely wondered why you did not receive an agenda for this meeting. Perhaps each may feel that others have been informed already, thereby inferring a certain amount of politics." His eyes, set deep in a craggy, inexpressive face, surveyed the men sitting around the table. "I can assure you that the Chief of 8341, Admiral Hung, and his Chief of Staff are the only ones aware of my reasons for bringing you here." The Minister of Defense spoke slowly, savoring each word as older men often do with a captive audience.

"General Yuan," he was referring to the head of 8341, "came to me recently with some interesting facts that make this meeting urgent, even if you may already be aware of some of them. Foremost is a buildup of Soviet infantry and artillery forces on the border, especially above Urumchi." That was the only city of any consequence in the northwest of China, and that was also the location of the headquarters for nuclear testing. "We have also noted an increase of forces in Mongolia, even though the leaders in Ulaanbaatur have rejected my queries about this." Yeh looked at the faces around the table, each impassive, each waiting for him to continue. They knew the Russians had been moving forces in and out of these areas for years.

This couldn't be the reason they were called in.

"While that isn't a matter for provocation at this time, I might also add that they have new T-72 tanks and artillery in position, the latter capable of firing tactical nuclear shells. And, we know they have also adapted chemical and biological shells for their heavy weapons. As far as we have been able to learn, one of the factories making the chemical weapons has been making shipments to border units. We know for a fact that Mongolia won't allow that type of weapon within her borders." He then read from a list the names of Soviet units and their new positions.

Yeh removed his glasses, blinking at the men waiting for him to continue. He smiled for the first time. "I'm talking to you the same way General Yuan first approached me." Then he struck the table gently with his fist. "And that is because he didn't believe the Russians were preparing for an attack across the borders either. No self respecting aggressor is going to send a message so obvious to his enemy." That statement was the end of his short speech, and he nodded at General Yuan.

Out of respect to the aged Yeh, the General stood up, making a barely perceptible bow with his head in the old man's direction. "I would have hesitated to waste the Minister's valuable time if our code breaking section hadn't effected some marvelous advances recently. As some of you may be aware, the Russians use a variety of code systems, the most complex for operational orders, the simplest for everyday logistics. Now, the French in

World War I and the Americans in World War II achieved amazing success in anticipating enemy force movements from analyzing movements of supplies over land or by merchant shipping. Against the Japanese, the U.S. Combat Intelligence Unit in Hawaii turned this into an art form.

"We are, in our own way, endeavoring to accomplish the same thing." Yuan hesitated, choosing his words carefully. "We have a small unit of cryptographic analysts, a group of men and women we selected a few years ago through a series of examinations, who have exhibited remarkable capabilities. These people have succeeded in breaking the lower grade code systems used primarily by the Soviet rear services, and this is the reason I came to Comrade Yeh."

Admiral Chen shifted uncomfortably in his chair. The room was hot and without air conditioning, as were most PLA administrative offices. The temperature might have been a bit lower than that outside the building, but he was comforted by noting the damp uniforms and sweating faces that the humidity was oppressive to all. He wished Yuan could complete his self-compliments and come to the point. Each man at the table knew that 8341 was gaining power.

Yuan continued. "There are certain surface ships from the Soviet Northern, Baltic, and Black Sea Fleets that are now, or will in the next month or so, shift their homeports to the Pacific. While some of them appear to be transferring to

Vladivostok, our intercepted messages indicate
others are not. Cam Ranh Bay and Da Nang are
likely choices since the Russians have made so
many ships' visits there in the last year or two. We
think they have invested a great deal in modernization even though the Americans left most
everything intact. Also, Soviet merchant shipping
scheduled to stop at those ports in the next few
months has increased considerably. Even as we
meet here, ships are waiting for days off Cam Ranh
Bay for dock space to be unloaded.

"And, comrades," Yuan leaned forward placing
his hands on the table, "those ships are carrying
primarily military supplies, or supplies destined to
be used by other than Vietnamese people. At Da
Nang, they are offloading spare parts for Soviet
ships and aircraft, since the Russians have apparently begun to transfer fighter aircraft
squadrons to that base. Also," and here he began
ticking off the elements on his fingers, "we have
noted shipments of Russian canned foods, generally those types consumed by military personnel,
large amounts of ammunition for naval surface
combatants, and the actual transport of two complete units of their Construction and Billeting
Troops. That means they are building permanent
support facilities. And, finally, we have noted that
certain submarines are apparently being transferred from their homeport of Petropavlovsk to
Cam Ranh Bay."

General Yuan sat down, inclining his head toward Yeh to note that he had completed his segment of the meeting.

"One other item that may not be as critical as the others that General Yuan has mentioned," added Yeh, "is that the Russians are also doing the same at the North Korean port of Nijin, near Wonsan on their east coast. Admittedly it is close to their fleet headquarters, but it's worth noting that Vladivostok is operating close to maximum right now and could not be expected to handle more operating forces or supplies in a time of war."

Li Zhiang, an elderly member of the ruling Military Commission, was the first to speak. He gave no indication that Magnuson's letter had made him aware of the topic of the meeting. He spoke slowly and deliberately, as Yeh had before. "If you feel that the troop movements on the border are a sham, what is your interpretation of the changes in their Pacific Fleet order of battle? Have we been able to break higher priority traffic from the Russians?"

"My unit is small and newly trained," responded Yuan. "They are working twenty-four hours of each day, seven days a week. But their expertise, I am afraid, is not at the level of other countries. While they may be able to break down part of the higher priority systems, I think we will have to make use of our human intelligence gathering units in other countries. We still do better on a person-to-person basis, and we must continue to rely on that."

"General Yuan is correct," said Yeh. "If his small group can accomplish more, then we will be thankful. But it is a necessity to rely on additional intelligence gathering from our diplomatic corps.

My feeling is that the Russians have given up the
concept of waiting us out and that they will make
a move by the end of the year. Our greatest suscep-
tibility is from the sea. There could be no better
reason for their current plans. But, how they are
going to do this, and exactly when, is something we
must determine soon. They are not so foolish to
undertake a land war. That would take too much
time and would bring in other countries on our
behalf. They must move quickly, and they do nothing half way. It will come by sea and they will prepare their forces completely before they do anything. We have time, I believe."

If the men around the table had seemed passive
because of the heat, they no longer showed it.

Like Yeh, Mr. Li had also been on the Long
March, and had been a close associate of Mao's
ever since. Much of Li's time had been spent in
developing natural resources, for he was also an
engineer and had joined Mao in the early thirties
after completing his education. As a result, he had
been chiefly responsible for establishing an energy
program for his country and was considered an expert in developing China's rich oil reserves. He had
remained a respected member of the Military Commission at Mao's request, for the Chairman had
always insisted that this close advisor report the efforts of the PLA to him. Mao had appointed Li to
the Central Military Commission, the Party's con-
trolling agency, for life. As a Party member first,
and a PLA leader second, Li had been faithful to
Mao's desires. His power was also untouchable

and he was deferred to by the others in the same manner as General Yeh.

Admiral Chen nodded respectfully to both Yeh and Li. "I would think that we should also consider the fact that the American Seventh Fleet will be visiting Vladivostok at the end of the year. It seems to me an amazing coincidence that their visit falls at the same time that Comrade Yeh feels the Soviet Union may make a move by sea. This situation in Vietnam creates a disastrous change in the regional equilibrium for Asia, if you follow me, at the same time the American President makes a major commitment to renew détente with the Soviets." He looked first at Yeh, then at the others. "Am I being oversensitive?"

The raised eyebrows and shaking heads answered his question. It was a striking coincidence, one they hadn't anticipated. But, since the days during and after the last world war, when the U.S. had supported Chiang Kai-shek against the better judgment of so many Americans who understood China, there had been a lurking suspicion. It was harbored more strongly by the older people, those who had spent most of their youth dodging the Kuomintang, only occasionally able to strike back. And, after 1947, when they finally found themselves able to stand up to Chiang, there were the Americans pumping arms and ammunition into the losing battle against them. Most of those in the upper echelon, and especially those at this meeting, would therefore find Admiral Chen's question thought provoking.

Yeh spoke up first, carefully choosing his words. "I wonder what the advantage to the Americans might be if they were to turn against us at this stage."

"Perhaps that is a question with an easy answer," remarked the head of the Air Force. "Oil! That's obviously what the Russians want. There's no secret that our undersea reserves exceed both the North Sea and the Alaskan fields by a great deal, and even we don't know the extent of our reserves under the deserts in the northwest. Perhaps after the Soviets make their move from the sea, they will use those forces on the border, to get at that oil, too." The Air Force General was a southerner, shorter, lighter-skinned than his northern brothers, and with a quick temperament.

Li Zhiang, obviously the one most able to answer that consideration, spoke. "But the Americans have signed agreements with us concerning our oil exploration. We are already using their equipment, their technicians, and we have contracts on future fields that extend well into the next century. I understand your feelings, and I can't fully discount them, but there have to be more reasons than that." He stopped for a moment to choose his next words.

Admiral Chen interrupted before the old man could continue. "I think we should consider possible hidden negotiations between the Soviets and the Americans, perhaps as a result of their interminable SALT talks. We know the Russians prefer to contain us. They are severely in need of energy. They want Manchuria, its industry, and its ports back very badly. And, perhaps an end to the costs of maintaining arms parity with the U.S. would mean a great deal to them." He raised his eyebrows and added, "As it would, also, to the Americans."

The discussion moved back and forth across the table, each member allowed to offer a theory or question another. Yeh had been growing restless with the discomfort of the closed, humid room, his eyes occasionally blinking him back to alertness. "I think we could offer a variety of reasons for the Russian moves, and even for American perfidy. However, we don't know what the Soviets are planning, nor if the Americans are really cooperating with them. It could simply be an unintentional, awkward move by the President." Yeh did not like long meetings. "We will reconvene here in four weeks. In the meantine, General Yuan has been initiating queries through our diplomatic corps, especially in countries that might have their own access to Soviet or American intelligence."

Yuan agreed readily. "I have operatives both in the CIA and the KGB. They should be able to find something for us within that time.

"I also want to increase air and infantry surveillance on the borders and wherever there is increased Soviet shipping. There is no harm in having the Russians know that we are on to something. Perhaps that will force them to do something foolish.

"Li and I have already scheduled a meeting with the Chairman tomorrow to discuss these matters with him. One factor I think is more important now than ever before is to be suspicious of all Americans, both those now in the country and those requesting visas. Until we have more reliable information concerning U.S. intentions, every American should be suspect."

Admiral Chen spoke up at this point. "With the change in Soviet submarine movements, I would like to increase surveillance from Shanghai," he said. "My area of responsibility is by far the largest and that might also let the Russians know we suspect something."

"Agreed," answered Yeh. He included the Admiral from Zhanjiang also in his next order. "I would want the South Sea Fleet to do the same, especially in the vicinity of the oil fields. Perhaps the patrol boat commanded by Mr. Li's daughter will be the first to find a Russian submarine." He smiled warmly at his old comrade in arms.

A few minutes were spent passing the time of day with each other before they departed in their separate cars, senior members first. The washing by the earlier showers, combined with a bright sun, attracted attention to Admiral Chen's shiny, black Hongchi. The wet streets, steaming under the hot sun, were again filled with people and bicycles. The limousine and its occupant were noticed with respect by many as it went up Chang'An Boulevard past Tien'Anmen Square. The brilliant flags were drying in a pleasant breeze and the upturned roofs and gargoyles of the Forbidden City stood out against a blue sky.

Diplomatic cocktail parties in Washington, as

documented in the *Post,* are social events, but the main objective of most attendees is to acquire information.

The Netherlands Embassy was an excellent place for garnering information and contacts, regardless of the country one represented. The Dutch were very liberal, inviting diplomats from all countries, and always insisting that they bring along the young ladies that worked in those embassies. Their presence assured a good turnout.

The occasion for a particularly joyful party was the birthday of the United States, the Fourth of July. The Dutch Ambassador owed one to the American Secretary of State and he meant to put on a good show. State had sent over especially attractive secretaries from a variety of departments, including some of the White House girls who were so overworked they deserved something as special as this party.

SuAnn McCollum was fascinated with the Dutch Embassy. It was her first diplomatic party and she could hardly wait to write all her friends in Biloxi to tell them about it. No one ever threw parties like this in her home town, and she didn't believe she had ever known anyone who had been to one.

SuAnn was only twenty years old and she had not yet learned how to drink in her few months in Washington. She decided to drink champagne which she had heard was much lower in alcohol and was something one could sip at a party with no problems.

Her roommate had told her that the best way to

meet eligible men was to keep circulating and that was what she was doing. Therefore, she was most startled when a short oriental gentleman stepped up to introduce himself.

Mr. Kan was from the Peoples' Republic of China. He said he wanted to make a special point of thanking her for the trouble she had taken to get some information for him a few days before. SuAnn was puzzled, since she couldn't remember doing anything of the sort for anyone from China.

He assured her he never forgot a name, and he was sorry she had forgotten his. Mr. Kan insisted on keeping her in conversation and each time a waiter passed, the gentleman would take another glass of champagne off the tray for her.

The conversation got back to her job and she acknowledged that she did work for Mr. Benjamin. Much to her surprise, Mr. Kan explained that he was a close friend of Mr. Benjamin's. Just recently, they had been discussing something about American businessmen coming to China with the cooperation of the government. Mr. Benjamin had provided the names to him but they had inadvertently been discarded. Since Mr. Kan would be contacting Beijing this weekend about the matter, and Mr. Benjamin would probably be away for the Fourth of July weekend which he certainly deserved, would Miss McCollum be willing to check back in her office for those names and the necessary information Mr. Benjamin had provided?

It wasn't difficult for Mr. Kan to convince SuAnn how valuable she was to Mr. Benjamin and the White House. As a matter of fact, she was getting quite tipsy, but did not know to what extent since she had never had that much to drink before in her life. Mr. Kan said he would be happy to drive her over there himself and then deliver her to her apartment later on if she preferred.

This was SuAnn's first opportunity to do a favor for Mr. Benjamin and she wanted to help him so much. He was extremely tired and deserved not to be interrupted on this long weekend. Of course, she would be happy to help out.

Mr. Kan was waiting for her in a small Chevrolet Citation that was a few years old, rather than the black Mercedes she thought all diplomats drove. He explained that it was the People's Republic of China's desire to contribute to energy conservation in America and the best way was by using fuel efficient cars made by Americans.

The car pulled up beside the White House Executive Office Building on 17th, and Mr. Kan left the engine running while SuAnn showed her identification badge to the guard and then went on into her office, which was right next to Mr. Benjamin's. She was outside in moments with copies she had made from the material on her boss's desk. There was information on four men and she told Mr. Kan that she couldn't remember which ones planned to visit China and which ones were to go to Russia. Mr. Kan explained that it was of little importance since one of his assistants would remember the right names.

It was after dark when the Chevrolet drew up

near SuAnn's apartment building, and Mr. Kan insisted that as a gentlemen he must escort her to her door. She was in a nice area of Washington but, even there, reported attacks on young women were on the increase. By this time, SuAnn was beginning to feel ill. Her head ached and her stomach was upset, and she was thankful for the assistance.

At first light the next morning, a park police patrol reported sighting a body floating face down in the Tidal Basin. A few minutes later, they called on their radio to report bringing in the body of a woman. An ambulance was sent over to remove the body and deliver it to the coroner's office.

In tears, one of SuAnn McCollum's roommates identified the body. The coroner ruled that her death by drowning was accidental since blood analysis revealed an excess of alcohol, a probable result of an embassy party she had attended the evening before. The police never considered that the stolen Chevy Citation they found that day in Rock Creek Park had anything to do with the young girl's death.

SEPTEMBER 1984

CHAPTER FOUR

Maslov rarely relaxed in front of his juniors, but today the Admiral knew this slight indiscretion wouldn't go beyond Krulev. It was a warm day for Vladivostok, the kind of day that had Maslov wishing for the air conditioning that existed in some of the Moscow offices. His uniform blouse was hung neatly on a hanger on the corner rack, and his tie and collar were loosened. The Admiral's feet were on his desk, crossed at the ankles. With his hands locked behind his head, he appeared deep in thought as he watched KIROV, a nuclear powered battle cruiser, ease alongside the nearest dock, her crew paraded on deck. She was the first of the largest class of cruisers in the world, and it was required that a tug stand alongside. But today the tug proved unnecessary for it was dead low tide in Golden Hern Bay, there was no current, and the air was still. There was nothing to prevent a perfect docking.

Never once did Maslov look over at Pietr Krulev, who sat opposite the desk also watching

KIROV. Like many of the modern Soviet cruisers, her bow was rounded and arched high above the water, the deck housing and bridge set almost amidships to accommodate the array of weapons forward. To Maslov, his flagship was both a thing of beauty and grace and a pure weapons platform. Not only was she armed with a variety of missiles to counter submarines, ships and aircraft, but she carried helicopters and even the old-fashioned gun mounts that he had literally lived in as a junior officer. Now, he could hardly wait for the first voyage with her, for he believed much as Admiral Makarov had over eighty years before—"To be at sea is to be at home."

Maslov was constantly fascinated with the fact that there were no stacks on the giant cruiser. "Look at that, Pietr. He's jockeying her in, forward then back, and not a breath of smoke. It never ceases to amaze me."

The younger Krulev was not as amazed, taking nuclear power more for granted. "Yes. She represents a new era for our surface forces, certainly, though the Americans have had atomic powered surface ships for years."

"But nothing like her, nothing even approaching her firepower." Maslov smiled for the first time since Krulev had entered his office. Then, under his breath, he added just to himself, "My queen of the seas."

When KIROV's lines were secured and the tug had left her side, Maslov turned reluctantly back to his political officer, his feet once again under his desk, his face serious.

"I suppose we have to get back to these, Pietr." The Admiral fingered the manila folders on his desk, turning them on their sides to inspect the unfamiliar names once again: Royal, Jack M.T.; Loomis, Thomas H.; Miller, Robert F.; Goodrich, Bennett H. "Who are they? Why were we sent these? They mean nothing to me." He pushed the folders back in Krulev's direction.

"They are American service records, Valery. Perfect copies. Taken directly from the Bureau of Naval Personnel in Washington, copied, and returned to their place without anyone knowing the better." He smiled ruefully at his senior. "You shouldn't dismiss them so quickly. No other organization can accomplish that in such secrecy, and I'm sure there is no way the Americans could ever remove a complete service record of one of our officers."

"So," Maslov snorted, "maybe you're right. But I can't read those things. What do they say?"

"They say that none of those men have been on active duty in the U.S. Navy since 1967." The blond man shrugged and wrinkled his forehead, looking under his pale eyebrows at Maslov.

"Almost twenty years ago!" the Admiral exclaimed. "Why are they bothering me with this?" He reached over and picked up one of the folders, flipping through it quickly, paying no attention to the contents. "What do we have them for?"

"I am told they may be the keys," Krulev paused for a moment. "Or perhaps it's better to say, that the KBG seems to think they are." He shook his head. "They don't make many mistakes, and they say these are the people that the Office of Naval Intelligence have been interested in for their Operation Seagull.''

"That American humor. Gorshkov's code name. I don't think that's funny," growled Maslov. "It's disrespectful to a great man. They're jealous of Admiral Gorshkov, jealous that he surpassed their own Navy." He leaned forward, bushy eyebrows raised in question, "What is Operation Seagull, and why did they choose that name?"

"I think perhaps to antagonize you, Valery," Krulev laughed. "And it has worked again. They would be happy if they could see you now, fuming like this. I remember an American officer once telling me that sometimes we are so serious that they take great fun in tweaking the nose of the Russian bear. I think that's what they are doing now." Then Krulev became suddenly serious. "I also think that they are trying to hide something by using that name. Sometimes, advertising your ignorance can intimidate your enemy.

"Anyway they can't help but notice, if only from their satellites, that ships are changing their homeports to the Pacific. And they have agents, good ones, in all our cities. They must keep track of the change in surface movements and supplies reoriented in another direction."

"You think they're aware of our plans?"

"No. That's just it. Our own people have been busy in Washington, especially at their CIA. The Americans know something is definitely in the wind, Valery. It concerns us, but to what extent we don't know. What bothers me most is these files the KGB has sent us. Our operatives in Washington have simply said that these old files went to the CIA and that their Office of Naval Intelligence has also taken an interest in these men. Why? I don't know. They are simply businessmen as far as we know. I doubt they could find their way around on the deck of an American ship today." Krulev shrugged his shoulders in frustration.

"What more does the KGB say about these men?"

"They know almost nothing. One report said it was very hard to investigate American civilians when they have no government contacts. They work and live where they want and our people don't know how to analyze files when a situation like this arises." Krulev fingered another folder that had been sitting in his briefcase. "I have a preliminary report right here on three of them. All businessmen. None of them has ever been in the Soviet Union. They have nothing at all to do with defense industries that we know of. The fourth one, Miller, is even harder to find out about. Apparently, he lives far away from any city centers in America, some place called Vermont. The KGB said it was much more difficult to locate him and learn more. Perhaps he lives in the wilderness."

"That report you showed me the other day indicates that this Operation Seagull of theirs has something possibly to do with their Seventh Fleet visit here. Could these four men be involved?"

"That's what we're working on now. Perhaps it's

a ploy to distract us. On the other hand, I'm always suspicious whenever the Americans make something so obvious."

The Admiral pulled at a low door in the wall behind his desk, opening a small refrigerator and freezer. From the freezer he took two small glasses, then a bottle of vodka which immediately frosted on the outside as the warm air touched it. Maslov set the two glasses, now cloudy, on his desk. Then he poured two ounces into each one, quickly returning the bottle to the freezer.

"To Operation Seagull then, and to its demise." He lifted his own glass, signifying that Krulev do the same. They looked briefly at each other, raising their glasses silently, then drank the contents in a single gulp.

Krulev wiped his lips with the back of his hand. "To its demise," he answered. "An excellent idea on a day like this."

"It makes us think more clearly, Pietr." Maslov placed his glass on the corner of his desk, and strode over to his window, gazing out at the huge cruiser, now alive with working sailors. He then turned back to Krulev. "If the KGB says those nobodies that are in the folders are important, then they must be. I want your people in Washington to find out exactly how they are concerned with this Operation Seagull."

Four weeks had passed by quickly. It was the day that Yeh had selected for the next meeting at Security Group 8341.

Admiral Chen had drawn his friend, Captain Ma, Admiral Hung's Chief of Staff, aside before the meeting to discuss a matter he considered gravely important. "I have been thinking seriously for the past four weeks about what might happen with the Russians. It could come sooner than Yeh expects, and Hung just is not ready to relinquish his power yet. He knows he will give it to me, yet he holds back. The Soviets aren't stupid. They know our system and how it works. They know that Admiral Hung is old and tired and not ready to face them. If they strike suddenly, unexpectedly, it could all be over before Hung knows what's taken place."

"I have thought about that also," replied Ma.

Chen was nervous. He knew Admiral Hung's Chief of Staff was much closer to him than to his boss, but Chen wondered how Ma would feel about such a conversation. "I can't just come out and ask him to turn over everything to me now. Someone, other than me, needs to talk with Hung. He must understand that I can't simply walk through his door and give instant orders to the other fleets. Operational command means having everything at your fingertips. If my only concern is the East Sea Fleet until he decides to have me relieve him, it may be too late."

"And you want me to talk to him?" Captain Ma's reply was part question and part statement. He was a bit shorter than Admiral Chen, even though he was also a northerner, but he always stood back just a little so that he looked directly into the man's eyes without inclining his head upward. "It is possible that I could antagonize him. You do not remove a powerful man from his power easily, regardless of his age and inclinations. If his reaction to me became negative, perhaps he would change his mind about you also."

"Not a chance. Yeh wouldn't let him. I have talked also with Yeh, since we last met, but he won't intercede. He says Hung will know when it's time."

"I find it hard to argue with that."

"Come." Admiral Chen put his hand on Ma's arm. "It's time for the meeting to begin. Think about what I've said." He was close enough now to look down at Ma. "You know," he added, "you would make a good commander of the East Sea Fleet . . . just as soon as I relieve Hung."

Captain Ma's brows rose slightly, the only acknowledgement that Admiral Chen's implication had registered. But Chen knew his statement wouldn't be forgotten.

"I had hoped," Yeh began methodically, "that we would have even more definitive information than has been made available to us. General Yuan's cryptographers have been working hard and have found more interesting Soviet logistical plans, but nothing to make any decisions on. However, our people in Washington have aided us.

"The Americans are planning something called Operation Seagull around their visit to Vladivostok. We don't know what this Seagull is, whether it is for or against the Russians, or perhaps even in conjunction with them against us." Yeh removed his glasses, placing them on the table and rubbing his eyes.

The Air Force general responded, voicing his previous theory, "They want our oil as much, if not more, than the Soviets. I think they would much rather take it than pay for it."

Li Zhiang answered immediately. He'd heard nothing further from Magnuson, yet he couldn't let the mood of the council turn against the Americans. "There is no reason for such suspicions. As I said at the last meeting, they have agreements with us that go into the next century, long after many of us are dead. They've proved to be our friends so far."

"So far," said the General. "Why should you trust them after everything they did to you years ago?"

"That was years ago, and the Americans were not to blame."

"So, the Kuomintang were, but what does it matter? They tortured you and your wife with American aid. I see no reason why you should support them now."

Li appeared thoughtful for a moment, looking up the table first at Yeh, then back to the General. "That was so long ago, and there are few people today in either country who can remember those bad days so vividly. When we get old," and he again looked up the table at Yeh, "we try to give new generations the benefit of the doubt. That in-

cludes not only the Americans but also you and
your generation. It used to be called wisdom." He
paused for just a moment, as old men do to make
a point. "I hope it still is."

The General looked at Li unhappily, but said
nothing, his brows furrowed.

General Yuan spoke up. "I appreciate what you
say, Comrade Li, and I sincerely hope you are correct. But, there is as yet no reason to dismiss completely what the General has said. Perhaps in your
desire to forget and in your wish to believe everything the Americans have said, you overlook the
many promises they have forgotten. My preference
is to accept both the opinions you have put forth
and those of the General, but I do not think wisdom should overrule caution."

"Comrades," interjected Yeh, "I suppose we
could argue the points of wisdom and youth for
hours, but that would appear to be a mistake. We
are not here to agree with each other, but to develop an intelligence network that will answer a
number of the questions from our last meeting.
Dissension has never been productive, and I am
sure in this case, it would be no different. General
Yuan, would you share with the others what you
have gathered?"

Yuan smiled slightly, which was excessive for
him. Each day, he had the opportunity to show the
increasing value of 8341. "It seems that other intelligence networks are still the best source of intelligence. Somehow, neither the KGB nor the CIA
can keep their secrets to themselves.

"Right now, they are both going to extreme methods to learn what the other is planning on Operation Seagull. I have no idea what the Soviets call it, but I'm satisfied to use the American name. At this stage our people in Washington and the Kremlin are watching a frantic interplay between the two organizations that could eventually compromise some of their best people. We should encourage this in our own way."

Li Zhiang leaned forward a bit to look down the table at General Yuan. "How do you encourage these large organizations with your little one?"

"We are small and relatively young, and just learning the ways of these sophisticated spies. So there is no reason to imitate them. I would call their methods of intelligence *active*. They are making policy, or at least influencing it in their respective governments. This influence becomes interference in other countries. I would call our method of intelligence *passive* at this point. We are not doers. We are listeners, and very good ones. We will change, of course, as we mature, but the Americans and the Soviets have shown us what we do not want to do.

"Right now, we talk with their known agents and their diplomats, and we listen to what they have to say. By piecing together a number of differing conversations, we can begin to get a picture. The fact that the Americans have already queried the Japanese about moving new fighter aircraft into their country, before the end of the year, to counter what they believe is a Soviet buildup, tends to make me follow Comrade Li's argument at this time."

"But we don't know for a fact," stated Admiral Chen.

"No, not for a fact," answered Yuan. "Comrade Yeh and I have attempted to place ourselves in the American position. They feel that whatever is best for them is best for everybody. If one considers the treaties and business arrangements that have been made between our two countries over the last few years, we tend to feel they do not want to interrupt our growth. A successful China would benefit them."

"Are you absolutely sure?" asked the skeptical Air Force general.

"We're not absolutely sure of anything," answered Yeh. "We will continue to suspect every American arriving in our country. We also intend to keep the Russians on their toes. Mr. Li, would you explain the vote of the Central Military Council?"

"While we cannot do a great deal to harass Soviet shipping, we can counter their troop movements. Very shortly, we will begin troop movements into northern Manchuria, along the Amur River, and all the way to the northeast corner across from Khabarovsk. We plan to show them a display of military exercises along with some fresh aerial tactics. It will give them something to think about, and I suspect they will decide that we're on to something."

* * *

TO: The President of the United States
FROM: Office of the Director of Naval Intelligence
VIA: Special Assistant to the President Benjamin
SUBJECT: *Operation Seagull*

Situation Report No. 1

At the request of Mr. Benjamin, and on a timely basis, this office will prepare special situation reports on OPERATION SEAGULL for your eyes only. This report should serve as a review up to the present date.

OPERATION SEAGULL is the code name for intelligence gathering activities relating to the U.S. Seventh Fleet's visit to Vladivostok scheduled over the coming New Year period. Preliminary indications are that American units involved in the Vladivostok visit may be used as a cover for a large scale Soviet operation. The mission of this office is to: 1) determine Soviet objectives; 2) analyze the developing strategic situation from both a regional and global perspective; 3) postulate how units of the Seventh Fleet might possibly be utilized by the U.S.S.R. on either a propagandistic basis or in a strategic/tactical sense; 4) ensure the safety of fleet units and personnel scheduled for that operation.

Intelligence gathering systems have confirmed a definite increase in activity directed to Soviet Pacific Fleet Headquarters in Vladivostok. This involves movement of military personnel, aircraft, surface and sub-surface naval units, weaponry, and logistical support for large scale operations well beyond any previous Soviet military exercises.

While neither strategic analysis personnel attached to this office nor our computer analysis team can es-

tablish an accurate projection of Soviet intentions,
certain aspects will be eliminated as the strategic picture develops.

Final analysis should consider Russian objectives.
It goes without saying that China has become a thorn
in Russia's side, more so than the United States.
Since Kosygin last met Chou in September of 1969,
when the final break was made between the two na-
tions, the U.S.S.R. has faced a double "Cold War"
front—U.S. strength and China's warlike posture.
The Sino-Soviet border extends for 4,200 miles and is
the longest and potentially the most explosive in the
world today. The Russians normally maintain forty-
five divisions on this border, a tremendous drain on
their military and an expensive economic factor. This
could better be spent on industrializing Siberia, which
is confronted by a rapidly industrializing Manchuria
that now has a population larger than West Germany. While Siberia is almost empty, it is potentially
rich, and could almost be a country by itself both economically and geographically, since the Ural Mountains separate this Asian Russia from European
Russia. The Chinese are aware of this.

Economics and energy, according to the CIA (the
Central Intelligence Agency provides this office with
economic and industrial output analyses), are the major factors involved in any Soviet military decision.
The one consumer item the U.S.S.R. has never been
short on is energy. Yet since 1977, the CIA has been
projecting a decrease in Soviet ability to meet its own
oil requirements and those of its satellites. This has
been disputed by many people, but the one fact that
remains is that demand will continue to increase
beyond Soviet capability to deliver. Russian oil pros-
pecting technology is projected to be thirty-five years

behind. While their current techniques boost short run production, they face severe problems in the future. Their decision to stand pat, as far as control of Middle Eastern oil fields are concerned, reinforces this office's assumption that they may see more long range possibilities in the as-yet undeveloped Chinese oil fields, both offshore and in China's western provinces. The latter are painfully unprotected from Soviet incursion. Within the confines of this report, it is safe to say the U.S.S.R. could consider what is already a U.S. long range objective.

As China grows stronger economically with Western cooperation, the chances of Soviet intervention will decrease drastically. Economic involvement with the PRC also will likely mean future Western military pacts with China which the Soviets would hesitate to challenge. It cannot be emphasized too much that foreign trade is an extension of foreign policy for China. Financing of their economy must be done by business expansion, the Chinese must export to bring development money into their country, and oil and gas must, in the final analysis, be the basis. And, on a domestic basis for China, energy is the key to industrial modernization and expansion.

This office must assume that the U.S.S.R. sees the current situation as an "us or them" position. My responsibility as Director of the Office of Naval Intelligence includes bringing to your attention the continuing hazardous developments that seem to be associated with Operation Seagull. Until the end of this century, energy (oil) will remain one of the major reasons any of the super powers would be willing to go to war. The second cold war front concerns the U.S. and is a global one. This office anticipates a Soviet effort at containment of the U.S., possibly by threat

with their ICBM force. The Seventh Fleet's visit to
Vladivostok at the end of this year provides all the
earmarks of potential U.S. involvement in a situation
that could create a Third World War.

> Respectfully submitted,

> Theodore Magnuson, Rear Admiral
> United States Navy

On the same day the President read Magnuson's
Situation Report, he scrawled a short memo to his
aide in longhand:

Mr. Benjamin—I recommend you do some research
before you report to my office at exactly 9:00 a.m.
tomorrow morning. I would like you to report to me
as to exactly who conducts foreign policy in the United States today, the military or the civilian sector.
You should also be prepared to offer any reasons that
Admiral Magnuson shouldn't be a civilian by the end
of tomorrow. Of equal importance would be an explanation of why you choose to support this
Admiral's contentions in direct opposition to the
stated goals of this administration.

Benjamin shuddered when he reread the memo.
He already knew the answers to all but the last of
the President's queries.

Jack Royal was a Senior Vice President in one of
the larger brokerage firms in New York, closer to
being rich through his own investments than the
exorbitant salary he commanded for his responsibilities. He had followed a career path familiar to
many of the bright early Sixties college graduates.

First earning his ticket from Princeton, he put in his three years in the Navy after an OCS commission, and then had gone into the investment business in New York. Royal was highly intelligent, able to smell sound business deals, sensitive to those around him, and very political when necessary, everything it took to succeed in a highly competitive job. His only marriage was to his business. He still maintained his tall, trim figure, though he claimed to all his friends that it was a battle to maintain his weight in middle age. His hair, which had turned white at the beaches every summer in his youth, now remained that color, complimenting its original sandy hue and his ruddy, Scottish complexion.

He hadn't expected to be sitting in Ted Magnuson's office two days before, but he was willing to come when he sensed the urgency in his friend's voice over the phone. They had been friends from years past and had enjoyed a lovely, lost summer as naval officers aboard a destroyer deployed to the Mediterranean. Ted opted to stay in the Navy twenty years before. Jack saw life more challenging on the outside. But they remained close, as close as two men could be when one made more money than he needed as a civilian and the other survived on a minimal salary in the dangerous business of intelligence.

The one thing Magnuson never forgot was the Peter Pan in his old friend, the gleam in the back of his eyes when there was excitement. So, like certain professionals in business and education who worked on occasion for the CIA, Jack Royal had agreed long ago to do the same thing for Magnuson if his friend were at a dead end. He had only been called once before. And now, he was sitting in the Admiral's office listening to a wild tale and loving every minute of it.

"All this sounds logical so far, I know," said Magnuson. "But there's something not quite right on the Russians' part. The President has agreed they can visit San Francisco next spring, and we know they're going to have a ball there. But, where would you go on the Pacific coast of Russia? There's hardly a playground there, not to mention any jewel cities."

"So, where?" asked Royal.

"Vladivostok."

"Lovely place."

"Sure. It's also their Pacific Fleet Headquarters. Nobody, I repeat nobody, ever gets invited there for any reason. So, we're suspicious, right?"

"Okay. You're suspicious. So. . . ?"

"They're up to something, Jack. They never do anything just for the hell of it. There's always a reason whenever the Soviets agree with us, and none of State's intelligence people can figure it out. Or, I should say most of them are baffled."

"You didn't bring me down here to leave me hanging. Who came up with what?"

"Don't think that there's anything simple here. We've done a lot of postulating, and most of this is based on theory, and some recent analyzing we've been able to do on Soviet military movements.

First, you know the Russians and Chinese are at each other's throats. They've been warning us for years about how dangerous the other is. The one who's telling us the story at the time is our friend and doesn't want us to trust the other."

"Okay. Go on."

"While the Russians are telling us the Chinese open door to the west is a lot of crap and we'd better prepare ourselves, the Chinese are saying pretty much the same thing about the Russians. But we seem to think the Chinese would kind of like to hold out as long as possible, since they still don't have the military technology the Russians do. That's one of the things they want from us."

"That's obvious. Any businessman can tell you that, while the Chinese want trade, technology exchange, and all the other things in their song and dance, they really want the technology and industrial expansion to kick the shit out of the Russians some day . . . and perhaps us right after that."

"Exactly. That's why the Russians are warning us every day."

"What's this all have to do with a ship's visit to Vladivostok? How many have been invited there?"

"Most of those that will be in the area at the time. So far, they're appeasing the President, making it seem that this time they're going all out to be good guys. They're willing to play host to the whole damn fleet if we want, even to the extent of opening up the one port that we've come to believe is their greatest naval secret."

"I think I see."

"Jack, we're so damn thin for ships now, we're spread all over the world. We can't be everywhere at once and the surface ships that will be around Japan or the China Sea or The Philippines are now scheduled to steam into Vladivostok between Christmas and New Year's. The Russians don't celebrate Christmas. New Year's is their specialty. But they're going to make an exception for the Americans."

"What's left to defend everything else out there?"

"Not a hell of a lot. If the available U.S. ships in that part of the world are showing the flag in Vladivostok while the Soviets are exercising a bit of sea control, you can imagine how we're going to look. If it doesn't appear contrived to most everyone else, you can be sure our hosts would point it out. A *fait accompli,* right? Moscow says that their new friends, the Americans, are even better friends now. Hell, they might even be able to threaten us somehow, since we'll be their guests."

"That's one of the most fantastic stories I've ever heard."

"Yeah, isn't it though. Except the more we look at the computer and what the Russians seem to be doing, it becomes a bit more logical."

"That's what you're in business for, Ted. But what the hell do you think I can do about this. I really don't give a damn which one of them wins. We'd all probably be better off if they wasted each other."

"That's the trouble with you civilians. So," and

Royal noticed his friend had never looked so serious before, "perhaps a little something extra will impress you a bit more. At least, I think it's going to be the kicker. Jack, since 1945, the Russians have been trying to one-up us. Do you think that they'd allow the Seventh Fleet to get away without doing something to take advantage of us with our pants down?" He answered his own question. "I think they're going to try to hold us up somehow . . . more than likely with their missile subs. I don't know how. Hell, I don't have any answers. But this will go a hell of a lot farther than just China."

"You *are* serious, aren't you?"

"I've never been more serious, Jack. The people that will still listen to me agree on the need for outsiders, people respectable beyond the Navy, people with solid business backgrounds. We need intelligence, a good cover, everything we couldn't do ourselves or with our own spooks. I didn't finger you right away. You just came to the surface without too much pushing on my part. Mr. Right," he grinned.

Finally, after a period of ten or fifteen seconds that had seemed like minutes, Royal remarked, "I suppose you really would have preferred a professional for this job."

"I always prefer professionals."

"I guess there's no doubt that everything might not work just like it's supposed to."

Ted Magnuson looked directly at him for an instant. "I don't expect anything. In my job I am suspicious of everything, and I expect anyone working for me to approach their job with the same idea. Old friendships aside, we're making a deal, a business deal if that makes it clearer to you. Whatever business you're looking for in Russia, the State Department guarantees support. It's an exchange between us, just like money passing hands. I didn't ever say I was giving you anything for free, did I?"

"Enough said."

Magnuson showed him satellite photos of the new construction in Da Nang and Cam Ranh Bay, along with Soviet supply ships standing off those ports waiting to offload. There was an impressive list of Russian war ships transferring to the Pacific. Classified reports on abnormal movement of supplies had been prepared.

Then, as if to add a note of caution, Magnuson showed movements by the Chinese. They seemed to be responding to an extent by moving forces in Manchuria toward the Soviet border near Khabarovsk, a city claimed by both sides. Reports of heavier anti-sub patrols in the East and South China Seas indicated that the Chinese were wary of something developing in their territorial waters, or at least waters that they considered to be under their jurisdiction.

And finally, adding another subdued note of caution, the Admiral said, "Our agents in both countries have noted a tightening of security. It's nothing that will affect you, or at least I doubt it. But it's worth keeping in mind. They might keep closer touch with Americans in the next few months."

"How do I get around Moscow? You know the Russians don't just give Americans free rein to wander around the countryside."

"I have a man in the Ministry of Internal Affairs, a Soviet version of a businessman, if you will. He'll be meeting you almost as you step off your plane. Both Intourist and the Ministry will let him shepherd you around. And, believe it or not, he's going to see that you're one of the first Americans to visit Vladivostok in about ten years. And then you're hopefully going to contact an agent on the Pacific Fleet staff who can tell you what Maslov is planning and when." Magnuson smiled at his old friend. "I'm hoping you'll be the first American private citizen allowed both in and out of Vladivostok and come back to talk about it."

"Ted," Royal sighed, "we see eye-to-eye on everything but your sense of humor."

OCTOBER 1984

CHAPTER FIVE

Autumn in Moscow can be lovely, but it is limited to a few glorious weeks. It follows a summer that can be as hot as the Russian winter is bitterly cold and it provides a very short respite to the Moscovites who know that the first snows will fall in November.

Jack Royal was enjoying one of those fall days, one that was comfortably clear and cool following a frosty night. Leaves that had been colorful the previous week now scurried down the streets of the Russian capital at the head of a strong breeze. The leaves were as brown and drab as many of the buildings they darted past. But the autumn sun, much lower in the sky even at noon, was bright and the American joined the Russians in Red Square raising their faces to these last warming rays.

Today was a day Royal had been looking forward to and dreading at the same time. The anticipation of surprising Bob Miller, half way around the world in Moscow, elated him. The fact that the meeting was a set-up inspired guilt feelings he'd not encountered in years.

Miller was the last of the innocents, the complete family man, the hard-driving, honest businessman making that final plunge to become independent in his own business. It was purely by accident that Miller's name had surfaced in Magnuson's office. But it was no accident that Bob Miller's name had been pulled off that State Department visa list. It had rung a bell with Ted Magnuson.

It was uncanny how Magnuson could extract a common name from a long list and know it was the same Bob Miller that Royal had shared a state-room with on a destroyer years before. Magnuson had been Royal's drinking buddy for only one summer. Miller had remained a life-long friend, the type whose door would be open in the middle of the night when you haven't seen each other for ages.

Miller was a computer expert, a genius according to one of the trade magazines. He had established his own company after years of threatening to go out on his own. It had taken everything he had saved in addition to accepting the psychological scars of giving up the security large organizations pander to their employees. Miller oriented his business to small companies who had access to the hardware but were not sophisticated enough to develop applications to modernize their businesses. He had come to the Soviet Union after a group of Soviet computer experts, touring the U.S., had visited his small company. They told him how welcome he'd be in Russia, and arranged his visit.

Bob Miller had no idea his name had turned up on a list in Ted Magnuson's office. He had even less of an idea that those things still happened in the United States. Miller had last seen Jack Royal on a hot Fourth of July weekend in Vermont earlier that year and never dreamed that the next place he'd see his old friend was strolling through the pathways of the Kremlin in the heart of Moscow. The reason for Miller's selection was a message Magnuson received a few weeks earlier and which confirmed his suspicions:

The key to Seagull remains secure in the computer. All operational planning remains in Vladivostok except for logistical planning assigned to Vol'sk School in Moscow. Supply plans can provide answers you need.

As a result, Bob Miller, the computer expert, had his name extracted from a final list of five. Neither Magnuson nor Royal had any idea how he might help, but the Admiral had an agent in the Soviet supply system. Even a one per cent chance was worth the gamble. With misgivings, Royal agreed with Magnuson. He would try to bring Miller into the fold.

Out of the corner of his eyes, Royal saw Ivan Petrov striding purposefully across Red Square, waving as he recognized the American. Petrov had been a shadow from the moment Royal arrived, recognizing him as he stepped from the plane, and greeting him at the foot of the steps. He explained in near perfect English that he was an economist from such-and-such a ministry and that he was re-

sponsible to the country to ensure Royal's visit was
an economic success. Petrov would also take a personal responsibility to see that he learned as much
as possible about the beauty and the culture of his
native land. Petrov was also Magnuson's man.
While they both knew it, nothing was said for the
first few days.

The early days were divided between meetings
with an interminable number of government officials and the museums and historic sites of Moscow and environs. Museums are the staple of Soviet cultural life. Schools provide a rigid curriculum
according to the desires of the state, but the galleries of Moscow offer the people as much of their
culture and history as they are likely to get. While
the economic and social history was limited to
post-1918, the paintings and sculpture went back
to the Renaissance, relating much of Russia's past
to Europe's.

Today's tour of the Kremlin, whose massive
walls faced Red Square, was a respite from the
boredom of the last few days of trying to do business in Russia. Now, the awesome beauty of the
cathedrals, Assumption and Annunciation especially, was in stark contrast to the mundane Soviet
system. Here were monuments to organized re-
ligion within a country that espoused no faith. Ivan
the Great—Tzar, Autocrat, Sovereign of All
Russia, Divine in the eyes of Almighty God—had
begun the monuments and they still reposed in the
Kremlin, seat of Communism and anti-God.

The Kremlin was breathtaking, and made
more so by Petrov whom Royal decided knew more

about guiding Americans than he did about economics. He was conversant on ancient frescoes, icons, and tapestries beyond valuation, the Armorer's Chamber where Ivan the Terrible's treasure still exists behind wrought iron doors, and jewelry, crowns, and thrones beautiful and precious beyond imagination. The Cross was strikingly evident in each of the buildings of the old Kremlin, its last haven in the Soviet Union.

The Ivans and Peter and Catherine and Nicholas were still fixed in their minds when once again they found themselves back in the bright sunlight. Resting on a granite frame near Archangel Cathedral was the King of Bells, two hundred tons of silence that had never rung.

"There has never been such a bell in the world," said Petrov. "It was ordered by Empress Anna in the early 1700's but was cracked by the water used to put out a fire in its own tower before it was ever hung."

"Why was it never repaired?" asked Royal.

"Come over to this side," commanded Petrov, beckoning. "Here you see where a segment of almost eleven tons broke off. It simply could never be repaired, but it stands as a monument to the glory days of the Romanov dynasty."

This was where Petrov had arranged it. He had been in touch with Miller's guide, explaining that the two Americans were old acquaintances and that it would be a wonderful surprise for both of them to meet quite by accident in the Kremlin. Miller's guide was neither especially bright nor ambitious. She found keeping up with the American was work and she decided Petrov's suggestion that perhaps he might handle both of the businessmen was an attractive proposition. Petrov bought her decision with an envelope of American money.

"Jack . . . Jack Royal . . . what in the world are you doing here?" Bob Miller had just stepped into the bright sunlight from the Cathedral of the Archangel and he was shading his eyes with his hand when he caught sight of an American tailored suit. Squinting through his glasses out of curiosity, he saw Royal standing by the bell.

"I'll be damned. I don't believe it." Royal responded as Miller crossed the short distance, his hand outstretched in greeting. "I had no idea you'd ever end up here, Bob."

Bob Miller wouldn't have stood out in a crowd of one. He was shorter than Royal by half a foot. Where the latter still had a firm middle, Miller's was beginning to bulge ever so slightly, when he wasn't consciously trying to hold it in. His dark hair was beginning to recede, and he still wore it in the short style common twenty years before. The afternoon sun had given his office pallor a reddish tinge and a few freckles were making a late season appearance. Even before he reached Royal, Jack noticed that he was pushing his thick horn-rimmed glasses further back on his short nose. It was a habit Miller had developed even before his Navy days.

The two Soviets stood back appreciatively, watching the Americans hug each other. Miller's guide remarked on the coincidence. Petrov nodded his agreement.

"It's time for a beer," said Royal. "The hell with

being tourists. We're due a couple of frosties."

"Great idea . . . but what about them," Miller asked, pointing at the two guides now engaged in conversation.

Royal shrugged. "Forget about them. Just a second. Ivan," he called waving his arm. "Come here for a moment, I want you to meet a friend." The two guides politely exchanged greetings with the Americans and Royal explained they simply wanted to have a beer together.

"May I suggest a place?" inquired Petrov. "Your friend's guide is willing to leave the two of you in my company, and I know just the bar Americans would enjoy."

It was all too easy. Miller, the family man, was lonely in Moscow. The companionship of an old friend was a shot in the arm. The fact that they were both in the impersonal, 6,000 room Hotel Rossiya was a plus. It was quickly arranged that Miller and Royal would travel together under Ivan Petrov's guidance.

Royal was uncomfortable. Miller was too nice a guy, too innocent, to be getting involved . . . yet Jack had agreed back in Washington to do it. And Petrov was Magnuson's man and Petrov reaffirmed that they didn't have a chance to get the information they needed without Miller.

That evening, while the three of them shared a bottle of vodka over dinner, Jack Royal explained why he was really in Moscow and what Petrov's role was. It was done gradually because the story sounded so outlandish at first. But Miller remembered Magnuson. And he also knew Jack Royal, the eternal bachelor, the man who was successful at whatever he touched, and it seemed logical that if anyone were to become involved in such a scheme it was Royal.

The romance of the situation amused Miller. The vodka helped to make it more attractive. The kicker was simply that Jack Royal said that the State Department would guarantee Miller all the business he could develop in the Soviet Union—no worry about competition or politics. The business would be his, and that would guarantee the success of his little company. Bob agreed to help even though neither Royal nor Petrov knew yet what was needed. But they explained the Russians were unaware of them and there was no danger. That was why Royal had agreed to help out Magnuson —a favor to an old friend!

Petrov knew a fine place for drinking beer, a very comfortable lounge at the Hotel National on Karl Marx Prospect, just outside the Kremlin walls. The beer was as bad as it had been the previous day, and Royal likened it to a local brew he had drunk in college that they had christened "swamp water." Petrov said nothing more about their other reasons for being in Moscow. He was as voluble and outgoing as ever about the places of interest still to be visited, and finished their conversation by outlining the appointment schedule for the following day.

"Now, let me drop you at the Rossiya. You need

a few hours in your room to yourselves." He had then leaned forward, elbows on the table, to snuff out his cigarette. In a very low voice, almost a whisper, he added quickly, "Remember, the walls . . ." and he had finished his sentence by pulling his right ear and nodding knowingly. Without losing a beat Petrov had pointed across the room to their waiter, indicating he wanted to pay.

"Thanks for the offer, Ivan," replied Bob Miller, pushing his glasses back. "I think we'd prefer to walk. I've read about a huge children's toy store and I thought I'd like to wander over there."

"Ah, *Dvitsky Mir* . . . Children's World," Petrov beamed. "Let me take you there then."

"No thanks. I don't mean to be impolite," Bob continued. "We could use the walk, sort of fit in with the crowd and see what the natives are doing."

Ivan laughed, almost a belly laugh. "Fit in with the natives!" he exclaimed. "You should see yourselves. In your American clothes, you might just as well go naked." He laughed again. "Take off those clothes of yours and go off down Karl Marx. The store is only about five blocks from here and you wouldn't stand out any more than you do right now." He grinned at his little humor.

The Americans strolled down the sidewalk of the wide thoroughfare, a chill beginning to tinge the air as the sun fell behind the spires and onion domes of the Kremlin. Petrov had been correct. They might just as well have been naked. Some of the austerely dressed people in the street simply stopped and stared, while others consciously moved farther away to give the strangers ample room.

Royal was in the right spot to sense the danger first. It was the terror in the eyes of a woman reflected in the display window he was looking into. They had just crossed Zdanova Street to the Dvitsky Mir block. Roual had stopped at the display in the first window while Miller, always the tinkerer, wandered to the edge of the wide sidewalk to examine an ancient Soviet truck apparently stalled in the street.

Jack Royal would never forget her eyes. The woman's face was exploding in anguish, eyes saucer-like, mouth torn open in a never-ending scream. As Royal whirled, he saw a black car bearing down on the sidewalk, racing directly at Miller. A little girl, not more than five years old he thought later, had wandered away from her mother's grip, staring at Miller's funny clothes. Royal's own voice echoed that of the woman's as she screamed at her child, he at Miller.

The little girl half turned toward her mother, then stopped, immobile, as she saw the car bearing down. Miller, in the same instant he heard Royal and became aware of the car, instinctively dove for the street, landing half under the stalled truck.

Royal, welded to his spot by the window, saw the car's wheels bounce over the curb. He felt time come almost to a halt, the world become slow motion, as the child's body was slammed by the left fender of the car. Then he saw a small shoe float

one way and a little red beret another as the tiny
body arched through the air toward the plate glass
window. The crunch of metal against the body cor-
responded with a second scream of anguish from
the mother. She had been running toward the girl,
still in slow motion in Royal's mind, the pain of
loss already evident in her eyes he thought, as she
saw the impact. Then the car continued on, hitting
the woman, mashing her body against the side of
the building as it came to a stop.

Slow motion returned to normal time in a flurry
of action and noise. He was alive, untouched. Feet
still planted, Royal heard screams from passersby,
stared at the child's bloody corpse in the display
window, red-smeared glass covering much of the
tiny form, saw the woman's crushed body sticking
grotesquely from under the car, her skirt ripped
from her by the impact.

Then he saw the driver.

That's what kept coming back to him later, between the replays of the horror before his eyes.
Perhaps he had expected to see an older person
slumped over the wheel, dead from a heart attack,
or maybe a hysterical driver in tears over the accident.

Instead, he saw a fairly young man, well attired
in a jacket and tie, first try the door on the driver's
side. Yanking at the handle he found the door
stuck. Jack saw no expression on the man's face
other than calm as he slid across the seat to open
the passenger door. But the driver stopped in mid
motion. The door was open. Another man, equally

expressionless, had opened it and was peering in, face set grimly, Later, Royal would think he saw the driver almost smile. But if he did, the smile turned instantly into fright, perhaps from recognition of the other. Then the driver slumped back toward the wheel.

The entire incident could not have taken more than fifteen or twenty seconds at most, though the picture seared into his brain seemed an eternity. Then he was lunging through the people at the curb, searching for Miller.

Bob was sprawled in the street, still partially under the truck but now up on one elbow, eyes fixed on the scene as people milled around the wreck. He had not been touched.

Royal turned back to the car, thinking suddenly of the man he had seen leaning in the passenger's side. No one was there. The door was shut, window up. He grasped the handle but the door was locked. The driver was slumped in the seat, eyes and mouth wide open in death.

With a ringing of bells, an ambulance appeared on the scene, attendants pulling stretchers from the back. Police began moving the crowds back. That was another thing that Royal questioned later— why had emergency help arrived so early? They were there less than a minute after the accident, taking charge, removing the bodies of the mother and child. It was too quick. A policeman had come up to them, obviously to ask questions, but had left them alone as soon as he realized they could not speak Russian.

Royal remembered afterward, as the shock wore off, that he had wanted to tell someone about the driver and the unidentified man who had opened the passenger door. But the mess had been cleaned up, the wrecked car gone, even the broken plate glass window was being repaired. The crowd had dispersed and those walking down the street were already paying more attention to the strangely dressed Americans than they were to the broken window or the once red smears on the sidewalk now turning black under pounding feet.

Petrov came to the hotel promptly at seven that evening, ringing Royal's room since this was the first time they were not already waiting for him in the lobby. When the Americans stepped from the elevator, the look in their eyes was all that was necessary. He knew what had happened, but listened politely to a short explanation. Then he went back outside. Leaning in the window of the taxi, he pulled money from his pocket, handed some bills to the driver and waved him on to a couple who had just come through the doors.

He came back to the two Americans, sliding an arm around each of their shoulders, guiding them over to the stairs leading up to the mezzanine and a V-shaped bar. It overlooked the lobby. With mirrors behind it and bottles stacked in tiers, the Rossiya had made an effort to make western tourists more comfortable.

Petrov was in control. He pulled out two barstools. "Sit down, relax. I have just the thing for you, something to relax the nerves before we dine tonight." He spoke quickly in his native tongue to one of the bartenders, who looked quizzically at Petrov for a moment and then nodded his assent to the request. Shortly, he returned with two old fashioned-type glasses, each brimming with ice. He removed a large frosted bottle from a block of ice behind the bar, filling each glass to the lip with the clear vodka. Then he placed an aperitif glass in front of Petrov, filling it with the frozen vodka, ready to be drunk in the traditional way.

Ivan turned to his two guests. "Eh, let's drink up." He raised his own glass, waiting for them to do likewise, then he downed the vodka in one gulp, exhaling and smiling at the same time. "See," he said to Royal and Miller, "just like America." He pointed at their glasses. "Just like your American martinis, eh? That will make you feel better."

They said little. The conversation was disjointed. Ivan asked a few questions about the accident. Then, after they had downed two of the huge vodkas, he announced it was time for dinner. "Tonight we will walk. It's not far, just back to where we were this afternoon, the National. They have one of the best dining rooms in the city. And it is a lovely night for a walk up there. Frost is in the air and it will clear your minds and make your appetite big for dinner. After today, you need something to restore your spirits."

On their way to the National, as they crossed an almost empty Red Square, Petrov stopped them for a moment. With the brightly illuminated tomb of Lenin behind them, the hammer and sickle flags spotlighted on the Kremlin walls, Petrov remarked quite simply, "That was no accident today." He looked first at Miller, nodding his head grimly. His eyes caught Jack's. "I think you are already aware of that, but I have done some checking. It wasn't the KGB either."

"Oh," murmured Royal. "You're sure?"

"I'm sure. From what I can gather, it's the GRU."

"What the hell is that?" asked Miller.

"It's similar to your ONI . . . to Magnuson's organization. They are military intelligence." He jerked his head to indicate that they should continue walking. "It makes no difference. They're just as dangerous."

"Will they try it again?" asked an incredulous Miller.

Petrov shrugged. "Who knows? They wouldn't have any idea about you." He inclined his head toward Royal. "More likely you. Perhaps they will wait to see if they scare you off." He was quiet as they trudged down a quiet street. Then he continued. "It seems we might cooperate with them."

"How?" asked Jack.

"I was contacted tonight . . . by Magnuson's other man. He said all logistics activities are being transferred from Moscow. They're worried about agents here, so they're even moving the Vol'sk group away."

"Where are they going?"

"Irkutsk . . . a very safe place, and very beautiful. Much closer to Vladivostok than to here, and in the middle of Siberia. If there are any foreign agents there I would be surprised. It's a wise decision . . . for all of us. You see, you American businessmen are now scheduled to visit the Irkutsk industries."

CHAPTER SIX

A brilliant glowing sun blinded him momentarily as he raised the shade. At first, the scene below was like any other landscape Ben Goodrich had ever seen in his travels. There were tinges of brown amidst the green of cultivated fields, tiny villages arranged near muddy rivers.

Until the plane descended low enough for Ben to see that the fields and villages were indeed vastly different from anything he had seen before, minutes seemed like hours. Then the land came up rapidly and the jet was bumping down the runway at Beijing's international airport. Once again, there was the thrill of things new and different. Buildings, service vehicles, ground crew uniforms, all were unlike anything he had experienced previously. The excitement was compounded as he stepped into a reception area teeming with Chinese. The people were smaller, their dress different, the sounds and language odd to the ear. Even the aroma of the cafeteria foods offered a unique sensation.

Goodrich had been tired on the plane and now he stretched muscles tight from hours in the cramped seats. Standing momentarily on his toes, he appeared taller than his six feet. This drew even more attention to his short, curly Afro hair style. There was no loose muscle around his middle and his ruddy complexion, coupled with dark eyes and hair, would make it difficult for anyone to guess that he was already over forty. He had grown up during an era of crew cuts and discipline and only his hair offered any hint that he was relaxing strict personal standards. Even at this hour of the day, he exuded an aura of confidence and success.

Ben failed to notice the imperceptible nod the customs official made to a little old man as he returned his visa, and he was unable to answer for a moment when the old gentleman stepped up, smiling and nodding his head, and said, "Mr. Goodrich . . . I welcome you to the People's Republic of China." The perfect English from the tiny man in the Mao-style, high-necked jacket was incongruous with the scene around him.

The little man was not more than an inch or so over five feet tall, and he might have weighed 120 pounds, being a bit stocky like many of the people around him. He was not bald, but his white hair was thin. His round face failed to give away his age, which might have been anywhere from fifty to seventy-five. There was a sense of dignity about the man, the way he held himself erect, his slow, metered English, the way his eyes looked directly into Ben's.

"I am not mistaken?" he questioned, a quizzical smile on his round face. "I am correct? Mr. Goodrich?"

"Why, yes. I'm Ben Goodrich." He awkwardly extended his arm to shake hands.

"I am Li Zhiang." He grasped the American's hand briefly in his own little one.

"I hadn't expected anyone to meet me at this hour," said Goodrich, looking at his watch. "Why, it's only seven o'clock."

"Early for you perhaps, sir, after traveling all night. But we Chinese arise early, with the sun generally." He again smiled, thoughtfully this time. "We have so much to do in a very short time." He turned, beckoning Ben to follow him, and another much younger man fell in step behind them. "That is our driver. He will help with the luggage. Let me assist in obtaining your bags. That tour group on your flight will create confusion and you might wait hours on your own."

It is difficult for anyone arriving in a totally different environment to catalog initial impressions of the first few hours. And it was no different for the American. At 8:00 a.m. the People's Republic of China was fully awake and working. It had been on the move for a couple of hours, its people already industriously involved in another day.

From the fields outside Beijing to the teeming streets of the capital city, the populace was either going somewhere purposefully or already there and involved in their duty. The mix of ancient habits with modern methods was what struck him initially, while Mr. Li maintained a continuous chatter, pointing out various sights he would have to see again.

Mr. Li was an official with the Petroleum Ministry. The old gentleman explained that he had been involved with coal, and then the natural gas and oil industries in China, and was also involved with the government in an official capacity. This was the reason he had been selected to meet the flight and coordinate his visit. He would work with Mr. Goodrich, whose field of interest was obviously the rich oil reserves of China.

The Beijing Hotel is on the main thoroughfare, Chang-An, near the heart of the city, close to the Great Hall of the People and Tien'Anmen Square. A large hotel, it is host to most of the foreigners visiting the city. Only those native Chinese doing business with these foreigners are allowed inside, and Mr. Li was one of those who entered without challenge, taking Ben directly to reception to check in.

After following him to his room and ensuring for himself that all would be comfortable, he said, "Mr. Goodrich, this has been a long hard trip for you and I'm certain you are very tired. I will leave you to catch up on your sleep, since it would be beneficial to all of us for you to adjust to our time as quickly as you can. I will call for you this evening at six. You are free to do as you please after you sleep. Beijing is a fascinating city and our people welcome you."

With that, Mr. Li excused himself politely, leaving Ben Goodrich completely mystified with the warm reception. Nowhere around the world had this occurred before.

Ben woke with a start, lost for an instant. The room, barely discernible with the curtains pulled tight, was alien to him. Rolling on to an elbow, he saw at the curtain edges that it was still light outside. The morning arrival in Beijing came back to him. His watch on the bedside table read two-thirty.

He rolled out of bed, stumbling over his shoes on the way to the window, and raised the shade. Below him lay an immense boulevard. Multi-colored flags waved in the sunlight and an orderly mass of humanity was flowing in both directions by bicycle. There were few automobiles. Two blocks down the street he recognized the Great Hall of the People from the many pictures he had seen. Smiling at his great good fortune to be in Beijing, he lay back down in bed, his hands behind his head and considered how fortunate he really was. . . .

Ben Goodrich was a consultant in the petroleum industry, and a maverick. He'd put in his time with more than a couple of the oil giants. He moved from place to place, company to company, until he knew enough of his business to be a manager—but he remained enough of a roamer that he never landed in the executive suite. The money was in exploration, the discovery of new fields, and entrepreneurs paid people like Ben a great deal of money for his knowledge.

He tried to settle down once. It seems like ages ago, he thought. She had been a lovely girl, one who wanted a home in the suburbs and a family. And Ben tried. But the traveling and commuting were rough and he finally convinced her to move back into New York, just to experiment with it for a year. It hadn't worked. The more each of them tried, the farther they grew from each other. And one night when he came home to their apartment, there was a note on the mirror. It was simple and straightforward and Ben knew she was right, but he refused to acknowledge it.

So, he attempted to return to his old ways again. The drinking and women took their toll and affected his work. It took a friend to convince him of what he already knew, that he was getting too old to burn the candle at both ends, and he found himself in front of his mirror the next morning admitting it.

"Goodrich," he told the lather-covered face looking back at him, "nothing turns you on any more. Not money, not work, not even women. Think of that!" The red rimmed eyes looked back at him. "You don't even get excited by bringing a broad home anymore. You were once the scourge of the U.S. Navy, but that was twenty years ago. Now you don't even like to compare notes the next morning. That's how bad you've gotten. Sooner or later, one of them's going to ring your bell for the last time. She might even stick a knife in your ribs —and you'd deserve it. *You* don't even like yourself these days." He winced from the hot water. He hadn't noticed that he'd turned it on.

As he splashed cold water on his face to rinse off the remaining lather, he conceded, "On a human level, and at the ripe old age of forty-three, you've screwed up forty-three years. Are you going to do the same for the next forty-three?"

That morning, Goodrich went to the library at the Petroleum Institute and sat down with all the information he could find on China. He knew it couldn't be proven, but his assumptions were reinforced as he read further. There seemed to be more oil reserves in Western China and under the South China Sea than the Arabs ever thought of. But the Chinese lacked the technical skills and entrepreneurial abilities to get it out of the earth successfully enough to make it pay off. They needed American petroleum technology and even more, they needed people like him. Before the day was over, he had written to CITIC, the China International Trust and Investment Corporation, the private agency desperately trying to attract money, business, and businessmen from outside China.

Within two weeks, he received a letter from Rong Yiren, the resurrected capitalist who established CITIC. The man put Goodrich in touch with China National Gas and Oil Exploration and Development. In less time than he could have dreamed, they had made arrangements for him to visit China. It literally seemed that they couldn't get him there fast enough.

It was his last chance to start over again, to

forget the booze and the women, to make a name for himself again . . . perhaps even to find that love that had so far eluded him.

The decor in the Fangshan Restaurant was exquisite. Ben knew it was a very special place, for there were no other foreigners. The Chinese were most discreet in looking over the American. None could be caught staring as the people along Chang'An had done that afternoon. He had even been followed briefly, at a distance, to study his strange clothes.

"The expression we use, Mr. Goodrich, is 'gan-bei.' It means 'bottoms up' or something close to that in your language." Mr. Li was responding to Ben's question about offering a toast. "Normally, the individual stands and makes his toast, then it's . . . gan-bei."

Goodrich stood. "I'm a bit awkward at this sort of thing, but it's the only way I know at this point to say thank you to you and your daughter for your courtesy and hospitality. I have never felt so comfortable in one day in a strange country before." He smiled briefly at both of them, then followed with "gan-bei." The mao-tai liquor was high in alcohol content and they already were feeling its effects.

"You are most kind, Mr. Goodrich." Their cups were immediately filled by a waitress hovering near their table to ensure there was always enough to drink.

Mr. Li had met him promptly at six in the lobby.

With him was his daughter, Li Han, on leave from the military. He had explained that she would serve as hostess this evening since his wife was crippled and unable to move freely beyond their home.

Li Han was beautiful, decided Ben, as they proceeded through the many dinner courses. She was slender and taller than her father. Her face was wide at the cheekbones, setting off sparkling black eyes. The eyes were not slanted as Americans often believed. They were actually almond-shaped and, when she smiled at some of his expressions, the wide high cheekbones, coupled with the dancing eyes, heightened her beauty. Her command of English was equal to her father's. She explained that everyone in the school she attended had to learn English to graduate.

Ben wasn't sure it was proper for an American but the mao-tai had given him the courage to finally ask Mr. Li about the Long March. He had read a great deal about it and wanted to find someone he could talk with about the ordeal.

"You are dining with him," answered Li Han, looking proudly at her father. "My mother also was one of the thirty women to join in the march."

"Mr. Li, you would make my visit if you could tell me about that experience," said Goodrich.

"I am pleased that an American would want to learn about our own revolution. Your country supported Chiang Kai-Shek's Kuomintang, our opposition. I doubt that we are that popular with your countrymen even yet."

Ben smiled, "You're correct, Mr. Li, to an extent. Our government assisted Chiang, against the recommendations of General Stilwell and many others. Once we get into something, we hate to admit we're wrong, or at least that we're sticking our noses somewhere they don't belong. So good money followed bad and then we found ourselves watching Chiang rape his own country."

Li Han's eyebrows raised. "I never expected to hear an American say that, since the United States still wants to assist the expatriates on Taiwan, thirty-five years after the revolution."

"Don't misunderstand me, Miss Li. I am willing to acknowledge that there are two sets of Chinese people under two different governments. You see only one. This is our disagreement."

"And that is a statement I don't believe I have ever heard an American make to a Chinese. Your people do not talk about Taiwan when they visit us." Mr. Li folded his arms, tilting his head quizzically to the side.

"Perhaps most Americans you meet are associated with our government or have been cautioned not to mention that sore point if they want to make business deals with your country. I'm not involved with the government. I'm on my own, sir," Ben replied with a smile. He felt a surge of pleasure, the feeling that comes with new people and new challenges, the excitement of a new country.

"Perhaps that is the case, Mr. Goodrich. Since you are so interested in our Long March, I will be happy to discuss it with you. But not tonight.

You must be still tired after your long trip, and I am very tired after a long day. I'm not as young as you." He smiled. "In my youth, I had your energy, but now I'm content to sleep when my body tells me I am tired. Tomorrow evening, you shall come to my home for dinner. My daughter will help her mother prepare a dinner that few Americans have ever experienced, a feast of country foods. Then, I will tell you about the Long March, if you'd care to hear an old man dredge up memories."

"I'd be delighted, sir," said Ben. "I was told that few Americans are ever invited into Chinese homes."

"That's true, Mr. Goodrich. Let's say that I have a special interest in you. I also respect a man who will talk to me directly, who will say what he thinks rather than what he hopes I want to hear."

Li Han added, "My father has never invited Americans to our home, at least when I have been in Beijing." She smiled a warm, happy smile at Goodrich. "It will be an honor to have you, and a chance for me to practice more of a disappearing art. The people in some sections of the nation still eat the food my father mentioned. The recipes are the result of preparing whatever they could during the years of the revolution. The food is simple and often highly spiced. I have learned from my mother how to prepare many of the dishes so that she does not have to move around. This is an art, something I would also lose in time without practice. It is a tradition I want to preserve so that my own children and their children eat as their ancestors did during those days. It is one way of preserving history."

At the rear of the dining room, a musician began playing a plaintive song on a strange instrument. The dining room quieted immediately. Mr. Li explained that it was an erh-hu, an ancient two-stringed instrument, similar to the violin, and that the woman was playing music from far back in Chinese history. The sound was strange to the American ears, but soothing.

The evening ended early, and as Ben rose from the table, Mr. Li pointed at the crumbs and spots from the various courses they had eaten. "There is an old Chinese proverb, which loosely translated in your language means 'the tablecloth should look like a battlefield after a good meal.' You have eaten like a Chinese on your first night in our country. I think that you will be a good guest and will enjoy yourself in my home."

As Goodrich stepped from the car at the front of the hotel, Mr. Li said, "Tomorrow is a very busy day for me. My daughter has agreed to guide you on a tour of the Great Wall, and perhaps the Ming Tombs if you have time. I look forward to your visiting my home tomorrow night."

As the car pulled away, Ben mused to himself, "That Li Han is one of the most beautiful women I've ever met. It's not only her features, but the way she expresses herself." He shook his head in wonder as he remembered that she also had explained she was a naval officer, on leave from her command at Zhanjiang in the south of China.

*   *   *

Ted Magnuson bent forward over his desk,
stretching his arms behind him, rereading the
memorandum Benjamin had sent over by courier.
It had been issued by the President to all White
House aides. Its meaning was obvious:

> I consider my efforts to date to again achieve deqtente
> with the Soviet Union to be of the highest
> priority. If there is to be a hallmark of this office, it
> will be this effort. I have an understanding with the
> Premier of the U.S.S.R., worked out over many
> trying days at a conference table. It bears my signa-
> ture and that of the Premier, two honorable men who
> will stand by their word. The visit by units of the Sev-
> enth Fleet to Vladivostok over the New Year
> portends the arrival of a new era in Soviet/American
> relations. I personally look with disfavor on those
> who would disturb this fragile relationship by in-
> timating that the leaders of the Soviet Union are us-
> ing this country's military forces to effect a new
> strategy in the Western Pacific. It should be under-
> stood that further efforts in this direction or in active-
> ly planning undercover military operations in
> Vladivostok will invite termination of responsibilities
> within this administration.

Benjamin's handwritten note accompanying the
copy of the President's memorandum said, "In
other words, he means screw off!"

Magnuson considered Benjamin's scrawled note
for a moment more. Then, he outlined the message
he would send to his Shanghai contact, Jack
Darby. Jack would be in Hong Kong in a week, on
one of his normal business visits to anybody who

might pay attention to the old Englishman. He'd welcome the opportunity to do a bit of undercover work again. Admiral Magnuson decided it was important that Darby get to know Loomis. It was odd how those names from the past had a way of popping up on the State Department's visa list. Tom Loomis was the same vintage as Royal. Magnuson had forgotten Tom long ago. He'd never really cared for him. But the man was another maverick, and he might just be of some use to Darby.

Magnuson smiled to himself as he sealed the note, the President's memo still on the corner of his desk. He had no proof the Chinese were to be the ultimate victims of Seagull at all. But his sixth sense had usually been correct. If not, he would experience a "termination of responsibilities" in the near future.

CHAPTER SEVEN

The ever-present black car was waiting at the front entrance of the Beijing Hotel at precisely six o'clock the following evening. While the driver spoke only Chinese, his courtesy and desire to please were infectious as he smiled and bowed his passenger into the back seat.

The evening was cool, much like a typical autumn evening in New England, thought Ben Goodrich. When he was young, fall days and nights smelled of burning leaves. In Beijing, the city smelled of cabbage for it was harvest time in the communes. Fresh supplies of giant cabbages came into the city every day, lining the sidewalks and attracting hordes of flies, with only the refuse left at the end of the day to perfume the air. Before morning, even the rotting leaves would be scavenged by withered old ladies to be replaced by the next day's harvest.

In the fading dusk, the old men were bringing in briquettes made of coal dust and water. During the day, they packed them by hand and left them to harden in the sun. As darkness fell, they brought the black cakes in, stacking them in neat piles near their stoves. They burned more slowly than natural coal and provided the only heat for much of the city's populace. They also created thick smoke that would turn the winter skies gray and cover the city with a layer of soot.

Earlier that day, Li Han had provided him with this information as their car wound through the streets towards the outskirts and on to the main highway to the Great Wall. Peasants waved to the black car from the fields, knowing that someone important must be inside. The sun, in the perpetually cloudless autumn sky, warmed the passengers as Li Han explained their surroundings.

While he took in every sight, asking questions, Ben couldn't resist studying Li Han out of the corner of his eye. She looked so fresh. Her eyes expressed as much as her voice, punctuating every word, her eyebrows rising with each point. Her black hair was cut short, almost American in style, something she had laughed about the night before when she explained that her sea duty required her hair to be shorter than most. But not a hair was out of place. And she wore brighter clothes than most of the women he had seen during his very brief stay in Peking. They were cut tighter, fitted to her small body, and Ben decided that contrary to what he had been told before they left the U.S., Chinese women could be very sexy. She was beautiful, unlike any other woman he had met before, and he intended to be very good friends with her.

The Ming Tombs are just off the main road, not too far from the Great Wall. It was here that thirteen emperors of the Ming Dynasty had been buried with all their servants. The road into the tombs was lined with full-sized pairs of statues of men and animals. They looked out at enormous weathered white elephants and camels and lions as they followed the same approach made by solemn funeral processions hundreds of years before.

Much of the Great Wall lies in disrepair, but the section that tourists are shown at Badaling is only ninety miles from Peking and is in perfect condition. Planned 2,000 years before and built of mud, it once snaked almost 4,000 miles across the mountains. It was intended to keep the Mongol hordes from disturbing the serenity of the Central Kingdom. Seven hundred years before, the Ming Dynasty had begun to cover its twenty foot barrier with brick and stone to ensure the permanence of their rule.

Li Han told stories of the ghosts of the more than 300,000 people who had built the wall, and of the woman who came back over the centuries to wail for her husband who had been buried alive inside it for a minor crime. Her knowledge of every detail amazed him.

"How did you learn so much about this, Li Han," inquired Ben. "You sound like a tour guide."

She smiled appreciatively. "You might say I have acted as one from time to time, mostly for my father. He is responsible for many important people visiting China. When your President Nixon made his first visit here, I was called up from duty in Shanghai to be one of his guides for a few days. I brought him to this exact spot." She turned to point northward, her arm sweeping in an arc. "I told him about the fear of the barbarians, and how I knew my people were as worried then about invasion from the north as we are today."

"The Russians?"

"Yes, the Russians. We are as concerned with their invading our country today as my ancestors were of the Mongols."

"You said your father arranged to have you guide Mr. Nixon. What puts your father in such a position, Li Han?" asked Ben.

"He's with the Petroleum Ministry. He was a friend of Chairman Mao, as you know, from the Long March. They were very close. Mao saved his life at the Battle of Tsunyi."

"Mao has been dead for many years. Who does your father know now?"

"He still has many friends in the government," she answered defensively, turning across the battlement to another vantage point.

That was the end of Ben's attempt to learn more about his host. Prior to sleeping the night before, Ben had realized Li Zhiang was more than simply an old gentleman involved in the developing Chinese petroleum industry. Wherever he had gone, there had been more than simple deference to his age. Doors were held with much scraping and bowing, and it was obvious that his face was known to most every citizen.

Now, as the car pulled up before his destination that evening, it was even more obvious. The Li's lived in neither an apartment nor one of the thousands of row houses so common to the city. Their home was a separate building, small but regal, with well kept gardens and flowers blooming gorgeously even in October. He remembered that Mrs. Li was crippled and her husband was a busy man. Servants must have maintained this appearance, and servants were not common in Beijing.

Mr. Li and his daughter appeared at the door as Goodrich stood admiring the gardens. "Are you a gardener?" the old man inquired as he came out to greet Ben.

"No, I live in the city, in a high rise . . . a tall building," he clarified. "The people who garden have little flower boxes outside the window or sometimes a small terrace where they grow a few things in wooden planters. But nothing like this."

"I'm sorry to hear that," Mr. Li responded. "There is great peace in flowers, a hobby that relaxes you."

"Do you take care of these gardens by yourself?" Ben inquired.

"No," was the wistful answer. "I wish I could. I dabble at it, and try. But I must have a man help me." He looked directly into Ben's eyes. "I pay him for his work." He turned and led him back to the door, adding as they went, "My wife has been looking forward to meeting you very much. As you may know, most of our women do not become involved with foreigners, but my wife learned your language with me many, many years ago. Her fervent wish when she learned you were coming to China was to meet you."

"I'm pleased my visit is considered so important, sir," replied Ben. "But, really, this is simply a business trip."

Again, Mr. Li turned to meet Ben's eyes directly. "We consider it that way also, but your business background is different from most of the Americans that come here. They are salesmen. They want to expand their company's profits by our backwardness. You are more than that, I think. We believe you may be able to help us quite a bit more."

Ben was escorted down a short hallway that entered into a room similar to an American living room. Mr. Li touched Goodrich's arm lightly. "We can discuss business in more detail tomorrow. Tonight we celebrate new friends."

In the middle of the room, buried in a deep, soft chair faded by years of wear, sat a tiny, gray haired woman, whose wrinkled face made her appear much older than her husband. She wore an embroidered black dress, tailored much like her daughter's clothes, yet she seemed to disappear within the shiny cloth, her gnarled hands barely peeping from under the sleeves.

"Mr. Goodrich, may I present my wife." He moved quickly to her side, a hand at her elbow as she rose slowly, almost painfully, to a height of perhaps four and a half feet. She took no more than a halting step to meet him, her hand appearing from the sleeve as she extended her arm.

"I am honored that you join us this evening." Her English was as perfect as her husband's, her words as slow. She rolled each word individually. As she waited for Ben to come to her, her shoulders visibly straightened. She smiled a sincere welcome and, as she did so, her eyes sparkled from the wrinkled face with youth and vitality.

Aware that she was greeting him in the American fashion, he took her hand in his own, surprised at how tiny it was as it disappeared in his grip.

"I consider it a great honor to be invited into your home. Few Americans are honored in this manner."

Mrs. Li returned to her deep chair, very slowly sinking into it with the assistance of her husband and daughter. "I do not have the opportunity to speak English often. It's a very complex language and so easy to forget. My family speaks it with me on occasion so that I can take part in the conversation when we have guests." She thought for a moment, then added, "We have had only one other American in our home since the President's visit. Isn't that correct?" she asked her husband.

Mr. Li inclined his head slightly, "Yes, and that was a few years ago." He murmured a few words imperceptibly to her in their own language, then turned to Goodrich. "Let me show you our home, while my wife and daughter finish preparations for our dinner."

"I think, Mr. Goodrich, before I begin, we

should understand a little about each other's history."

To the American's surprise, after the women of his family had prepared an exquisite meal served by a maid, Mr. Li offered brandy and cigars. He explained that Chinese custom currently did not favor luxuries of this nature, but it was allowed when entertaining foreigners.

He continued. "I have studied your country's history closely, especially your own revolution. Are you aware of the vast similarities between our struggles for freedom?" He raised his hand to note that he hadn't finished. "Perhaps I should qualify that. We fought the Kuomintang for over twenty years, and even joined them against the Japanese, while your battle with the British was much shorter."

"I'd be foolish to answer that question, wouldn't I. Only our scholars have easy access to modern Chinese history. My knowledge is limited."

"I didn't mean to put you in an awkward position. It's just that I think the Americans should know how similar our struggles have been. Our revolution was Communist, and your people have been trained to think all communism is Russian. Am I correct?"

"Generally," Ben answered, "but communism in this century has meant bloody revolution wherever it's appeared. Our country has existed for more than two hundred years. You must admit that war two hundred years ago was quite different from today."

"Perhaps my beginning to this story was inadequate," replied Mr. Li. "Let me begin again by stating that Mao had no more business raising an army to fight Chiang than George Washington did against the English . . . . except each man thought he could rally the people of his country behind him.

"Our army was getting beaten as badly as General Washington's, every time. I have read your history books, and the Long March I'm going to tell you about was no different than the early years of your own revolution. Our escape from the Juichen base was a victory just like your Battle of Trenton." Here, he paused just a moment for emphasis. "It allowed us time to escape from the probability of early defeat."

Li Han spoke for the first time. "Mao was surrounded at Juichen. The forces of the Kuomintang were closing in. The only element left was surprise."

"The Long March was nothing romantic to begin with," continued Mr. Li. "It was a headlong flight from encirclement and certain torture and death. Your winter at Valley Forge was our Long March." His voice had risen, emotion evident for the first time since they had met. "I was an officer then and I believed in Mao more than anything else in my life . . . then or now. Others did not. They deserted or went back to their farms, just as Washington's men did. War wasn't in their blood. Your ancestors fought Hessians. I looked into the skies on many days to see German aircraft flown by German pilots strafing my men. We had to live off the countryside, depending on what little food there was from the peasant farmers . . . . just as Washington's army did. And often there was nothing to eat!"

Mrs. Li was sitting up in her chair, her face composed, and when she spoke, her words were much faster than earlier in the evening. "You will understand that it is still sometimes difficult for my husband to discuss this subject. We are emotionally involved, more than you can imagine, for we actually took part in our revolution. Yours was long ago and the history books explain it to you in print, unemotionally. Oral history is emotional. Events can be colored by what one saw or thought he saw in an instant. There has not yet been time for the writers to compile their records and present them in a factual order."

"I know that," Ben answered. "I couldn't have put it in the same words, but that's why I *am* interested."

Mr. Li began, his eyes fixed on an invisible spot on the ceiling. "There were a hundred and twenty thousand of us when we broke through. Twenty-five thousand of our men were killed, just in smashing Chiang's lines so the rest of us could escape. And when we did, we had to cross the Hsiang River, where the main force of the Kuomintang Army waited . . . . the *main* force! We lost thirty thousand more just in that crossing. Even after that, they never let up. We broke out in October, 1935. By November, it was bitterly cold and we had no winter clothes, none at all. We moved directly west towards the mountains, and when we first rested two months later, after leaving Chiang's army behind," and here he spread his hands in despair, "there were only thirty thousand men left of all those who had broken out. Think of that. Ninety thousand of our small army slaughtered in about two months. Chiang's hatred of Communists led him to only one solution: annihilate us!"

The old man went on without interruption, living each step of the March, suffering with the loss of each man, explaining the politics that changed constantly, until Mao, after taking Tsunyi for the first time, called a halt. While his men rested, he exerted his leadership, with Chou En-Lai's aid, and had himself elected as Chairman of the Revolutionary Military Council. That was when he took over command of all elements of the Party for good and established the principles that would lead them to victory in 1949, fourteen years later.

"Excuse me just a moment," interrupted Goodrich. He turned to Li Han. "Didn't you say that your father was saved by Mao at the Battle of Tsunyi?"

"Yes, I did," she answered quietly, looking at her father. The old man's eyes had filled. He chose not to speak.

Again, his wife spoke up. "Mr. Goodrich, when a man is against such odds, cold, starvation, bullets, day after day, month after month, he loses his will to survive unless some factor in his existence maintains that will to live. No matter what our government later says about Chairman Mao as an old man, he was a leader, like few in history. He dressed no better than his people. He ate no more. He slept less than anyone. His leadership meant everything to us. When the men were in action, Mao was beside them.

"To attack Tsunyi, we first had to cross the Wu River, over three hundred yards wide, then scale the cliffs on the opposite side, always under fire. My husband was in Mao's boat. A shell exploded close aboard, killing some of them outright, and tipping the rest into the water. Mao was unhurt. As soon as he came to the surface, he was concerned for his men. He went to each floating body to determine if they were alive or not. My husband was one of those. He had grasped something floating in the water, but apparently had given up. Mao swam to him, held his head above the water, and told him he would not let a friend die, especially one as loyal as his friend, Li Zhiang. My husband remembers Mao insisting that he, too, help to rescue others, that they could not risk losing any more men. When Mao swam away, and went to the next man, my husband could do no less than the same thing. It took four days of battle, but does that explain why they were then able to scale those cliffs and capture Tsunyi?"

Nothing was said for a moment.

"Our glasses are empty. I don't mean to be a poor host." Mr. Li, his face a mask against any emotions from the story his wife had just finished, rose and refilled the snifters, adding an equal amount to his own.

Ben Goodrich swirled the amber liquid, holding

it to the light, then sniffed it gently. "I never expected to see a glass of brandy during this visit, Mr. Li. You are a very gracious host."

"It was always a joke of Mao's that I could never rid myself of some of the capitalist habits I picked up during my organizing days, before I became a soldier. I worked with Chou in Shanghai, and spent much time in the International Settlement explaining our side to the British. They taught me to also enjoy the good life." He smiled, raising a snifter in salute, "To the British. There were some very fine men among them."

"There seems to be quite a bit about you beyond your oil interests that I don't know."

"There is a great deal I don't know yet about you, either." Mr. Li was not smiling when he added this. "But let me get back to my story."

The old man told of Mao's now firm conviction that he must escape once and for all from Chiang's pursuit so that they could reorganize. The Japanese invaders were taking advantage of the civil war in China to take over vast tracts of land in the rich northeastern provinces. If they could defeat the Japanese, then the people would support the Communists. But first, he must settle with Chiang, and at the same time bring together the factions from many of the independent northern and western warlords.

The winter was cold, and Mao spent much of it wheeling his army in many directions, drawing the Kuomintang troops into traps set by his much smaller forces. Twenty enemy divisions were destroyed that winter as Mao moved into the western mountains bordering Tibet, then north. The primitive tribes in these western provinces were hostile to all armies and they ambushed Mao's troops with spears and boulders.

"We moved north and west, dividing our forces into smaller groups. Chiang would have less of a chance of major victory against an army separated into smaller units. Then, intelligence sources learned that Chiang was planning a stand at Luting, using the Tatu River as a barrier. Part of our force was sent southeast to cross the river on barges, as a diversion, for we knew that much of the one major bridge over the Luting had been destroyed. The river cuts through a mountain range leaving a series of deep gorges. It could be crossed neither to the north nor to the south, except in the well defended flatland area where our men used the barges. They were met with stiff resistance and we hoped perhaps Chiang might think this was the main attack and send all his forces there. But, when we arrived at the bridge, much of it was destroyed, and they were waiting. . . ." Again, Mr. Li was forced to stop, his eyes brimming with emotion. He looked at Goodrich, his eyes blinking, but said nothing.

Mrs. Li looked first to her husband, then to her guest and said, "You must excuse us. It is late and my husband does not care to continue. It has been difficult to talk of the old days." She rose slowly from her chair, moving painfully, step by step to her husband's side, placing her hands on his shoul-

ders, massaging them softly. Mr. Li looked up at
her. He said nothing, but took one of her tiny
hands in his own, gently pressing it to his cheek.

Li Han rose from her place at the table. "If you
will excuse me, I will see my parents to their
room."

Goodrich also stood. "Excuse me . . . I didn't
realize the hour," said Ben. "I'll find my way out.
The driver is waiting. I didn't mean to
overstay. . . ."

"No, not at all," responded Mr. Li in a new,
small, soft voice, almost a whisper. "We could not
allow a guest to do that. My daughter will be most
pleased to see you out. I . . . I'm sorry to leave you
like this. As I become older, the memories become
more difficult. Please . . . please excuse us." He
stood and took one of his wife's arms as Li Han
took the other.

"We are so pleased you could join us," Mrs. Li
smiled, inclining her head in Ben's direction. "I sincerely hope you will join us again. It has been
a most pleasant evening for me . . . for all of us,"
she said, as she slowly turned and left the room,
back again straight against the pain of movement.

"Please help yourself to more brandy, if you
wish," said Li Han. "I will join you again in a moment."

Ben picked up Mr. Li's brandy bottle and removed the cork. He paused momentarily, thinking
how difficult it must be to acquire such a fine bottle
of brandy in China. With the bottle still poised
over his glass, he realized Li Zhiang was no minor

official from the Petroleum Ministry. If he was at the right hand of Mao in the early days of the revolution, he likely remained there up to Mao's death. Mr. Li spoke too easily of Mao and Chou. He had lived within the corridors of power, survived the purges, and now lived a very gracious existence. He must still be well placed within the Party. Why is someone like that so interested in me? It disturbed him.

Then, Ben thought about Li Han. She was a totally new experience, beautiful and charming and innocent. Yet at the same time, she seemed to take him, as a man, for granted. He had come to the Orient to renew himself. Quite unexpectedly, and in a very short time, Beijing offered new and exciting challenges.

He poured himself a healthy draught of brandy.

Li Han sat down in her chair again, smiling pleasantly. "I hope you don't mind my parents leaving, or their being so concerned about it. They are modern Chinese but their manners still go back to the old days." She laughed aloud. "Especially when their guest is an American whom they're supposed to be suspicious of. For some reason, my father seems to feel you are here for more than business." Her eyebrows raised, as if in question.

"Where would he ever get that idea?" Now he was on the defensive for a reason he didn't understand.

"I'm sure I don't know," she answered.

"It would seem he was fairly close to those in

Mao's government," persisted Ben. "Does he still see those people?"

"Oh, I'm sure he's still in contact with some of his old friends. One doesn't get away from those experiences easily." Then she changed the subject.

"Would you like to hear about the bridge at Luting? I doubt my father will ever be able to relate that to an outsider, at least I don't think he's up to it any more."

Ben said nothing, raising his eyebrows in question.

She nodded. "Memories like that become more intense, or perhaps emotional is a better term, as people grow older. Years ago, the veterans of the March could sit up all night and tell such stories, with firmness and pride. They still saw themselves as soldiers. Now, with so many of their comrades gone, it is difficult for those that remain to maintain the same tough front."

"Please, if you are willing to take the time, I'd like to hear it."

"I always have the time, Mr. Goodrich. I am an officer of the People's Liberation Army now, and it is a tale I will tell my comrades. I will also tell it someday when I have children of my own. During your visit to our country, you will find that much of our pride comes from such stories that quickly become folk tales. It is the strength of the oral history we discussed earlier."

She took up the story where her father had left off. . . . "They found much of the bridge destroyed. It seems that it consisted of thirteen enormous chains spanning a gorge two hundred feet below. The Kuomintang had removed all the planks to a halfway point and this bridge was long. On their own half, they had kept the planking so that they could set up machine guns.

"Mao waited with his men, hoping the force that had crossed the river below might attack from behind the bridge defenders. While they waited, Chiang's men lay down an artillery barrage that had begun at first light and continued into the morning. It was difficult for our men. There was little place to hide and spotters were making the fire more accurate. Mao knew he could not withdraw. His men had not yet made contact with the enemy on the opposite side.

"There was a meeting of the senior officers. Mao said they must attack anyway, even if the diversionary group never showed up. All knew it could be a suicidal effort, seemingly impossible even if the enemy were attacked from behind. It became a matter of asking for volunteers to lead the first wave, to try to lay down boards towards the middle of the bridge. As they were finalizing plans, a messenger came in to tell them that there was firing from the other side of the gorge. Our other group, pitifully decimated, had made it and were engaging the enemy. But they could not hold out for long.

"My father then asked that he be allowed to lead a small group in the first wave. He said that to try to lay down planking to the middle would be foolish. There would be no chance. His idea was to lead a small band by swinging across under the chains. They would be harder to hit and might have a better chance if the machine gunners on the other side were engaged from the land. Mao respected my father, as you know, and allowed him to select a group of volunteers. He picked twenty-two, each of them men that he had led in battle before and that he knew were brave and would not turn back. They carried hand grenades with rifles slung over their backs. It was agreed that any man that was hit would be replaced by another."

She took a deep breath, her eyes reflecting the horror of Luting. "Of the original twenty-two men who started out, seventeen died in the machine gun fire. As a man fell into the gorge below, another would take his place, working across the chain, hand over hand, toward that halfway point. My father remembers stopping for a moment as a man fell, compelled to watch the body until it hit below. I couldn't tell you how many men died, but they did reach the halfway point and then charged Chiang's machine gunners and took that end of the bridge. Their comrades then laid down doors taken from the houses of the villagers on the south side and the remainder of the army marched across to take the city." Li Han's eyes now had traces of tears in the corners. She looked directly at Goodrich. "That is the story of the taking of the Bridge at Luting. It is much longer and told in much more detail among our people. But do you see why my father could not continue the story for you?"

Ben nodded. "I am not one of you," he said softly.

"That was May 25, 1935. They had been on the March for almost eight months, eight months of almost continual battle. After that, my father was even closer to Mao, always at his elbow whenever decisions were being made."

Ben whistled softly under his breath. "You hear of men like that, but you rarely meet them."

"You're correct." Li Han sat upright. "But he would be the first to tell you not to forget my mother. She marched every step of the way and fought like a man when she had to. The women had to be as strong as a man then."

"Li Han, your mother moves with great difficulty. Was she wounded during the March?"

"No, not at all," answered Li Han, her eyes flashing. "She came out of the entire March unscathed. Strangely enough, all of the thirty women who started survived. Her injuries came later, when she was briefly a prisoner of the Kuomintang. They tortured her and tried to make her denounce my father. They had been married that winter of 1935, at Yanan. She was in their hands only for a short time, for she escaped during a raid on Kuomintang headquarters where my father knew she was being held. In those days, it was better to die trying to escape than be held prisoner, for they tortured men and women alike. You see, we were a vicious people at war, Communist and Nationalist alike. Mao's second wife, like my mother, was captured but in 1930, well before the Long March. But she was not as lucky, for she was tortured, then executed. Mao lost a great deal personally. The Kuomintang also executed his brother just before the March began. He adopted his brother's son, but the boy was no luckier than his father. The Kuomintang buried him alive only three years before the Revolution was finally over."

She paused for breath, seemingly unable to stop talking. "You understand why my father wanted to either free my mother or see her dead? Fortunately, she is a brave, intelligent woman. She was able to get away somehow when the attack began. How she did it I don't know. Her legs even today are masses of scar tissue, but she somehow managed to get far enough away from her captors so my father could bring her back. She followed him through every campaign until Liberation in 1949. It was not until then that they would even consider having a child."

She stopped with as much haste as she had been talking, rising to stride uneasily back and forth across the room. "It is difficult even for me to talk about those days sometimes."

"What you've told me tonight, Li Han, is fascinating. Every nation has such stories, but the endurance of those men is so fantastic, considering the odds."

"There is so much more that could be told, or perhaps should be told, to outsiders. My father may be willing to do so someday again," and here she glanced at Ben curiously, "since he seems to be attracted to you for some reason. . . . After Luting, Mao led his men north through the Snow Mountains where so many that survived the battles died of exposure and pneumonia. They were attacked again by a major force at the treacherous, flooded

Great Marshes. And, finally, as they were turning northeast on what was to be the last leg of their journey, they were attacked at the Waxy Mouth Pass by forty thousand Kuomintang troops. There were only eight thousand men left, and they were so poorly armed by this time that many fought with knives and cut glass . . . against cavalry, if you can conceive of that! As they entered Shenxi Province and the end of their ordeal, they were forced to fight a warlord's cavalry. When they reached safety, there were only seven thousand left out of one hundred and twenty thousand who began the Long March." She paused, then added, "I am very lucky to have my mother and father. They are the history of my country."

The days in Beijing passed quickly for Ben Goodrich. The pleasant moments as a tourist became limited as he spent more time with Mr. Li at the Petroleum Ministry, meeting officials there, analyzing new seismic data the Chinese had already prepared for him. Exploratory efforts seemed to indicate that the oil fields in the South China Sea were not only abundant, but no estimate could be made of the vast amount of oil that existed. Technology was the answer, he found. The Chinese were willing to work with outsiders to a degree, but they needed capital and technology if they were to become a major exporter. It would be profitable for those willing to help them. There was money to be made, lots of it, for someone like himself.

Evenings, and occasional afternoons, were spent

in learning more of Beijing and its surroundings. Always, Li Han was at his side, leading the way, pointing out the little things a tourist wouldn't have the chance to see, and relating moments in Chinese history that meant so much to her and her people yet would go forever unnoticed by the rest of the world.

They stopped at sidewalk stands for *jao-tze*, the savory dumplings from the north, and *panguar*, an ice cream on a stick that was equally as tasty as the Good Humors Ben remembered as a boy.

She took him shopping at the tourist's Friendship Store to buy souvenirs. Then she served as his interpreter on Wangfuching Street, Beijing's main shopping boulevard, where he bought clothing for himself. The native ready-made clothes were generally too small, so Li Han arranged an appointment with a tailor, insisting that he bring along one of his own suits.

"If you let him fit you, he'll make it too big. Clothes are always made that way for winter, so you can wear lots of things underneath to keep warm. So few of our rooms are heated." The suit she chose for him to bring was a summer weight, ". . . . because it fits you so well," she said. "You are a handsome man and wear clothes that are well tailored. This American style makes you look so young," she smiled shyly. Then, she insisted on picking out the cloth.

She found a small store on the main street to buy him some sweaters. He had not anticipated the chilly fall weather. And, finally, she took him to a store where he was fitted for a Mao-style suit, similar to the ones her father wore. "You will find them very comfortable. There's a reason for wearing them," she laughed gaily, and he found later that it was one of the most comfortable outfits he owned.

He dined many evenings at the Li home, gradually learning more about the family and finding himself accepted by her parents. She took him shopping on the side streets, where produce from the communes lined the sidewalks. There was almost no refrigeration so people bought their food once a day. Food and its preparation were an event in each family, and the Li home was no exception. Ben experienced foods that few Americans had even heard of in their travels. The family went out of their way to ensure that each meal was an adventure, never the same offering twice.

Near the end of Li Han's leave from her ship, Mr. Li announced one evening that he was making arrangements for Ben to travel to the Gulf of Bohai, a functioning oil center on the Yellow Sea. He was sorry that the only time he could schedule was over the coming weekend, the last one that Li Han would be in Beijing.

Ben said nothing, knowing that once things were arranged in China there was no way to change them. He glanced over at Li Han who said nothing, idly picking at the food on her plate.

Mr. Li noticed her unspoken disappointment also. "Mr. Goodrich will need an interpreter with him," the old man said to his daughter. "I know this is your last weekend with us, but your mother and I would not object if you were to travel with Mr. Goodrich and translate for him."

Li Han brightened, looking first to her father and then her mother. The old woman smiled slightly and inclined her head.

"I have already contacted an old comrade of mine in Petaiho. That is a vacation retreat on the Coast," he said to Ben. "It used to be a summer resort for foreigners . . . before Liberation . . . and was used by diplomats, businessmen, and missionaries who built huge villas. After 1949, our government took them over and we now use Petaiho as a rest area for our military and government people." He laughed out loud. "You'll like it Mr. Goodrich. It is lovely and offers just a taint of capitalism in our socialist country." Ben had noticed the old man's eyes twinkle before when he was joking with someone, and now they sparkled with this little joke. "My daughter has also enjoyed your visit, and I think this little vacation before she returns to the rigors of her military life would make her happy. And I notice she has enjoyed being a tour guide," he teased.

The train trip to Petaiho is a bit more than six hours. Ben found that the food and the amenities of first class travel on Chinese trains rivaled that of the Europeans. When he saw the buildings of the resort for the first time, he knew what could spark a revolution. Compared to the peasant's wheat fields and the commune just outside the town, there was an instant change to shiny well-painted shops, rich orchards, and beautifully kept estates surrounded by hedges and high walls.

The car that met them at the train, another large, black model similar to the one in Beijing, whisked them to one of these estates overlooking the Gulf. The sunporch looked out over well tended gardens toward sparkling blue water. The smell of pines and salt in the air contrasted with the cabbage and gray smoke of the city.

"You did not expect something like this in China, did you?" questioned Li Han. She had come up beside him, linking her arm in his, her head resting lightly on his arm, the breeze sweeping strands of hair across her face.

Ben looked down at her. "I have rarely seen such an unspoiled place like this in my own country," he answered. The wind toyed with the hair drifting across her face, reminding him of American girls on similar beaches years ago. But he could not remember one so lovely, nor one he had felt more attached to. Strange, he thought to himself, that I have never even kissed her.

They walked through the gardens, hand in hand as lovers do, to the edge of the bank looking over the pink sand. A stairway led to the beach below. "Come on," she said, coaxing him down the stairs. "I have never walked a beach like this before. We have only a weekend."

"Wait," he called as she released his hand and skipped down over the sand. "We have a wise habit in the United States if we're going to run on the beach. We take off our shoes if the sands aren't too hot." He caught up to her, helping her remove her shoes.

Ben tied his sweater around his waist by the sleeves, an odd sight that amused Li Han. He grasped her hand again, and together they wandered down the beach, drawing strange glances from foreigners and Chinese alike.

It was difficult to believe he was in a strange country half way around the world from his own, strolling down an idyllic beach with the most beautiful and gentle woman he'd ever known. He was happier than he'd been in years, perhaps even in his lifetime.

The evening was as full of surprises as the day had been. When he came downstairs after his shower, a bar had been set up in the front room next to the sun porch. Dusk was settling over the water. An almost full moon was rising above the horizon. Through the open windows came the soft sound of waves lapping the beach.

Li Han's voice came from behind him. "Is this more like your own country?"

Ben turned to a sight that stirred his heart. She had never been dressed formally in his presence before, and he found that he was holding his breath. Li Han was wearing a tight-fitting, ankle length oriental dress, a deep fuchsia color to contrast with her golden skin and black hair and eyes. A scent of unfamiliar perfume filled the air. The real life dream seemingly would have no end.

"Believe me, Li Han. I have never lived like this

at home. But I'm not complaining either," he smiled. "Just wondering how all of this can continue to happen to me."

"Don't concern yourself with that," she murmured softly, pirouetting to show off her dress. "Let us both silently thank my father for arranging this for us." She moved over beside him, clasping his hands. "This is not common in China, you know. Women who consort with foreigners are often treated as evil. It used to be that a girl's father arranged her marriage, but never, oh never, a weekend like this." She smiled coyly. "Even though I am a woman now over thirty, it was not something I would have imagined from him, even a week ago. And it's certainly not something I would have expected for myself, or even thought about, a few weeks ago. You have caused me to surprise myself many times since you arrived in our country."

"Li Han, I've surprised myself more than once since I've been here. But this," he let go of her hands and walked over to the window, staring out over the sparkling waters, "This is not something I would have thought could happen to me again, even back home." He turned back, fascinated with her beauty and her confidence in the situation that surrounded them. He knew that Chinese women did not find themselves in such a position, but she seemed so comfortable this evening. "May I make you a drink?"

"No, thank you very much, but I do not drink your whiskies. There should be some wine there. I will have a little glass of that."

He brought drinks over to a modern, western-style couch. Ben was about to sit next to her, then thought better of it. Instead, he bent down and gently kissed her, for only the briefest moment. "That's to say thank you for your kindness since I've been here . . . and also to say that I'm becoming very attached to you. Back home, I had made a rule for myself that I would never become involved with any woman again. I was so afraid of being hurt by someone else. And believe me, I'm very strict about promises to myself."

"Then I'm glad you are willing to break your own rules." She stood up in front of him, reaching up with one hand to pull his head down to hers, rising on her tiptoes as she did. Kissing him gently in the same manner, she said, "And this is for changing my life in such a short time. Chinese women do not dream of such a thing. I, too, have now broken some of my own promises, so you have made me one of the lucky few. We have so little to remember in our personal lives but I now have a handsome American whom I will always keep in a corner of my mind. And I promise I will keep you there always, Ben, to remind me that there is truly a reason for caring selfishly for someone. I hope so very much there will be more weekends like this one." She kissed him again, this time pulling his face down with both hands before wrapping her arms around his neck.

They were served a fine French wine and an exquisite dinner. The fact that he was in China slipped further to the back of his mind as dessert, accompanied by imported liqueurs, was served. And, as they finished, a cool breeze came off the water inviting them back to stroll at the edge of the sea.

The moon's beams skipped off the surface to reflect in Li Han's eyes as she smiled happily up at him. Ben held her hand at first, then slipped his arm around her shoulders. Every few moments he would stop to pull her tightly against him, their kisses lasting longer each time. The awkwardness of holding a strange, new person disappeared as they quickly sensed how their bodies reacted to each other. It seemed as if they had been together forever, strolling that same beach in the moonlight, pausing to mold their bodies into one form, straining against each other to become closer.

The breeze chased an occasional cloud across the moon, and when Li Han shivered a second time, Ben knew it was time to return to the villa. Retracing their steps, they paused to kiss again at the same places that their sandy footsteps faced each other. Ben couldn't remember such a feeling before, yet he recognized that emotion called love, that ache he had long ago forgotten. He wanted to lift her off her feet and race back, never stopping until they were upstairs in their villa.

But she stopped him at the top of the beach stairs, tiny tears in the corners of her eyes. "Ben, one thing I cannot do now is join you in your bedroom. That is not something common in China, and that will take me a longer time to overcome." She reached up on her tiptoes to kiss him goodnight. "I know your women are different, but give me more time to learn about you and myself. I do care for you so very much. You will be back again, and perhaps I will become more Americanized by then."

"I care enough for you, Li Han, so it is not necessary to change for me. Don't try. Be yourself. I will come back sooner than you think, and we will let time decide who will change . . . if someone must change."

Then she ran ahead of him into the house, not stopping until she threw herself weeping onto her own bed.

On the following Tuesday, Mr. Li allowed Ben Goodrich to join him in seeing Li Han off on the plane. She was in uniform and would fly back to Zhanjiang, headquarters of the South Sea Fleet. Though he shook hands formally with the officer before him as if saying goodby to a friend, he was seeing the lovely lady in the fuchsia gown strolling arm in arm with him on the moonlit beach.

In the car on the way back to the city, Ben asked Mr. Li about his daughter's duties in Zhanjiang. "It's funny now that I think of it. We never discussed it and I don't remember asking her about it."

"She has been very successful in the military for a young person," Mr. Li answered. "She has her own command, a small one, of course, for so young an officer. It is a little torpedo boat, but one of the modern ones with hydrofoils. They patrol the oil fields between the mainland and Hainan Island." The old man leaned back into his seat, a smile of satisfaction on his face. "She is very proud of her success and we are very proud of our daughter, too."

Ben remarked, "In my country, we have women in the military but they don't become involved in combat units." He was silent for a moment. Then, he added an afterthought, almost to himself, "I never thought I'd see the day when I could become so attached to a person."

Mr. Li understood him completely. "My daughter has also become very fond of you, Mr. Goodrich. That is most unusual because we have been a suspicious nation and do not normally become involved with foreigners. But in your case, Mrs. Li and I are quite pleased." He looked out the window at the passing fields. "As a matter of fact, I'm especially glad that it will bring you back to us more often."

Mrs. Li knew her husband hadn't yet been asleep. The pain she lived with caused her to sleep lightly and she awoke silently each time her husband rolled over. She remained awake when he finally got out of bed and went to his writing table. He shaded the single bulb, not realizing she was watching him.

It took more than an hour to compose the letter. He wrote in English so infrequently the past few years that the phrasing came to him with difficulty.

After reviewing what he had written, he crossed out much of what was on the paper and rewrote it. The second effort was satisfactory. He turned out the light and slipped quietly back into bed.

"You were writing Ted Magnuson," his wife whispered.

"Yes."

"What did you tell him?"

"I told him the truth. I told him that America has few supporters at our meetings . . . that the Seventh Fleet visit to Vladivostok has convinced many that America will support the Russians against us."

She waited silently, knowing there was more.

"I also told him about Li Han . . . and that she has fallen in love with the American, Goodrich. I said that I had returned his trust over the years by introducing Mr. Goodrich to very important people and that he was returning to America with a wealth of knowledge and enough contacts should Magnuson ever require that they be used." Li Zhiang sighed deeply, grasping his wife's tiny hand under the sheet. "And I said that her mother and father would be most deeply in his debt if Goodrich could be left out of whatever will be happening."

Li Han was their only child. They had waited so long as soldiers during the revolution, and her injuries had allowed her only that one. Mrs. Li squeezed her husband's hand, wiping a silent tear away with the other.

CHAPTER EIGHT

Promptly at 10:00 a.m. the "Rossiya," the trans-Siberian express, cleared the yards at Moscow's Yaroslavl Station with a blast of its whistle and began the long journey to the Pacific Ocean. The modern steel and plastic coaches of the Rossiya contrasted with the older wooden cars and steam engines still evident in the railyards in Moscow.

The train would carry its passengers for a week to cities with familiar names, Kirov, Sverdlovsk, Omsk, Novosibirsk, and Irkutsk. Yet for days they would also see cities and towns and villages that the rest of the world would never hear of.

Bob Miller had learned in the early stages of his visit that computers in Russia were poorly utilized. As one manager had explained to them, "they are still treated like fast adding machines." Lack of a sophisticated telephone system meant that expensive and highly capable computers were unable to communicate with each other. Industrial applications of the computers, Miller's specialty, were generations behind the U.S.

*

As the Rossiya rattled into the vast, empty spaces of Russia, Bob Miller had more than enough time on his hands to analyze his opportunities in the Soviet Union. He was not an adventurous soul. One segment of his brain told him to go home, to forget the gold at the end of Magnuson's or Royal's rainbow . . . whatever that rainbow might be.

But the other part of his brain was the greedy, less cautious side and it impressed upon him that this was an obviously hungry customer desperately in need of his abilities. Contracts with the Soviet Union, guaranteed by the US government, could bring financial success and that independence from large corporations that he dreamed of.

But there was still something cautious and deliberate lurking in the back of his mind, a gnawing doubt that kept telling him it was better to forget the Soviet opportunities, to get out of Russia before it was too late. Ivan Petrov had told him, one night when they had drunk too much vodka, that amateurs rarely survived in a high stakes game. Bob had mentioned Ivan's remark to Royal one day when they had been wandering the streets of Moscow, away from their room and able to converse openly. Jack had understood, even agreed that Ivan made a very good point, but he had not accepted the premise. In retrospect, Miller realized that they looked at the situation from two very different perspectives. While Bob was involved because he was looking for a way to establish himself as an independent, Jack already was. Royal was a loner, no family to worry about or to miss during long trips. And most of all, Jack was not concerned with the responsibilities that came with a wife and children.

Across the compartment, Bob noticed that Royal was dozing, too tired to concentrate on the scenery rushing past the window. The pace had caught up with him also. Bob's thoughts drifted back to that warm July night when Royal had flown up to Vermont. Perhaps Jack had known about this even then. No, he couldn't have. . . .

Bob Miller leaped out of the driver's seat bellowing to the whole airport, "Jackson, my boy, we were afraid you'd melt away down in the caverns of New York." He came around to the rear of the car, pushing his glasses back on his nose with one hand, extending the other. "You old son of a bitch," he exclaimed. "Jesus, it's good to see you." He squeezed Royal's hand with both of his, then clapped him on the shoulder.

"You couldn't keep me down there in this heat. Christ, Bob, my feet were sticking to the streets and the garbage stunk just like you always said it did." He inhaled a huge gulp of air. "I've been needing this. And," he grinned, as Miller took his brief case, "I've been having a hell of a time finding someone to outdrink, so I decided to take you on."

Bob called to his son, "Billy, just toss that stuff in through the back window. I left it down. And go up front there and show your Uncle Jack how you handle a car." He opened the car door on the right

hand side, gesturing with his hand. "You've come
to the right place. Jump into the back seat there,
and we'll see who's going to outdrink who."

Royal felt a slap on the rump as he stepped up
into the high vehicle. The lights from a car just to
the rear of the Blazer illuminated its interior. They
outlined a large collie dog panting and drooling on
the seat. It greeted Royal with a sloppy lick and a
blast of warm, smelly breath.

"Go on, Jackie, way back," shouted Miller, waving his arms at the dog. The collie gave Royal's
face another slobber, then leaped gracefully into
the back end. "That's how long you've been away,
Jack. We had to name a dog after you. Almost two
years old now. Give him a pat before he takes your
arm off. He only wanted to see how you tasted
first." Royal slid toward the opposite side of the
car, through the dog fur and slobber, eyeing the
animal in the darkness while it licked the arm he
rested on the back of the seat.

"OK, driver," called Milled to his son, "take us
home, and be gentle on the corners so you don't
spill anything back here." He reached into the luggage area behind the seat, opening a large cooler.
"What'll it be, stranger? Beer to kill the thirst, or
are you man enough to hit the martini trail right
away?"

"Just a beer to start." Jack eyed the cooler filled
two-thirds full of ice, beer bottles just barely peek-
ing through. There were also two glasses chilling in
the ice, along with a closed pitcher, which he had to
assume contained the martinis.

"Aha! A brew first! Getting careful in your old age," answered Miller. He turned forward for a moment and added, "Your old Uncle Jack is gun shy . . . not like he used to be."

"Thanks," nodded Royal as an extremely cold, dripping bottle of beer was placed in his hand. "No one's treated me this way in a long time. This is quite a greeting."

"Dad's been waiting for this for a week, Uncle Jack. Mom says the little kid in him is coming out again."

"The kid's right. I have been looking forward to this visit. It would have been a dull Fourth of July without you, Jack." Bob raised his own beer. "Here's to a hell of a good visit. Welcome back to your second home."

"My favorite second home," answered Royal, lifting the bottle to his mouth and taking a deep swallow. "Lovely, lovely," he gasped, looking critically at the label. "A great way to welcome a tired sailor. I'll say that for you."

"Hell, I don't get much of a chance to do this anymore," answered Miller.

"You know, Bob, I feel relaxed already. Not five minutes into my visit, and I feel like a new man. It must be the Vermont air."

"No. It's the friendly people. No doubt about it. Here, suck up that beer. I want to make this trip one that only royalty would respect. We have in this pitcher," and he lifted a pitcher from the ice, "the finest frozen Tanqueray martinis that man has ever tangled with."

"Looks lovely," Royal answered between swallows. "But wait a minute. I can't inhale this stuff like I used to . . ."

"Dad said you'd never admit something like that," came a laugh from the driver's seat. "You're supposed to be the last of the iron men."

"When we have a chance, Billy, you're going to have to repeat everything your father's said about me. Then we'll decide what you're supposed to believe."

Bob reached back into the cooler. "Olives, onions, a twist perhaps?"

"Hell, I'm hungry. A little bit of everything while you're at it." He watched the condiments appear from a plastic cup buried in the ice. "You know, you're really serious about this, aren't you?"

"Of course I am. We treat all our guests this way. Don't you know that?"

"I don't know. It's been so long, I'd forgotten."

"That's exactly it. Too long, Jack. Margie and I were so happy when you called. This is fun but it's just the beginning." He raised his glass in toast again. "Cheers. We needed you up here. It does get kind of quiet out here in the boonies, and a friendly old face from the past brings a lot of memories we sort of miss." Royal was amused by the sheepish smile on his friend's face as they passed under a street light. "I guess we'd better not drink these too fast, or we're going to miss a great dinner that Marge has put together for you."

Miller's reverie was interrupted by a sharp rapping on the compartment door. Jack's eyes opened as Petrov entered.

"Aha," smiled Ivan pleasantly, "catching up on your rest, eh? Can't keep up with the Russian nights." He laughed as he flopped on the seat next to Jack. "Perhaps this trip will help you regain your energy."

Royal grinned pleasantly at him. "Is it Russians in general, or you in particular, that we have to keep up with?"

"My friend, you will find that I'm one of the more subdued Russians." Ivan's brows lifted sadly. "I'm afraid I can't drink vodka like I once did, although I try," he beamed. He leaned forward toward Miller. "That's why I interrupted your dreams. It is close to lunch and I thought a vodka or two might be just the thing you both need to get you back on your feet."

Bob glanced at Jack, a sad look on his face. The other nodded in agreement. "Go ahead without us this time, Ivan. Perhaps tonight we'll join you for drinks. Right now," he sighed, "I think we'll just kind of nap until lunch time."

Petrov nodded, shrugging his shoulders with a smile. "Have it your way, my friends. I tried. You're not making it easy for me to turn you into good Russians." He raised his eyebrows again. "You're just not going to fit in, but I've tried."

"You've been very good about it, too," Jack responded. "Now get out of here and let a couple of Yanks suffer quietly."

Ivan backed out the door, hands raised in defeat,

still smiling. Jack Royal's head sank back against
the cushions, his eyes closing almost immediately.
Bob Miller's troubled thoughts again returned to
that visit of Royal's when life had been so
simple. . . .

After dinner, the three adults had settled beside
the new swimming pool at the rear of the house.
Like most Vermont nights, even in the hottest
weather, the air had cooled to a comfortable temperature, much drier than when Royal had arrived.
Stars were twinkling in a clear sky, now lit at midnight by a waning moon just risen over the mountains to the east.

"How about a refill, Jack?"

"Oh, Christ, no. I've been watching that old
moon up there, trying to get it into focus." He
pointed upward. "I couldn't tell you which way the
cusps were pointed unless I looked again." Royal
was silent for a moment, then added, "But I guess
you could talk me into a good-night beer."

"I'll get it," Marge offered. Bob's wife was short,
blonde, slender and still attractive. She had welcomed Jack that evening almost as heartily as her
husband, with a kiss and a long hug, the kind reserved only for an old friend.

"Never you mind, my dear. This cooler resting
at my feet contains some of Canada's finest, chilled
just for this occasion. Nothing too good for our
famous guest."

"Famous? Hell, just drunk. Smashed. Wiped
out. And with a full tummy, too. That dinner was

just great, Marge, super. You could make a fortune in the city."

"That's not such a bad idea," answered Marge. "The fortune, I mean, not the city. But your old buddy keeps complaining how quiet life is up here. No action outside of the office. The high rollers haven't found Burlington yet."

"Oh, now, Marge, it's not that bad," said Miller, pushing his glasses back.

"You can always go back to Armonk," added Royal. "You'll be close to the action there."

Bob Miller took a long sip of his drink. "Now that you mention it, forget it. Maybe the action's down there, but the peace and quiet is right here." He sighed, took another sip, and added, "Where could you get a view like this?" He spread his arms out to encompass the dark mountains to the east. "Right in your own backyard. Right?"

"You know," whispered Jack, breaking a sleepy silence, "it's very drunk out and it's barely midnight. What kind of drinkers have we become? We used to be just starting at about this time."

"I'll tell you what I'm going to do to solve your little problem," Bob answered. "How'd you like to get your ass tossed into that pool? That'll wake you up."

"Now that's not a bad idea. I'd like that," Jack said slowly, pondering the idea. "But, if I go in, everybody goes with me."

"Now wait a minute," said Marge. "I'm sober enough so I can't get this outfit soaked."

"Well, take the goddamn thing off," her husband

answered, removing his glasses. "We'll skinny dip. Jack's not embarrassed, are you?"

"Nothing embarrasses Uncle Jack any more," he answered. "That is if it doesn't bother little Margie," he giggled.

"Aren't you two something else when there's only one woman around," Margie said, standing up and heading for the pool, her hand already reaching for the buttons on the back of her blouse. "I guess you both forgot the last time Jack was up here, and we all went skinny dipping in the falls down in Bristol one night. You were both just as drunk then and you both giggled like a bunch of high school boys when I suggested we jump in. You're never going to grow up." And she removed the last of her clothes and leaped into the pool.

Royal stood up, taking a final pull on his beer. "Women have changed a lot since we were kids, haven't they?" He began unbuttoning his shirt.

"Or maybe we have," pondered Miller, rising unsteadily to his feet. "You know, women are going to take over the world soon, at least it seems that way to me if they keep taking off their clothes so fast." He stopped for a moment as he reached to untie his shoes. "Now what did I mean by that?"

"It means you can't handle it anymore, you turkeys," yelled Marge, splashing noisily around the pool. "The first thing women can do is outdrink the two of you."

Royal looked at his friend, as they balanced unsteadily on the side of the pool before diving in. "Maybe she's right."

* * *

There is nothing like a parade . . . except for a small town parade on the Fourth of July. Everyone takes part. The local politicians, plus maybe a congressman or two, lead it off. They are suffered silently by the citizens on the sidewalk, for everyone knows the fun is about to begin. Then follow old cars, homemade floats built by every organization from the local grocery store to the women's club, and music by the local high school band, a nearby drum and bugle corps, and maybe some older amateur groups. Interspersed are marchers galore, the Cub Scouts and Brownies, the local legionnaires, a black power group complete with muskets and frontier dress, the high school boosters collecting change for football uniforms. The parade is always finished off by fire engines, their sirens screaming while children peer from behind their parents' legs at the source of all the noise.

It is uniquely small town and is always followed by a gathering down at the town baseball field to award prizes and listen to the bands play and show off their talents after the street parade. Kegs of beer empty as fast as they can be replaced and the children take time out from their sack races and egg tosses to eat and drink all the hot dogs and soda they can.

Jack Royal stood sweating near the judge's box on the main street, the three smaller Miller children alternately pulling at his arms or sitting on the curb until the parade got to them. He'd been there for the Fourth before, and was willing to sit on the curb with anyone's kids—just to be there, even though he was hung over. The bugles had been rough enough on his sensibilities, and the muskets were certainly intended to punish him for the night before, but he was convinced the fire engines were howling for him and him alone. Margie had marched at the head of the Cub Scouts and Brownies. Billy Miller was with his football team, waving at all the girls in the crowd. And Bob had led his Cameron Pipers, kilts swirling, down the main street, his face red as his bagpipe saluted the Fourth of July. Bob Miller and bagpipes were synonymous across northern Vermont. He was devoted to his hobby and would play in the foulest weather or on the hottest day of the year, or even with a raging hangover.

At the end of the parade, when Royal sauntered down to the baseball field, trying to keep track of the three children and their balloons, Marge caught up to him, still dressed in her den leader's uniform. "How you doing now, big fellow?"

Jack grinned at her. "I don't know whether you're just rubbing it in or if you're looking for a partner in pain."

She laughed. "Both. You have to pay the piper, you know, if you still want to be the swinger you used to be."

"I'm paying. Believe me, I'm paying. How about you?"

"Me, too. But who cares? It's the Fourth of July and it's a gorgeous day to be alive, even with a god-awful hangover. Imagine how your buddy feels blowing his brains out into that squeaky bag under his arm."

Royal turned to her. "You should have seen his eyes when they went by us. It almost made me feel good again, just to look at him. My God, I thought he was going to cry right there with his cheeks all puffed out and that wailing coming out of the end of that thing to compound it all."

"Yes," Marge answered, "and he does it every time. I don't know how many parades he's marched in when I thought his eyeballs were going to pop right out of his head. The piper keeps paying, and keeps paying, and I don't know if he's ever going to stop. But that's his problem."

The first and third base sides of the field were lined with spectators, many with plastic cups of beer drawn from the kegs under the trees behind the backstop. Bob Miller's Scottish pipers waited in marching order at one end of the field. A voice boomed from a jeep equipped as a sound truck to quiet everyone, and the band marched onto the field. Each member was dressed in kilts displaying the colors of various clans. They went through their routine with drums pounding, horns blaring, and the bagpipes mournfully wailing through marches, reels, strathspeys and laments. The final number was for the lone piper, Miller, now at the far end of the field. . . . "Amazing Grace." Then they marched off, never missing a beat until they reached right field, when they broke as one and raced for the kegs.

Jack Royal was in line for another draft when

the pipers arrived. The head of the line was their due after their performance. Miller was at the front of the pack and the first to arrive, his military blouse soaked, perspiration visibly running down his body.

"Lovely show, lovely," said Royal. "How about an encore?"

There was no answer until Bob drained his first beer completely. "Oh my God, perhaps I'm not going to die after all." He looked at Jack, pushing his glasses back and rolling his eyes. "I thought I was going to drop right in my tracks. Cold sweat, spots in front of my eyes. The whole thing," he exclaimed. "Oh shit, I would have been embarrassed. I don't think I ever felt so shitty for a parade." He lifted his second cup in toast. "Thank goodness you only show up every few years. I couldn't survive any more than that."

Royal pointed at his friend, smiling, "I don't remember anyone holding you down and pouring it down your throat."

Marge came up to join them, the three smaller children trailing behind her. "Face it boys. You're never going to grow up. But your children still love you, dear." She winked at Bob. "They thought Daddy was just terrific out there today, all dressed up like a madman in his skirts and making those outlandish noises."

"That's music, kids, music to march and dance to," he answered as he drew another beer.

A sharp knock on the door, followed by Ivan's

face peering into the compartment, brought him back to reality again. Outside the window, the flat Russian countryside raced by.

"Lunch my friends," announced Petrov. "We are close to the Volga, so we will toast the crossing over lunch, eh?"

Jack Royal peered through still sleepy eyes. "You know, Ivan, you're setting a tough example for us. We don't usually drink at lunch back home."

"So now you're on vacation. For the next couple of days we have nothing to do but look at the beautiful scenery, and it will get beautiful as we climb into the Urals. Sverdlovsk is two days away. It is time to relax, to drink vodka, and," here his eyebrows lifted again and his smile waned, "talk of more serious things." His face again broke into a smile. "Come, I have saved a table for us."

The dining car was two coaches forward, and the passage between cars was chilling. October was a foreboding of Russia's early winter, one that presaged heavy snows even in November.

Over a lunch of greasy soup, the ever-present garlic sausage, and cheese, washed down with a watery red wine, Petrov talked of the factories and the people they would meet in Sverdlovsk. He had warned them on the way up that the dining car was not a place to discuss anything else, for there were too many ears. While they were unable to pick out the KGB-types that Ivan insisted would be travelling wherever they went, he was correct about the military people. It seemed that wherever they went, the uniform of the Red Army was evident in great numbers. It was no different on the Rossiya. The brown uniforms were everywhere and Ivan explained that the army moved their people by train whenever possible. It was too expensive to transfer them by plane. And so many of them seemed to be heading east. At this last comment, Petrov's eyebrows again rose, pleased with this bit of information.

When they returned to their compartment, it had been ransacked. Nothing was missing, but nothing had been overlooked. It was a thorough job. The linings of suits had been slashed. Heels of shoes had been neatly removed. Petrov's eyebrows said it all. Someone was still keeping track of them.

Bob Miller slept poorly that night, but it was not the rocking and clacking of the Rossiya that disturbed him. In his lifetime, he had experienced the fear of bullies and the adolescent fear of girls, and as he grew older he had been afraid of doing poorly at school or in a job. But he had never experienced a fear of the unknown. Now, almost as if it had been planned well ahead of time, he found himself involved in some clandestine scheme he knew nothing about and traveling across the heart of a country that inspired terror even in its own citizens.

He remembered telling Royal during that July visit why he decided to go out on his own—"I want to get up on a Monday morning and, instead of going to the office after breakfast, I want to race for a plane that's going to take me to New York or Montreal, so that I can catch a bigger plane that's going to take me overseas. I want to land in Moscow and Paris and Tokyo and I want to do it for myself. I don't want to do it for some big, goddamn company. I want to be met at those airports as Mr. Robert Miller, himself, not Mr. Miller of the company!" It was a romantic image. And Royal had said, "Welcome to the circus."

As the Rossiya rumbled and lurched across the stark, Soviet steppe, a vision of his youngest daughter kept appearing before Miller's eyes. She was four years old and whenever the illusion stole into his mind, she climbed up into his lap, smiling up at him with those large loving eyes . . . Suzanne, a tiny, blonde bundle of love. She would grow up to look just like her mother. God, how he missed them all. . . .

Jim MacIntyre remained in his chair, concentrating on the back of Magnuson's broad shoulders. The Admiral was staring out the window, his hands behind his back, fingers continually knotting into fists.

It had been a lousy day. Benjamin had come in that morning before going on to the White House. His visit had lasted only two or three minutes, but they had been very unpleasant ones. Someone had gotten the President's ear. They explained that Magnuson and ONI were still involved in Seagull, that they were using people in the Soviet Union. If the Russians got wind of it . . . that was all they needed to say. Furthermore, Benjamin had been seen in Magnuson's company. The President, himself, had sent Benjamin over to deliver the twenty-four hour ultimatum. Drop it or quit.

"All right, goddamn it, tell him we quit . . . tell him he's right and we're wrong . . . tell him any goddamn thing you want to!"

Now, a message from Vladivostok had come in confirming that the logistics information they needed to support their contentions, to prove there was justification to continue Seagull, had been moved to Irkutsk for security purposes. The message confirmed that Royal had made contact with Miller, that the two Americans had survived a suspicious accident, that Royal, Miller, and their guide had been seen boarding the Rossiya and that eventually they would arrive in Irkutsk.

Magnuson turned from the window. "Jim, somehow Petrov's got to get hold of the information on that tape. I don't know how but they have to get it out in some form with Royal or Miller. Get that to Petrov. And I don't want anyone, not Benjamin, not anyone else here to know what we're doing. Do it yourself."

CHAPTER NINE

After the Rossiya turns east from the Volga, the landscape changes gradually. From the foothills and birches of the Urals, it rises into beautiful, mountainous terrain. The city of Sverdlovsk marks the departure from European Russia and modern industrialization as the train descends from the Urals into the vast Siberian taiga. From then on, there is little variation in the land. The only life seems to be the stunted Siberian cedar. After the snow-covered Urals, boredom becomes overwhelming. Only Novosibirsk, the Chicago of Siberia, and small industrial sites break the monotony. They are clothed in an impenetrable smoky fog cover, a manmade roof of soot that filters what little sun exists during the long winter.

Irkutsk, therefore, resembles an oasis to a traveler on the Rossiya. It can be seen from a great distance, outlined by its flaming industrial chimneys. There is little that might be considered suburbs, for the edge of the city is lined by tarpaper covered bungalows shuttered against the biting cold. Almost as quickly as the mind can comprehend a city in the midst of the barren taiga, the train is among the factories and high rise apartment buildings that look suspiciously like cellblocks.

Royal and Miller had fallen into the same habits as the Russians, just as Petrov had predicted. They could read for only a short time, for the unchanging scenery and clickety clack of wheels would hypnotize them. Their compartment, too warm or too cold, but never comfortable, depended on the status of the coal fired boiler in the front of their coach. At first, the *provodnik*, the Soviet version of a porter, had served *chai*, the strong, black Russian tea whenever they requested it. But as Ivan had said, they found themselves joining the drinkers, which included most everyone in the car. Petrov was the only other speaking English, but this didn't bother them or any of their traveling companions. There was an unspoken comfort in steady drinking. They drank whatever seemed appropriate at the time, cognac, beer, wine, vodka. They finally settled on the vodka, just as Ivan had said they would, because the cognac tasted like hair tonic, the red wine was similar to cough syrup, and the beer was warm and sour.

So Irkutsk, a grimy city they had never thought they would welcome, became a mecca to the two Americans. It also meant a change of scenery, new people to talk with, and an opportunity to again exercise their minds.

Petrov was equally pleased to be off the Rossiya

for a few days. "No work today, my friends," he beamed. "I have planned that we can tour the city and show you the places of interest. No factories today, none at all! Irkutsk has art galleries, museums, universities, everything. It is the cultural center of Siberia."

"I never knew there was one in Siberia," remarked Royal sarcastically.

"Oh, yes," responded Ivan. "Most definitely. There are seven universities, four theaters, a circus, a philharmonic orchestra, a planetarium . . . whatever you desire," he said, spreading his arms to encompass the city before them. "I must confess," he said after a short pause, "I learned that from the tourist booklets before we arrived. But, I promise you it will be a change," he added, expelling a blast of frosty breath into the frigid air.

Their arrival at the Intourist Hotel, one of the two decent hotels in the city, cast an ominous note on a day that was to be relaxing. As usual, they turned over their passports to the clerk at reception. The man looked at them, at their passports, then back at them before stepping quickly into an office behind him. In answer to Royal's inquiring look, Petrov shrugged, "Let's wait for a moment. You're a novelty. Few Americans visit Irkutsk." Miller unconsciously pushed his glasses further back on his nose.

In less than a minute the man returned, sliding registration cards across the desk. "Ask him what his problem was, Ivan," said Miller.

After a few sentences had been exchanged with

the clerk, Ivan said, eyebrows raised, "Why didn't you tell me you had so many friends in Irkutsk? We could have called ahead and had them meet the train." He was beaming at his little joke.

The two Americans looked at him curiously.

"No. Forget it. I am just joking, but it is not so funny, eh? It seems some people have been asking about Mr. Royal . . . some people other than the business contacts we are to see."

A note had been waiting for Petrov when they arrived at the hotel. Soon after settling in their rooms, he excused himself, explaining that an old friend had heard he was in Irkutsk and wanted to get together for a couple of drinks. As he had often done before in public places, he grasped his ears to show that perhaps eavesdroppers could be listening.

That evening, as they were strolling through the park along the Angara river bank, Petrov explained his meeting. "The special logistics group from the Vol'sk School is using the computer facilities at the Academy of Sciences here in the city. It is the equal of anything they have in Moscow, but Vladivostok does not yet have the capacity they require." He looked at Miller. "There will be only one chance. No more. We have to be sure about gaining access to the system. Of course, the equipment here is modeled after your American computers. We don't need to design our own if your people do it for us."

"If the Academy is like any in the U.S., there will

be a series of remote units. All I need is the basic information from your man, use of a tape drive . . ."

"Yes, yes," answered Petrov irritably. "Please, you are getting beyond my understanding. My contact did say that we have units that can gain access and that one of his people will have what you need. But somehow, they have special guards . . . electronic guards, or something like that. He says it is like a warning bell . . . or something like that." Petrov shrugged his shoulders, his usually pleasant demeanor gone.

"I think I know what you mean, Ivan," Miller responded. "Our own government has exactly the same warning systems for defense programs, but it's surprising how innocent people have fallen into the middle of them purely by accident. It can be done." Bob was animated by the knowledge of how close they might be to their goal. For a moment, he had forgotten his fear of this strange, unfriendly country. Perhaps everything could be done quickly and they could leave Russia.

"That's what I am told," Petrov answered, "that it is easy once we know how." Again he shrugged his shoulders. "Now, I am uncomfortable. This is something I don't understand, and what we are doing . . . or not doing right now . . . is very dangerous. We could do it tomorrow. It could be five days. The longer we wait for our chance, the more dangerous it becomes." Then, as quickly as his attitude had become gloomy, his face brightened and he smiled. "What am I disturbing you for? Come,

let's drink and eat. That will make us all feel better." He clapped them both on the shoulders.
"You are learning to like our vodka, eh?"

Unexpectedly, the city turned out to be a more
pleasant place to visit than they anticipated. People
were friendlier than in other sections of Russia.
Royal said it was just like the United States—
Americans got friendlier as one got farther away
from New York. Petrov agreed the same was true
as one drew east of Moscow. When they went to
examine the hydro stations under construction on
the Angara River, their hosts insisted on taking
them on the hydrofoil boat to Lake Baikal, the
deepest lake in the world and one of the most ancient. The plant manager at the truck plant that
was having computer problems insisted that he escort them to the History Museum. He wanted the
Americans to know more about the Yakuts and
Buryats, the Siberian tribes that were related to the
American Eskimos. He was even prouder of the
fact that people from Irkutsk actually founded the
first Russian settlements in Alaska and California.

The hospitality now meant a great deal to Miller.
He had expressed reservations about his involvement since the accident in Moscow. The incident at
the reception desk at the hotel had reinforced any
lingering doubts, and Petrov's worry the first evening didn't help. He missed Marge and the children, more than even he had anticipated. It was
one thing to be traveling in the United States or
even in Europe on company business. But those
trips were short. Most people he did business with

in France or Germany spoke English, and he was able to call Marge most evenings when he was traveling in the United States. In Russia, the climate, the dress, the buildings, everything was different, and few spoke English. Many of the people were intimidating, almost rude to a person unable to speak their language. This was especially true of the government people. The Siberian taiga, vast, open stretches of land, was even more difficult to be comfortable in. To Bob Miller, it might as well have been the other side of the moon. It was somber, uninviting, and the dream he had the first night on the train of being lost in Siberia, coupled with the repeated vision of his youngest daughter, came back to him on succeeding nights.

The manager of the truck plant invited them to his home, one of the old, intricately carved wooden houses in the city. He spoke broken English and was overjoyed to test it on these new acquaintances. He was difficult to understand. His burly wife spent the evening staring unsmilingly at them, as if they were intruders. But, in return they invited him and his wife to dinner, and were overjoyed when they learned she could not join them.

The Angara Restaurant, named after the adjacent river, "the beautiful daughter of Old Baikal," was Irkutsk's finest. As usual, the evening was devoted to the favorite Soviet pastime, drinking frozen vodka.

"You know," said Royal, looking first to Ivan and then their guest, "I'm beginning to enjoy this custom."

They were drinking the vodka neat, in long

stemmed glasses, returning the bottle each time to a block of ice. The silvery liquid went down in one swallow, ice cold over the tongue, smooth in the throat, exploding warmly in the stomach. With salty caviar or smoked fish, it was even more exquisite than by itself. It also went down faster.

Their dinner was superb, one of the finest they'd had during the trip. Couples danced on a small wooden floor to an animated orchestra.

"Now, my friends, we all dance," bellowed Ivan.

"Dance, yes," agreed their guest, knocking over his chair as he leaped up to pirouette around the table.

"See, now you will know the Russian love of music and dancing. But first you have to come all the way to Siberia," gurgled Petrov, tossing off another glass of vodka.

"Perhaps we'll just watch you," mumbled Miller, none too happy at the prospect.

Royal looked about him at the single women in the room. Most were dressed the same way, dark sweaters, dark, long skirts, and poorly executed makeup. They wouldn't get far in New York, he decided, but what the hell.

"Okay, Ivan, what do I do? Just go up to one of them and offer my hand and point to the dance floor?"

Petrov looked thoughtful for a moment, almost sober. "I suppose they would know what you had in mind, but no, that's not the way it should be done." He grabbed Jack's arm. "Come, show me which one you want. I will introduce you formally." He grabbed Miller at the same time. "Everybody has fun tonight."

"Perhaps I'll just watch," Bob repeated uncertainly. "My wife says I'm not a very good dancer, and I really don't feel too well right now."

"Nonsense, you wouldn't want to make our guest feel badly would you?" The plant manager was already dancing happily with a woman at least as big as he was.

Jack shrugged his shoulders. "I don't blame him. At least she smiles."

"Correct. Everybody has a good time tonight." Petrov led them across the floor in the direction of a couple of tables of women. "You trust me. I will pick out the best for you, my friends." He took them to a table of four women, letting go of their arms long enough to bow drunkenly to the ladies. He said something in Russian, causing them all to laugh and stare at the two Americans.

"Ivan, what are you saying to them?" asked Bob.

"I figure since you don't speak our language that I must make you very important." The women were eyeing them appreciatively.

"Fine, but what did you say?"

"I hope you don't mind," he said sheepishly. "I explained that you are U.S. Olympic hockey players here on a good will tour. Hockey and hockey players are very popular out here." He raised his eyebrows, grinning his infectious little boy grin. "Maybe you will fall in love for a night, eh?"

"Oh, my God," said Bob. "What's he getting us into now?"

"Look at it this way," Royal answered. "You

don't have to talk with them and. . . ." he smiled lecherously, "when in Russia . . . ."

"I'm not comfortable."

"For Christ's sake, try. You're halfway around the world and you've got nothing else to do but have a good time. You're getting drunk, aren't you?"

"Very."

"Well, blame it on the booze. Lose control!"

Ivan had been happily engaged in conversation with the women, and at this moment waved Royal to join him. "I would like you to meet Vera," he said, one arm around Jack's shoulders, the other stroking Vera's neck. "She is very lovely, isn't she?" He launched immediately into a discussion with the lady, which caused her to smile at Jack as she rose from her chair. Her smile was half metal teeth.

"What did you say to her this time?"

"Nothing serious. Nothing at all, my friend. I told her that you had been watching her all evening and that you simply had to be introduced to her." His face became mock serious. "It is the least I can do for you, Jack. You have been living like a priest since you arrived in our country. What more could a friend do for you?"

Royal was unable to answer as a smiling Vera led him onto the dance floor, engaging him in a bear hug the moment they began to dance.

Bob Miller had turned back toward their table in a feeble attempt to escape Ivan's good will. It was too late. "Bob Miller," Ivan's voice boomed out.

"This Ludmila has been eyeing you all night and she is enchanted to learn that you have been doing the same. I think perhaps you have something in common."

Bob saw there was no escaping Ludmila or the good will of Petrov. He found himself dancing with an enthusiastic partner, also equipped with metal teeth.

When the orchestra took a break, Petrov invited all of the women back to the table, at the same time waving gleefully for another bottle of vodka. Ivan told a story in Russian that brought gales of laughter and admiring glances from the women. Their guest leaned over to shake both their hands, clapping them on the shoulder and mumbling in a heavy accent, "unbelievable . . . . unbelievable."

"Ivan, what have you done to us now?"

"You will be the toast of Irkutsk by morning, my friends. I have explained that your athletic prowess goes beyond the hockey rink. You will be pleased to know that you are now famous in Moscow not only for your ability to drink large quantities of vodka, but because the ladies of our capital city were sneaking into your rooms after your reputation began to spread."

"Oh, my God, Jack. We don't stand a chance. That madman will be the death of us."

"I seem to remember years ago," Royal said with a smile, "maybe twenty-two or twenty-three, that a young ensign did the same thing to me at the Viking in Newport. I had my girl up for the weekend, the first time she'd ever been to Newport or met anyone on the ship, and she was expecting to be very impressed. And if you remember that night, Mr. Miller, I couldn't understand why all those girls kept coming up to kiss me or sit in my lap as if it was the most natural thing in the world. Unfortunately for you, one of them finally gave away your name. So, live it up, and perhaps no one will send any pictures back to Vermont."

Royal had seen the photographer coming. They roved the nightclubs of Moscow, and apparently did the same thing in Irkutsk. Before Miller could react, the women were seated in their laps, arms around their necks, and the flashbulbs popped three times to record the event for the happy participants.

Their guest leaned over to pat Bob's knee. "You Americans know how to have a good time," he said drunkenly, the words barely recognizable as English. "Ivan says you stay a few more days. We do this again." He laughed happily, banging the table with his fist.

Ludmila happily planted a wet kiss on Bob's lips before he understood what she had in mind.

"That's it, my friend," giggled Petrov. "For a minute, I thought you might be serious about being boring. But I was right. Americans know how to have a good time."

The evening progressed with more dancing, more vodka, and no escape from the party. Ivan and their guest, with the cooperation of the band, climbed upon two tables to present their awkward version of the Russian saber dance. They were rewarded with rhythmic applause from their audience.

Petrov then insisted Jack join him on another table and to the amusement of the crowd, taught him vaguely how to do the same thing. Then, as if on cue, they both tumbled from their tables, raucous, happy laughter greeting them.

Bob Miller, with the added courage of more vodka, decided there was no point in being a wet blanket. He joined in with the fun and drank more than he had since his arrival in Russia. Time seemed to have no end. Then, the room began to spin. His stomach churned. Slipping away from the table, he weaved into the men's room and for some reason noticed his watch read ten minutes after midnight. A split second later he saw Petrov, and that time became chiseled on his brain forever. Ivan was lying on the men's room floor, his head at an impossible angle from his neck, a trickle of blood flowing from his nose. His sightless eyes stared at the uncovered bulb on the ceiling.

The next day and a half were a whirl, cloudy and foreign. They found their suddenly quite sober guest from the truck factory handling affairs with the police, his English now more than adequate. He escorted them back to their hotel after promising to whisk them through court the following morning.

A hearing was held before a magistrate. The plant manager seemed to know the legal system quite well, explaining their position, providing witnesses who placed them on the dance floor during the period Ivan was killed.

Since Petrov's brief meeting the afternoon they

arrived in Irkutsk, he had never been contacted again. It was discussed in brief, private moments each day but Ivan had explained to them that nothing could be done. "Be patient," he explained. "We will be contacted when the time is right."

Now Petrov was dead, and they were alone in a strange city in the middle of Siberia. They had no idea who Petrov's contact was, or if the person might somehow try to get to them. As Miller pointed out to Royal, they were in the same position as an astronaut hurtling across space toward a planet no one had ever seen before and, like the astronaut, they had no idea what to expect.

The plant manager took care of everything. His efficiency under stress marked him as much more than he claimed, but he was helping and there was no way they could determine what he might know about them. They did learn there were no choices as far as their next move. They were told that space had been reserved for them on the next train through Irkutsk to the east. They were never told why they couldn't fly. Their reason for being in Irkutsk had failed, and they were now under new control, or it seemed that way. Had it ever been any different?

The Rossiya swung around the southern tip of Lake Baikal, sweeping down toward the Mongolian border, then paralleling the low hills on the edge of the Gobi desert. The landscape, as tedious as the taiga, varied from flat and treeless to rolling foothills with small cedar. The winter's snow had arrived in some sections, the whiteness already tarnished by desert dust.

Earlier in the century, Manchuria had been Russian and the Trans-Siberian railroad had run directly across the province to Vladivostok. But wars change borders and the Soviets had lost Manchuria. The Rossiya was forced to take an extra day, following the Amur River along the now-Chinese border, first to the northeast, then back down again to the southeast to terminate in Khabarovsk, a more lonely and desolate trip than the previous day.

One night was spend in Khabarovsk, the city disputed by both China and the Soviet Union at the confluence of the Amur and Ussuri Rivers. Though autumn lasted longer here than most sections of Siberia, neither the warmer climate nor the city interested them at all. The horror of Irkutsk was still much too vivid. And always, always they were under someone's eye—prisoners without chains.

On the following day, they were escorted to an entirely new train. They were told this would be the final leg of their journey. And for a brief interval they were swept back into another period of time. The train was called the Vostok, and it was totally different from the Rossiya that had been both their home and prison. Their compartment was Victorian in style with mirrors, carpets, brass fittings, varnished wood, etched glass globes, red velvet tassled curtains, and goose feather pillows.

They were headed south now, and there was no longer any snow.

Bob Miller stared out the window at the flat landscape, broken only by an occasional small, wooden bungalow. There were few settlements, no roads, and the few stations they passed were old wooden, gingerbread-peaked buildings covered with posters. It was no different than when they left Moscow. The unknown was still before them. For the first time, he began to wonder if Royal had told him everything.

"Get them out! I don't give a shit how it's done. Just get them the hell out of there." Ted Magnuson rarely lost control of his temper, but this was one of those times.

When the message was brought into his office, it had been slightly garbled. He sent the radioman back to clarify it. This gave him time to think. His decision came instantly when the correct message was on his desk. It stated essentially the same that the other copy had—Petrov was dead, the GRU had control of Royal and Miller. Magnuson's people had been at the airport in Irkutsk, while the two Americans were being placed on the train. There was no trail. For days, it was thought they were either being interrogated in Irkutsk or dead. Then the agent on Maslov's staff reported they had unexpectedly turned up in Khabarovsk—under Maslov's control. Magnuson knew Krulev would get what he wanted from them.

"Do you want them moved to Japan?" asked MacIntyre.

"Japan, Korea . . . I don't give a shit, Jim. If they end up in Vladivostok, they're dead men. Do anything you have to. And for Christ's sake make sure none of this gets out to the White House!"

* * *

Their train's destination was Nakhodka, Russia's main Pacific port now that Vladivostok was closed. All foreigners went in and out of Eastern Russia via Nakhodka. Officially, there was no longer a Vladivostok for non-Russians.

As they stepped from the Vostok, an escort awaited them, pointing out the car that would take them the ninety miles back to Vladivostok. It was all very cold and official and reinforced the feeling that Ivan Petrov would have been the only friend in this strange and forbidding country.

The road to Vladivostok followed the coast, sweeping north just when they could look across a wide expanse of water to the hills and factory chimneys of the city and the unmistakable outline of ships. Bob Miller experienced an odd sensation deep in his stomach as he realized that he was one of the first Americans to see that sight since President Ford's visit almost ten years before.

The day was cold and raw. Showers swept across the gray waters onto the shore, diminishing their view of the Soviet countryside. Gusts of wind kicked up whitecaps, diverting gulls to the cover of coastal rocks and trees.

Neither American thought anything of the vehicle ahead of them off to the side of the road. One wheel was jacked into the air. A spare tire leaned against the side of the car. Through the windshield wipers, they could see a man next to the car waving a white cloth.

The driver pulled their car over to the side of the road. He and their escort got out, pulling their col-

lars up against the wind-driven, icy rain. The man
with the cloth came toward them, smiling good na-
turedly, and wiping his hands. As he slid the rag
into his pocket with his left hand, his right casually
dipped into the other pocket and, quite suddenly,
there was a gun in his hand. His expression
changed menacingly as he barked orders, his free
hand gesturing.

Their escort, lunging to one side and shouting at
the driver at the same time, was in the process of
pulling his own gun from a shoulder holster. As he
did so, a second man rose from a crouching position behind the other car, his gun leveled with both
hands.

A series of shots exploded around them. The action covered no more than a couple of seconds.
The surprised Americans had no opportunity to
protect themselves. Their escort never had control
of his gun as far as they could tell. He hit the side
of the road heavily, rolled down into the drainage
ditch, and came to a stop with his head face down
in the gurgling water.

The driver had no better chance. Even as he
made a motion into his coat, the other man was
firing. The bullets struck the man as he stood near
the front of their car, driving him backward against
the windshield. For an instant, their vision was
blocked. Then the body slid to the side, finally
slumping off the hood onto the ground. He left a
red smear across the windshield.

The closest man dropped his gun into his coat
pocket and casually sauntered over to their car,

pulling open the door on Miller's side. "Which one of you is Royal?"

Neither of them moved, the shock of what they'd witnessed paralyzing them. Finally, as the man leaned patiently on the door, waiting for a response, Jack leaned forward from the waist. "I am."

"Will you both come with me, please?" he asked politely, jerking his head toward the other car. His partner already had dropped the car from the jack. "We have little time."

They remained immobile. While a choice obviously did not exist, the violence of the past few days had numbed their reactions. They'd been given no reason to move, no assurance that the same fate didn't await them as soon as they left the security of the car.

"Please, both of us," the man nodded toward his partner who now had the other car ready, "are taking our lives in our hands as it is. We have orders from Admiral Magnuson, if that will help you at all. He wants you out of this country. Considering the situation you're in right here, does it matter much whether you take a chance on me or let the GRU do what they will and when they want?"

Royal looked at Miller, shrugged his shoulders helplessly, and gestured toward the door. "Thank you, gentlemen," the man said. "Our time is very precious."

As their new vehicle moved off, the man giving the orders said, "I can assure you I understand your hesitation and I'm glad you appreciate your position. You really had no choice. I'm going to get out of the car before the next village. It wouldn't do my career, or my neck, any good to be seen with you." The man leaned over the back seat, glancing at each of them to make his point. "You're lucky. Admiral Maslov would never do the same for his agents."

"I don't understand . . ." began Miller.

"That's all right, Mr. Miller. I know exactly what I'm doing. This car will take you back toward Nakhodka, where you came from. Arrangements unknown to me have been made to extract you to Japan. From there, the Americans are responsible for you."

"Who are you? If we get out of here, who do we say helped us?" asked Royal.

"You won't have to. He knows." They pulled over next to another vehicle under a patch of trees. The man stepped out quickly and disappeared into the other car, which pulled away instantly.

"Where are you taking us?" asked Royal.

In barely understandable English, the driver said, "I do not speak your language."

Later that same night, somewhere off the Russian coast, not too far from Nakhodka, a fishing boat picked them up soon after darkness had fallen. The weather had deteriorated rapidly. By the time the small boat heaved to hours later, six-foot waves were tossing it about in fog and heavy rain. Kept below, the Americans were virtual prisoners. None of the crew spoke English. They were offered nothing to eat.

Then, as fear of the unknown was progressing to despair, the roar of engines came to them. A crewman flung open the hatch, gesturing anxiously for them to follow. On deck, they could feel the beat of rotors from a helicopter hovering off the stern. A flashlight blinked upward through the haze and the helo moved just over the stern, a cable descending into the waiting hands of a crewman. Miller was grabbed roughly by two crewmen, his arms thrust into a sling, and he was swept up and away from the tossing boat. His next sensation was a man in a black wet suit and helmet sweeping him rapidly into the helo. The sling was yanked off his body and dropped quickly through the hatch as Miller fell into the corner. A moment later, Royal appeared in the hatchway and was just as roughly shoved next to him. The helo banked sharply and surged away from the little boat, racing across the ocean just above the waves.

Once the helo steadied on course, the helmeted crewman crawled over to them. "Arc you okay?" he bellowed.

"Where the hell are we . . .?" Royal shouted back.

"Don't worry. First stop USS TARAWA. Then you're on your way home!"

CHAPTER TEN

Shanghai, the largest city in China with close to eleven million inhabitants, has come full circle since the Revolution—once again, it is a great international commercial center. While it was the birthplace of the Chinese Communist Party, it is even more important to the country today because more than half of China's exports pass through this port city.

Though it rests close by the confluence of the Yangtze River, Shanghai is set fifty miles inland from the East China Sea. The river widens into a tremendous delta pouring cloudy silt from thousands of miles inland into its ever-changing entrance. The city, therefore, is well protected from attack by sea. Shanghai, itself, sits on the banks of the Huangpu River, a tributary to the immense Yangtze delta. From the air, the first time traveler can trace the path of seagoing traders from around the world as they wend their way to China's export center.

The neatly dressed Chinese gentleman had no trouble identifying the tall American he'd been sent to meet among the mostly oriental passengers. The three piece suit and single color tie contrasted with the man's physical appearance. Tom Loomis could have been a Pancho Villa sidekick, a Serbian partisan, an Italian gigolo, anything other than the American businessman he was. His thick, gray-black hair, dark eyes, and drooping black mustache set off sharp features. He was a few inches over six feet tall, dark, and had a perpetual five o'clock shadow. Acquaintances were well aware of his quick tongue and a temper that matched his appearance.

The man sent to meet Loomis was a junior employee of CITIC (China International Trust and Investment Corporation) whose English was equal to that of any tour guide. Mr. Rong Yiren, the Chairman of CITIC, had personally called Mr. Cheng and asked that he escort Mr. Loomis during his stay in Shanghai.

While many of the Chinese Loomis had met in the past were silent, responding politely to any questions, Cheng was voluble. From the time their black Hongchi exited Hongqaio Airport until they arrived at his hotel, Loomis was treated to a steady stream of facts about the area, complete with place names and dates. Cheng was one of the more engaging Chinese he had met.

Loomis learned that the People's Liberation Army had come from the west of the city when Shanghai was finally liberated. As a matter of fact, for obvious reasons, the airport was one of the first points captured. The PLA swept down the very road they were now on, arriving in the city almost without firing a shot. Chiang Kai-shek had already escaped to Taiwan, taking the wealth of the country and his army with him. There had been only token resistance, and those few Nationalists left behind had surrendered before any harm could come to them.

Cheng brought him down Nanking Road, once crowded with foreigners, now a thoroughly Chinese shopping area. The famous Shanghai Racetrack, where rich white people once bet millions of dollars, was now the Renmin People's Park. Each location they passed was identified as it used to be and as it had become. Loomis sensed Cheng's pride as he related how Shanghai had brought China face-to-face with Western commerce and culture. He would learn very quickly that the Chinese worked respectfully with foreigners, yet retained a hatred for what their city had once been.

"And here we are, Mr. Loomis." Cheng swung the car around a corner onto a broad boulevard bordering a wide, busy river. Small freighters were tied up alongside the road. The river bore every type of floating craft imaginable, from modern foreign ships to ancient sailing junks. "This is Zhongshan Road, formerly the Bund before 1949. The Bund was one of the most famous streets in the world. If you had been a sailor, you would have known about it even if you'd never been here. The Bund was the commerce center of Asia, and a sailor could find anything he'd ever dreamed of within a few blocks." Cheng looked back over the seat. "It's not like that anymore, but it's always what foreigners are most interested in hearing about. And this is your hotel."

The car pulled up before an imposing, marble-fronted building capped by a shiny spire. "This is the Peace Hotel, Mr. Loomis, the finest in the city. Mr. Yiren insisted you stay here. He requested a room on the front looking over the river."

"I take it Mr. Yiren has even more influence than I assumed."

"Yes sir." Cheng had already stepped out of the car, signaling a doorman to take Loomis' baggage. He came around to the rear door before Tom could step out. "Mr. Yiren was once mayor of Shanghai before he was asked to go to Beijing."

The scene stretching out before him was impressive. The bustle of craft on the river, the Huangpu (Whangpoo) he was told later, the traffic on the street, and the European architecture were all totally different from the China he had come to expect. This was part of the old International Settlement, a segment of a city actually carved out by foreign nationals to the exclusion of the natives of that city. Just thirty-five years before, this had been legally separated from China, a part of a great city that a Chinese would not have dared to enter unless he was on official business. Now Shanghai was functioning much as it had before, only today the natives were in charge.

Loomis looked up at the hotel. The sign over the entrance was translated by Cheng as the Heping

Hotel, meaning peace. "It was the Cathay Hotel before, Mr. Loomis. I've never had the opportunity to see any of the rooms but I'm told that many of the suites used to have marble baths with silver taps." He shook his head in wonder. "Imagine that, just to get clean."

Cheng walked up the steps with Loomis, his never ending monologue continuing. "The most famous people in the world stayed right here, and if they were really famous they had a suite named after them. One of your people, a writer, stayed here and wrote one of his famous plays . . . now what was his name?" Cheng looked perplexed for an instant, but answered his own question, "Coward. That was his name, Noel Coward." His face lit up at remembering the occidental name.

"I'm afraid he wasn't one of ours, Mr. Cheng. He was British."

"Oh, yes, British," he mused. "Well, all the same. They were all foreigners then. But, don't misunderstand me, please, Mr. Loomis," he assured the American. "Everything is different today."

Cheng escorted him to the reception desk, explaining proudly to the clerk who Loomis was and who had arranged for his room. "I think you will be most comfortable, Mr. Loomis. I am assured by this gentleman that Mr. Yiren has been able to obtain a sixth floor room with an excellent view of the river. That is an honor."

"I will have to remember to thank Mr. Yiren then."

Cheng changed the subject. "You have nothing scheduled today. The rest of the afternoon is free. If you care to rest, I will leave you alone. Or, if you'd like to see more of the city, I am available for the remainder of the day to escort you."

"I appreciate that. What I'd really like to do first is take my luggage to my room and wash up. Then, if you've no objections, I'll accept your offer to see the city." An idea came to Loomis. "Since you've never been in the rooms here before, would you care to come up to mine for a moment?"

Cheng shook his head. "It is preferred that Chinese do not visit in a guest's room, especially in hotels that cater to foreigners. And," he smiled wistfully at Loomis, "I think perhaps I don't care to familiarize myself with such luxuries at this time. Perhaps when I am Mr. Yiren's age I will have earned that privilege."

Tom nodded. "I think I understand. Are you a native of this city?"

"I was born here just before the Japanese occupied Shanghai in 1941. I was too young to remember much about the Japanese, except when they surrendered." His face clouded for a moment. "Then the others returned again."

"I think I do understand you, Mr. Cheng, and I'd be delighted to have you show me about your city. I've heard so much about it and it would be an honor to join a native of Shanghai."

Cheng beamed.

That afternoon, Loomis saw more of Shanghai and learned more about the city than most visitors

would in a week, and from the front seat of the
Hongchi. He had quickly earned Cheng's respect,
and was able to approach the man on almost equal
footing. Whenever possible, he interrupted the
steady patter about Shanghai's lore to ask a bit
about the people he would be meeting during his
stay. The foremost name was Lu Zhong, the person
who was meeting him for dinner that evening, the
manager of CITIC's Shanghai office.

Cheng, who was also a very thoughtful person,
brought him back to the hotel so that he could
shower and relax before going out that evening.
The marble tub and silver fixtures were impressive,
even if the water pressure in the Peace Hotel left a
little to be desired. After a needed shave, Loomis
stretched out on his bed. As he dozed, his mind
drifted back to a meeting with a potential partner
and perhaps the heaviest investor in his new
company . . . .

He was explaining his upcoming visit to Shanghai. "Hotel construction in Beijing, Shanghai,
Canton, any of the growing money centers, is
booming. And I can tell you right now, the Chinese
know how to get those damn buildings up in the
air. They can also furnish them, and they can make
each one plusher than the next. But the one thing a
guest can't do with much success when he's settled
down in that room is call out for an appointment,
or call for a dinner reservation, or even call the
room next door. It's the old two-tin-cans-and-a-
piece-of-string routine.

"They need PBX systems, or their equivalent, in hotels, universities, business centers, government complexes . . . everywhere. They can build nuclear weapons, fire ICBMs seven thousand miles, but they can't do shit with surface communications."

"I'm surprised the telephone company isn't over there en masse."

"We've got enough of our own problems. It's the entrepreneur who's going to make the big score this time," Tom answered.

"And you see China as the big score?"

"Mister, it's the chance of a lifetime. I've got a piece of a little company that's been putting together a PBX-type system. It's miniaturized and does everything the Bell System's unit will do and more. If I can guarantee them those sales in China, we'll get a major interest in that company. That means it comes out of someone else's pocket and into a company that belongs to us. And if that company can take away business from the international giant of the industry, can you imagine where we go from there?"

"It sounds lovely."

"It certainly does, but everything in China sounds easier than it really is. You can't believe the system you've got to go through to find the person who makes a decision."

The man nodded in agreement. "But I understand that they're trying to make business easier for outsiders, too."

"Oh, they are trying. But have you ever seen a bureaucracy that made anything easier?" Loomis

continued without answering his own question.
"To change a system, they set up a new system. I'll
tell you, their parents and grandparents and great
grandparents were suspicious of the westerner, and
times haven't changed. Mao made sure that they
aren't going to forget the white devil for years to
come . . . and that means you and me. . . ."

There was no problem in identifying the Chinese
financier in the lobby when Mr. Lu entered the
Peace Hotel that evening. Lu Zhong was a handsome man, taller than most of his people, his black
hair cut in western style and streaked with gray.
The autumn weather in Shanghai was still in the
sixties, and he was dressed much like a westerner,
with an open necked white shirt and sport jacket.

"Mr. Loomis, I have heard so much about you.
How pleased I am to finally make your acquaintance." Lu's English was slower than Mr. Cheng's,
and occasionally he halted to search for a word.
While polite, he did not defer to Tom as so many of
the other Chinese had done. He considered himself
an equal from the start.

"If you don't mind, I have reserved a table right
here in the hotel. It seems some of the best food in
Shanghai is still right in this building. When the
British were here, the eighth floor dining room was
the most exquisite in all of China. It boasts a beautiful river view, Chinese cuisine from five regions,
and I am sure the best cream puffs in China. For
some reason we didn't ruin that tradition over the
years." He smiled at Tom's questioning glance. "I
worked with the British also. It's hard to get rid of

those wonderfully decadent habits once you've acquired them."

Mr. Lu's charm matched his appearance. As they stepped from the elevator, a head waiter appeared instantly at Mr. Lu's side. They were led to a table with all the flourish that might have been accorded royalty. Shanghai and the Huangpu River were alight and in motion through the vast windows.

A bottle of the heady mao tai appeared between them as they were seated. Mr. Lu's desires were anticipated.

"I'm impressed," said Loomis, gesturing first out the window and then to the table.

"Thank you, Mr. Loomis. It is my pleasure to ensure that you are not disappointed during your visit to Shanghai. Your expertise in communications systems could mean a great deal to us."

"That's kind of you to say. I hope I can be of some help."

"There's not the least bit of doubt. Here," he reached for the bottle, "I hope you'll join me."

Tom lifted his glass to his host, sensing that the man across the table felt some kind of power over him.

"No, please, the honor is mine." Mr. Lu smiled sincerely. "It would be rude of me not to propose a toast to a new friend." He looked out the window thoughtfully. "I think we should drink to your health, Mr. Loomis." Lu looked back from the river lights directly at his guest. "Yes, that's a good idea. I would hope that your visit here is strictly business and there would be nothing else that could interfere with that or affect your health in the slightest." He raised his glass. "Your health, sir . . . *gan bei*!"

Tom never took his eyes off Lu's as he drank the fiery liquor. Putting the glass aside, he leaned forward, elbows on the table, his chin on his hands. "I'm not sure I follow you, Mr. Lu. Is there something I should know?"

The Chinese leaned back in his chair, arms folded, returning Loomis' stare. "I would hope not, though I can't really answer that yet." He refilled the glasses. "I am drawn to people like you, Mr. Loomis, and I go out of my way to learn as much as I can about them before I ever do business with them. Sometimes I learn more than I should." He lifted his glass, saying nothing, a slight smile on his face, and downed it in a gulp. "I have many suspicious countrymen, and I think you ought to be aware of that. There have been some discreet questions asked about your visit. Both Rong Yiren and I are businessmen and interested in making money by building business for our country."

Tom pulled on his mustache, straightening it, thinking as fast as he could about the man across the table.

"Our problem in China is security. Russia is our enemy and we have information that they are creating a number of intimidating movements in our direction. Your Seventh Fleet is scheduled to visit Vladivostok in a couple of months. Certain people in our government suspect that maybe the United States and Russia are involved in this as yet unknown effort together. Therefore, all Americans arriving in our country are looked at with suspicion. Do you see why I'm asking you this?"

"It couldn't be any clearer, Mr. Lu." Tom took a deep breath before adding, "While I appreciate what you're saying, I am what I say I am, and I'm here to make money, as much as I can."

Lu smiled. "Then we do understand each other. Now you can tell me a little more about your background. You work for the telephone company in the United States, but you also have developed your own business. Correct me if I'm wrong."

Damn, this man was sharp. Loomis looked closely at Lu Zhong sitting across from him. No doubt about it. The man represented the big score. He was a decision maker, and he took the trouble to know as much about the American as possible. Tom preferred to deal with men like that.

"Mr. Lu, you seem to know enough about me that you're aware I have an interest in a much smaller company, one that's years ahead in a micro-PBX system that can move the communication requirements on your new construction projects into the next century."

Mr. Lu smiled appreciately. "You overestimate me. I am aware of your little company, and assumed that was part of your reason for coming to China, but I don't know a great deal about this new system." He picked up a menu that had discreetly been left at the table. "If you will allow me to order some of the rare specialties this restaurant is known for, we can discuss the details over dinner."

As they dined, Tom Loomis took over the conversation, explaining the advantages of the new system, its less technical details, and why it would be better for the Chinese to deal with a small, new company rather than the giant corporation he currently worked for.

Mr. Lu asked a few simple questions while they awaited a very special after-dinner drink he had insisted on ordering for them. When it arrived, he explained what it was, raised his glass to the American, and sipped thoughtfully.

"Would I be wrong, Mr. Loomis, in assuming that your present organization would be upset if they knew what you were selling to me this evening."

Tom looked at the other curiously. "Yes, you could assume that."

"I do think we can reach agreement on your new system, not so much because you have convinced me that it is better but because I think we can do favors for each other."

Loomis said nothing. Sipping his drink, he looked out at the lights of the busy river, then back at Lu, waiting for the other man to continue.

"I plan to retire soon. Unlike many of my associates, I have no intention of slowly killing myself for the sake of socialism. And they don't give you a watch in China when you are finally unable to work any longer, Mr. Loomis. They bury you." He paused to emphasize his point. "So you see that I can't really retire in my own country either. I have to go somewhere else. And, as I'm sure you're aware, the Chinese *renminbi* is pretty much worthless scrip in the rest of the world."

Why the son of a bitch is no better than I am, Tom thought. "And if you take my PBX system, I become the key to your retirement program." Tom already knew the answer.

"Gold or precious stones are the only true international currency today. I have access to this and I want it out of China. Any Chinese citizen would have trouble taking anything of value out. You assist me and, in return, you will have a contract delivering profit even after I'm gone. To ensure we can trust each other, I will work out a system that repays each of us from the other's wealth, a kickback if you will. That term was coined by you Americans but it's a worldwide business method."

"Do you expect me to agree to this tonight?"

"Not at all, Mr. Loomis. I want to understand you better so that we can smooth out details. There are a lot of things I need to know, and I would hope you feel the same way. One evening doesn't establish a relationship, but honor among thieves doesn't require a marriage either."

"The terminology you choose isn't especially attractive, but I agree we should talk again. Smuggling is not something I'm adept at."

"Call it what you will."

"When will we get together again?"

"I'll be in touch."

"Mr. Cheng has a fairly busy schedule for me."

"He is new to our company and will arrange whatever is necessary for me."

Loomis' eyebrows were raised. "Oh, from talking with him, I would have thought he'd been with you for a long time."

"He is a native of Shanghai," answered Lu, "but he was just recently sent to us. I have no idea why, since he seems ill prepared for business with foreigners." He smiled. "That's why we assigned him to guide you." Then he added, "It is lazy of me not to find out more about the man. I will say good evening to you now, Mr. Loomis. We have both had a busy day."

They shook hands as Loomis stepped from the elevator at the sixth floor. Vaguely, as he was fumbling with his key at the door, he noticed an unpleasant odor. He knew he had smelled it in the past but couldn't imagine where. It slipped from his mind as he pushed open the door.

Stepping into the room, he sensed something was wrong before he was sure what it was. He had not left the lights on. Now they were ablaze. With two more steps, they revealed the contents of a drawer strewn across the middle of the floor. Before his senses could react further to halt his progress into the room, he was grabbed from behind, his arms pinned at his sides. At the same time, a cloth was jammed roughly over his face, his head pulled back painfully.

He could neither move his arms nor make a sound. His neck was being twisted at an odd angle. It was impossible to shake off the evil smelling cloth stifling his breath, barely allowing a trickle of air into his nose. Then he remembered that smell.

It came back to him from school laboratories and hospital corridors. Ether! He tried to bite the hand holding the cloth, but this just caused strong fingers under his chin to pull sharply back. The pain of stretched muscles came to him as the room began to darken. He was passing out. There had to be at least two of them. He was sure of that.

Gradually the room regained its shape. He was on his back. His eyes traveled from the ceiling fixture to a wall, down the wallpaper past a window to the floor. He moved his head. There was a dull pain. Then he recognized the bed where he had carelessly tossed his coat before dinner. It was in shreds. One of his suitcases was open on the floor, the insides slashed open.

He rose to one elbow, his eyes finishing their cataloging of the room, his room, in the Peace Hotel in Shanghai. Nothing was left intact. Even the furniture had been ripped apart. He hadn't been in the room more than a few hours. What the hell were they after?

Rising first to his knees, head aching, mouth dry and evil tasting, he stood up shakily. My God, he realized, while I was out they searched me. His pants had been pulled off. His shoes were on the other side of the room, where someone had relaxed in the easy chair while prying off the heels.

Stumbling over to his bedside, head and eyes burning, he picked up the room phone. It rang and rang on the other end. Damn phone systems! Finally, a voice with just enough English to be understood, explained that he should hold for the manager. Feeling a sudden need to vomit, he left his room number with the operator, explaining it was an emergency.

And then it was upon him, his throat opening uncontrollably, the stink of ether returning and gagging him. He ran. Slamming open the door to the large, ancient bathroom, he aimed at the commode, vomit spewing from his mouth as he tripped over something on the floor, sprawling to the side of the toilet. Missing the first time, he pulled his head up to the bowl, emptying his stomach. Then as the heaving began to subside, he recalled stumbling as he lurched through the bathroom door.

Turning his aching head, still grasping the bowl with both hands, he observed a leg hanging limply out of the tub. Most of the bath curtain was torn away from the rod, much of it splattered with blood. Rising to his knees, he looked into the vast marble tub at Cheng's lifeless eyes. One side of his skull was brutally crushed. A trail of blood ran under the body where it then collected in a puddle in the torn curtain.

The phone in the other room came to life, ringing incessantly.

Loomis was depressed and unable to function normally the next day. He had covered the events of the entire evening in detail for the consulate, and they had taken detailed statements for the local police. He was assured that he was not a suspect in the death. And for some reason, the local government was avoiding discussion of anything about

Cheng's background. Loomis was advanced some money for personal items, and had spent much of the afternoon out at the stores on Nanking Street, attempting to find western style clothes that would fit.

That evening, Loomis sat alone at the bar in the glass-ringed eighth floor dining room of the hotel. The sun was setting behind him, colorful rays dancing across the windows overlooking the bustling Huangpu, when an older occidental gentleman perched himself on the adjoining stool.

He waved at the bartender, an elfish grin on his round, reddish face, "Scotch if you will, mate . . . one ice cube." He rubbed his hands together as though he were drying them and turned to Tom, "Mr. Loomis is it now?" He extended his hand. "Darby's the name, Jack Darby. Very pleased to meet you."

Surprised as much at the man's old-boy approach as he was by the unexpected interruption, Tom shook the man's hand, looking into sparkling black eyes set deeply into a round, jowly face. Darby couldn't have been more than five foot six or seven, and he appeared reasonably slender for a man of his years, though even the man's age was indeterminate. He could have been seventy years old, Tom thought, but his spriteliness was that of a much younger man. The white hair had receded, but still appeared thick enough to be holding its own. The accent had been very British. The bright red ascot around his neck contributed a regal mein to his expensive looking clothes.

"Should I know you, Mr. Darby?"

"Not at all, old fellow, not at all. But I think we'll get along famously." The scotch arrived and the little man immediately downed most of it. "Ah, wonderful. Can't let it get too cold or too diluted now, can we?" He grinned at Tom, finishing off the remainder of his drink and sliding the glass back to the bartender, nodding for a refill.

"No, Mr. Loomis, you aren't supposed to know me at all. But I'm willing to wager that too many people already know you. Right?"

"That unfortunately seems to be the case."

"Now, now, old man, don't be feeling bad about everything. There's an old saying in Shanghai, a very simple one, one word—*maskee!* See. Very simple . . . *maskee*. It means everything's going to get better . . . the spirit of eternal optimism. And you probably need a bit of that right now. It was a term that the coolies used years ago, when they were probably wondering if life was all worthwhile." The older man raised a hand to make a point. "I was here way back then, and I don't know if it really was worthwhile for them. Ah! A miserable life from the day they were born to the day they died. *Maskee* was the only hope they had. Then the white man even stole that from them. Twisted it a little bit as they twisted everything else. Used it to mean that profits were going to improve, or the weather was going to change for the better. Imagine that! Stealing a damn fine word that really had quality to it. *Maskee!*"

It brought a smile to Tom's face, the first time

something had amused him that day. "*Maskee . . . maskee*. All right, Mr. Darby, I'll remember that. Maybe everything will improve."

The Englishman's second scotch arrived and he motioned to the bartender, "Another for my friend . . . on my check please."

Tom fumbled with a swizzle stick on the bar. "I suppose you could tell me who you are since you're buying me a drink."

"Why certainly, old man. No problem. Your consulate is aware. You've been involved in a bit of a problem here, not the normal introduction most outsiders need the first night in Shanghai. You might need a friendly face beyond the local authorities who'd be happy to help you."

"Yes, I guess so." Loomis looked questioningly at the other.

"Well, I'm him, dirty socks and all," he said, one eyebrow cocked slightly higher than the other as he turned on the stool to face Tom. "I've been known to have some contacts with the American intelligence network, but I suppose you wouldn't expect someone my age involved in that undercover stuff, would you?"

"Not really."

"Where the hell do you think professionals come from in this business of ours anyway? Not youngsters, by God. They're just learning. You're looking at a survivor, right? So I must have a hell of a lot of something going for me." His second scotch disappeared as fast as the first.

"There's something you should understand right

away. I'm no professional. I have no desire to be one. I'm a businessman. And if last night is any indication of the daily hazards of your business, it's been nice knowing you."

Darby clapped him gently on the shoulder, patting him as a coach would a player. "Now don't you worry yourself about things like that as long as we're working together. See," he poked himself in the chest with a thumb, "solid flesh and blood. A survivor. Don't take chances or you'll be in trouble, just like poor Cheng."

"Cheng?" Tom whirled on his stool.

"Poor bugger." Darby bowed his head. "He was one of ours. But that's what I mean. Not professional enough. Took one too many chances, or he never would have ended up in your bathtub, Mr. Loomis. And things like that tend to upset the local authorities. Doesn't matter whether the police are communists or capitalists, they hate to have outsiders messing around their bailiwick, because bodies always start turning up."

Tom looked at Darby incredulously. "Cheng was messed up with you? He wasn't with CITIC?" What was left of the day was deteriorating rapidly.

"Of course he was with CITIC. He had a job with them. I made sure of that. That's what I'm trying to explain to you Mr. Loomis, about professionals. You don't have to worry when you're with the best. Cheng simply wasn't ready to play with the big boys, but we were running out of time and agents. Simple as that!" A third scotch disappeared as quickly as the other two.

"I didn't bargain for this." He thought he'd been humoring the Darby fellow who wanted to buy him a drink. Now Tom was beginning to feel the man might be serious.

"None of you ever do." His merry eyes sparkled. "But never mind. I've been a babysitter before." The raised finger to the bartender meant two more drinks. "Now, Mr. Loomis, we're going to have to get serious this evening. It's nice of you to accept my invitation to dinner. Don't worry." He raised his hand to interrupt Loomis before he started. "I've already cleared it with the Consulate. You can leave the hotel and go anywhere you want, as long as you're with me."

"I seem to have no choice."

"I beg your pardon," Darby said in mock seriousness. "You couldn't have a more engaging partner. I know Shanghai better than most Chinese. We'll get out of here and find a native place for dinner. There are a lot of places where we can't be watched."

"Watched?"

"Naturally. You don't expect to be involved with what you were last night and run around Shanghai like a bloody tourist, do you?" He picked up his new drink, touched glasses with Tom, and said, "To a fine meal tonight. Lu Zhong fed you well in this room last night, and it's okay for foreigners. But I'll take you to some places white men have never seen before . . . other than myself, of course. And," he giggled, "I promise you won't paint your walls with your dinner like you did last night . . . as long as you stick with me." The scotch over one cube disappeared.

"Lu Zhong. You know Mr. Lu?"

"Do I know Lu Zhong? Lu Zhong and I go way back together, and I assure you neither of us have ever trusted the other. So it's an amicable relationship." Darby's jovial face became suddenly serious. "I suppose he's already made his offer to you?" He looked over at the stunned expression on Loomis's face. "No. Don't tell me about it. I can see it on your face. I'm good at that, too. He's a bit younger than me, and that makes him a bit faster . . . and I'm sorry the son of a bitch got to you before I did." Darby waved his hand. "No, don't tell me about it now. You come tell me about it at dinner, when we're by ourselves. Come on now, mate. Drink up. You're one of the slower Americans I've run into . . . and after last night, I'd like you to have some fun for a change."

Ted Magnuson was having a good day, the first one in quite a while. In the past twenty-four hours, he'd received contact messages from Li Zhiang in Beijing and Darby in Shanghai. And an old friend, the Captain of USS TARAWA, reported that Royal and Miller were aboard and in good health.

The first stage of his plan seemed to have worked, though he wouldn't be sure until he talked with Royal. Eventually, Li would have an opportunity to get in touch with more detailed information on Goodrich. It might take more time to hear from Darby, but Jack always filed a detailed written report whenever he touched down in Hong Kong.

Magnuson estimated that he had eight to nine weeks. He couldn't be sure. It was impossible to establish firm dates when Maslov refused to set one. Or, if he had, it hadn't gotten down to the level of Magnuson's agent. If he could just get the tape, and the software he had hoped Miller would pick up, they'd be able to project the date in Washington. It was the only way he could ever get to the President again. Benjamin had told him recently that he doubted his White House job would last much longer. He was out of favor. Too many people knew he was maintaining contact with Magnuson.

But, it remained a day to celebrate. Magnuson had four fresh, unknown men in position, or close to it, for Seagull, even if two of them hadn't the vaguest idea about it.

CHAPTER ELEVEN

It was the first small car Loomis had ridden in since he arrived in China. Standing next to it the roof came somewhere below his chest and, inside, his knees rested against the dashboard. If he had to drive, it would have been impossible to shift.

"I must admit, it's not much of a car. But then, how many foreigners have you seen driving in this country," said Darby.

"None that I've noticed."

"That's because the authorities don't want you behind a wheel. Gives the natives the idea that you've got something over them and they never want that to happen again. And, it's just as well, believe me. With the laws here, a foreigner might spend half his life in jail before they figured out how to get him to court."

Tom winced as they hit a bump. The cars the Japanese were exporting to China had little to offer in the way of springs or shocks. "Am I being naive in asking why you're driving?"

"Not at all, old chap. I know the right people."

"And how does one get to know the right people?"

"Well, first you have to speak the language. Not just a passing ability, but like a native. And it helps if you've lived around here for forty or fifty years."

This interested Loomis. It gave him an idea of how old Darby really was. "You were here before the war?"

"Which war?" Darby laughed. Then, thinking better of it, "I'm sorry. I don't mean to be sarcastic. It's just that there was always war in this country from the beginning of the century until Liberation in 1949. Local joke . . . my apologies." He took a deep breath. "Yes, I was here before the war, Mr. Loomis. I joined the International Settlement Police in this city in 1932 and stayed with it until '35. I was in my early twenties then, a young bloke looking for action. For anyone in the Far East in those days, that meant Shanghai."

"You came out from England?"

"Originally, yes. Not to join the force though. My family had holdings out here, like so many other Brits then. Plantations, that sort of thing. Before and after Shanghai, I worked in various places, Malaya, Borneo . . . it was Sarawak then under Rajah Brooke and an exciting place to be . . . New Guinea, and a bit of time in Ceylon. I even ran a rubber plantation on a tiny island in the Solomons for a year, but that was a dead life. After Shanghai, one always has to come back. You can't stay away. Here now, let me show you some of the sights while we're driving. You can learn about me when we've sat down for a good dinner."

The car wound through broad, busy boulevards, thronged with people, and back streets barely wide enough for two tiny cars to pass. There were strange names for every place he pointed out, and even stranger stories that he'd mention for a moment before they arrived at the next spot. Loomis soon lost track of direction. He had no idea how near or far he was from the Huangpu River. The farther they got from the business center of the city, the deeper they were into a world unknown to occidentals. It was at once alien and beautiful and frightening, for he knew white men never walked these streets.

Quite suddenly, Darby turned the little car down an alley even darker than the unlighted street they'd just left. Piles of rubbish marked a dead end.

"Okay then," said Darby, as he switched the lights off, "all ashore." He stepped out into the darkness, then leaned back in, noticing Loomis hadn't moved. "Come on man, aren't you hungry?"

"All I see is a pile of trash."

"Never fear, now. I must admit, it certainly doesn't look like the Peace Hotel, but the food's better. Come on then. We don't want to keep our hosts waiting. I did call ahead."

Cautiously, Loomis opened the car door, unwinding himself from the tight seat, stretching stiff muscles as he stood up. The smell of the alley was overpowering.

"Good God, this place stinks."

"Well then, that's what must attract the natives, because it smells just lovely inside. Follow old Jack and you'll have no problem. Come along now."

Darby led the way to the street, walking no more than ten yards before turning into an unlighted doorway. Looking back, he motioned to Loomis. They passed down a long, barely lighted hallway, stopping at a door just past a staircase. The air was changing rapidly to some delightful and unusual aromas. Darby pushed the door open, and Loomis saw that they had just entered a bright, noisy room full of happy, laughing Chinese gathered around tables heaped with an abundance of food.

The din quieted momentarily as the inhabitants of the room examined the two foreigners. Darby was recognized, for some people waved or said a few words as they began to weave their way through the tables. The voices picked up as quickly as they had died.

The change in noise level had brought a very round, happy looking, older Chinese woman from an adjoining room. She skipped over to Darby, and welcomed him with a motherly hug.

As they were settled at a rear table, a bottle of scotch appeared between them, along with glasses containing one cube of ice each. In apparently perfect Chinese, Darby spoke to the waiter, pointing at Loomis' drink as he did so. "Extra ice," he translated. "He understood when I told him Americans weren't quite civilized yet."

As the meal progressed through twelve enticing

courses, Darby explained more of his background. He had been in Malaya when the Japanese moved south and he'd been captured early in the Campaign. He enjoyed making a joke out of it. "I went to the Navy first, and they told me that with the sinking of the PRINCE OF WALES and the RE-PULSE, they'd run out of ships. So I decided the RAF was the next most romantic place for an adventurous character like me, but they said that anything that hadn't been shot down had been destroyed on the ground. So, I didn't tell the Army they were the last on my list and they greeted me with open arms. That was the end of '41, and wouldn't you know the Japs got there before I'd figured out how to wear the uniform. I spent the next four years as a prisoner of war building the Burma Railroad. I had my card all punched when you were just a snotty, old boy."

Darby's life was a travelog, always ending up in Shanghai. "I learned the city like the back of my thumb from the seat of a Harley-Davidson. We were the toughest police force in the world then, and we went wherever we pleased in the city. That's the way I met some fine people, Mr. Loomis." He stopped here, as if suddenly remembering something very important. "Just why in the hell am I calling you Mr. Loomis when we've become such fast friends?" He raised his eyebrows in an innocent, cherubic expression. "Jack's the name, and Jack it shall be."

"Everyone calls me Tom. Okay?"

"Almost makes us blood brothers, doesn't it?"

Darby laughed at his own remark, pouring another scotch over his shrinking ice cube.

"You're wondering what keeps getting me back into Shanghai now that the communists run it, right?" Without waiting for an answer, he continued, "Before the war, I spent some time with the old firm of Jardine Matheson, the trading company that helped open up this god-awful, lovely city. I was with them after the war for a while before I went back to sea to get some of the wanderlust out of my blood. When I came back in 1950, they'd run off to Hong Kong. The communists made life so hard for them, they barely got out with the clothes on their backs. No one here had anything against Jack Darby, and a lot of Chinese I knew were doing pretty well under the new regime, so I could come and go as I pleased. After all, the communists had to put on some type of show to make everyone think they weren't down on all white men. When the Jardine people in Hong Kong found that out, they made me their representative. No dummies there, mind you. They knew Shanghai would come back again. For all intents and purposes, and a damn good front if I do say so myself, that's where I hang my hat today."

The man was a storehouse of knowledge about the past fifty years of Shanghai. He talked about the death of commerce after Liberation, the new growing pains the city went through after 1949, industrialization, the new power brokers, and always how he managed to know enough people to come back whenever he wanted. His friends were not other occidentals. They were Chinese and their loyalty was to Shanghai, just as much as Darby's.

"I know the city, Tom. I know the people, whatever they do, no matter the language. That's why I also work for your people, not to mention the pay's not so bad either." The little black eyes sparkled as he smiled. His cheeks had become a bit rosy. It could have been the scotch, or perhaps his pleasure at being able to monopolize the almost non-stop conversation. Whatever, he had charmed his American counterpart.

"I hope you don't mind not talking about you, Tom. I already know all there is to know. And," his index finger made an imaginary circle in the air, "so does our friend, Lu Zhong."

"Christ, I'm getting sick of being at a disadvantage. I feel like someone else is pulling my strings. I don't know a damn thing about anyone or anything."

"Just as well in this business. If someone thought to ask you some questions, especially if they were to use a bit of pressure, I'm sorry to say, you wouldn't know a thing, would you?"

"I wouldn't know what the hell to do."

"Relax old chap. You'll stay healthy that way. You were just on the receiving end of a warning last night, and I'm sorry to say they were a bit ahead of themselves." Darby smiled encouragingly. "You can't resent a simple upchuck now can you? That was the easy way out."

"Let's talk about something I understand. Lu Zhong. You seem to have the advantage over me again with him."

"Now that takes a bit of doing, and I'm going to have to ease you into that chap. He doesn't have a shadow. That's part of your education, old man, the kind of education that could save your ass later on." He paused for a second. "Just a question or two. You talked with Lu about the new Rainbow Hotel they're building?"

Loomis nodded. "Another month or so and it would have been too far along to use our system."

"Good, good. Any other construction?"

"We discussed a couple of others."

"What do you have to do in return?"

Loomis was caught unexpectedly by that question. "In return . . ."

"Yes, old chap. Now come on. Come clean with Old Jack. I told you I knew Lu from way back and I doubt he's changed his stripes at this late date. He'll have asked a favor."

Tom thought for a moment, his brain slightly impaired by the scotch he'd consumed. But, as always, he regained his composure. This was business, not something that involved this intelligence matter Darby alluded to.

Or was it? Lu Zhong intended to leave China. He had mentioned precious metals and stones, which the government would never knowingly allow him to take out. The deal smelled from the start, but it was not an unheard of way to do business overseas. Or was he being set up? There was something about Darby that inspired confidence. What the hell, he decided.

"He wants me to take something out for him."

Darby's eyes narrowed, his lips pursed. "The

diamonds!" It wasn't a question or even a statement. It was the answer to something that had been running through Jack's mind for some time. He knew that Lu had to get out soon. Then he relaxed, saying barely loud enough for Tom to hear, "I knew he had to be making plans, but this one I might have overlooked." He looked up at Tom. "I would have expected almost anything from that man, but I guess he's got the biggest balls of all, as you Yanks would say."

Jack pulled a sheaf of paper from his breast pocket, and handed it to Loomis. "Here, read this if you get a chance. It'll give you a better idea about what you're getting into." He pointed to the title on the first page— *Triple Murder* by d'Esterre Darby. "Don't pay attention to my pen name. Just something I wrote after the war when I thought I might become an author. Tried to sell it to Wide World and got thumbs down on it. Don't bother now, but give it a read when you have a chance. I'm just sorry I couldn't find the clippings from the old North China Daily News that I'd saved. They'd of told more than this, but it ought to get you thinking about what you're getting into." He stood up. "Let's move on and get a drink somewhere." There was little indication in his movement of the amount of scotch he'd consumed.

Tom had put the *Triple Murder* story on his bedside table when he emptied his pockets. As he reached to turn out his light, he again noticed the front page, and couldn't resist picking it up. He read . . . .

TRIPLE MURDER
by
d'Esterre Darby

In the late Summer of 1934, there occurred in Shanghai an astounding, if not the most astounding, case of murder in the annals of that city; and certainly in the records of the International Settlement Police.

I was serving at the time with the Settlement Police, so can vouch for the truth of this almost unbelievable affair.

In this incredibly cold-blooded series of murders, a mysterious patient was shot dead in bed, in a public ward of a public hospital, in full view of a nurse and numerous other patients.

A Chinese detective was shot down inside the same building, and died almost immediately. And a Chinese constable from the French Concession Police was shot dead in the entrance compound of this same hospital.

These three murders were carried out in little more than the equivalent number of minutes. As some indication of the speed with which they were executed, it might be mentioned in passing, that when the gang entered the hospital, a lift had just left the ground floor. When that lift returned from the fifth floor, three people were dead, and the assassins had disappeared.

The gang worked with speed, smoothness, and efficiency and having accomplished their task, they apparently displayed no signs of undue hurry, and took themselves off from the hospital at quite a leisurely pace.

Each murder was witnessed, the whole affair took place in broad daylight, and the assailants got clean away.

This all seems quite impossible, but it is cold hard fact, not fiction, and can be verified in the records of the Shanghai Municipal Police, and in the files of the Shanghai daily newspapers at that time.

Lung Koh-woo, the mysterious patient, arrived in Shanghai probably in the latter half of August or early September 1934; although he told the police that he had come from Hangchow only the day before. Chinese dectectives, however, later established the fact that he had been in Shanghai for at least three weeks when he was shot the first time.

Yes, this man had already been shot at and seriously wounded on September 16, at the Cheh Kya lodging house in Shansi Road.

Shortly before midnight on that date two men called on him at this lodging house: on opening the door one of the men immediately opened fire, and Lung Koh-woo was wounded in the chest, neck and mouth. His assailants left him for dead. On arrival of the police he was removed to the Lester Hospital, Shantung Road, a hospital for Chinese but in the International Settlement.

There Lung was put into a ground floor ward. A Chinese detective, Han Nyah-kok from Louza Police Station, was detailed to stand guard over him.

Lung Koh-woo refused to disclose the nature of his business in Shanghai, to attempt any identification of his attackers, or to suggest any motive whatsoever for the crime. In the face of this stubborn silence, first rate detectives from the Special Branch were quite unable to prise any information at all out of him. The only thing about which the detectives seemed certain was that Lung was using an assumed name.

It was about a quarter to four in the afternoon of September the 26th, and visitors to the hospital were laughing and chatting to their friends in the ground-floor ward, quite close to the entrance lounge of the building.

Lying in the first bed from the door into the ward was Lung Koh-woo. He had no visitors and was reading a book.

He faced down toward the other end of the ward: his features could not possibly have been seen from the door by which one entered the ward.

A Chinese nurse was attending to a patient a few beds away from him.

Immediately adjacent to the ward, in a small guest room off the main entrance lounge, sat Han Nyah-kok, the Chinese detective. At the enquiry desk, a Chinese youth of some eighteen years was on duty. Apart from the unobtrusive detective, everything was normal and running with the usual smoothness one expects to find in a well conducted hospital.

Four men, all wearing the long gowns favoured by the Chinese, entered the lounge. The boy at the desk, naturally assuming that they wished to see some friend in the wards, asked one of them for his visiting card.

The man addressed suddenly whipped out a pistol and ordered the boy to make no sound or he would be shot instantly.

The boy had sufficient sense to obey this order, and returned to his seat near the door; he was closely followed by the gunman who had not re-placed the pistol in his pocket, but still kept his hand on it ready for immediate use. One of the other men sauntered over to the entrance to the guest room and stood before it. The remaining two made direct for the door of the ground-floor ward.

They entered the ward in a leisurely manner, and walked straight to the bed occupied by Lung Koh-woo, who, apparently oblivious of the fact that two men stood in front of him, continued to read.

The murderers bent down to identify their victim. Their momentary scrutiny must have satisfied them on this point, for the one closest to Lung produced a pistol and fired twice in quick succession.

Lung Koh-woo must have been completely immersed in his book, for he never once looked up, and died instantly.

The visitors, the other patients, and the nurse, must either have been petrified with fear or too flabbergasted to move or speak, for no one made any attempt to raise the alarm. Remember, this was no out of the way house in the country; it was a large public hospital in the centre of a great city, with scores of people moving in and out of, and around, its precincts all day long.

The murderers, however, appeared quite unconcerned, and walked out of the ward in the same leisurely way they had entered it.

Meanwhile, in the lounge, and following immediately upon the two shots in the ward, another coldblooded murder was about to take place.

The man standing guard over the boy at the enquiry desk once more produced his pistol and ordered him to stand behind the counter with his arms above his head. The youth, again luckily for him, obeyed instantly.

But Han Nyah-kok, the Chinese detective sitting in the guest room just outside the ward, on hearing the shots, jumped to his feet and made for the ward reaching for his automatic as he went.

He never completed the movement. The other member of the gang, standing in the lounge alongside the guest room door, turned on him with a Mauser, hitting him in the chest and stomach. The detective crumpled to the floor—dead.

All four men now made for the main entrance to the building, and passing through it to the compound beyond, started for the gate by which they had entered.

Just as they did so, however, a uniformed Chinese constable from the French Concession Police came through the gate, accompanying a man who had been injured on the road. The constable, of course, knowing nothing of the murderous attacks which had only a moment or so previously taken place in the hospital, proceeded calmly on across the compound.

The assassins, however, were taking no chances; he was brought to the ground with a single shot; and then one of the gang—so far as could be ascertained from the bullets found on the scene of the crimes afterward—the same one who had shot Lung only minutes before, went up to the constable struggling gamely to rise to his feet, and cooly and deliberately fired at him twice at point blank range. The constable staggered to his feet, tottered to the hospital entrance, and there collapsed—dead.

The gunman, without so much as a backward glance, tucked his pistol into his gown and rejoined his companions.

This third murder in almost as many minutes

was also witnessed; by the gateman, and by a European member of the hospital staff who had been working on the accounts.

This accountant was fairly busy at the time and did not pay much attention to the initial shots fired—those from the ward.

Shanghai is an extremely noisy place at the best of times, and an explosion might be anything from a motor car tyre to a Chinese firecracker.

The shots from the lounge, however, echoing through the corridors of the hospital, brought him to his feet and out on to the nearest verandah, which happened to overlook the compound.

And there before his eyes he saw the Chinese constable on the ground, struggling to rise and draw his pistol, and the gunman deliberately shoot him down at point blank range.

The only remaining obstacle now in the path of the gangsters' escape was the gateman at the entrance. He, although unarmed, and having just witnessed the murder of the police constable, did make an attempt to close the gate.

The murderers, however, were not prepared to stand for any of this sort of nonsense, and two of them levelled their pistols at him.

The gateman, considering discretion the better part of valour, and with good reason, let them through, and the four men passed out into the main road beyond.

Here they were joined by two others of the gang who had been posted close to the hospital gates to keep watch for the police.

There were many small shops in the vicinity of the hospital, and here again all movements were witnessed.

Shop-keepers saw the four killers come out of the hospital compound and join up with the two sentries. All six of them made off towards the French Concession, and were soon swallowed up in the crowds which continually jostle in the streets of Shanghai.

The Police of the International Settlement, working in conjunction with the French Concession Police, acted swiftly; and the following day, having sifted a mass of information which had been pouring into Chengtu Road Station overnight, carried out half a dozen or more raids in widely scattered parts of the city.

Their prompt action was, up to a point, rewarded. Five men and four women were arrested. Two suitcases containing twenty-five pistols, some thousands of rounds of ammunition, two hand grenades and a dagger, were collected as a result of these raids.

Under the expert scrutiny of members of the Police Ballistics Department, two of these weapons were identified as those used by the triple murderers. Bullets picked up on the scene of the crime were subjected to microscopic examinations, and particular rifling marks and other minute irregularities established without doubt the connection between these two pistols and the killers.

The markings also tallied with those on bullets found at the Shansi Road lodging house where the first attempt on Lung Koh-woo's life had been made.

A further result of these raids was that large quantities of Communist literature were discovered, and seemed to provide the police with a possible motive for the murder of Lung Koh-woo. But no admissions of connection with any shootings in the city could be obtained from the nine arrested persons.

Very shortly after this, I left the Settlement Police and Shanghai. Up to that time and so far as I know up to the present day, no trace has been found of the perpetrators of this remarkably audacious, and probably unique, crime.

They vanished, in broad daylight, after committing three murders in little more than as many minutes, in a public hospital, and in one of the most densely crowded cities of the World.

Jack Darby showed up for breakfast a day later. "Sorry to have missed a day, old chap. Things got a bit tacky over our friend, Cheng. Seems the locals dug up a bit of dirt that tied him in with some of your people, someone at the American Consulate. Took a bit of doing, but you'll never guess who gave you a clean bill of health."

"Mr. Lu?"

"Correct the first time. You know, you might just make a good undercover man after all."

"Forget the humor, Jack. Why Lu?"

"Because you mean so much to him, old chap. And he didn't want you associated with anyone like that. Of course, I had to call and let him know your name might be dragged through the mud."

"I see." Loomis was no longer surprised at anything in Shanghai. "You said you went back a long way together."

"Right. Did you read that little work of art by d'Esterre Darby?"

"Yes, but I'm not sure what the purpose was. That all took place about fifty years ago."

"Do you know what was happening then?" He interrupted his own question. "No, don't bother. You weren't even a gleam in your old man's eye then. There are a couple of things you should know. Lung Koh-woo was a phony name, as the police surmised. The murdered man's name was Lu Koh-woo." He emphasized the Lu.

"Lu Zhong's family?" asked Loomis.

"The very same. His father, no less. Secondly, the people who did him in were discovered to be communists, right? But they couldn't locate the real killers. That's because they were brought in as an assassination team. And for the communists to go to that expense, they'd have to be pretty excited. Believe me. They had a lot of faith in those days, but very little money. As a matter of fact they were even missing some.

"Now, the big organizer around Shanghai in those days was Mr. Chou En-lai himself. Brilliant man. He knew that Chinese money would eventually have about as much value as chicken feathers, so he decided that they'd hoard gold, diamonds, things like that. A man could get anything he wanted with those valuables, especially weapons, and the PLA needed weapons desperately in those days. Chiang Kai-shek had it in his bonnet that the only way he was ever going to stop Mao and Chou and his people was to wipe them out, and they knew that. Without something solid for exchange, they were lost."

"I'm afraid I'm getting the picture."

Darby waved him quiet. "Not so fast now. You're probably right about some of it. Chou had an old friend, a northerner who had grown up in Mao's village. It was Lu's father, Lu Koh-woo, and Chou had entrusted him with making sure a large supply of diamonds, mostly swiped from Europeans in the settlement, was secure. But in the summer of '34, Chou began to get suspicious about just how many diamonds they had. He was no dummy, you know. Chou was trained as an economist. He figured that his trusted friend was actually siphoning a bit off the top, and he was absolutely right. Now, Lu's father had been working outside of Shanghai in those days, staying pretty close to Mao. When he heard that Chou was on to him, he figured the best place to hide was in Shanghai, right under his nose.

"It fooled Chou for a while, but not forever. One of the local enclaves had a girl who spotted Lu one day and trailed him to his rooming house. She brought back the information and Chou decided the best way to solve the problem was through an assassination team. He figured that would throw the police off because he didn't want them getting involved with any family problems within the Party. If they'd done a good job the first time, no one would have been the wiser. But they screwed up. I've heard, and this is a story that's been around for fifty years, that Chou was wild. First, he was going to kill the supposed professionals himself. Then he decided they would have to go back and finish the job. Only, they had to go right into the Lester Hospital and do it there. I suppose he figured they'd be knocked off by the locals and the trail would stop right there. But after screwing it up the first time, they did it up jolly well the second time, even taking a couple of others at the same time as old Mr. Lu. And they got away.

"Well, I guess Chou was outraged when he found out they'd done in two police also, because he knew this would bring the locals down on his head. And it did, as you saw in my little article there. Apparently, they almost got Chou himself, one of those cases where he was going out the back door as the authorities were coming in the front door."

Darby paused for a moment.

"Why weren't the police able to find the killers?" asked Tom.

"Chou got to them first. For such a quiet little man, he was known for a terrible temper. I heard rumors that he killed them himself, then had them chopped up and dumped in the Huangpu. Of course, it would be hard to prove, because people were always being tossed in the river in one or more pieces. That was just part of Shanghai in those days."

"The diamonds?"

"Chou never did find them. Old Lu's family had moved on, probably on his instructions, and Chiang Kai-shek was hot on the heels of the Communists in those days. I imagine Chou was glad to get away with the stones he had."

"And everyone forgot about the diamonds," Loomis mused.

"Most everyone. There was an inspector on the

force in those days who had some friends that were pretty close to the Communists. He got wind of it. He learned that the dead man was really Lu Koh-woo, where his family was from, that sort of thing. The name of that inspector was Darby, Jack Darby, and to this day he's never forgotten about that. You might say I almost pissed in my pants when I first met Lu Zhong and figured out who he really was. I've been waiting a long time, old boy. A man could retire comfortably on those diamonds."

"Did you know you're quoting the venerable Lu Zhong?"

"I thought as much. But remember, I'm a bit older and therefore more deserving."

Tom Loomis sat back in his chair, folding his arms across his chest, and stared at Darby. He was thinking as fast as he could, analyzing each of the curves he'd been thrown. There was no doubt about what Lu Zhong was—a high class crook with a superb front. But Darby was different. Tom couldn't figure out what he was. There was little, if anything, the old man didn't know, and he obviously was in tight with all the right people. Tom's own choices were simple. Deal with Mr. Lu and take his chances. Deal with Darby and take chances he hadn't even been told about. Or get the hell out . . . if they'd let him go. The latter decision would be the safest. But he'd never walked away from a profitable deal before, and these were the highest stakes he'd ever seen.

"Okay," Tom finally responded. "Now you tell

me what kind of a deal you're offering."

Darby flashed his elfish grin. "I knew we were out of the same mold. I just wasn't sure how high you were ready to fly." He looked at the table top, sketching an imaginary face on its surface with a finger, then glanced back at Loomis. "Mine comes in two stages. One's straight. The other's got a slight bend in it, but you're a man who understands corners sometimes have to be cut."

"I'm listening."

"You're familiar with a man named Magnuson?"

Tom looked at him ruefully but said nothing.

"A name from your past, right?" Darby added. "You know what he's doing now?"

"An old friend of mine said Ted was still in the Navy . . . an admiral now, I believe." This time it was Darby's turn to nod. "And, I imagine he's still in intelligence." The picture suddenly cleared.

"And, on occasion, I still work for him," Darby finished.

"I suppose this is why you perched yourself next to me at the bar the other day, and why I'm indebted to you, and why it seems that the Chinese are overly interested in me."

"I'm sure you understand the answer to all your whys now." This time there was no smile. "But there is a bit more beyond that and it's past your control, or even mine or Lu's. Look," he continued, "the Chinese are convinced that you Americans are getting tight with the Russians for some heinous reason. At the beginning of the year, a big part of your American Seventh Fleet is going to be in Vladivostok as part of your President's new détente policy. I'm not privy to all the details, but the big men in Beijing seem to smell a rat and the end results aren't supposed to be good for the Chinese. So, any American coming into China these days is considered a top prospect as a spy of some kind. Not very nice I must admit, is it?"

Loomis was silent. Nothing came easy, but intrigue wasn't the game he was interested in at all. Money was valueless if you were too dead to spend it. "Where do I come in?" he asked in a monotone.

"Well, it doesn't look too good to be an American just arrived in the country and have a dead body turn up in your room. So here I am, a trusted friend of China from the thirties saying you're clean, and Lu Zhong, a respected businessman from way back telling them he's a bit worried about you, and in the same breath telling you he wants to make a deal." Here Darby shook his finger at Tom as if he were scolding him. "And you'd better believe me, he's going to be playing you like a fiddle."

"You have a great interest in me because an admiral back in the States got you on to me. I'm beginning to get a rotten feeling in my stomach. Mr. Darby," Loomis asked angrily, "who's playing who like a goddamn fiddle?"

"My friend, you are right in the middle." He raised a hand to keep Tom from interrupting. "I work for two bosses, myself and your government. I think the latter wants a young buck like you involved because Ted Magnuson feels I'm getting a bit too old for some of this stuff. And, I'm the first to admit that I'm thinking about retiring and would like to have a bit more to live with than the proverbial nest egg. If you leave China without some promises of coming back, you'll never get back in . . . if you get out," he added ominously. "And I can assure you that Lu Zhong will see those PBX contracts go elsewhere, plus your own company might even get wind of what you were doing here for yourself on their dollar. I don't think it's just a shot in the dark that you might not even get out of this country if old Lu doesn't have some pretty solid assurances that you're going to help him."

"That covers Lu. What about yourself?"

"For myself is just the same as for you. Go along with Lu. I think it's a lovely idea." Darby leaned forward. "Only I plan to make sure that you and Jack Darby, rather than you and Lu, share those diamonds. And in return for my insuring that everything turns out for you right down the line, I'm going to want your help. Nothing serious, mind you. It might even be considered patriotic for you later on because Ted Magnuson knows his country isn't going to help the Russians in anything. But somebody here has to convince the Chinese of that. The only one in the States who realizes the prospect of leaving the Chinese by themselves cán lead to war is our good friend, Ted Magnuson."

"Your friend. I haven't seen him in years.

There's no love lost between me and the military."

"Well, he seems to know you well enough. He figured you might get yourself in hot water here and need a bit of help from an old China hand like me. So . . . my help in exchange for your helping him. That is, if you want my help."

"It doesn't look like I have many choices."

"You're very calm for someone who's just grasped the shitty end of the stick."

"I don't lose my temper unless there's someone to lose it at. It's just like a fart," Loomis grinned. "It's not half as much fun if there's no audience."

"For as little as has been said, you really are quite perceptive."

"Poor Cheng comes to mind. He makes it quite clear to me."

"So right," sighed Darby. "Without the proper assurances in the right places, that's exactly the way you'll end up."

NOVEMBER 1984

CHAPTER TWELVE

In the more than twenty years they'd known each other, Royal had never seen Ted Magnuson discouraged before. He knew Ted had no intention of throwing in the towel, but the odds against him in Washington were now tougher than overseas.

"Benjamin's gone, Jack. Fired. He went last week. There was no fanfare, no official announcement, nothing. The President didn't even talk to him. Just had his Chief of Staff call him into the office at the White House and explain his services were no longer required. Just like that." He drummed a pencil on his desk, shaking his head morosely. "He stopped by here afterward to let me know."

"Did you ask him what he said?"

"Sure. I'd been hoping if we both laid low he'd be my last ace in the hole. Benjamin did ask for details and the Chief said it was a matter of undermining the President's policies toward Russia, pure and simple. The Chief wished him luck, told him to clean out his desk that same day, and sent him packing with a handshake. That's the way it is in the White House . . . easy come, easy go."

"Do you have any idea how you stand?"

"I suppose I'm lucky to still be in this office. The shit came flowing downhill here the same day. The President called the Chairman of the Joint Chiefs, the Chairman called the CNO, the CNO called me and said I'd better come up with something firm on Seagull fast or plan on early retirement."

"Which means . . . don't tell the President what he doesn't want to hear."

"Not unless you can nail down the entire scenario, I guess. But shit, Jack, look at this." Magnuson slid a paper across the desk. It bore TOP SECRET stamps in each corner. "This is what I've been digging for, the key I expected—this is what the President has to give a shit about and I still can't say this is it forever and ever, Amen. We can break their damn codes, but the code words within the messages are killing us. Until we know what they mean by those terms, we can't nail down anything."

The message was to all Soviet submarines attached to the Pacific Fleet. It indicated they should be in newly assigned stations no later than "Delta minus five." The code words for missile targets would be continued in publications to be distributed at a later date by courier. It also referenced American ships scheduled for Vladivostok and pinpointed the most recent stations of American missile subs in the Western Pacific. Krulev had issued the message.

"The Delta date, Jack. That's what I need first. If I had that computer tape, or even a partial copy, to establish the date and the plans Maslov has, I might get to the President. All the other agencies are in the dark and the President has scared the shit out of them." His fist came down on the desk in frustration. "You know, a couple of months ago I had Benjamin on my side. We at least got into the Oval Office . . . explained that the Soviets having the Seventh Fleet in Vladivostok would literally make them hostages if the Russians moved against the Chinese or anyone else. It didn't matter that I got thrown out. He knew something was up, like it or not. Now, that latest message of Krulev's assigns new stations to their missile subs, probably off the West Coast, and pinpoints the last stations we've assigned to our own subs. Christ, we might just as well include Maslov in our planning. You know what . . ." his voice trailed off.

Royal waited silently. Magnuson snapped his pencil in half.

"It's wild, Jack. In the last few years we've been putting all our eggs into NATO and the theory the Soviets will move across Europe. Maybe they've been quietly planning on the Pacific. Since we've been concentrating on Europe and the Middle East, they logically decided to make their move on the opposite side of the world. The untapped energy and mineral sources! They don't want a missile exchange, Jack. For Christ's sake, no one with any common sense does. So, bang, they surprise us on the other side of the world, literally have us hostage, and then they make the new rules for the ball game." Magnuson raised his eyebrows. "If you were President, would you buy that theory?"

"No, and I think I'd look for a new head of ONI."

"Jack, I haven't changed my mind about stealing what we need from that computer. My own boys can get those code word lists and do the regular crap they're experienced at. But somehow, I've got to have that tape." He drummed his fingers on the desk, the broken pencil swept to the side. "Will Miller help again?"

"After what happened to us?"

"Shit!" Then, "I guess I don't blame him."

"I'll talk to him."

Less than a week after returning to the U.S., Ben Goodrich knew he had to go back to Peking, to Li Han, and he'd written her. Almost by return mail, she answered . . . .

It seems so long ago we were together on the beach at Petaiho, yet it has been less than a month. There is so much to be done in China that time has always seemed to pass with the speed of a rabbit. But now that I have someone to love for the first time in my life, I count the hours of each day until your return.

I am sure you remember my words that last night on the beach and I shall never forget them. Life is so different in China that it takes much longer for a woman like me to understand a man, especially an American. Your women do not think as we do and I know you expect so much more from them. I do not want to be like one of them but I think you will be surprised when we are together again. I will always be Chinese, but you will be amazed by the woman I found inside myself these past few weeks.

You will be happy to know I will be home for the beginning of the year when I am told you will return to Beijing. My father seemed to know even before you did, when you would be back here once again. Anyway, I was able to get leave for that time, and I think perhaps my father had something to do with that.

We are so busy now I don't know how often I will be able to write you. We are at sea often, more than ever before, and that is very hard on the crew of a small boat. For some reason, our senior officers feel that the Russians may do something drastic, so we are often patrolling off Hainan and around the oil fields. I so hope nothing happens that will keep me from seeing you soon . . . .

Magnuson read the carefully printed letter again. The hand was slow and painstaking, the letters inscribed one by one. Each sentence was important, but two stood out as if underlined in red: "Your Mr. Goodrich has written to say he will be back at the end of December," and "I hope your man is of good faith as he and Li Han have become much in love with each other."

The Admiral rested his head in his hands, his elbows on the desk, and sighed to himself. He was well aware of Ben's personal life. If Goodrich followed his normal instincts, it could become a very personal problem for Magnuson.

* * *

Royal turned left off Madison, bending his head slightly and leaning into the wind. A red sun was setting across the Hudson behind the Palisades, its last rays sharp in the crisp autumn air. Jack dug his hands deeper in his coat pockets against the chill as papers and dust devils chased each other down 48th Street.

A couple of doors before Fifth Avenue, he turned into their favorite watering hole. Ratazzi's had never been quite the same since Mario had left. Joe, the new bartender, was equally adept and was beginning to grow on the steadies as Mario had. Perhaps he, too, would become an institution.

Jack squinted into the abrupt darkness of the bar. A thought passed through his mind that Miller was so pissed he wouldn't show. But it passed quickly. Bob could be depended on whether he agreed with you or not.

Jack had phoned him twice. The first time, Bob had politely said, "forget it." That was shortly after Royal had last been in Magnuson's office. Waiting a week, Royal called again, taking a different tack. This time, he never mentioned Magnuson or Russia, just that they ought to talk. Royal was willing to fly to Vermont, but Miller preferred New York—"away from the family," he said.

Royal ordered a martini, then called Joe back and changed it to a bourbon and water. This was business. Ratazzi's martinis should only be taken for a celebration. He dawdled, spinning the ice cubes with his finger, the idea that Bob wouldn't show continuing to run through his mind.

The lights from the street flashed in the bar mirror as the outer door swung open. Bob Miller stepped inside, blinking his eyes against the darkness as he searched up and down the bar. He saw Royal's arm waving.

Miller slid onto an adjacent stool. "Nice to see you again," he said extending his hand.

"I was afraid you might not show."

"I haven't changed, Jack. I'm a man of my word. You know that."

"Yeah, you're right. You always were. Haven't changed a bit." Royal toyed with his ice cubes. It was going to be difficult to look Miller in the eye.

Bob ordered a drink and, while he waited, they were silent, like two people at a class reunion not knowing quite what to say to each other after the initial greetings.

"I suppose my credibility leaves something to be desired . . ." Jack began.

"Hey, forget it. It wasn't like you didn't warn me. There's a bit of the romantic in me. Margie still says that."

"No, no, that's not it. It was what I got you into. I didn't tell you there'd be any chance of getting hurt . . ." He raised his hand to keep the other from interrupting. "Mind you, I wouldn't even get involved in this stuff . . . and I certainly wouldn't ask you to . . ."

"I said forget it, Jack. I've done a lot of thinking about everything. No hard feelings. Believe me. And I know damn well the reason for calling me twice is to get me to help you again." He put his drink down and turned to Royal. They hadn't been looking at each other before. Now Miller held Royal's eyes. "Perhaps we'll have that opportunity."

Royal's head snapped around. "Huh?"

Miller shrugged. "Remember what you said in Moscow, about that guarantee of Soviet business? I need it."

"You got it anyway. Ted won't renege."

"Good." It was Miller's turn to poke at his ice cubes. "I was a bit worried . . . nothing on paper, you know. And it's kind of hard to trust the government these days."

"No, believe me, Bob. Whatever you were close to picking up is yours. The government will confirm it."

"Well, I need more . . . in the next three months. I got problems . . . quality control, cash flow . . . whatever you want to pick. I can tell you . . . being independent isn't everything it's cracked up to be. Everything can turn to shit so fast." He looked up from his ice cubes at Royal. "I won't bullshit you, Jack. As fast as things looked great, they've turned to shit and my back's against the wall. No one needs what I can deliver more than the Russians. My bank wants to see contracts, and the fastest way to assure the bank that I can get my shit together is through government licenses."

"You mean you'll listen to Magnuson?"

"I don't want to, but I've got no choice. Look, Jack, two weeks ago I wouldn't even have talked to you if you'd called. Then, when you called a week ago, I figured I didn't really need you even though I was getting these hints from my friendly banker. The next time you rang me, I'd just come out of a meeting at the bank where they'd outlined the basis of my recovery when I didn't even know I was down that far. And I can tell you, when you consider going broke, those episodes in Russia are suddenly far, far away. I can't tell you why—because I don't know myself—but that bank was impressed with the government approving contracts between me and the Soviet Union. So, you tell me when I have to go to Washington. I don't know how things will be then, but I've got no choice. I'll listen."

Admiral Magnuson was feeling good. It was quite a change from the previous day. MacIntyre was cataloging the days and the bad ones far outdistanced the good. It was a pleasure to be in the office when the boss was in a good mood.

Darby's report from Hong Kong had just arrived. It was what the Admiral needed to renew his spirits. Tom Loomis had been convinced to stay in Shanghai for another eight weeks. The message didn't bother to explain what influenced the decision, but Magnuson knew Darby was behind it. His old friend was teaching Loomis the secrets of bypassing the government to get things done. Loomis was meeting the right people. Jack had introduced him to Admiral Chen at a reception. It was critical that they get to know each other if Magnuson's plan was to have any chances. Chen knew enough of the Englishman's background to know the American could be critical to him if Darby took the trouble to bring them together. While Chen was especially suspicious of the United States, he was willing to culture an American whom Darby indicated had the proper contacts back in Washington.

Magnuson was smiling to himself as MacIntyre entered his office. He'd just hung up his phone. "That was Royal calling, Jim. He and Miller are coming in tomorrow. And read this." He slid Darby's note across the desk, grinning like a cat. It was nice to have a few victories to balance the defeats of recent days. Perhaps things were changing for the better.

"Before we really get into this," said Magnuson, "I want you to take a look at this. Do you recognize this sailor?" He dropped a photograph on his desk.

Royal shook his head.

"You might have if you were experienced at this job. All you would have had to do was notice him once out front. His name was Sam Butler, and he was one of my best yeomen, been with me a long time, very trustworthy." He unfolded a newspaper article. "This small report from the *Post* says he was killed because he was involved in drugs. The police dismissed it with a nod." He looked carefully at Bob Miller. "I knew the boy well. He wouldn't have a thing to do with drugs. He had a nice family, just like yours. Our people traced it back a little and I think I know why he was killed.

He was responsible for your old service records. That's how I think the Russians found out about you, though we may never know the details. I'd like to think he died trying to protect them." Magnuson played it for all it was worth.

There was silence in the office.

The Admiral opened another file, placing another photograph on the front of the desk for them to look over. "Pretty girl, isn't she?"

They nodded.

"They found her floating face down in the Tidal Basin. The coroner's office said she was so drunk she probably fell in. And, I suppose no one here ever would have paid any more attention to it except that a guard over at the Executive Office Building had remembered the oriental gentlemen who had escorted her there. You see, she worked for someone in the White House who was familiar with this operation. We had to make a check." He shook his head sadly. "It was just by accident one of my people happened to question that guard or we never would have known." He was silent for just a moment. "So I called her father down in Biloxi to let him know that what the papers said wasn't true. And let me tell you, it took a lot of talking to convince him that someday what happened to his daughter—his only child, as a matter of fact—would be made public." His face hardened perceptibly. "That she didn't get shitfaced and fall in a mudhole, but was killed trying to help her country." Magnuson leaned forward, hands folded on the desk, eyes bright. "I hope I can do that someday soon for Mr. McCollum."

"Why are you giving us this song and dance?" Miller asked, irritated.

"Because I'm desperate. Because I don't have anyone else right now who can get into Vladivostok and steal the information I need. Because I'm out of options." Magnuson raised his eyebrows. "Satisfied? Now all my cards are on the table. Jack knows that," he added, nodding at Royal. "If I can't get the information on that tape, which . . ." his fist slammed into his palm, ". . . which seems to be the only hard goods the President will accept, well, we'll just have to wait and see what the Russians have in mind. We won't have the advantage of even partial intelligence, other than that they're getting ready to beat the shit out of somebody."

"Why can't your man in Vladivostok get what you want?"

"That man in Vladivostok is so high—so high— he can't take a chance on anything like that. We can't gamble on compromising him. Please, just accept the fact that he's so important that we know we'll need him again in the future, even considering the impact of Seagull." Magnuson frowned. "It's a gamble. The gamble is that we'll come out of this in good enough shape so that we'll actually have need of this man again in the future."

"If not?" asked Royal.

"That's part of our gamble. If not, he's got the best of both possible worlds. They win and no one's the wiser about him. He comes out smelling like a rose."

"I've already told Ted what you need," Royal

added to Miller.

"No problem, Bob." Magnuson spread his hand magnanimously. "It's worth it to us." He handed Miller an official looking letter displaying the seal of the Department of State. "There it is, in writing. Just like a license to steal. You let the person who signed that letter know of the contracts you want approved and they'll take care of the paperwork for you." The Admiral grinned. "Provided we're still doing business with them after this is all over."

Miller was skeptical. "Do you have any better idea of what I'm after? With Petrov, we were being led by the hand. Now we seem to be on our own."

"I wish I knew exactly. There will be ports, ships' names, departure dates, positions they're headed for . . . maybe a lot more, but it will all be based on their supply system. With that, I'll know exactly what, when and where. All I need is proof . . . just enough proof to get the White House to believe me. Even with twenty-four hours left . . . twelve even . . . we could throw a monkey wrench into this." Magnuson thought for a minute, then added, "I can tell you that we have intercepted one message, signed by Krulev, that was sent to their submarines. A number of them are taking up new stations off our West Coast. How about that? We're a target of some kind. I've got to know!"

"Just this once," Miller whispered. "Just this once, I'll go along with you. And then, Ted, I don't want to ever hear from you again."

As November faded into a gray December in

Washington, satellite reports piled higher on
Magnuson's desk depicting the movement of
awesome forces in the Far East. The Soviet Pacific
Fleet was almost double its size from the previous
year. Vladivostok could not handle all of these
ships, and many utilized the North Korean port of
Najin. Helicopters were pictured daily between Najin and Vladivostok, likely ferrying staff officers
back and forth. Cam Ranh Bay and Da Nang were
busier than they'd been when the Americans were
there. A new Soviet carrier was conducting maneuvers south of the Chinese island of Hainan, in the
midst of the vital South Sea oil fields. Supply ships
increased in number. A more menacing note was
the appearance of amphibious ships with full com-
plements of marines.

Not to be intimidated at sea by this buildup, the
Chinese Navy conducted a series of exercises from
the Strait of Tsushima on the north to the southernmost point of Vietnam. Naval intelligence indicated that at least two thirds of the more than
one hundred Chinese submarines were constantly
at sea. China was preparing for something. Beijing
issued a terse warning to all countries. She would
patrol her seaward borders intensively. Any foreign shipping within a preannounced line would
hazard the chance of being sunk if their movements
were not first cleared.

On the Sino-Soviet borders, posturing was approaching the critical stage. Both countries moved
new divisions into place, especially in the vicinity
of the sensitive city of Khabarovsk. Daily border

incidents became increasingly ominous.

Magnuson paced in front of his chart of the western Pacific, scratching on it from time to time with various colored pencils. He could not make up his mind. Maslov was a brilliant strategist and Magnuson couldn't take a chance of proposing a theory. He had one opportunity, and only one, and it had to be the right one.

DECEMBER 1984

CHAPTER THIRTEEN

Jack Royal paused in awe at the head of the pier. The sheer majesty of the ship before him had become more apparent as he rounded the corner of the street from the officer's club. He had remembered and tried to resurrect that old cockiness from his days as a young ensign, but the size and power of the ship overwhelmed him.

USS TEXAS was feminine. Her lines, from the sharp bow bearing the single designation "39" to the square stern, were clean. Unlike the old, gunbristling destroyers he remembered, the first third of her deck was smooth, broken only by deck fittings. A missile launcher and an automatic, five-inch gun mount were both trained perfectly in line to the bow. Her deck housing reared up majestically amidships to support a complex array of electronic wizardry, yet there were no dirty stacks to mar the vision. She was nuclear powered. The after section of TEXAS was equally clean, the sleekness again broken only by another gun and launcher.

Her destructive weapons lay within the giant hull. He could picture her charging across the open ocean, bow waves sheering cleanly to either side, a fine salt mist rising in her wake. TEXAS generated respect rather than fear. She was sleek, gray, fast, and nuclear and her silent authority was humbling.

Jack Royal and Bob Miller meandered up the pier, their winter-white arms toasting in the hot tropical sun of Subic Bay, gold braid and insignia too clean to be part of the deep water navy. They stared in admiration at the cruiser, their ship for the next few weeks. This time Magnuson had cast them as naval reservists, ostensibly made part of this good will cruise. He wanted to surprise Maslov with their presence, for whatever shock value it might provide.

"They sure do keep her clean, don't they." Royal was the first one to comment in awe. "Not a speck of red lead showing. Just like she was polished."

"No stacks, so no soot. There's a nuclear reactor humming away down deep in that hull, just waiting to get up steam." Bob Miller was equally impressed. "No oil, no fire boxes, just a couple of cadmium rods to bring the core up when they want heat."

To each of them, TEXAS offered her own meaning. They had been away from the sea for more than twenty years. Not only the ships, but the entire Navy had changed. It was smaller, more professional, technologically decades ahead of anything they had experienced. When they served, the Navy was still having trouble escaping from the too-old weapons and tactics of World War II. Royal and Miller had sailed on ships that they had read about as kids and saw fighting in WW II movies. They were familiar and comfortable. These new, sleek, silent ships were of another age, and they had not yet proved themselves in battle. They were an unknown, symbols of a new generation, and they inspired fear and awe at the same time. Turning to Royal, Miller remarked quietly, "I have this feeling that time has passed me by." They had arrived at the gangway leading to the quarter deck.

The apprehension of once again boarding a warship disappeared as they reached the quarterdeck of TEXAS, put down their bags, and saluted first the American flag at the stern and then the Officer of the Deck. Each mouthed the traditional "reporting aboard for temporary duty" as they faced the OOD, both feeling an unexpected, almost adolescent, surge of pride at boarding a warship once again.

Prior to leaving the States, Admiral Magnuson made each of them temporary Lieutenant Commanders. They wore new uniforms, not the ancient, worn outfits that a reservist would maintain until they were threadbare. They could tell by a glance that the OOD knew they weren't what their orders indicated.

"The messenger will show you to your quarters, gentlemen. You'll have half an hour to get settled per the Captain's orders. Then he'll send someone to escort you to his cabin."

"That's quick," remarked Royal. "I didn't expect we'd see him for quite some time. Does he always treat reservists this well?"

The OOD grinned. "None of us do. But apparently you two are considered special.

"As a matter of fact, you don't even have service records. And the kicker is all the secret messages that have been generated on your behalf to the captain." He shook his head wisely. "Ships are too small for secrets to last. I don't know what you're doing here, but it's going to be fun to find out." He turned to a waiting sailor to escort them to their quarters. He picked up the phone on the quarterdeck desk. "I'll call the CO to inform him you're aboard."

The commanding officer of a nuclear powered, guided missile cruiser is a full captain, one grade under rear admiral. The job is demanding and carries tremendous responsibility. The man that holds this position is qualified to manage a nuclear power plant, and is also a weapons expert, an acknowledged mariner, and a leader destined for flag rank and major responsibilities in the service. There are only a dozen such cruisers in the world, eleven of them American. The surface officer that earns command of such a ship is an exceptional individual.

Captain Walter Haven, who looked the part completely, greeted them in his cabin. Times had indeed changed. Many admirals had not enjoyed

such spacious quarters. A warmly carpeted sitting
room, bedroom and dining area, much of it pan-
eled, surprised them. Captain Haven was no older
than they were. Of medium height, lean, a touch of
gray at the temples, skin bronzed by the tropical
sun, starched white uniform with knife edge
creases, he was an advertisement for navy recruit-
ing.

"Gentlemen, I'm most pleased to welcome you
aboard TEXAS," he said as he rose to his feet,
pushing back from a large, paper cluttered desk.
Smiling, he met them half way across the room repeating each of their names as he shook their
hands.

After coffee had been served by a steward who
disappeared as silently as he had arrived, Captain
Haven sat down at his desk, rolling the chair
around to face them. "I've been anxious to meet
you since Ted Magnuson called to say you'd be
joining us."

"You're acquainted with Admiral Magnuson,
sir?" asked Royal.

"Oh, by all means. We go back quite a way together. We were junior officers in the Sixth Fleet
years back . . . had a hell of a time together. And
occasionally we'd end up at the same duty station."
He picked up a pipe from his desk, tamping it
adroitly before lighting it. "The last time was the
Naval War College. That was before he took over
that desk in Washington. Then I got TEXAS. I
suppose we're not close friends in the true sense of
the word, but you know how the Navy has a way of

bringing people together even if they rarely ever see each other.

"One of the things he said that tickled the hell out of me," he continued after relighting the pipe, "was that he wasn't sure whether or not I'd ever speak to him again after he had dumped you on me. It seems neither of you are known for your love of the Navy." He raised his eyebrows in amusement.

"Perhaps that's not quite fair, sir," answered Bob Miller. "This isn't something we planned all by ourselves, but we could have avoided it if we'd chosen to. We're here of our own will, if that's what you mean."

"Actually, right now this is a rather exciting experience for us." Jack Royal leaned forward slightly. "I think everyone who's ever been in the Navy would like to be back on a ship like this, maybe not on permanent duty but just for the thrill of it. I know I feel a bit like a kid again." He paused momentarily to choose his words. "What concerns us more is just what Admiral Magnuson might have said about our temporary duty with you. Our understanding was that we were sent as reservists and we'd be treated as such. Apparently there's no secrets about us as far as I can tell from what the OOD said when we came aboard, and what you've just mentioned."

"It's pretty hard to keep secrets in our current status, Mr. Royal. Since every command in the Far East has been made aware of the current Russian buildup, it's rather difficult to hold even small secrets. I can't keep my officers in the dark about the Russians when we're literally preparing for wartime steaming conditions."

Miller's head snapped up, "Wartime?"

"It's necessary, Mr. Miller, when you have as much firepower in these waters as the Soviets do, and a China that's stated quite simply that it may not hesitate to use submarines. Who's to know what conditions the Chinese are going to settle on to decide what qualifies as infringing on their security?" He wasn't looking for an answer. "We can't take chances, regardless of the fact that the Chinese are our friends and we tell them of every ship's movement in the Pacific. If I was chasing around in an ancient submarine in those shallow coastal waters, even I might be trigger happy. Thus, wartime conditions, until otherwise notified."

"Who established this?" asked Royal.

"It doesn't matter," Haven replied sharply.

"Sorry, sir," replied Royal. "That's the civilian side of us Admiral Magnuson probably warned you about." Captain Haven nodded silently. "We're just concerned about what's been revealed about our assignment."

"No one on this ship, other than myself and the executive officer, should be aware of your orders." Haven hesitated. "You didn't expect me to know about them either, did you?"

"Frankly, no," said Miller. "We've kind of considered ourselves as independents."

"I'm sorry. If things hadn't changed, perhaps it might have been that way." He relit his pipe, looking back at them sternly as the smoke rose above his head. "Things have a way of changing, and we have to roll with them. You do, too. As a matter of fact, I'm not especially happy to be telling you how much they've changed." He reached under a pile of papers, extracting one which he handed to Royal. "This was sent to my care, but it's for you. It's not going to make you happy, but that's why those of us who need to know have been part of this thing you're doing . . . because you're going to need backup," he added w   finality.

The message explained quite clearly that an American agent had disappeared in Vladivostok. His whereabouts were still unknown, but it was assumed he had been taken alive. That agent knew they were aboard TEXAS. It was possible he could be forced to surrender this information. However, until intelligence was received to the contrary, they were to continue on the assumption that the Soviets were unaware of their mission.

It seemed nothing was going to come easy. It wasn't the piece of cake they kept expecting. Magnuson was getting a solid day of work from them for the profit they expected.

"Mr. Royal, if the Soviets do in fact have positive information about your mission, you could be targets from the minute your feet touch Russian soil, regardless of the guards around you." Haven paused, tapping the stem of his pipe on his chin. "I'd hate to think one of my own sailors was on their payroll . . . but it's happened before on other ships."

* * *

Jack Royal relaxed comfortably against a stanchion near the bow of TEXAS. He savored the clean salt air flowing past his face. The sun had already climbed high enough to warm the humid air. Luzon was just a speck beyond the stern, almost invisible in the still, morning haze.

Royal had loved getting underway on those early mornings years ago. He remembered waking in the middle of the night to the familiar sounds of a ship preparing for sea—boilers being lit off, machinery tested, the dawn bustle of the deck force as the ship was made ready.

He had risen this morning before sunrise, the old thrill still in his veins, this time as a spectator to watch TEXAS and her men prepare for sea.

Too soon, he learned that he had arisen much too early. There were no boilers, no ancient machinery to be coaxed into functioning long after its intended life span. TEXAS was today's Navy, her engineers trained at shore-based nuclear reactors before they ever came aboard ship. She was built to function with fewer sailors and designed to get underway literally with the touch of a button.

The sea detail had taken their stations a few moments before they were scheduled to depart. Lines were taken in efficiently. There was a minimum of noise as the hull shuddered gently to the bite of the screws. The only engine sounds came from the tug alongside, assisting TEXAS with the tide that had been invisibly pushing her against the pier. The radar antennas had begun their quiet, interminable rotation against an almost cloudless sky. And then she was standing out to sea, a gentle hum the only indication she was under power.

Over coffee the night before, Haven had covered the details of the Seventh Fleet's operation plan for the Vladivostok visit. There was comfort in seeing that the Navy had laid it out like a war game, as prepared as they could be in a sensitive political position. What hadn't been planned and what couldn't be programmed accurately was the Chinese reaction. Battalion size flareups were occurring now along all borders with the Soviet Union. Aircraft on both sides had been shot down. A Soviet destroyer was missing near Taiwan. U.S. sources indicated it had been inside the boundary the Chinese had established. Another Russian ship had attacked a contact in the water, claiming a torpedo had been fired at them.

A message had come in to Haven just before their dinner. It had simply verified that the agent in Vladivostok was now confirmed to be in Soviet hands. He had been seen and he was alive. He was therefore capable of talking. It was something they could think about as TEXAS steamed north.

The agitated voice sounded clearly over the ship's speaker, interrupting the last sounds of the general quarters klaxon. "Fire in Main Control Switchboard, fire in Main Control Switchboard. All hands to general quarters." The klaxon wailed again.

Bob Miller sat bolt upright in his bunk, the acrid smell of electrical smoke in the air. He could hear the clanging on the PA system outside the door to their stateroom.

Fire. Aboard ship, there was no place to go. You stayed with the ship or went into the sea. There was no getting away. It could spread rapidly, fueled by paint and oil and too many flammables that were overlooked in peacetime. There was no place to hide from flame and smoke at sea. Fire was a sailor's most frightening experience.

Royal stirred, reaching over his shoulder as he heard the sounds. He flicked the switch on his bunk lamp. Nothing happened.

"No lights, Jack," snapped Miller. "There's a fire in main control . . . electrical switchboard."

The echo of running feet came to them. The sharp clap of watertight hatches competed with the shouting voices outside their room in after officers quarters. Royal found a match. The brief light gave them a bearing on the first necessity—shoes. Shoes compete with fresh air as a necessity when metal decks are heated by flames.

The smoke was becoming heavier in their stateroom. "We must be near that switchboard," said Royal.

"Christ, the way it's pouring in here, we must be right over it."

The PA came to life again. "Damage Control Central, call the bridge. Medical team report on the double to main deck, port side, forward hatch to main control."

"The goddamn door's jammed!" Miller was tugging on the knob with both hands.

Royal lit another match, stumbling over by Miller's side, pants still around his knees. "Give it a good yank."

"I did. Look, the knob's just turning in my hands." He let go. "Try it yourself."

Jack dropped the match, grasping the knob as the flame flickered out on the deck. In the darkness, they could hear the futile sounds as he pulled at the door. "Shit . . . double shit! It's just not going to budge."

Miller's voice cracked through the smoke. "Where the hell are the battle lanterns? Aren't they supposed to go on automatically when you lose power?" His voice trailed off coughing.

"Yeah, there was at least one on the overhead that I noticed."

"Well the son of a bitch isn't working now."

His pants now secured around his waist, Royal struck another match. Smoke was choking them, tearing at their lungs.

"Don't let that go out," yelled Miller. "I'll call the bridge."

"Shit," bellowed Royal as the match singed his finger.

"Come on. Light another. I can't see the buttons."

Another match flared. The smoke, thick and white, filled the room. Royal inched his way over to the bulkhead where Miller was holding a sound powered phone, squinting at the designation over each button.

"Bring it closer, dammit! My eyes!"

Jack moved to the side. "There it is. Two buttons over from your finger."

Bob jabbed at the button . . . once . . . twice . . . three times . . . four times. "For Christ' sake . . . answer up there." God, someone had to be there. The phone had to work. The wait was no more than a few seconds. A voice answered on the other end. "This is Mr. Miller . . . in after officers. We're trapped in our stateroom . . . we can't get out . . . the smoke's getting thick." His lungs strained for oxygen.

"What'd they say?"

"Nothing . . . not a goddamn thing. There's nobody on the other end . . . at least I don't think so." Then he heard a voice. It was Captain Haven.

"That's right, Captain." Miller shouted back into the phone, coughing, "We can't get out of here . . . the smoke's getting thick."

As the phone slipped from his hands, swinging at the end of its wire, the PA sounded again. It was Haven's voice. "Damage control three. Men trapped in after officers compartment, starboard side, frame 127. Heavy smoke."

Miller was succumbing now, slumping to the deck, his breathing becoming shallow. "This stuff hurts . . . down deep," he gasped. "Get down on the deck. There's still some air down here." Then he became silent.

Voices were heard in the corridor outside. "Stay clear of the door," someone bellowed and began smashing at the door.

Above them, they heard the clank of metal

against metal, the sound of a wheel turning. A light cut through the smoke. "Anyone down there? This the compartment?"

Royal looked up at the glow. A small hatch in the overhead had been opened. "Yes," he gasped, coughing fitfully.

"You can't get through here, but this'll clear some of the smoke. They're coming through your door."

With a crash, the metal door ripped from its hinges, crashing at Miller's feet. Right behind were sailors with battle lanterns, their faces masked in breathing apparatus. Picking their way through the smoke-filled compartment, they dragged the two men back out, down the corridor, and through a hatch into the open air.

"Oxygen, over here . . . quick, quick." Miller heard the demanding voice. His eyes hurt. He couldn't see the man leaning over him. Then, something was clapped over his face. "Breathe man . . . suck it down . . . breathe deep." There was pressure on his chest. He felt his lungs expand almost unconsciously, then deflate. Again, he breathed deeply, this time aware that he was doing the inhaling on his own. The gas in his lungs was clear. There was no smell to it. No taste. He opened his eyes, blinking back the tears, to see two sailors bending over him. He wanted to ask about Jack, attempting to push the mask from his face. "No man, no . . . just keep on breathing." Miller twisted his head to try to rid himself of the mask. The sailor's hand was firm.

Frantically Bob jerked his finger back, pointing back into the corridor. They understood him. "No problem, man . . . take it easy . . . he's out here . . . you're both okay."

The man eased the pressure slightly on the mask, nodding to Miller's left.

Jack Royal was in a sitting position, his back against the bulkhead, wiping smoky tears from his eyes.

Looking over the sailor's shoulder, Miller caught sight of a destroyer close aboard, her lights blazing. On her decks, he could see sailors manning fire hoses, ready, if necessary, to assist TEXAS.

"It galls me to admit it could happen on this ship, but I have no choice." Captain Haven's face was solemn, almost sad at the realization that the fire had been set. "I suppose I could look at it as simply a case of sabotage, a disgruntled sailor getting even with the Navy." He took a deep breath and sighed, his jaw set. "However, there's no doubt about the real purpose, is there, gentlemen?"

"It seems to follow us," said Miller despondently.

Haven nodded. He'd just reviewed the report from his chief engineer. The fire in the main board had been started by a simple timer triggering a short circuit. The Damage Control Officer's investigation found that the venting system leading by their stateroom in after officer's quarters had been tinkered with, the smoke diverted into their stateroom. And going one step further, even though their door had been smashed by the fire axes, he was able to take apart the lock. There was no way they were ever expected to get out of that room.

The fire had never been intended to disable the ship. Its purpose was to create a blackout, smoke, confusion, just enough to suffocate the inhabitants of that particular stateroom. Whoever did it had overlooked one item, the sound-powered phone system.

Captain Haven smiled wistfully. "I wish I had some Marines on board."

"How's that?" asked Royal.

"Just some wishful thinking. I'd prefer to have Marines guarding you. Sailors are superstitious about carrying people like you fellows. They always have been. The fact that one of their own did this just makes it worse. Marines would keep you separate from the ship's company. As it is, I have to use members of the crew to protect you now. But I have no choice. I'm responsible for getting you to Vladivostok alive. Somehow I'm going to do that."

CHAPTER FOURTEEN

The balance of the cruise to Vladivostok was uneventful. Miller and Royal were virtually prisoners aboard TEXAS. An armed sailor was with them at all times, in their stateroom, when they were allowed on deck for exercise, and even as they ate in the wardroom. The only space on the ship considered safe was the Captain's cabin, and Haven became an understanding jailer. He often invited them to dine with him in his quarters, taking the time to update them on the changing strategic situation as TEXAS and her small force moved north.

In deference to Chinese wishes, TEXAS remained to the east of Taiwan, avoiding the tense strait between the mainland and the Nationalist island. South of Okinawa, they altered course northwest, entering the East China Sea via the Nansei Shoto. Then, they headed due north toward the Strait of Tsushima to join with the other major American task group on the last step of the journey to Vladivostok.

Captain Haven called them to the bridge for the

rendezvous with the nuclear carrier DWIGHT D. EISENHOWER and her escorts the day after they entered the East China Sea. It was a magnificent sight for destroyer sailors who had left the service before the advent of the nuclear surface navy. Royal identified the island of the massive carrier well before the mast of ARKANSAS, a sister ship to TEXAS, came into view, even though she was miles ahead of the carrier. On the radar screen before him, Jack could see a number of smaller cruisers, destroyers, and frigates each on station with the carrier. On a given signal, the two forces merged, EISENHOWER becoming the center of a screen that stretched for miles to every point of the compass. It was an imposing display of power for the bystanders, too, for both the Chinese and the Soviets were on hand to observe the ships and their movements.

The task force vanished in the darkness. The lights of Japan and South Korea glowed on the horizon to either side as they passed through the Strait of Tsushima. The force turned slightly west of north for the final leg to Vladivostok. It was less than a thirty-six-hour run to the Russian city, and the task force commander on EISENHOWER intended that his ships would be standing off Vladivostok the following day at first light.

Ted Magnuson's walls were papered with charts. His once impeccable office no longer existed. The crisp, military aura of efficiency had evolved into organized confusion. MacIntyre used scraps of note paper to identify appropriate stacks of reports as Seagull became a reality.

It was well past midnight. The Admiral, in shirtsleeves and with tie askew, had made a decision. He had not come to it wholly by himself. Senior officers from almost all of the Navy's departments had been in the Office of Naval Intelligence at one time or another over most of the past twenty-four hours.

What Magnuson had anticipated, the strategic plan he had been evolving over the past few months in counterpoint to Maslov's efforts, was actually falling into place. It was confirmed by the final position of Maslov's ships already at sea.

There were still some doubts. Maslov's flagship, KIROV, and an impressive array of capital ships, remained in Vladivostok as host to the American Seventh Fleet. How the final elements of the operation would come about and when they would commence remained an uncertainty.

China was the initial Soviet objective, step number one in their strategy. The Soviet Union could make no moves toward the U.S. until the Chinese were at least neutralized. Time lost in fighting with the Chinese would upset their plans.

Step number two was perhaps more complex and involved both the Seventh Fleet's arrival in Vladivostok and the repositioning of Soviet missile subs off the U.S. west coast.

Magnuson was not only sure that the Russians had no intention of commencing a land war with China or the U.S., he was positive their moves would be entirely psychological from a global standpoint. For once, the Premier of the Soviet Union had kept his mouth shut and allowed the entire strategy to develop where it was least expected. The NATO countries were no longer the key to Soviet strategy, although Russian divisions continued to be strengthened in Central Europe as a master feint.

Instead, the Russians were going to solve their Chinese problem once and for all, not by warring with China but by neutralizing her through blockade. What should have been obvious to Magnuson all along was how they could use the Seventh Fleet. It was all in the timing. The presence of U.S. warships in Vladivostok at the same moment the Soviet Fleet was surrounding the Chinese coastline would prove to Beijing that the United States was in league with the U.S.S.R. It wasn't necessary to substantiate such a theory once the Russians moved. Just the fact that the U.S. ships were there, and that this supposedly innocent ship's visit had been planned by the U.S. President and the Soviet Premier months before, would seem evidence enough during the confusion that would follow.

Most frightening of all was Magnuson's next conclusion. Maslov's intent was to hold the Seventh Fleet hostage while Soviet submarines would be used as the hammer to force the U.S. to negotiate from the weak side of the table.

The advantage belonged to the Soviet Premier. Timing was critical. Maslov's ability to carry out the plan was the key. Vladivostok was simply a cat-and-mouse game, a place on the map where a war of words would be fought. Timing revolved around that vital computer tape that Magnuson knew existed.

And here he stopped. The shock of recognition left him breathless. What had been his goal for so long, the confirmation he had longed to place on the President's desk to justify himself, was no longer a necessity. What he had to prove was already unfolding. Proof was no longer necessary. Response to events as they occurred over the next forty-eight hours was the key. Suddenly the tape he coveted wasn't needed. He had failed to compromise it, and now he had to keep Royal and Miller from digging further.

It was imperative that the Seventh Fleet take the initiative and weigh anchor before the Soviets made their move. But the key to continued coexistence was still China, a China supporting the United States. Right now, Magnuson had to acknowledge that the Chinese Military Council would conclude U.S. cooperation with the U.S.S.R. would be a fact within twelve hours. The powers in Beijing could see the pincers closing. Once the Seventh Fleet steamed into Vladivostok's Golden Horn Bay, there would be no doubt in their minds that their recently acquired friend, the United States, had turned on them.

The plan formulating in Magnuson's mind was bizarre. Yet months ago, he had quietly begun to manipulate four people without being sure what they might eventually contribute or what might happen to them. Now they were in position at the right time. Perhaps they were the only right thing he had done during Operation Seagull. As he prepared his message to Li Zhiang, he preferred not to consider the odds.

The message read:

U.S. has no part in Soviet strategy. President is unaware of events leading to blockade. U.S. is in as much danger as China. You must convince Defense Ministry. Seventh Fleet will assist you. Absolutely essential you have Goodrich in your headquarters and Loomis at sea with Chen for communications with the U.S. forces when conflict breaks out. Your judgment is essential in determining time that China initiates declaration of war against U.S. I will coordinate in Washington. Repeat, U.S. is not moving in conjunction with Soviet Union. More to follow.

The only man he could trust to encode and send the message was MacIntyre. It was a tremendous gamble.

Sea detail was set at dawn. Royal and Miller were on the starboard wing of TEXAS' bridge as they prepared to enter port. Familiar landmarks, seen only briefly from a car that never reached Vladivostok, appeared through the dusky light. Breaths created frosty clouds in the icy, gray-white morning air. The short sleeved shirts of Luzon had changed to windbreakers north of Taiwan and then foul weather gear in the icy Sea of Japan.

Vladivostok is one of the best protected ports in

the world. There are land masses to the east and west to protect the city from the open ocean. To the south of Vladivostok's Golden Horn Bay, just across the East Bosphorus Strait, is Russki Island, again a shield against the ocean storms.

The Seventh Fleet ships steamed north through occasional ice floes that would become heavy pack ice by February. They turned west into the East Bosphorus Strait as they came close to Cape Basargina. Through binoculars the city rose into hills from the water's edge, much like San Francisco. It was silhouetted through a frozen sea fog by an orange-red, midwinter wun.

The Americans found no difficulty in taking advantage of Russian hospitality. The party in the officer's club at day's end was a pour-your-own affair.

The Russians knew their guests had missed their traditional Christmas holiday in transit, and were more than willing to start their own New Year celebration early. Tables neatly covered with white cloths were positioned down the center of the room. Each one supported heavy cakes of ice with just the necks of vodka bottles peeping out. As fast as a bottle became empty, it was replaced with another. Heaping platters of food circulated around the hall. U.S. and Soviet officers in dress uniforms were generally unable to communicate with each other and couldn't have cared less if a bilingual member of the group joined them or not. There was no need to understand each other at this point.

Jack Royal was part of a small, elite cluster made up of Admiral V.P. Maslov, Commander of the Soviet Pacific Fleet, on one side and Admiral Harry Pickett, U.S. Task Force Commander, on the other. The mood was jovial, the participants cautious of each other.

There had been no further communications on the compromised U.S. agent, nothing about whom it was, the extent of his knowledge of their activities, or even if he was still alive. Royal could not imagine that it could have taken this long to dredge out whatever information the man had. He assumed that had been done quickly and efficiently.

Krulev, noting the U.S. Marines' intent on staying close to Royal, sidled up to him. "I was curious about the very extraordinary occurrence of your being selected by the Navy to visit Vladivostok, especially after your sudden departure recently." The Russian's smile was cold but not unfriendly. Krulev felt in complete control. This was his show.

The son-of-a-bitch knows a hell of a lot more than he's letting on, thought Royal. "I'm afraid I don't understand your question, sir. This is purely a special assignment."

Admiral Pickett interrupted. "Our governments are quite different, gentlemen. In this case, I personally requested people such as Mr. Royal to join the force for this visit."

"I see," said Maslov, looking up at Pickett. "You are the one who arranged for Mr. Royal and his friend to join you on this cruise."

"I'm afraid I didn't request them specifically. Just someone who was familiar with the Soviet Union. I learned later that they do business in your country, if that's what you mean." Pickett smiled cooly. "I only requested men who were friendly to your country, Admiral Krulev."

"I appreciate your sensitivity, Admiral Pickett." Maslov could play as well as the American. He turned to one of his aides and requested something of the man, slapping him on the shoulder to hurry. "I have a special treat for you gentlemen, something that not even Mr. Royal or his friend have enjoyed in our country yet. Because this is a new era, it's time we celebrate."

As quickly as he'd left, the aide returned with a waiter bearing a silver tray with two bottles of vodka and frosted glasses. The drinks were poured and handed around.

"Gentlemen, to your Navy," said Maslov. "And to our success in improving relations," he said caustically, his glass raised high.

One of Maslov's aides explained the significance of the Admiral requesting two of his special bottles. "This vodka is a very special brand, gentlemen, made only near Vladivostok. Admiral Maslov believes that the vodkas from the factories are good, but this is special . . . and for special guests."

"Mr. Royal, isn't it?"

Jack turned to find a Soviet Army colonel at his elbow. "Yes."

"I am Colonel Yuri Bespalov." His English was

halting but understandable. "I am a member of the rear services." He pointed to the insignia on his sleeves. "It is similar to your quartermaster corps."

"Oh . . . yes . . . I see." The man detached himself from the group, indicating that Royal should join him.

"You do not understand why the Army is here?" Bespalov continued. "An operation like the one we are undertaking requires a great deal from the rear services. In fact, it could not even be considered in this magnitude without us."

Royal did not understand the man, but he smiled politely. "You mean the plans for this visit, Colonel?"

"No, Mr. Royal, I think you will understand if I simply explain that Admiral Magnuson knows me." Then he added, "Seagull . . ."

Royal was caught by surprise. He stepped back abruptly, involuntarily, as if the man had threatened him. When Magnuson said someone high up would be in touch, he had assumed it was a naval officer. Why in the world would he pick someone from the army during a naval operation?

"I'd really appreciate it, sir," said Bespalov nervously, "if you'd laugh or do just about anything but act like either a fool or someone talking to a fool. Admiral Maslov has eyes in the back of his head." The colonel laughed heartily.

Royal responded weakly, "Yes, I do know him . . ."

"Mr. Royal, I was ordered to make contact with you for any number of reasons known only to Admiral Magnuson. If it were up to me, I'd remain anonymous.''

"I see.'' Royal could not even think of what to say. Magnuson had told him someone other than Petrov would contact him last October. Nothing had happened. Now, when he least expected it, a Soviet Army officer, as cool as could be, was standing before him and talking about an intelligence assignment as if describing his wife's rose garden. Christ, I'm no good at this, thought Jack. What the hell am I supposed to do now?

"There's absolutely nothing to be done now,'' continued Bespalov, reading his mind. "There is something you should know at this point, and I'd appreciate it if you'd try to control your facial expressions.'' Bespalov picked up another glass of vodka and handed it to Royal. "Here, if you'll just hold that and act like we've having a pleasant conversation, it would help. First, it's too late to utilize any computer tapes. You are ordered to break off. Next, there is an American named Loomis in Shanghai who you apparently know. Maslov has a contact there who has found out about· this Loomis.''

Royal's vodka disappeared in one gulp. Bespalov handed him another, clinking glasses cordially as he did: "Not only do I suspect that leak is aware of your friend's efforts in Shanghai, but this someone has been very close to senior level officials in Beijing. He has learned that the People's Liberation Army is aware of Soviet intentions and of their plans to respond. All of this has been coming right back to Vladivostok. I have no idea if a date was ever set for our fleet to move in force, but I am sure that date has been changed now to confuse their intelligence." He paused. "You see, the PLA's security group also has people here."

"I see," Royal mumbled, doing his best to smile politely.

"Yes, as you might suspect, this town is likely running over with agents right now. Some of them probably are working for the same country and don't even know of each other. Imagine that!" he exclaimed with a smile.

"Oh . . . yes," answered Jack.

"It is important that you explain this to Admiral Pickett."

Royal nodded dumbly. "It is important that your ships maintain their readiness. I'm sure Maslov is planning on our people celebrating New Year before we move, but he is full of surprises." Looking over Royal's shoulder, Bespalov broke into laughter, tossing off his vodka, and taking two more from the table for them. "Yes, my friend, can you imagine her saying that?" He was looking over Royal's shoulder.

Peitr Krulev joined them. "Why, Colonel, I had no idea you spoke English."

"Most definitely, Admiral. That's becoming an increasing requirement of our rear services school also. Perhaps they have in mind happy occasions such as this one."

"Perhaps so," answered Krulev. He turned to Royal. "Admiral Maslov is making plans for a tour of the base and some of our ships tomorrow with Admiral Pickett. He asks that you join us. Excuse us, Colonel."

"Certainly . . . most pleasant to talk with you Mr. Royal. I hope we have the opportunity to discuss your business again. Good evening."

"Good evening," Jack answered, relieved to break away, even if with the inscrutable Krulev.

The snatch, if it could be called that, occurred late the following day. Kidnapping, Royal decided, might have been a better word. Though whatever one called it, it was subtle and went unnoticed until Bob Miller failed to show up on TEXAS after the final group returned from the tour of the base.

The sun sets early in the heart of winter on the Siberian coast, and darkness in a strange, forbidding country is ominous. Royal shivered from the cold as the icy wind cut through his heavy bridge coat. The messenger on the quarterdeck had just called his stateroom to report that a Russian officer was on the pier and wanted to talk with him. The man refused to come aboard.

Jack was unable to recognize the man as he peered from the comfort and security of the quarterdeck. The figure waited just beyond the circle of light from a high lamp post. Initially, he hoped it might be Bespalov, but the uniform was navy, the man too short. Royal hesitated, the realization that Miller was not aboard and a Soviet officer was waiting for him taking on a new meaning.

The man turned, looking up at Royal on TEX-

AS' high deck, and beckoned impatiently to him to come down, stepping into the light as he did so. No other figures could be seen on the pier. After another second's indecision, Royal drew a deep breath of frigid evening air, and crossed to the pier.

"Mr. Royal?" The man was agitated.

"Yes."

"My name is Chursin . . . Captain Second Rank Chursin." The name sounded vaguely familiar from the night before. "I am logistics coordinator on Admiral Maslov's staff and I have worked closely with Colonel Bespalov for the past six months." The heavily accented words came rapidly and, as Jack looked more closely, fear was etched on the man's face. His lips were drawn tight over his teeth. His eyes blinked rapidly. Royal could see the hands twisting nervously in the pockets of his thick bridge coat, like little quirrels trying to escape. "I have no time . . . none. I have taken it upon myself to come here. I could have been followed. I don't know." The words came out in a swift, high pitched succession. "Krulev . . . or I should say the GRU . . . has taken your friend."

"Where . . . ? Suddenly the light they were standing under seemed to pulse. But it was only Royal's reaction to those words . . . GRU. The dreaded GRU! Miller . . . how had they grabbed him? It couldn't be! Not with the marines constantly around them. Royal's heart was racing. He began instantaneously cataloging all the reasons it couldn't have happened, yet his heart was racing because he was sure it was true. It was what he feared most when he learned that a Russian was waiting for him on the pier.

Royal's eyes refocused on the frightened man before him. The light from above, that had pulsed only in his mind, still shone down on them, casting their bulky shadows toward TEXAS' gray hull. The Russian's mouth was open, as if to say something, and then Royal realized he'd interrupted the man in midsentence when he'd barked "Where . . . ?" Only an instant had passed and Jack recognized that the words were still coming from the man.

"They also have Bespalov . . ." The Russian shuddered visibly, his body shaking clearly even under the heavy winter coat hanging below his knees. Now the speaker was breathing in short gasps, the icy wind and the shock forcing phrases from him in staccato blasts. "They found out about Bespalov somehow . . . I don't know when . . . but they waited until all of you were touring the base . . . my yeoman saw it happen . . . he has no idea why . . . he said that it was all very quiet . . . they came to the office . . . talked to Bespalov for a moment . . . he nodded and took his hat and coat from a closet . . . went out with them as if nothing was happening . . ."

"How do you know it was the GRU?"

"Believe me, Mr. Royal, everyone knows when it is them. My yeoman looked out the window and saw your Mr. Miller in the same car."

"Oh shit, oh double shit," groaned Royal. He grabbed the Russian's arm. "We've got to explain this to Admiral Pickett." Royal turned, his arm interlocked with the other's, as if to board TEXAS. But the arm was yanked away.

"No . . ." Chursin backed off, moving out of the light's glare. "If they see me board an American ship . . . even for a moment . . . I am a dead man." His speech was becoming so fast and clipped as to be unintelligible. "I have to go . . . I can't be seen."

Royal couldn't let the man go. Reason began to take over from the fear that crept into his veins when he first saw Chursin on the pier and then had run rampant through him when he heard the words "Miller" and "GRU." It seemed to Royal as if warmth, out here on the frigid, wind-swept pier, was settling over him. It began at the top of his head, and sank slowly down through his body. He didn't know if it was his imagination playing tricks, just as it had made the overhead light seem to pulse moments before, or if he was finally approaching this frenzied situation with calmness and logic. But he did know he couldn't let this Chursin get away yet.

"You said they have taken them away . . ."

"Yes," Chursin interrupted. "Most probably to their headquarters." His body visibly shuddered again. "There . . . the GRU will learn whatever they want . . ."

"Why did you come to me, Captain Chursin?" Jack found his voice calm. For reasons unknown even to himself, he knew exactly what he wanted to say, what he had to find out from this man who was verging on hysterics.

Chursin, who had been studying his own feet, looked up at Royal. "I don't know . . ." He cocked his head to one side, seeing Royal as if for the first time. "I . . . there is no one else that knows other than Bespalov and myself . . . no one else . . . or at least the Colonel never told me of anyone . . . I didn't know where to go . . ." The man's shoulders slumped. His whole body sagged as if he was about to collapse. Royal stepped toward him. Chursin came erect, nimbly hopping backward. "No!".

The man was terrified. Royal understood Chursin might crack at any moment, and then he would be useless. Jack also realized he knew nothing more than that Miller and Bespalov had been grabbed. How they managed to separate Miller from the others he might never know, but he knew who was behind it . . . Krulev.

It was abruptly clear, now that Miller was gone, that working with Magnuson, or returning to Vladivostok, was romantic nonsense. Nobody in their right mind would have done such a thing. And, he knew, after Bespalov had identified himself the previous night—something Magnuson would not reveal—and had endangered himself by personally relaying an order from Magnuson to break off, they should have remained on the ship.

A strange thought passed through Royal's mind. Perhaps he was becoming irrational again, relapsing to an alter ego that would once again react without thinking. But his inner self insisted, against a myriad of contrary arguments running through his mind, that all of this was entirely his fault.

Something as wild and foolish as Miller being carried off by the GRU was totally Jack Royal's responsibility. It was Royal who had talked this naive, rather immature friend of his into taking such a crazy chance. And Miller had lost! Royal was to blame! It was therefore Royal's responsibility to try to get Miller back. The man belonged snug in his house in Vermont surrounded by his family, not off somewhere in a godforsaken Siberian city in the middle of winter. It seemed so logical.

"Do you know where GRU headquarters are?"

"Yes," Chursin responded.

"Can you get me there?"

Again, fear was in the man's voice. "The GRU . . . ? Why . . . ? No." He stepped further away from the circle of light.

"What will they do to Bespalov?"

"Make . . . make him talk." The voice faded off.

"About you?" The man nodded slowly. "If you could get us there, perhaps we could do something . . . anything . . . before you are known to them. Otherwise, you are a dead man, too. Both you and Bespalov could have sanctuary aboard our ships. If we go there, perhaps there is a chance . . ." Royal heard his own voice fading. Perhaps it was because he knew the idea was outrageous, or better yet, maybe that inner self was working overtime to convince Chursin there was a chance.

"I do have a car. Over there." Chursin pointed. "By my office." The direction he was indicating was near Maslov's headquarters.

Perhaps Royal should have realized then that Chursin had agreed much too soon, considering his reactions of only a moment or two before. But it made sense that Maslov's staff logistics officer should now fear for his life enough to undertake something irrational.

The Officer of the Deck aboard TEXAS thought nothing of the two officers, one American and one Russian, wandering up the pier—not until the messenger pointed out that Mr. Royal had been gone for five minutes. Then it was too late.

CHAPTER FIFTEEN

Ben Goodrich was disappointed when Mr. Li was not at the airport to meet him. He had developed an affection for the old man. His spirit, his wisdom, and his humility, coupled with the tenderness Goodrich felt for Li Han, had meant a great deal to Ben in the past weeks. Ben's return to the United States in October precipitated a mental struggle. On the one hand, there was the world he was familiar with—New York, the challenge of business, the security of a life that was comfortable. This clashed head on with an alternative life he felt he must turn to—Li Han's world, part dream and part reality, but one that he could build with her. In the end, Li Han's world had won. Her last letter convinced him of a new life that could be his last opportunity for happiness.

Ben recognized the man that met him, a junior official from Mr. Li's office. His answers to Ben's questions were monosyllabic. He would say only that they were going to one of Mr. Li's offices. It was evident he would volunteer nothing. The ride into the city was rapid. The driver explained that traffic was restricted, since the military required instant access to the roads. Goodrich noted that the lights hadn't been darkened. Missiles could see in the dark.

An empty Chang'an Boulevard appeared wider than ever. The banners lining Tien'Anmen Square stood out starkly in the breeze. The ancient Forbidden City was dark, the upturned roofs stark against the night sky. The black car raced by the Square unnoticed, turning up the street to PLA Headquarters. Ben had suspected this might be the case, that Mr. Li was still involved with the military, but the recognition was still frightening. The guard outside was doubled, the only indication anything was amiss.

It was quiet inside. The PLA did not operate chaotically. He was led into a small anteroom before a PLA colonel, busily working at a tiny desk.

"Please be seated for a moment." He never looked up. Only an electric heater in one corner offered warmth to the cold, bare room.

It was deadly quiet.

The jangle of a telephone on the desk caught the American by surprise. The colonel listened attentively, responding only once. "Mr. Goodrich, you may go in."

The colonel went to the door at the rear of the room, knocked softly twice, and pushed it open for Goodrich. Ben entered another small, bare, windowless office, dimly lit, a small heater in one corner struggling against the winter cold. Behind a larger desk sat Mr. Li, appearing even tinier in quilted winter clothes. His face was drawn and tired, his eyes sad, almost lifeless. Ben might not have recognized the old man on the street, a man he felt so close to in such a short time. Mr. Li had aged in just two months, as if ravaged by disease. He stared wordlessly back at Ben.

"Mr. Li," Ben began, "I'm so pleased to see you again . . ."

Li waved him to silence, extending a hand toward a chair before the desk. "Please, Mr. Goodrich, sit down." There was a pause. "You will excuse me if I don't get up." The words were hollow, each seemingly a strain for him.

Goodrich accepted the proffered chair, unable to comprehend the change in attitude. He had sensed, almost assumed, a silent understanding between them, a bond. It was a sentiment forged by their affection for Li Han, a sharing not expressed but mutely implied.

Silently, Mr. Li leaned forward, picking up a sheet of paper displaying Chinese characters. His eyes dropped to the sheet, then came back to rest on Ben. The old man pushed the paper across the desk, gesturing for Ben to pick it up.

There was no way the American could read it. He looked at it for a moment, shrugged his shoulders, and dropped it back on the desk. "I'm sorry. I can't read your language."

The sad eyes surveyed Ben from behind the desk, a tear forming in the corner of one of them. The old man's lower lip quivered slightly. He picked up the sheet of paper again, staring at it, then slowly flattened it and folded it in half. His eyes came back to Ben. "It is about my daughter, Li Han." A tear ran down his weathered cheek. "I will read it for you." He opened the sheet, smoothing it mechanically with his palm. " 'We regret to inform you that your daughter Li Han was killed in action this date when her patrol boat was sunk during an engagement with Soviet forces off Hainan Island.' " A tear rolled slowly down through the wrinkles of the other cheek. "I thought you should know, Mr. Goodrich. She was back for a last visit with us just two weeks ago. She knew she was going into action . . . there was heavy submarine activity in the oil fields . . . it was her duty. And it is my duty as her father . . . and as your friend . . ." The words came slowly, his voice almost a whisper, the emotion stressing each word. ". . . to tell you that she loved you very much. That is hard for a father to put into words." Mr. Li intended to say more but his mouth closed. He would not allow his voice to break.

Ben stared blankly across the space between them, hearing words he couldn't accept. The world that he had been creating in his mind had suddenly collapsed. Li Han's youth and beauty and love had triggered something deep within him that he had once thought was lost forever. Few people realize such an opportunity. Fewer still had a second chance. In an instant, it had been wiped out.

"Mr. Li . . ." He could think of nothing to say. His mind raced wildly. He wanted to express something that would describe the loss they shared. At

the same time that Mr. Li seemed so close, Ben
became aware they were worlds apart. For a brief
moment, they had shared a love, the love of a
woman . . . one man's daughter . . . the other
man's dream. And, in an instant, they were left
with a memory.

The old man stood up, drawing his slumped
shoulders erect. "Mr. Goodrich, there is nothing
that can possibly be said that I can't see in your
eyes. I understand more than you can know." He
came around from behind his desk, wiping away
the trace of dampness on his cheeks with a handkerchief. "She was my only child . . . and it is as if
my heart had been torn out of my chest." He took
a deep breath, exhaling slowly as he refolded the
cable from South Sea Fleet Headquarters, stuffing
it inside his jacket.

Mr. Li looked up at the tall American beside
him. "You are alone . . . so alone. We have all been
there before and I assure you it is the loneliness,
even more than the loss, that is deepest.

"I am going to go home to be with my wife.
Would you please join me?" The old man's eyes
became shiny again. "Mrs. Li would agree with me
and be very upset if she found I left you. We do not
want you to be that man alone tonight. We must
share our grief together."

Ben could find no words that could adequately
express what he felt. He nodded his head in assent.
The old man took his arm gently. "Thank you . . .
thank you very much," Ben finally managed.

* * *

Peering down at the Chinese coastline, silhouetted by an orange, early morning sun, Tom Loomis recognized the Yangtze conveying its never-ending flow of mud through the delta into the East China Sea. Under the wing were the nearly empty piers of Admiral Chen's East Sea Fleet headquarters. Smoke drifted from the stacks of the few remaining ancient destroyers. A few miles inland, the stone facades of Shanghai's financial empire reflected the sun onto the busy Huangpu.

Jack Darby's shiny black eyes and white hair caught Tom's eye as he came through the passenger gate. The Englishman's jolly smile reached out to him after the three almost sleepless days he'd just spent at the Canton Trade Fair.

"Certainly is pleasant to see you, old man. Things have been getting a bit nasty around here." He looked across at Tom as they drove into Shanghai, an amused grin on his face. "To be honest, though, I really haven't had so much fun in quite a bit. When you get to be my age," he sighed, "you're afraid everything may have passed you by. And, lord knows, I'd hate to be put out to pasture too early, especially when we're about to hit the big one."

"Big one?"

"The diamonds, old man. Chou En-lai's diamonds, or Lu's, if you will. The reason you convinced yourself to get into this mess."

"I did a lot of thinking about it. I can tell you that, especially when I could look out and see Hong Kong in the distance."

"I'm sure you did, but there really wasn't any doubt in my mind that you'd be back."

Loomis considered Darby out of the corner of his eye, saying nothing.

"Call it what you will, old chap," Darby continued. "Greed. Patriotism. Maybe a little of both. We're very much alike, you know. And, I've actually become rather attached to you. We'll have a good time together in the next few days."

Darby continued the one-sided conversation into the city and then right up to Tom's room at the Peace Hotel. He explained how Russian submarines had effectively closed off the Nansei Shoto, the only really open water between the southern tip of Japan and Taiwan. Admiral Chen Liang's ancient ships, many of them relics of the days when the Russians were building the PLA fleet, were now facing overwhelming forces. Chen, it seemed, felt he could do enough damage to make the Russians think twice. He had only two major concerns—the weak link in his intelligence system relaying vital plans to Vladivostok and the American Seventh Fleet. What was their commitment?

"You see, old man, there's just a bit more you have to know before you get forty winks. I know you wish I'd go away, but there's not a hell of a lot of time for sleeping in this game." Loomis was removing his clothes, the bed already turned back. "I'm afraid I made us a luncheon appointment and you don't have much choice. It's with Admiral Chen and you can imagine what Ted Magnuson would say if you turned down lunch with an Admiral who was already losing ships in a war you're part of, like it or not!"

Loomis, his pants over one arm, stood before the little Englishman, the first smile in twenty-four hours creasing his face. "That gives me almost three hours sleep, and I can survive on that." He tapped the watch on his wrist. "But if you don't get the hell out of here and leave me alone, neither of us are going to be there for lunch, because I will have tossed you out the window. Jack, go away . . . please go away. Come back and get me at noon. You can tell me everything while I have a shower and shave. I promise . . . I'll be bright and cheery and crow like a goddamn rooster if you want. But, please go away."

"Right then, old chap. Message received. See you at noon."

Admiral Magnuson reread the report his staff had completed only an hour before. He had asked them to cull the mass of data compiled over the past few days into a short succinct analysis he could offer to the President:

As of this date, satellite intelligence indicates that Chinese forces are expanding considerably on the northeastern Manchurian border to confront a similar Russian buildup. The heaviest concentration appears to be near Khabarovsk, a city that rests on the confluence of the Amur and Ussuri Rivers. This is a center of controversy since both countries claim the city. It is the economic capital of the area and is considered strategic to the Russians since they have not developed this part of

Siberia to the extent that the Chinese have indus-
trialized Manchuria. Any land battles in this zone
would be fought to the bitter end by both countries. The Soviet Union must keep Khabarovsk if
they are to maintain (1) the security of the Soviet
Maritime Peninsula, (2) their Pacific Fleet Headquarters at Vladivostok, and (3) the vital port city
of Nakhodka. The latter city is the gateway to
Siberia and the Pacific terminus for the Trans-
Siberian Railway, in addition to being a major
shipbuilding center.

The loss of this section of Siberia would be similar to losing our Pacific coast states, and the military and industrial centers of San Diego, Los An-
geles, the San Francisco Bay area, and Seattle. The
U.S. *would not* relinquish that territory and the
Russian attitude is no different. The Chinese see
the value of this area to the Soviet Union and are
aware that success would mean a great deal to ending the harassment by their northern neighbor.

The divisions facing each other on the borders
are equal in manpower, but the Russians are vastly
superior in weaponry. Soviet power in tanks and
artillery are as imposing as Hitler's Blitzkrieg
forces in 1939. The PLA lacks air power in every
capacity: speed, weaponry, and training. If there is
a balancing factor, on the land situation, it is that
the PLA will follow the tactics that made Mao so
successful against equally superior forces during
the revolution: (1) draw him ahead of his supply
lines and then harass those lines; (2) retreat until
your enemy is trapped; (3) annihilate the enemy at
each opportunity, always on a small scale, never in
a major battle. A future report will take into consideration the use of tactical nuclear weapons, a

distinct possibility by the Chinese.

The situation at sea is evolving well beyond the expectations of this command. Again, the Russian Navy is superior to the PLA naval forces in every respect. The Soviets have moved every type of combatant unit into this area in the last four months to supplement an already superior force. While thé Russians will make use of many of their nuclear submarines, it should be noted that China has the third largest submarine force in the world, and they seem to have developed it on the same defensive strategy that Admiral Gorshkov did for the U.S.S.R., though he has now succeeded on the offensive level also.

What the Chinese may lack in size and sophistication of their fleet is made up for somewhat by a high level of morale and an almost suicidal desire to win at all costs. Sacrifice has always been a source of pride to these people. It should also be noted that the senior cadre in the PLA naval forces were originally trained by the Russians. The Russians are predictable in their tactics since their on-scene commanders do not often make their own decisions. The Chinese know this. Unlike our own Navy, Russian officers tend to remain with the same units or in the same fleet throughout their career. So the Chinese are familiar with many of the people they are facing and this could be a factor in their behalf.

Current Analysis: No recommendation can be made by this command at this time concerning U.S. decisions and/or assistance. Chinese intelligence operations have reached a level of sophistication we were not prepared for, including deep incursions into both Soviet and U.S. agen-

cies. Their Security Group 8341 has come of age.
This ability has reduced the Soviet element of surprise to zero.

At this stage, the Chinese are vastly outnumbered, outweaponed, and surrounded. However,
with the U.S.S.R.'s loss of surprise, there is the
possibility the PLA may be able to hold off Soviet
blockading efforts long enough to gain world support. They may also be able to inflict enough material damage and personnel loss to the Soviets to
force withdrawal. The Soviet High Command will
not accept heavy losses unless the Motherland is
endangered, nor will they allow themselves to
again be drawn into sustained military operations.

Sources at the Japanese Military Self Defense
Command have been in continual contact with
this office and are in touch with developments via
their own intelligence system and pass through
from U.S. satellite services. The events directly related to Operation Seagull will influence Japan's
economy and relations with its neighbors for the
remainder of this century. Japan will not allow
itself to become an Asiatic Finland. As a result,
Japan is now conducting large scale naval exercises south of the island of Kyushu. These forces
are in a prime location to provide assistance.

Magnuson slid the report into the special folder
he'd been compiling for his last effort with the
President. The Staff at the White House had activated the War Room, but more for an informational purpose. The President remained firm.
Magnuson knew what was going on in the minds of
the Military Council in Beijing. While PLA fleet
units prepared to face totally superior forces, their

leaders worried about what the United States would do. American ships were in Vladivostok, their crews happily rubbing elbows with the Russians.

The U.S. President remained aloof. Perhaps he would respond only to a declaration of war.

Admiral Chen was also operating with little sleep. Not only was he manipulating a small fleet of ships under wartime conditions, but he might have to go to Beijing at any time. Admiral Hung seemed ready to relinquish control of the Navy to him.

Admiral Chen leaned forward in his chair, his hands grasping the edge of the table. "Just before you came here today, I received a message that both saddened and angered me. One of my old destroyers, KUEI YANG, disappeared this morning. Not even a trace of her exists at this point. Two hundred men . . . gone. That saddens me because I've lived with those men for many years. What angers me, Mr. Loomis, is that so very few people knew where that ship was going or her purpose. There were—and still are—American fighter planes in the area where she went down and I don't know whether your people or the Soviets sunk my ship."

"That's an incredible statement." Loomis felt an icicle touch the base of his spine. "Why should American aircraft do that?"

"I don't know, Mr. Loomis. I was hoping you might answer that for me, but I'm not sure who you Americans are supporting. Mr. Li in Peking, whom you've never met, assures me that I should trust you, and Mr. Darby claims you are most important to us. But I can't understand why you aren't in touch with your government through the official routes."

"Excuse me, Admiral," Darby interrupted. "Mr. Loomis' employer is the U.S. Navy, not the government."

Chen was perplexed.

"We operate quite differently in the United States, Admiral," Tom answered. Darby had carefully prepared him. "We have a government intending to renew détente and that's why our Seventh Fleet is in Vladivostok now. My limited understanding of the political aspect is simply that our heads of state do not believe the Soviets are going to make war on you. They find it hard to believe that our own ships could be used even for propaganda purposes. The Navy isn't so sure about that. That's where I come in, Admiral. I'm supposed to help our Navy if we, for some reason, become involved in your affair with the Soviets." The icicle remained, its chilling effect spreading.

"On what side?" asked Chen. "The one that sank KUEI YANG?"

"I don't understand why I should know, or why you should even think the U.S. would have done anything to your ship." said Tom, angry and defensive.

"That ship was headed for the Strait of Tsushima. It was my spy ship, the one that would warn me exactly how many Soviet units would be coming through there and exactly when they would appear. I don't have the intelligence system your government has, nor do I have the aircraft or satellites to use. The United States has all that available and I have no doubt they knew exactly where KUEI YANG was from the time she left here." Admiral Chen was tired. He rubbed his eyes for a moment, blinking them before turning them directly on Loomis. "Not only do I not know what your country intends, even though I should assume their visit to Vladivostok right now means complicity with the Russians, but there are other people who would implicate your country."

"That's absurd." Loomis reacted impatiently. Looking at Darby, he knew the Englishman was troubled. Chen was supposed to accept their proposition and they hadn't yet had the chance to offer it.

"It may be absurd to you, but I have other reasons. If you will join me for a few minutes, you will understand."

They followed Chen downstairs into a sub-basement. At the end of a long, dimly lit corridor he pushed open a door, holding it for them. Three of Chen's men jumped up from chairs at one end of a putrid smelling room. A still form, naked, was crumpled face down on a blanket on the floor. Loomis' stomach reacted instantly to the odor. The blanket underneath the form was smeared with blood and vomit. The individual had been rolling in his own feces. As much as he wanted to turn away, Loomis' eyes were riveted to the blanket. Tom could tell by its angle that one leg had been broken. Fear now crept up from his bowels. He swallowed involuntarily.

"This is one of the few people who knew about KUEI YANG and her mission," said Chen. "I've had reason to wonder about this man from time to time. Turn him over," he ordered one of the guards.

The face was mutilated. Loomis was struck by the abomination before him that had once been a human being. An arm dangled oddly from its shoulder. Much of the body had been horribly abused. Tom was unable to believe a human could live after so much suffering.

"I can see you're unhappy with my methods, Mr. Loomis. When you're at war, you can't take chances. You have to follow your suspicions."

"You mean . . . you didn't know whether this person had the information you were after?" Loomis asked incredulously.

"It was a chance I had to take." He turned to the Englishman. "You're familiar with these methods aren't you, Mr. Darby?"

The color had gone out of the old man's face. His bright eyes had become dull. His jowls sagged as if he had aged twenty years. "Yes, I remember seeing people just like that," he answered, "In Jap prisoner of war camps."

"That's correct," said Chen. "I saw them do this to many of the people in my village during the war, when I was just a boy. I never forgot how long it lasted, or how much noise the victims made. You see, Mr. Loomis," he said, eyeing the American, "you were probably my age then, but America was never occupied. If even the slightest chance existed that your country could be invaded, you would be willing to go to any extent, even this, to prevent that possibility."

The body on the floor moved, shuddering uncontrollably for a moment. Chen nodded to one of the guards. A bucket of water was dumped on the bloody figure. The body jerked, broken limbs grotesquely out of synchronization. A low moan escaped from a hole in the face. At the same time, Tom involuntarily gasped, his belly churning. Blood had made him ill before.

"I'm really sorry to upset you like this, Mr. Loomis, but my men had a great deal more trouble than usual in getting the information we wanted from this man. But, I want to show you graphically what we've learned." He jerked a thumb at one of the guards.

They maneuvered a small machine over by the blanket, taking care not to touch the body as they attached small wires to its skin with metal clips. The clips pinched cruelly, yet there was no reaction from the man.

Chen leaned down closer and asked quietly, "Will you tell me what you told my men? Who did you tell about the KUEI YANG . . . who's paying you?"

There was only a low moan, blood rolling from the lips. Chen jabbed a button on the machine with his index finger. The whole body jerked, a cry of pain escaping.

"KUEI YANG . . ." Chen repeated. "Tell me

who you gave information to and there will be no more pain . . . just tell me what you told the others.".

There was a cough from the body as it gasped for a breath. Blood sprayed Chen's uniform. The Admiral never moved. He seemed oblivious to the darkening stains as he waited. The eyes flicked open as Chen again moved his hand toward the machine. The torn lips moved, and a whisper came from a toothless mouth. Loomis strained to hear, unable to discern any words. Yet there was a look of triumph on Chen's face.

He looked over his shoulder, "Mr. Darby, bend down here, you can understand our language and I'm sure you will tell our American friend what the man is saying."

Darby moved closer, his face expressionless, bending slightly at the waist to look over Chen's shoulder. The Admiral pulled him closer. "Come, come, Mr. Darby. He can't hurt you. Bend down here. I want you to hear this." His eyes and voice were cruel. "Tell us again," he shouted at the person on the floor. "One more time."

Loomis heard a whisper, but was unable to see past the two men huddled over the victim.

Chen and Darby straightened up at the same time. Chen's face was triumphant, Darby's stricken.

"Tell him what you heard," ordered Chen.

"The Americans," Jack said, his voice so low Loomis could barely hear him. "He said it was the Americans."

Loomis heard, both times. He was unable to

comprehend this room or remain any longer near the ravaged body on the floor.

Torture.

He'd read about it, but it was never something that registered in his mind. It happened in other countries to other people, uncivilized people who spoke strange languages, people who murdered and raped, but never in America.

It was never intended that he be involved in something like this, not with this Chinese Admiral smiling through tormented eyes, not a care at all for the man on the floor.

"What am I to believe, Mr. Loomis?" Chen was speaking to him. Tom could see his lips moving. He could hear the man clearly, yet his mind wouldn't accept what he had just seen. He felt the chill spreading through his body. His bowels were loose now.

"He says he was working for the Americans," Chen continued. "He offered a good deal more information to my men, but I felt you should hear that for yourself." The Admiral hesitated just a moment for effect. "I'm sure if that traitor had a mother, he would have offered her to my men at that point. It's strange how men react under pain . . . very curious." Chen was making up his mind.

Tom couldn't answer. He felt his eyes blinking involuntarily. His throat, he knew, was dry. Awareness of the stink in the room caused his stomach to churn once again. A cold sweat broke out on his forehead and neck. The room was wavering, growing smaller. Oh no, oh God, no, he thought. I can't pass out now. I'll never leave here if I do. He heard Chen talking to one of the guards in his own language, gesturing toward Loomis. He saw the man move toward him, something in his hand. Tom wanted to move backward, away from the guard, out of the room, get out of the building, breathe fresh air.

The guard lifted a bucket under Tom's chin just as he bent slightly, spraying the contents of his stomach into it. He grasped the bucket, yanking it from the guard, turning his back to Chen and retching until his muscles ached. He never turned back. He took a handkerchief from his back pocket, wiped his mouth and folded it and swabbed his face, his senses coming back as quickly as the shock of the room had dulled them. There was no reason for him to be there. He had done nothing. The Admiral was testing him. Chen knew he had succeeded, too. The evidence was stinking in the bucket. There was only one way he could get out, and that was to calmly open the door and walk out.

Loomis never looked back. He took the few steps to the door, turned the handle, and pulled it open. "Admiral Chen, if you want to discuss this, we can do it decently in your office. I will not be a part of this." He stepped into the corridor, leaving the door ajar for Chen and Darby. He had no idea what would happen until he heard their steps behind him, then heard the door shut.

Admiral Chen was the first to speak when they were seated back in his office. "You are a very brave man, Mr. Loomis. With what that man revealed, you might have taken his place."

I'm not a brave man, thought Tom. I'm a roaring asshole getting myself into something like this. Only an asshole would be sitting here right now. I am a roaring, screaming asshole.

"No matter what that poor man said," Tom answered, "I know nothing about it. My job is to help you and that's what I'm here for. I don't know why he said what he did . . . I don't believe it if he did, because a man would say anything if he was tortured like that . . . just to stop the pain."

"I have no understanding of your country, Mr. Loomis, but I must accept your word. I don't think you are lying. And I have to believe Mr. Darby because he has been a friend to my people for so many years. He would never work for your government. But, I do not trust what your Seventh Fleet will do in the next day or so. If there is the slightest suspicion that they will become our enemy, I can promise that you will be convinced that poor wretch down in the basement was a lucky man . . . believe me."

The remainder of their discussion continued as if the episode in the basement had never occurred. Chen showed them a message from Mr. Li in Peking, stating that Loomis would be required to stay close to Admiral Chen. He would act as a liaison with the Americans if the Soviet fleet passed through Tsushima into the East China Sea. The Seventh Fleet would be astern of the Russians, but not to support them. Chen was still unsure if the

Americans would be favoring China. But, he clarified, Loomis would be beside him.

Jack Darby was silent most of the way into the city. As they neared the turn to the Peace Hotel, he finally spoke. "I've seen that man before . . . the one they were torturing. Such a mess I could barely recognize him. But I did."

"Who is he?"

"I don't know his name, but I've seen him at Lu Zhong's before. Perhaps he has two jobs," Darby said. "One with the PLA and one with Lu Zhong. I think we have to be very, very careful about Mr. Lu."

CHAPTER SIXTEEN

The telephone jarred Loomis out of a deep sleep. "Sorry to wake you from your beauty rest, old chap. It seems to have worked." Tom fumbled for his watch on the bedside table. Almost 6:30 in the morning. Darby sounded as if he'd been up for hours. "It appears that there will be a slight change of plans, I'm afraid." Darby had said he was going to check further on the man in Chen's cellar.

"What's that?"

"It seems the Russians are supposed to pick you up on the high seas rather than your own people. Now what do you think of that?" Darby's voice was cheery. Loomis could imagine the bright eyes and pink cheeks, the ascot fastened at his throat. "That *was* one of Lu's men Chen was torturing."

"Jack, why don't you come over here and tell me all about it when I'm more awake. I'll meet you in the lobby in thirty minutes."

"Perfect, old chap. I was beginning to feel a bit hungry."

Shanghai was wide awake and busy at seven in

the morning. The lobby and coffee shop in the Peace Hotel were crowded. Darby decided on a little restaurant a few blocks away from the river, one that served a western breakfast yet not a soul understood English.

"What makes you so sure that Lu Zhong sent that message," asked Tom.

"Well, there aren't too many people who know Chen will be aboard XIAN, and no one in Shanghai knows you're going to join him. The kicker was simple. It seems Lu has an old friend up there in Vladivostok, someone who knows about those diamonds. The message said that the American would be carrying the precious cargo . . . not diamonds, mind you, but precious cargo. Even Chen knows nothing about that. Neither do any of his people." Darby's eyebrows rose in question, his forehead wrinkled. "What do you say about that, hmm?"

"It seems there's no doubt in anybody's mind about who the whore is, is there?"

"Now, now, don't be so rough on yourself, old man. Americans are always surprised when they hear the rest of the world's viewpoint. It's not really you that's doing all this. You are a very brave man, willing to go to any lengths to ensure the security of your country . . . even to smuggling if necessary. Doesn't that sound a bit more palatable?"

Loomis sipped his strong black tea. He had grown attached to it during his stay in China. Tea penetrated to the nerve centers more quickly and it looked like one of those days.

"Okay, Jack. We seem to be more than halfway there. Now what do we do? I'm sure that your plans don't call for you to wave a hanky at me as I head to sea with Chen and all those diamonds."

Darby cocked his head to the side, eyes sparkling. Tom had found this amusing affectation was about the same as a snake preparing to strike. "Not at all, old chap. My job's to find out a little more about how old Lu gets his messages back and forth. I want to convince the right person that you didn't get away with those diamonds after all. There's no point in everybody fighting over you if they think you're clean, now is there? I just want to see you back in the United States, welcoming me at your door with open arms and a healthy checkbook." He cocked his head again. "That's what friends are for, isn't it?"

"Am I going to see you again before then? Or are we off on our separate ways after this morning."

"I wouldn't expect we'd be keeping any social appointments after this. We've both a lot to do, and precious little time to do it in."

Loomis sighed deeply. "Nothing ever comes easy, Jack. Well make out somehow."

"No doubt, old chap."

Just as Lu Zhong had promised the previous day, a car was waiting for Tom at 8:00 p.m. at the front entrance of the Peace Hotel. The Chinese never allowed foreigners to drive in their country, but Loomis wished he could get behind that wheel now. He did his best thinking when he was driving.

Chen expected him no later than ten that night and Mr. Lu, aware of everything, had promised to deliver him to Chen at precisely that time. Nothing seemed to escape Lu. He was a traitor to his own country, an enemy of the United States, and there was no telling how much the Russians could trust him once he got the precious stones in his hands. Tom had even considered killing Lu that night. Wasn't that his job? Lu was as much a threat to him as he was to anyone else. How could he trust Lu if they met in New York? But the thought of using a gun, or any other weapon, wrenched his insides as much as it had in Chen's basement the night before. There was no doubt in Loomis' mind that he'd make a lousy spy. What a hell of a way to go about starting a new business!

The ride to the Shanghai Industrial Exhibition was a short one, a few blocks along the river, then down Yan'an Road to the outskirts of the city. Lu's warehouse was only two blocks from the Exhibition grounds and located in a clean, pleasant neighborhood. Another black Hongchi was already parked at the front when the driver pulled up to the door.

The outer office was similar to the business entrances to any warehouse. A long counter covered the front of the room, a series of paper-cluttered desks behind, secretarial chairs pushed tightly against them. At one end of the room was an unmarked door and this was the one the driver pointed to.

Tom put his hand hesitantly on the doorknob, looking back at the man. The driver nodded and Tom twisted the handle, pushing the door inward. He squinted in the sudden bright lights of the inner office.

"Ah, right on time, Mr. Loomis. Come in, come in." Mr. Lu was seated behind another ornate desk. The room was much like his downtown office, the furniture in American and European style, the trimmings oriental. The balance was effective. It gave a sense of both power and style at the same time, a curious blend of money and culture. Financial power was an oddity in China.

"I like your style, Mr. Lu. There seem to be a number of similarities between us. This place is as exquisite as your other office. You live graciously."

"Somehow, in another time or place, I think we could be very effective partners, Mr. Loomis. However, as I say, I am too old to continue. There are things of the heart and mind I want to do now, and that means leaving the business world." He came from behind the desk, stopping before a richly detailed silk screen painting, tilting his head to the side to offset the reflection from its surface. "Perhaps, if we manage everything properly, you can have my offices when you return to China in the future." He beamed at Tom. "I don't intend to return here, and I'm sure your communications business will blossom in the next few years. My offices could be your second home."

He's also one of history's great liars, thought Tom. He no more plans for me to be alive three days from now than the man in the moon. But he pulls it all off wonderfully. "That's very kind of you. I'd like to make arrangements for that when we meet in New York. It would be a fine way to celebrate."

"In an hour and a half, you must be in Admiral Chen's hands. We can't waste too much time with small talk this evening. Do you have your luggage with you?"

"In the car."

Lu reached over his desk, pushing a buzzer impatiently. He spoke quickly over an intercom to his man in the outer office. "I asked him to bring in your luggage. I want to be sure we pack so that nothing is obvious. Diamonds are so tiny they will take up less room than a pair of shoes, but we don't want to give them away when we are so close to success. You will be carrying about a million and a half dollars worth in American money."

Lu Zhong lifted the print Tom had been admiring to reveal a wall safe. Spinning the dial rapidly, he pulled back the door, and removed a green felt cloth. Though he unwrapped it slowly and gingerly, a small object still slipped out, glittering as it bounced across the desk.

Lu smiled as he picked the diamond up delicately between his thumb and index finger and held it up to the light for Loomis to examine. Then he dropped it in Tom's hand. "Go ahead. Study it. It's real . . . and beautifully cut, and there are many, many more."

Tom watched the older man remove fourteen

more packets, each wrapped with the green cloth. Lu made three stacks of five each on his desk. They occupied an insignificant space for their value. It would be no problem to fit them into his suitcase. So little volume for such a fantastic opportunity. It was worth the chance.

Lu pushed his buzzer impatiently, jabbing at it with his index finger, anxious for his man to bring in Tom's bag. When the door to the outer office did open, Lu looked up at Jack Darby's bright eyes and then into the muzzle of a snub nose revolver. Loomis whirled at the sharp hiss of Lu's breath.

"Don't move a muscle, Lu. Don't breathe. Don't blink. Not even the slightest move toward that desk," he snarled. In a lighter voice, without taking his eyes off the Chinese, he said to Tom, "Sorry, old chap. Didn't mean to frighten you like this. Time got too short to do things the proper way."

"I don't . . ."

"Don't bother. Maybe I can tell you on the way to Chen's. The problem now is with our friend here, who would cut my throat if I took my eyes off him for a second." He never wavered from Lu. "Maybe our rich friend would like to explain what he had in store for you." Darby spoke in Chinese to Lu.

Tom watched Lu's eyes narrow. His brief answer to Darby was barely heard. Lu dropped his arm just a fraction of an inch, still watching the gun. Jack's finger tightened on the trigger. The arm moved back up.

"I had to explain to him that his man outside had a serious neck problem," said Jack. "I think he expected him to come back in at any time to surprise me. Hard to figure how someone so smart can be stupid about people like me."

"Jack, let's not waste time being cute."

"It's a damn good thing I showed up, old chap. It seems our friend here never did plan for the Russians to get hold of you. Your driver, the one outside with the slightly damaged neck, was going to go right on board with you. Old Lu had it all cleared with Admiral Chen right down the line. The driver is a sailor on Chen's staff, and the Admiral had no idea how well Lu had infiltrated there. I doubt if you ever would have seen the sights of Tsushima, my friend. Lu had you scheduled to be fish food before XIAN ever arrived there."

Lu Zhong's eyes wandered from Darby to Loomis and back again.

Tom was openmouthed in amazement. "Admiral Chen . . . how much does he know about this?" The relationships were too intricate. His mind was oriented to organization, patterns that fell into place. Nothing about the last two days made sense. Nothing fell into place as he expected it to. He had no control over his destiny.

"Don't worry . . . don't worry," Jack replied soothingly, his eyes still riveted on Lu. "Just get those damn diamonds in your kit there, and get the hell outside. Chen's all taken care of. I saw to that before I wandered over here. You'll be welcomed

with open arms. But I'm afraid his staff, whether
they're hooked up with this character or not, aren't
having a very pleasant evening. They were headed
for Chen's basement when I said my good-byes."

Cautiously, Darby moved away from the suitcase, careful that Loomis was never between Lu
and the gun. He gestured slightly with the weapon
towards the wall, quietly explaining in Chinese
what he expected of Lu. As the Chinese faced the
wall, placing his palms flat against it, Darby
stepped closer, pushing the man's body against the
flat surface, forcing him to raise his hands higher.
Jack muttered again in Chinese, then began to run
his hands down one of Lu's sides, carefully patting
for a weapon.

If either of them had looked at the door, then
turned away before looking back, there would never have been visible evidence that it was moving, so
slowly did the person behind it act.

Tom was the first to sense motion. It was neither
a noise nor a movement by the door. It was a shadow on the office wall, thrown by a light beyond the
door.

"Jack . . ." Tom's shout echoed through the
room at the same instant a form hurtled through
the doorway and across the room, even as Darby
was bringing his gun to bear on the door.

"Get flat," Jack bellowed, leaping away from
Lu, turning toward the flying figure. As Darby
leveled his gun, there was a flash from the
intruder's hand, his body still in mid-air. As he descended, there was a second flash. The shock of the

explosions registered with Loomis as his own body headed for the floor. Time had stopped. He felt suspended. If he couldn't descend faster, he'd stop one of those bullets. They didn't depend on the fickleness of gravity, now a slow force that seemed to him to be reversing itself.

Before he hit the floor, the sound of more shots came to him. Was it three? four? five? Then he landed solidly on the rug, the breath whooshing out of his chest.

He was aware of the assailant crashing into something solid. One of the floor lamps was falling. Noise echoed from every direction—from Darby, from Lu, from the intruder, from furniture crashing. Tom rolled to his right, coming up on his stomach, his hands under his chest, just as the lamp finally hit the floor, bulbs popping like firecrackers.

Tom's eyes settled on the man who had just hurtled into the office. He was slumped on his side, a section of his face gone, blood spurting in a fountain. Turning to his left, Tom saw Jack propped on one elbow, his shoulders back against the opposite wall, a dazed expression on his face. His gun had landed about three feet from his body, in Lu's direction.

To Darby's left, partially hidden by the desk, Tom was aware of Lu. He had reacted exactly as Loomis, hitting the floor instinctively. Now he was on his hands and knees, eyes on Darby's gun.

Time again seemed to halt. Darby was watching the proceedings. There was no doubt about that.

Tom saw his eyes moving from person to person. But not a muscle moved in the Englishman's body. Jack's eyes darted to his nearby gun, to Lu, then back to Tom. Lu was scrambling on his hands and knees toward Darby's gun.

The image of the body behind him came back to Tom. The gun was still in its hand. He remembered that it had been pointed in his direction. He would have been next. Pushing up now with both hands, Loomis turned his head, his eyes riveted on that gun. He lunged, landing on his elbows, his hands scant inches away from it. His right hand shot out, grasping for the weapon, yanking it from the hand that still cradled it.

Tom rolled onto his right side, falling heavily against the body. His fingers fumbled with the gun clumsily, unable to get the index finger through the trigger guard. Then he had it.

Lu had reached Darby's gun. He was in a squatting position, knees drawn up, holding it with both hands, aiming it at Loomis. Their eyes met, each for an instant sensing the horror within the other, the feeling that chills the spine as one looks down the barrel of a gun aimed directly at him.

Both guns roared simultaneously. Tom had no idea how many shots he fired. Even as he realized Lu was hit, there was the thud of a bullet striking the wall scant inches above his shoulder. A second followed, almost at the same instant. Tom became aware his gun was empty when his arm no longer bucked each time he squeezed the trigger. He never knew if Lu fired more shots for he was watching the man's body.

The first bullet hit square in Lu's chest, the impact slamming his body backward on his butt, legs flat on the floor, eyes shutting from the impact. The second caught him in the neck, snapping his eyes open before his head whipped back, crashing into the wall. Blood was spouting before Lu's body stopped.

He had killed his first human being.

The gun slipped from Loomis' hands. He watched it as it landed in a spreading pool of deep red. Then Tom realized he was lying in that blood. It was flowing from the body he lay against. His stomach contracted. His muscles tensed, his mind reacted to the horror of the moment and he felt that same cold feeling that came over him in Chen's basement torture room. Instantly, he was in a squatting position, unsure where he would move next.

"Come on, old chap." It was Darby, his voice rasping. "Get hold of yourself."

Loomis' eyes settled on the Englishman. Jack had not moved. He was looking directly at Tom, a red stain spreading across his chest. Another was forming just above his belt.

Tom moved over to Darby's side, lowering himself to one knee beside the man. He reached out tentatively to touch Jack's shoulder.

"That's it, my friend. Grab something." The voice was almost a whisper. "Once you do that, you'll be all right. You don't have the time to worry about your guts right now."

No . . . No. Tom heard the words in his mind, but they never came from his lips. Jack was right.

No, nothing in the room was right. He did have to get out. He had to get Darby out . . . get him help. "I'll get you to the car." He slid one arm under the little man, as if to lift him up.

"Stop!" The voice was as sharp and firm as it had been minutes earlier. Tom yanked back his arm in surprise. The voice was tired and weak. "Don't even try, old man. My back is spread all over the wall behind me . . . can't move a muscle. But don't trouble yourself," he added. "I can't feel a thing either."

"Oh, for Christ sake, Jack . . ."

"Shut up and listen. If you keep losing control of yourself, you're going to end up like me one of these days." A faint smile came to Darby's lips as the clouded, black eyes looked up to Tom. "Just get those diamonds the hell out of here. You've been around Shanghai with old Jack long enough to find the way now, haven't you?"

Tom nodded. "Sure."

"Chen knew I was coming here to get you. He knew what I was planning for Lu, so there's no problem there. Just get yourself to his quarters as fast as you can." Darby looked up at Tom, his face contorting into a weird smile. "Why don't you get that damn coat off. The natives worry enough about the white devils without having to run into one covered with blood."

Loomis looked down at the jacket. It was smeared with the blood of the man he had fallen against. He ripped it from his body as if he were on fire.

"That's better, old chap. That's the way I like to see you move. Don't worry about the car. I left it running. I didn't expect to be here too long." Darby's voice was trailing off, his breath coming in short gasps, cutting off his words.

Tom zipped up his bag, the diamonds secure inside. He lifted it experimentally. It remained a very innocent looking suitcase.

He turned back to Darby to say something, but halted, his lips moving without the words coming. The bright little black eyes, now filmy, were staring blankly at the ceiling.

He bolted out the door, nearly tumbling over the body of his driver. The black Hongchi purred quietly. Slipping behind the wheel he eased onto the dark, quiet street. It appeared to be raining out as he turned onto Yan'an Street. He fumbled for the windshield wipers. They scratched back and forth noisily over a dry window.

He wiped his eyes with a shirt sleeve enough to see the road ahead. Tears of rage and tears of affection still clung to his cheeks.

CHAPTER SEVENTEEN

Chursin was a lousy driver. Royal had no doubt about that. Within minutes after they left the naval base, the little Zhiguli was careening down the dark streets of Vladivostok as if its driver was possessed.

Royal's right hand clung with a death grip to the armrest on the door, and his left continually shot out to the dashboard. His fear of what might be happening to Miller was replaced for the time being by concern for his own health. This was re-affirmed as the car slid on a patch of ice, bouncing off the curb before proceeding down a steep hill.

It seemed almost as if the Russian thought he was being followed, but Jack had checked behind them repeatedly. There were few cars on Vladivostok's darkened streets. Royal kept close track of the course Chursin had taken since they passed through the gates of the base. He had developed the habit as a youngster, a sort of mental game to see if he could return to the starting point.

"Captain Chursin, is it necessary to kill ourselves before we ever get there?"

Chursin's hands held the steering wheel in a

death grip, his knuckles white. "You are a fool if you think we aren't already missed." His voice was high pitched, his rough English spoken through tightly clenched teeth. His eyes left the road for a moment and caught Royal's. "I'm not sure what might happen to you if they catch us, but I have no doubt what would happen to me. We have a small chance if we have already lost them. Perhaps they might not realize we were heading for GRU right away. Then we might be in and out before they happen to check. On the other hand, if we die in this car before we arrive, Mr. Royal, it may be a more comfortable death."

There was no need for an answer. Jack held on tightly as they raced on through the night, looking occasionally over his shoulder. Chursin was full of it. No one was following.

As they reached the top of the next hill, Royal confirmed exactly what till then had been part of that childhood game. After the winding course through the side streets of the city, they were due north of their starting point. The masthead lights of the ships at pierside stood out clearly, and he could pick out the massive silhouette of EISEN-HOWER. He could still have returned on his own and won his own little game as always.

Jack was thrown against the door again as the car whipped down a street to the left, coming out of a slide at the last instant. Three blocks later, Chursin brought the car to a halt at an intersection. They were no more than five minutes from the base.

"There it is." The Russian pointed at a darkened building halfway down the next block. Like most of the side streets of Vladivostok, this one was unlighted. Dim bulbs burned occasionally over doorways, throwing dark shadows in their wake. No one was in the street. "We'll walk from here."

Jack stepped from the car, slipping on an ice patch on the sidewalk. Cursing under his breath, he said, "There doesn't seem to be any life around here."

"There isn't. Mostly death," Chursin mumbled under his breath.

"What the hell do we do when we get to that door?"

"Ring the bell . . . or knock."

"Just like that? Is the GRU used to strangers stopping by?" Royal asked sarcastically, shivering against the cold and his mounting fear.

"I'm not a stranger to them, Mr. Royal. I have worked with the GRU in the past. We are familiar with each other."

Jack stopped, his hand on Chursin's arm. "They'll know you?"

"If the right people are there, yes. They may even accept my claim that Admiral Maslov sent us to pick up the two prisoners and return them to his jurisdiction. On the other hand, if Krulev has already missed us . . ." His voice trailed off as they came to the door.

A light across the street barely illuminated the number on the plain wooden door. There was no sign identifying the occupant. Chursin pulled the bell cord. If it rang, they could not hear it. The door was thick and heavy.

It was bitterly cold. The interminable seconds magnified Royal's heart beat. He had time to realize exactly what they were about to attempt. A bright spot shone from the middle of the door indicating someone was looking them over. Then, the door was pulled open. There was no retreating now. They were committed.

"Captain Chursin, come in." A sergeant major swung the door back for them. "We didn't expect you, Captain . . . it is a rather odd time of the night for visitors." He looked over Royal's uniform curiously, his face expressionless.

"Is Colonel Shelest here?"

"He's upstairs, but I believe he may be unavailable."

"Well, tell him I'm here," barked Chursin. "On Admiral Maslov's orders. You have two prisoners that I am supposed to return to the base."

The sergeant considered Royal again, then faced Chursin, undecided.

"He is authorized by Admiral Maslov to be here, sergeant."

They were led upstairs to a brightly lit office. Diligent looking uniformed men hovered busily over desks. There was an aura of efficiency and discipline. A few eyes turned up to nod at Chursin and stare curiously at the American uniform. The sergeant disappeared into another room. Royal's heart pounded and he could feel the sweat running down over his ribs.

The sergeant returned quickly, an Army colonel ahead of him, a dismayed look on his face. "Captain Chursin! I had no idea you were expected here this evening."

"I had no plans, Colonel Shelest." Chursin was surprisingly calm and relaxed, his attitude modified from the wild drive of moments before. "Admiral Maslov sent us here." He half turned to Royal, as if he had forgotten him. "Oh . . . excuse me. Colonel Shelest, this is Lieutenant Commander Royal of the U.S. Navy . . . one of the Americans visiting for the holidays. The Admiral insisted that he make the trip out here with me tonight. Too bad . . . with such a fine party." He redirected his attention to Shelest, totally serious. "It seems your men made a serious mistake . . . they brought two men, Colonel Bespalov and an American, out here. Admiral Maslov insists Bespalov be returned to him so that he may conduct the interrogation personally. It was a grave mistake to have taken the American into custody at all. His own people promised Maslov they would discipline him."

Shelest's face fell. He peered first at Chursin through thick glasses, then at Royal. Nervously, he licked his lips, eyes back on Chursin. "This is embarrassing, Captain. Does this gentleman speak Russian?"

"A bit." Chursin was now the picture of cordiality. "Not enough to follow our conversation completely."

"Then would you please tell him," Shelest said,

turning partially in Royal's direction, clicking his heels formally, "that the Americans have our deepest apologies . . . that a formal note will be sent to his Admiral and to his government expressing our deepest regrets. The error is ours, completely."

Chursin translated Shelest's words while the Colonel waited expectantly, his face indicating both regret and seriousness. Everything appeared too simple to Royal. Chursin's personality changed too quickly. "Where's Miller?"

"The Colonel will have him released and brought to us at once," Chursin answered after a brief conversation with the other. "I have never seen the Colonel so upset before," he said apologetically. "The GRU, you should know, never makes such mistakes. He is very concerned . . . especially when your visit is so important to Admiral Maslov."

"Does the Colonel speak English at all?" asked Jack.

"No, I don't think so, but I will ask him."

Royal watched closely, but the answer was already evident. Shelest had shaken his head, no, before Chursin had asked the question. They were anticipating each other. Chursin could not have become so calm after the ride from the base. And Royal couldn't comprehend a GRU colonel so ready to apologize. It wasn't their nature. This scene was too well orchestrated.

"Mr. Miller will be right here in a moment," said Chursin confidently. "He's fine. He was just detained . . . not questioned."

Bullshit. Shelest had never left the room, never spoken with anyone since he had come out of the other room. And he was still making no move whatsoever. Jack experienced that same icy chill again, similar to the one he'd experienced outside GRU before Chursin had pulled the bell. He stood tense, waiting, while the two Russians talked.

Royal's mind imagined a dozen different ways the evening would end, each one punctuating a heart beat, a pounding that he felt increasing as they waited. When the side door to Shelest's office was opened, Jack knew no more than thirty seconds had passed since the last time Chursin had spoken to him. His mind had raced over everything that might occur from that point on, yet he had not come up with one solid idea. His heartbeat seemed so loud that the other two must have heard it. They all turned as the door swung open.

Bob Miller entered the room, blinking in the light. Only an escorting guard was with him. Miller's uniform was neat, his hair in place, his coat over one arm. The face was pale and tense as Jack had expected. Bob stopped as soon as the guard released his arm. His eyes passed over each of them, halting only for a second. There was no recognition, at first, no differentiation between them. Then he said expressionlessly, "I'm glad you're here, Jack."

"He's been drugged, Chursin. The bastards have drugged him!"

Chursin spoke sharply to Shelest. The answer

was just as pointed. "The Colonel says Mr. Miller was drunk when he was detained. He thinks Mr. Miller was sleeping during the short time he was here."

"Bullshit!" Royal's word fell out with no hesitation. "Tell the Colonel that I don't for a minute accept the fact he was drunk. Miller was touring ships with a group when he was snatched. That man has been fed some goddamn drug . . ."

Shelest's response to Chursin was equally as sharp. "If the gentlemen will bear with me, I can offer something personally which will bring this man to his senses fairly quickly. Tell him I use it myself when I have been drinking." Shelest was sticking with his story.

Chursin's translation to Royal was pleading. His look said that they had to get away.

"Mr. Royal, please believe me. We must leave before Krulev calls here. I am familiar with what the Colonel is referring to. It is widely used in our military and, believe me, it does wonders when you've been drinking. So go along with him. Please . . . give him the opportunity." Chursin's eyes were imploring. "It will get us out of here more quickly. Please, we must get out of here. It's a matter of minutes before it may be too late." He looked as if he might cry. The consummate actor, thought Royal.

Jack nodded and Shelest smiled his approval. There was no waiting. He had been carrying it in a little tin in his pocket. He pressed a small white pill into Miller's palm.

Bob raised his hand slowly, looked at the pill curiously, then at Royal. His reactions were pitifully slow, but there was recognition. He was aware of what was taking place.

"Swallow," Shelest said gruffly. "Good for you . . . you'll feel better." His eyes never left Miller's face, never looked over at Royal whose eyes were burning into him as the Russian spoke in rough English.

"We must hurry," pleaded Chursin.

"Go ahead, Bob. You'll feel better."

Miller slowly placed the tablet on his tongue, bobbed his head in Jack's direction and swallowed. This produced his first facial expression since he entered the room. It was as if he had bitten into a lemon. The pill tasted sour. He screwed up his face, his eyes expressing displeasure with the sensation.

"A glass of water," barked Shelest.

"It does taste awful," Chursin said apologetically. "I suppose it's a combination of caffeine, and other things that stimulate the body. It's bitter. I should have had them bring some water before."

Miller's lips were pursed as he showed his distaste for the pill. "Awful stuff," he said slowly, ". . . tastes awful."

He drank the entire glass of water, and asked for more. "I'm thirsty, Jack . . . very thirsty." Each word was pronounced separately, dragged out through each syllable. "I must have an awful hangover . . ." He smiled slightly. ". . . feels like last summer . . . in Vermont." He raised his eyebrows slightly, wrinkling his forehead. "Christ . . . what a headache."

Shelest looked triumphant, nodding at Chursin, and speaking again in Russian.

"He says there's no doubt about it, Mr. Royal. Your friend is suffering from a hangover."

"Yes, I heard. The Colonel can tell us all about it tomorrow. Come on, Captain, let's get out of here. I don't like him or this place." Royal knew now that there never had been anything to fear as they approached the door to GRU headquarters. Now his mind was searching. What was Maslov's next step?

Chursin and the Colonel again spoke to each other with Shelest smiling and pointing at Miller as they were moving to the outer office. "He asks that you put on your coat, Mr. Miller. It's a very cold night outside." He nodded to Royal. "They will bring back Bespalov themselves. We can go now."

Bob stopped, laboriously pulling on the heavy coat, and turned to stare at Shelest as they were passing down the hallway to the street door. Jack noticed him look curiously at the man once, then again. Royal thought he saw a trace of recognition in Bob's eyes, then it was replaced by a sense of fear. It was gone as he slowly turned his head back to Bob. "Thanks again for picking me up." Whatever he had seen had already passed from his mind.

Then they were on the sidewalk, their breaths clouding the icy air. "Hurry," said Chursin. "Perhaps our luck will hold."

Their fast pace became a trot, Royal holding Miller's arm, leading him to the car. "Your Colonel speaks English, Captain, almost as well as you. You knew that. And you no longer seem so concerned about Colonel Bespalov. Why the game?"

"Mr. Royal," panted Chursin, "this is no game. We are racing against time and Admiral Maslov right now. We will talk about all that later." They were at the car. "Let your friend have the back seat. He will be more comfortable."

The car roared into life, Chursin's foot jamming the gas pedal to the floor. He had the vehicle into a sharp turn instantly, heading back in the direction they had come from. It was the same trip again, a tense Chursin behind the wheel, taking corners too sharply, driving as if he, too, had been drugged. His reactions were delayed, more than they should have been. Then, in a flash, Royal realized the answer, what had been bothering him since he first got in the car with the Russian. This ride was pre-planned. Chursin knew he wasn't being followed. He knew where he was going. The turns were not made at the last moment by a poor driver. They were being executed by a man who knew exactly what he was doing. He wasn't nervous. It was all part of the show he'd been putting on since they'd met. Chursin wasn't a lousy driver. He needed acting lessons.

Jack realized all this as he leaned over the seat to talk to Miller. Bob was reviving quickly now, as Shelest had promised. His eyes were sharper, his voice clearer and more expressive. His head still ached and he kept turning it in a circle, rubbing the back of his neck.

"I swear, Jack, it feels like one of my all time hangovers. I don't know what the hell hit me . . ."

The voice was firmer. His color was returning. Chursin's driving also helped to bring Bob around, using his arms and legs to brace himself against the corners.

As they talked, there was no doubt in Jack's mind about the man behind the wheel. Chursin was full of shit. He had been ever since they first met. The course they were taking was in the general direction of the base, but Chursin's driving was eating up a few miles for every half mile they advanced. He wasn't planning on delivering them to Admiral Pickett. That probably had never been the plan. Maslov, or Krulev, wanted them badly. When they failed to grab Royal at the same time they got Miller, they had to work out another method. It was a matter of revenge, bitterness that the two Americans had disappeared only weeks earlier, just before arriving in Vladivostok. Bespalov must have arranged their escape then. Royal had no doubt that Bespalov had been compromised and was likely dead now. They were next.

So, there were no plans to return them to the base, but Chursin was being very dramatic about it all. But what now? That chill returned, scaring him even more than before. It had to happen soon. He looked into the back seat. Miller was still rubbing his neck and stretching his shoulders. Never again, Magnuson, you son of a bitch, never again, Royal muttered to himself.

Then he saw it ahead. Chursin didn't need to point it out.

"Up ahead . . . look." The car slowed as they

came around a corner. A red light revolved
ominously ahead. Their headlights picked up a
heavily clad army officer, waving his arms over his
head. As Chursin braked the car, Royal noted the
automatic rifle slung over the man's shoulder. The
soldier waved them around in front of the car with
the blinking red light. Jack saw another car across
the street, soldiers on either side of it, all armed.
They were stamping their feet on the ground as
Chursin brought the car to a halt. Now, they
stopped their movement, attentive to the vehicle
and its passengers. So this is how it's supposed to
end, thought Royal.

Chursin appeared stricken. "I don't know what
it is . . . what they want. Maybe it is not us." His
jaw hung slackly as he looked imploringly at
Royal. "You stay here." He'd already swung his
door open. "I'll talk to them. Perhaps there's nothing at all." And he was gone, slamming the door
behind them, striding over to the officer who had
been approaching the car.

Royal had made up his mind, as he watched out
the rear window. Chursin had disappeared into one
of the cars, but one of the soldiers had just unslung
his rifle. "That son of a bitch isn't planning to
come back to this car again. Chursin's full of shit.
He has been all along. I don't know how they plan
to do it, but he hasn't the slightest intention of taking us back."

Their car had been left running to keep the occu-
pants warm. It was Chursin's way of keeping their
confidence—and his one big mistake. Jack slid
across the seat, slamming the car into gear at the

same time, the back end fishtailing as it roared down the street. If those soldiers were ready, he wanted to be a poor target.

There were no street lights and it was dark, too dark to see far ahead. He wanted to get off the street as quickly as he could. The back window shattered at the same instant the windshield on the passenger side spider-webbed. There had been no sound. But through the rear view mirror, Royal saw the pinpoints of light from rifle muzzles. If only they'd been armed with pistols. The rifles were too accurate, too easy.

Bullets thudded into the car's steel hide. The rear view mirror disintegrated in a shower of glass. If they got a tire, the game would belong to the Russians. This is what Chursin must have wanted. It would be much easier to report to Admiral Pickett that the two Americans had stolen a Russian vehicle. That they had broken through a roadblock. He imagined Pickett or one of his staff brought out to the scene. It would be too easy. Royal, the driver, crushed behind the wheel. Miller dead, too. It would show it wasn't a put-up job—they couldn't jam a body behind a wheel like that. Both killed in a high speed chase. He had to get off this street. Only seconds had passed but they had taken forever.

He barely caught sight of the alley on the left. He was almost on top of it, probably too late, but he threw the wheel over anyway. It was instinctive. Better to take a chance than a bullet. That son of a bitch Magnuson!

The car slid sideways, all four wheels still on the

pavement. His lights picked out the curb, and then they were bouncing over it. The sidewalk was covered with snow and they were still sliding, a solid wall coming up fast on them. Glancing off it to the sound of torn metal and broken glass, the car bounced back into the street, fishtailing again before Royal could control the wheel. He took his foot off the gas, turned into the skid, gained control and crammed the accelerator to the floor.

There was no longer the thud of bullets. But something in the recesses of Royal's mind had also registered a primal sound, and perhaps delayed his acceptance of it until he had the car under control. It had only been an instant ago, and the tone terrified him.

Miller had cried out, not to say something, not in fear. It was a cry of anguish, of pain.

"Bob . . . for Christ's sake . . . Bob? Answer me! What happened?"

"Something hit me. I think they hit me, Jack." His voice was soft, unbelieving. "I don't believe this. . . ." his words trailed off.

Royal whipped the car to his right, taking a street toward the harbor. It was wider, maybe a main road. No good. They'd radio ahead, probably set up another road block. Krulev would never be willing to tell Admiral Maslov that they'd gotten away. Royal knew he had to stick to the side streets.

He looked quickly over his shoulder. There were street lights now. Miller's face was twisted in pain, his hand under his coat, below the left shoulder.

Blood was running down his arm, not in a trickle, but spurting out. His heart was pumping his blood out through the shoulder.

"Jack . . .?"

"Yes? . . . what?"

"There's a hole in my chest . . . a hole." He sounded skeptical, but then, "I've got my fist in it."

Royal ripped off his scarf, tossing it into the back seat. "Use this. Just cram it in, Bob. Anything. Just stop the blood." His mind was racing. That son of a bitch Magnuson. Nothing like this, he said. A lot of money for us in return for a little work for him. Bullshit. My friend . . . my best friend . . . is sitting in the back seat with his fist stuck in a hole in his chest. That son of a bitch.

"Can you stop it . . . the bleeding?" Royal heard himself shouting against the wind rushing through the car. The bullets had taken out the back window. The windshield had fallen into the front seat when the car bounced off the building. He realized how cold it was as the car raced on. Maybe that would stop the blood.

"I don't think so, Jack. But it doesn't hurt so much now." His voice was softer, sleepy. Royal could barely hear him. "You know, Jack, I remember that colonel back there now, the one that gave me that pill." The car bounced sharply over a hole in the road. Miller let out a gasp of pain. "Oh shit, that hurts."

"What about that colonel?"

"I remember talking with him somewhere . . . maybe in that building." He stopped, his chest heaving with deep gasps. "Jesus, it hurts to breathe." He paused, his head down for a minute as if searching for words. "I think I told him everything. I don't know why . . . I think I wanted to . . . don't know why . . ." His voice trailed off.

Royal glanced over his shoulder for an instant. Bob's eyes were closed. But Royal could see the lips moving, then stretching back across his teeth in pain. They crested a small hill. Before them were the mast head lights of ships. Many of them were American, too. The dark hulk of EISENHOWER stood out majestically. Safety!

The bastards! That's what they did. Royal muttered to himself. Gave him something, some drug, one that would make him spit out everything. A simple way to do it. No blood, no bruises, no mess.

He steered the car down another side street, inching closer to the piers, never staying on the same street for long. They must be out here, he thought. They must think I'm going to take a straight shot at the base. They can't wait right at the gate. By now, Pickett must know about us. He has to have Marines at the gate. Got to come in from the side until I'm just about on top of them, then just come at that gate like there's no tomorrow. If I can make it inside . . .

He took the car around another sharp corner. A moan came from the back seat and Jack looked quickly over his shoulder. Bob's eyes were open again, staring down at his chest.

Blood dripped off his hand when he pulled Jack's scarf away from the wound.

Royal glanced back a second time. Miller's eyes were riveted on him. They reflected a fear Jack had never seen before. It was the terror of a dying man.

"Jack?" The voice was weaker still, but high-pitched, frightened. "I'm scared, Jack . . . and I'm cold, awfully cold."

"They blew out our windows."

"No, not that way. It's sort of all over." He dropped the scarf to the floor. "I'm bleeding bad. I didn't know I had so much blood in me. Jack . . . a man can't live with this big a hole in him."

"Just hold on, for Christ sake." Royal's own voice startled him. He was yelling above the wind that whistled through the vehicle, and screaming at his own fear, screaming at Magnuson, that son of a bitch. He was trying to drown out the fear in his own mind of having to face Margie, Bob's wife, maybe one of the best friends he had after Bob. Bob's kids—not them either. Oh, shit, why, oh why did it have to happen to Bob?

"Can't hold on much longer . . . shit, I'm getting dizzy . . . I can't see much, Jack. What's happening?" The last was a passionate cry into the black, cold Russian night. Miller's mind had confirmed what was happening. His heart wasn't ready to accept it.

The car raced across the main street leading to the gates. Royal saw the bright welcoming lights. The way was clear, no roadblocks, nothing that could stop them. He cut down the next block, then back to the main street again. He saw a car coming, lights flashing. But it couldn't catch him in time.

Nothing could! He had the accelerator to the floor, the engine roaring. He heard a screaming in the back seat that grew in intensity, competing with the engine and the wind streaming through the car. The sound was cutting through him, tearing at his own heart. In the distance, he saw flashing red lights coming down the main road toward the gate, but he was going to get there first.

One hand left the steering wheel to pound on the horn, the harsh noise adding a new dimension inside the vehicle. He didn't want anyone standing in his way when the car arrived. He wanted to be inside. He wanted to be surrounded by Marines. If they weren't at the main gate, he'd keep going . . . until he got to TEXAS if he had to.

They were almost there, almost through the gates. He could see men moving to the side, readying weapons, unsure of this car. The screaming renewed and intensified until it was the only sound. It tore at his ears, digging down deep inside.

And then they were through and he was braking the car. There were American marines there. It was then that he realized the screaming was his own. Bob Miller was very still, staring wordlessly at Royal, unable to comprehend the sound from the front seat.

They were surrounded by Russian and U.S. guards, all with drawn weapons, and Jack was shouting at a major for a doctor. The marines had surrounded the car at the first sight of Jack's uniform. The Russians uncertainly formed an outer circle.

Royal pushed open the door of the car, placing one foot, then the other on the ground. He halted for a second, staring back at the major, neither of them quite ready to say anything. Then Jack stood up, his legs unsteady, holding onto the door. He looked around at the eyes watching him, then pointed at the Russians, his finger sweeping around half the circle. "Don't let those bastards anywhere near this car." He drew a couple of deep breaths, sucking the cold air into his lungs, blinking at the men surrounding them.

Then he looked into the back seat. Bob was gazing back, eyes clouded, mouth open, straining to draw even the shortest of breaths.

"Let me have your scarves, handkerchiefs, anything," he said to the closest men. When no one moved at first, he screamed, "For Christ sake. Can't you see he's bleeding?"

Instantly, he had a handful. Climbing into the back seat, he folded one of the scarves and gently pulled back Bob's coat. Jack wasn't sure what he had planned to do, for all that existed was blood, blood and raw flesh. There was nothing left of the chest. Very carefully, he folded more material together. Then, tenderly, he pulled back the coat again and covered the wound with the makeshift bandage.

"There, that'll do until the doctor comes."

"Doctor?" The word hissed out with a weak breath.

"Yeah. There's one on his way. Relax. We'll have you taken care of in a moment." A trace of a smile appeared on Bob's blue lips. "I guess we just made it in time, old friend."

"You're full of shit . . ." The eyes closed for a second. They reopened as he drew a breath. "Won't make any difference . . . they don't make plugs as big as that hole."

"Just be quiet."

"Screw it, Jack . . . you got to see Margie . . . got to explain what happened . . . why I wanted to do this . . ." The voice, progressively weaker with each breath, was a whisper now. Only a few words escaped between each painful gasp. The eyes seemed to stare right through Royal. "You have to tell her why . . . the reason for this."

There isn't any goddamn reason. Royal felt it inside, wanted to shout it to Bob, to the faceless silent men standing outside. I'll tell Magnuson. I'll make that son of a bitch go up to Vermont and tell Margie to her face. See how the son of a bitch likes that.

"Jack?" Miller slowly reached out a bloody hand. He stared into Royal's face, his hand grasping at the air. "Hold my hand . . . please . . . I don't want to be alone."

Royal took the hand in both of his, squeezing tightly. It was slippery with blood, and cold. He held on tighter.

"When you get back . . . please help Billy . . . you're more than an uncle . . . he needs somebody."

"Please, take it easy. You're going to be able to do it all yourself." Royal had so much more to say, but he didn't know how. He didn't know how one man says it to another. All he could do was hold Bob's hand to his cheek.

"You're still full of shit . . . Royal . . . but I love you . . . old friend. . . ." The eyes shut. The chest settled, then rose almost imperceptibly. The distance between each breath grew longer, the effort imperceptible.

Jack heard the siren screaming, listened as it got closer and watched the chest, counting each breath, knowing each one was shallower, the time between each greater. And then he realized there was no longer a siren. A marine was pulling open the door and a man dressed in white was climbing in back with him.

The doctor lifted Bob's eyelids, then grasped the wrist below the hand Royal still clutched. "I can't help this man."

The doctor stared at Royal. Jack was holding the hand tightly, still against his cheek, gazing into Miller's face, teeth clenched tightly to hold back the cry of anguish deep in his chest.

The doctor looked closely at Jack and saw the water forming in the corners of his eyes. More softly, he repeated, "I'm sorry, very sorry. Neither of us can do anything." Very gently he took hold of Jack's arm, drawing it away from his cheek, loosening the grip on Miller's hand.

Slowly, Royal turned his head toward the doctor, tears mixing with the blood. "I understand."

But he didn't understand. He wouldn't ever understand. That son of a bitch Magnuson.

TO: The President of the United States
FROM: Office of the Director of Naval Intelligence

SUBJECT: OPERATION SEAGULL

At 2:00 p.m. Washington time, the Soviet Pacific Fleet commenced exiting the harbor at Vladivostok. It is known that Admiral Maslov boarded his flagship KIROV a short time before departure. This office is in direct communication on an open line with Admiral Pickett aboard EISENHOWER. He has reported establishing contact with our operative in Peking. You should be aware that not only is one of our people personally involved with the Ministry of Defense of the People's Republic of China, as a representative of the United States, but another is also enroute with Admiral Chen, now Commander in Chief of the Chinese Navy, to his flagship XIAN. It is believed XIAN, in company with a destroyer squadron, is enroute to intercept the Soviet Pacific Fleet at Tsushima. Admiral Chen has determined that if the Soviet Pacific Fleet exits Tsushima into the East China Sea then the PRC will be unable to contain them.

While Chinese naval forces are weak, they remain extremely aggressive. The Ministry of Defense under General Yeh has stepped up its program of harassment of Soviet forces on land and at sea. A major land battle is underway in northern Manchuria for Khabarovsk. It is impossible to assess the outcome of that conflict at this time.

Chinese air strikes from bases near the Soviet Maritime Province have been underway for the past few hours, and it is possible one may be destined for Vladivostok. A warning has already been issued concerning U.S. naval units in that port.

Chinese aircraft capable of laying mines are also reported airborne, though their exact mission is unknown. Computer analysis indicates that their purpose would be primarily antisubmarine. Minefields could be established to limit access to the Yellow Sea in a line from the South Korean mainland to Quingdao and even from the Korean island of Cheju-do to Shanghai. However, results would be haphazard at best. Chinese mine technology is well behind modern capabilities.

Air attacks against the ports of Da Nang and Cam Ranh Bay in the last few hours have been turned back after minimal damage to port facilities. However, additional waves of Chinese bombers, supported by fighter aircraft, are reported airborne.

As with their sub fleet, they are attempting to accomplish in vast numbers what they are unable to achieve in quality. However, Chinese morale means a great deal and there seems to be no change in their methods, i.e., their personnel have no objection to suicidal methods to achieve their goals.

Analysis and recommendations:
It is urgently recommended that I meet directly with you in conjunction with the Joint Chiefs of Staff and appropriate members of your cabinet to discuss the following:

1)   Shifting the US Armed Forces from Wartime Readiness Condition Two to Condition One;
2)   The latest intelligence reports, along with an analysis of options that now remain open to the US;
3)   The utilization of operatives from this office now in sensitive positions with Chinese forces;
4)   A separate meeting, if necessary, with the Japanese Ambassador concerning combined operations with units of the Japanese Military Self Defense Force now in position off Kyushu.

Respectfully submitted,

Theodore Magnuson
Rear Admiral, USN

The President reread Admiral Magnuson's report, then handed it to his Chief of Staff with the curt order, "One hour from now!" After this was all over, he'd consider charging Magnuson with insubordination. In the meantime, he would have words with the Soviet Premier over the hotline. "That son of a bitch," he muttered, including both the stubborn Director of Naval Intelligence and the Premier in his thoughts.

CHAPTER EIGHTEEN

"Nuclear weapons?" Li Zhiang was appalled. The words the old gentleman wanted to blurt out wouldn't come.

"Yes," answered Yeh Chien-ying. "Precisely." The Minister of Defense removed his glasses, rubbing his red-rimmed sleepless eyes. "But tactical nuclear weapons. Small ones to be used in the field or at sea. Not our ballistic missiles. Those would be strategic."

"The size makes no difference," answered Li. "It's willingness to use them."

"Our purposes are justifiable. Soviet troops are massed on our northern borders. Their ships encompass our territorial waters." Yeh's voice rose. He was a stubborn man. "We didn't start this at all, my old friend. The Russians did. We are simply protecting ourselves and I must consider every possible option."

"Some day, when there is no longer such danger, we should examine our conflicting philosophy on these weapons," answered Mr. Li. "Right now, I say that the use of any kind of nuclear arms will only invite the Russians to retaliate in like manner. And I will assure everyone here, right now, that they will bury us." The men around the table were quiet. Li chose his words carefully. "They will use larger and larger weapons until we are subjugated. This is not the way to win. The way to win is to force the Russians to back down, to cease this military action and go home without accepting the role of a loser."

The meeting at PLA Headquarters continued for more than an hour. On the subject of nuclear weapons, the older men, with the exception of Yeh, were opposed at all costs. The younger ones would consider any means to combat the Russians. But the consensus was that they could not await the final Soviet move by sea. They would take the offensive. The one point that Li Zhiang was able to get agreement on was that they should step up their actions at sea. It was imperative to show the Russians it would not be the simple, decisive coup that Moscow originally conceived.

They would move against the Russian divisions on the Manchurian border rather than wait. They would take Khabarovsk, the key city to the Soviet Maritime Province, and thereby cut Vladivostok off from the rest of Mother Russia.

Yeh Chien-ying had said the Russians would not remain in any action, declared or not, that would drag on for a long time. They had learned their lesson in the past. Their military strategies were based on rapid movement, surprise, and devastation to the opponent. The PLA would be just as persistent as it had been forty years before, and the Soviet leadership could not afford that.

And, finally, Li Zhiang brought up the matter of the American, Goodrich. The discussion was heated.

"And now, it comes time to explain to you a series of coincidences that must have bothered you. Until now, you have had the courtesy to say nothing. It enhances my respect for you." Li Zhiang smiled ruefully at Goodrich, his eyes coming to reflect the sentiment of a father for a son. "You realized quite a while back that my responsibilities involved more than those with the Petroleum Ministry."

Goodrich nodded, waiting.

"I have been a member of the Defense Ministry for almost thirty years. I was initially appointed by Mao, first as a reward for my loyalty to him, then as his eyes and ears through the years of his critics, especially the Cultural Revolution."

"I understand that." Ben sensed that Mr. Li's uneasiness would be the source of even greater discomfort for himself. There had been an undertone of mystery, perhaps the word was evasion, ever since his first visit to Beijing in October. Perhaps it was meeting Li Han that enhanced his naivete. He realized, even back then, that things seemed to fall into place too easily. If they didn't function efficiently in America, why should they in China? The answer was simple. It was time to pay the piper.

"In many ways you have been used unfairly, Mr.

Goodrich. But I hasten to add that the culprit is your own country as much as mine."

"And Li Han? Was she a culprit, too?" That's what he must find out first. Had she also used him? Whatever he was about to be the victim of could wait.

Li Zhiang closed his eyes tightly for a moment, his arms folded across his chest. He inclined his head slightly forward, perhaps in respect to his daughter, then looked up directly into Ben's eyes. "I can assure you she never had any idea of the effort I have been involved in with your country. Perhaps if it is a crime that your country is using you as they will, it is even a greater crime that a father would mislead his daughter as I did. What brought you and Li Han together was something very beautiful. If I unintentionally initiated it, I also did not choose to stop it. She has often served as my hostess for visiting dignitaries. Therefore, I saw nothing amiss when I was contacted about your visit by Admiral Magnuson . . ."

"Admiral Magnuson?" Goodrich exclaimed.

"I had no idea how well you knew him."

"I don't know him . . . at least I haven't seen him in years." Ben's mind was racing. Where had he last heard Magnuson's name? Pictures of any number of people that might have mentioned the man swirled before his eyes. Then one image came back and he knew . . . Jack Royal!

Mr. Li's words came quickly, his demeanor changing to one of authority. "I do not question your relationship with the Admiral. Since you were somehow selected by him, then I remain satisfied with his choice. Because of the immensity of this operation, I was more than willing to allow Li Han to spend time with you when I realized her feelings. Through my daughter, I could learn if you could be trusted. And nothing happened to change my mind."

Ben's head snapped up. The little man's black eyes told him this was true. There was no time for kicking and screaming. Some freak accident of timing and planning, by a man back in Washington whom he'd long ago forgotten, had somehow maneuvered him into an incredible position. His own image of himself as a businessman or a grieving lover had been transferred to sucker in an instant, a flash in time that he had no opportunity to control. Would it have been any different if Li Han were alive? No. She had been as much a part of it all along as he was becoming.

"What might have happened?"

The old man's eyes were shiny as he said, "Nothing happened. You respected and loved her . . . you allowed her to remain a Chinese woman. I think perhaps Admiral Magnuson knew something about you that you may not even know yourself." To Ben's questioning glance, he added, "She was like a daughter to him when he was here. It was almost twenty years ago when he entered our country through Hong Kong, masquerading as an English businessman. I met him through another one of your sometime agents in Shanghai, Mr. Darby. Darby was an Englishman—but Chinese at heart.

This all occurred in the days when your Mr. Kennedy first considered resuming relations with our country, and that is how I got to know your Admiral Magnuson. He was a fine man, and he and Li Han were so close." He smiled to himself. "That's when she first began learning English . . . sitting on his knee . . ."

"She never mentioned any American to me."

"No, she never would," Mr. Li answered wistfully. "For he was never in China as far as anyone else was concerned. His mission failed, you see. That was near the beginning of our Cultural Revolution and he barely escaped."

Ben shook his head in disbelief. The story was preposterous, yet he did not doubt the old man for a moment. Through a feat of unimaginable manipulation, here he was in Beijing on the eve of what appeared to be the beginning of a major war.

"And I am under your control?" Ben asked.

"As you wish." He offered a sheet of paper to Ben. It stated simply that Mr. Li was acting for Rear Admiral Theodore Magnuson, Director of Naval Intelligence. And there was his own name— Bennett H. Goodrich—requested as a U.S. national to assist his country in time of emergency. The people, the letter, the place, the time . . . surreal! He heard Mr. Li saying, "Anything I might request of you would be as if it were ordered by the Admiral, who, in turn, is acting for your President. The chain of command is a bit odd, I must admit, but the situation, and Admiral Magnuson's perception of it, are even stranger. You were one of those he wanted here."

"And the others?"

"There is a man in Shanghai, working with Mr. Darby. Like you, he was also an acquaintance of the Admiral, Mr. Loomis . . . and another who was sent to Vladivostok with the Seventh Fleet . . . Royal is his name."

Ben nodded his head bitterly. Damn Magnuson. He knew. He remembered. But how the hell did he ever get us to follow his game plan? And then he nodded to himself, remembering . . . still a manipulator, the perfect spook. Now he's inventing the games instead of playing them.

"What do you expect of me?" asked Ben.

"Nothing that makes that tone of voice necessary, Mr. Goodrich. Admiral Magnuson realized quite logically that no American agent, no man that worked undercover and weaseled his way into our country, could be accepted when times were critical. He had to have an American in Beijing, one that arrived in China legally, and one that became attached to me and my family to challenge any criticism from my people. He wanted a man that could become Chinese, if you will. In that manner, perhaps he used you and Li Han, or better yet, he knew he was using us all. But, whatever the consequences, it was necessary to have someone here who could be in direct voice communications with both Washington and the American forces. You are a cog, but a valuable one. Admiral Magnuson could not predict what the Russians were going to do, not how China would react for that matter, and your President apparently would not listen to him. So he gambled. I'm one of the few who learned how much he did so. You are the right person. You are in the right place, and we hope the timing is correct. A great deal of time was spent considering you at the Ministry of Defense meeting today."

"Me? Who did?"

"Everyone there, and they all had an opinion. You see, I explained how you are intended to be used as a go-between with the Seventh Fleet and Admiral Chen. That only stirred up the question about which side the Americans really were on."

"Which side?" Goodrich shook his head in disbelief.

"If you were Chinese and had lived through the years that I have seen, you, too, would not be sure of America. A provisional declaration of war is right now being delivered to your Secretary of State by our Ambassador in Washington. It was American money that supported Chiang Kai-shek when the people of China opposed him. It was American guns that wounded me twice. I am telling you this as a friend. Imagine what some of the other old men had to say about Americans today," he added sympathetically.

"Wake up, my friend." Ben felt a gentle hand on his shoulder. "Wake up. It's time."

The American woke with a start, blinking up at Mr. Li's gentle face, the old man's eyes tired but still sparkling. Ben looked around the room. He had fallen asleep in an easy chair. Outside the window to his left, the sky was dark. Stars sparkled in the cold air. It was still night in Beijing. He couldn't have been asleep for long.

"I'm sorry. I didn't mean to doze. How long . . . how long have I been asleep?" He shook his head, running his hands through his hair.

"Not long. Maybe an hour at the most. You needed it. There was no need to wake you before . . . nothing you could have done."

"What's happening?" asked Ben.

"They're moving. The Russians are underway. The message just came through. Some of their screening ships have already departed Vladivostok. KIROV has just slipped her lines."

Ben shook his head, rubbing the sleep from his eyes. "How did you find out . . . so fast, I mean?"

"One of our submarines. She has been sitting on the bottom off Vladivostok. She came in under your own ships at the same time and hovered just off the bottom. Her orders were to listen and not to do a thing until she could identify the Soviet ships leaving the harbor."

"But she had to surface to call you."

"Yes. It was her first and last message. She was identifying some of the Russian ships coming out when they spotted her. The last transmission was cut off in the middle. It's started. We need you now to contact your Admiral Pickett on EISEN-HOWER."

"Your people trust me?"

"They have no other choice now. Come. We have no time to waste. I'll explain."

CHAPTER NINETEEN

Krulev had gone to Admiral Maslov's quarters to awaken him at 3:00 a.m. His tentative knock was answered by a booming voice. Maslov was already in dress uniform, freshly laundered, the creases knife sharp. His sword lay on the unused bed, the scabbard's brightwork sparkling. Maslov was taking the most powerful Russian fleet in history to sea, and he would do it in style.

Arriving at KIROV's berth, the Admiral went directly to the bridge of the battle cruiser, sending his aides below to prepare his quarters. The weather was perfect—cold, dry and clear. He intended to see each of his ships get underway. The organizational details could be handled by his aides and the computer experts.

KIROV's bridge was darkened, the only illumination coming from red night lights and the eerie green glow of the radar scopes. Few personnel were needed there until just before the ship backed away from the pier. Maslov marveled at the silence. In the days when he had commanded destroyers and cruisers, the hours before a dawn departure were busy, the clamor increasing as they made preparations for getting underway.

Maslov did realize men were busy in main control where the reactors were located. Yet there was only a distant hum, its location unidentifiable. There was no smoke, no hiss of escaping steam as the hour drew near, no vibration under the feet that hinted of power. But Maslov knew KIROV was ready to warp out from the pier at a moment's notice.

He strode back and forth across the pilot house, hands clasped behind his back, stepping occasionally onto a bridge wing to assure himself the stars were still bright, that no streaks of color were piercing the eastern horizon. He studied the nest of American ships at the other end of the harbor through his binoculars, then turned to the outer harbor to the immense outline of EISENHOWER against the night sky. He could see activity there. It was too late to alter anything. The Americans knew what was happening. One of his aides had confirmed that the Americans had ship's power available. This meant that the ships could switch from the electrical power provided by the cables from the pier to their own power. Pickett was simply waiting for a sign that Maslov and his fleet would depart.

He climbed to his flag bridge, one deck above and just aft of the pilot house. There his staff was laboring silently, rechecking their communication circuits, concluding checkoff lists, reassuring them-

selves that KIROV's departments were ready for
sea. It was something every Admiral's staff insisted
upon, and an irritation for the ship's company
whenever a flag staff came aboard.

Maslov peered at the glowing dial of his watch as
he stared out at the American carrier. His smaller
ships, the destroyers that would screen KIROV's
departure, should be getting underway now. He returned inside the flag bridge to check the surface
radar scope. Just as he had ordered, the destroyers
were underway. Green dots on the scope, each rep-
resenting one of his ships, gradually separated and
became distinct from the blur of the piers they had
been tied to.

Admiral Maslov again looked at his watch. Another moment to go. He stepped out on the flag
bridge wing. In the distance, the hulls of the American ships were outlined by the lights on the piers,
each one still powered by the electrical umbilicus
from the shore.

Abruptly, the lights on those piers and on the
U.S. ships were extinguished. The shore power had
been switched off. He knew it wouldn't surprise the
Americans, nor would it inconvenience them for
long, but it was just long enough for KIROV and
the remainder of the larger ships in the Soviet Fleet
to get underway. The nuclear powered U.S. ships
wouldn't really be affected at all. The conventional
ones would be inconvenienced for only a short time
until they could switch their electrical boards to
ship's power. But it was all the time Maslov required.

He heard the slap of the lines against KIROV's hull as they were tossed from the bollards on the pier. The distant hum increased and his feet detected, even before his ears, the thrum of the giant propellers biting into the icy water of Vladivostok's harbor. He thrilled to the increased noise level, the bellow of boatswains' orders to the deck forces, and the friendly calls across the water to the men left on shore. It would already be evident on EISENHOWER's radar that the Russians were underway, but Pickett could not react instantly. Maslov knew how long it took a carrier to get underway, and he also knew that the radar operators aboard EISENHOWER would be reporting new contacts off Cape Basargina. His submarines were now surfacing, some to provide a screen for the departing ships, and some to patrol menacingly outside the harbor until Pickett made his move.

KIROV departed Golden Horn Bay and turned southeast through the East Bosphorus Strait. It was a much faster exit than normally allowed, but necessary if his ships were to form up quickly. Maslov observed their running lights as they darted through the narrow passage, seeking open water and the security of unobstructed space from their sister ships. One collision could negate everything.

As he watched the dots on the radar scurry like bacteria under a microscope, Maslov also perceived order develop out of seeming chaos. There was no confusion. The Soviet Pacific Fleet was at sea and each ship was taking its assigned

position. To Maslov, it was much like the final act
of the ballet—after much chasing about, each
dancer arrived in his proper place as the curtain
fell.

An increasing glow in the east outlined billowy
fair weather clouds. "Well, Pietr," Admiral
Maslow questioned his Chief of Staff, "are the
Americans underway yet?" It was only for small
talk. He could see the movement on the scope himself. Their faces took on a reddish tinge as an edge
of the sun peaked over the horizon.

"Yes, Admiral," Krulev answered. He breathed
the cold sea air deeply. A brisk morning breeze had
sprung up, scattering white caps across the calm,
easy swells sliding under the ship. "Their frigates
have exited the harbor and apparently are sweeping across a line to verify if we might have left any
other submarines than those on the surface."

"Perhaps they are curious about mines?"
Maslov offered. It was an idea Krulev had
broached and Maslov had rejected. That would
have been an aggressive act, and there would have
been no way of predicting what the Americans
would have done if one of their ships had been
sunk or even damaged by one. Besides, that was
never his idea. He didn't wany any damage to come
to the Seventh Fleet ships. He wanted to keep them
just far enough behind him to give the appearance,
or at least the suspicion, they might be joining his
own ships. As long as the Chinese, or any other
observers for that matter, maintained even a trace

of concern about Seventh Fleet intentions, Maslov would be satisfied.

He acknowledged weeks before that any element of surprise had vanished. Chinese intelligence had compromised most of his plans. But he still held the one unknown and he was going to play it for all it was worth. Only he and the Americans were certain of the situation and he was willing to draw them on as long as he could—right through the Strait of Tsushima if possible.

"The Seventh Fleet is forming up faster than we expected, Valery." Krulev studied the radar screen closely. "It's probably better to recall the submarines now, and send the surface squadron to the rear. I'm sure Pickett's not going to take any chances with EISENHOWER getting too close to our subs." He looked over at Maslov, seated now in his bridge chair. "I'd say that Admiral Pickett's going to move frigates straight out and challenge them, and you said yourself one little mistake could ruin the entire operation at this stage."

Maslov waved his hand in Krulev's direction, never taking his eyes from the scene before him. "Fine. Go ahead. They're not in torpedo range of EISENHOWER, are they?"

"Not quite."

"Good. Don't let them. I'm afraid one of them might try to fire a torpedo if they thought they were in the least bit of danger. I never trust submarine captains," he mused. "They're too independent, and those Americans are touchy about their carriers," he added.

A radioman appeared on the flag bridge, saluting as he extended his message board to the Admiral. Scanning the message quickly, he beckoned Krulev over to his side.

"Look at this Pietr," Maslov said, his bushy brows raised in surprise. "Those Chinese are annoying."

Krulev scanned the sheet quickly, then reviewed it a second time in more detail. Chinese losses were heavy, but he sensed a determination the computers would never assimilate. The Soviet anti-submarine carrier KHARKOV had encountered numerous attacks as she steamed into the South China Sea. Repeatedly, the ship had been attacked by waves of aircraft from the Zhanjiang base, using tactics of forty years ago. Each time, her escorts had brought down all of the planes. Two Chinese submarines, obviously the old diesel type, had charged directly at her from the security of coastal waters. They never closed the range enough to fire torpedoes before they were sunk. And, the report indicated, an escorting destroyer had been seriously damaged in a surface attack by a squadron of torpedo boats off Hainan. All the boats had been destroyed.

Other Soviet units had not been as lucky. Two Krivak destroyers were missing to the east of Shanghai, and the amphibious landing ship IVAN ROGOV had returned to Cam Ranh Bay after surviving two torpedoes. It was apparent the Chinese were especially on edge over the possibility of the landing of marines. A nuclear attack submarine had not reported in over forty-eight hours, though Submarine Operations was unable to believe the Chinese could have detected and then sunk it. Other units had encountered resistance also, and their reports included fanatical assaults on the part of the Chinese navy.

Krulev glanced questioningly at his superior. "The computer will never be able to project this type of resistance. Have you determined the acceptable losses we can take?"

"We will finalize that when we enter the East China Sea, Pietr. If I'm correct, the Chinese will still see the Seventh Fleet right behind us . . . as if we were steaming together."

Admiral Pickett had not slept the previous night either. It was apparent the Russians' final concern had been the leaks within their own staff. That was why they had taken Miller, and why they had made the bungled effort to kill both him and Royal. It had been concern with their own intelligence weaknesses that had allowed the Soviets to wait as long as they had, but they had finally routed out the last of the American agents. When Royal had been brought back to EISENHOWER, Pickett decided the Russians would make their move at any time. The Russians had made a concerted effort to ply their guests with vodka the previous night, and the parties would have gone on forever if captains hadn't called their crews back.

So the Seventh Fleet had been almost ready,

ready for everything but the temporary loss of
power, and Pickett had only himself to blame. If
the conventional ships had already shifted to complete ship's power, they never would have lost precious time checking and realigning vital electronic
equipment.

Score one for Maslov, Pickett decided, as he
leaned against the railing on EISENHOWER's
open bridge. The orange sun climbing out of the
ocean provided little warmth. The Admiral pulled
his collar tighter. A breeze ruffled his hair, bringing
the sour harbor smells to his nose. The light wind
slowly swung the carrier's bow to the southeast, the
direction she would head when they lifted anchor.
He hoped it would increase as they went downwind
so he could launch aircraft even before they
reached open water.

To seaward, he watched the frigates scurrying
back and forth silently pinging the depths for signs
of submarines or even mines that Maslov might
have left in his wake. Pickett didn't expect mines.
That wouldn't make sense, for he was sure Maslov
wanted to draw them into the open ocean. Out
there, he would either turn to face them and block
southward movement, or he would lure them toward Tsushima.

Pickett was aware someone had come out to the
bridge wing. He'd heard the pilot house hatch open
and shut quickly. Feet shuffled around the wooden
grating, stopping behind him, but the Admiral never reacted until addressed. "You sent for me, sir?"

He recognized the voice, even beyond the

speaker's tired monotone. Pickett straightened up and faced a haggard Jack Royal, shoulders hunched against the cold early morning air, hands jammed deep into the pockets of his foul weather jacket. "How are you feeling this morning?"

"All right, I guess . . . sir."

"Good, I'm glad to hear that. You weren't quite yourself when they brought you aboard last night."

Jack remembered very little after he'd driven through the gates of the base, only that in the bloody back seat of a car a doctor told him Miller was dead. The rest was vague. He was aware of being close to hysteria when the launch brought him out to EISENHOWER. But now it came back, certain incidents illuminated by a series of mental flashbulbs. They raced through his brain and in seconds the previous night was vivid, much too clear. And one of the pictures was of Admiral Pickett waiting on the quarterdeck as Jack wearily climbed up from the launch. He knew what Pickett was referring to. He recalled arms waving . . . he remembered shouting . . . but it was himself, Jack Royal, doing the raving. His emotions were out of control. He was heaping all the blame on the Admiral in front of a stunned audience. For a second, Royal was withdrawn from the scene, watching a blood-spattered lunatic screaming at the calm, understanding Pickett.

"I'm very sorry, Admiral. I . . . I wasn't myself when I came aboard last night. I'm not sure what I said, but I apologize. I'd be happy to make a formal apology."

Pickett's stern features softened for an instant. Placing both hands on Royal's shoulders, he said, "Forget it, Jack. There's no anger involved. I just want to make sure you understand that you're still attached to the U.S. Navy and that you're aboard a warship. We need you . . . I need you . . . on top of yourself." He clapped Royal on the shoulders a few times. "You have two old friends in China, one in Beijing, one probably going aboard a Chinese destroyer. I've already been in touch with Mr. Goodrich in Beijing. He needs to hear from you, too."

"You've been talking with Ben?" The name alone refreshed him, reality seeping back into his veins.

"That's right. There are secure voice circuits. The Chinese are still doubtful of us . . . uncertain of what we're all about. I'm pretty sure they'll come around." He paused, his eyes narrowing, any softness from the previous few moments gone, as he looked directly at Royal. "What ultimately will contribute to that final acceptance may have a lot to do with your friends, Goodrich and Loomis, and their contact with me . . . via you, Mr. Royal. I don't think I could make it any clearer."

The bastard is just like Magnuson, Royal thought. "No, nothing more needs to be said, Admiral. I'm okay."

"Fine . . . fine." Pickett clapped him on the shoulder again.

"Admiral Pickett . . . I was just wondering. Do you happen to know Admiral Magnuson . . . Ted

Magnuson, in the Office of Naval Intelligence?"

"Why I most certainly do," the other smiled. "Ted and I go back a long way. As a matter of fact, I was attached to that office my last tour in Washington."

"I should have known."

Pickett winked at him, nodded knowingly, and put his binoculars back to his eyes again to survey his scurrying frigates.

"Admiral?" an aide called through the pilot house hatch. "Admiral, message from frigate group commander reports all clear to seaward. The Russian subs are drawing to the south. Looks like a squadron of their destroyers are moving up."

"I can see that from right here," Pickett growled.

"Yes, sir. Request permission to transmit the sortie message."

"Permission granted." The aide disappeared back inside the pilot house. "Well, Mr. Royal, would you join me out here to watch this display? Might keep your mind off other things."

"Thank you, sir. I appreciate it."

"Good. Get back in that pilot house and have them get you something warm to wear. That sun doesn't rise very high out here . . . no heat to it." Pickett's voice had again become as friendly and as accommodating as Magnuson's. Royal was familiar with the approach.

Ben Goodrich sat back in the easy chair provided for him at Mr. Li's insistence. Awkwardly, he blew a smoke ring, an oval shape that faltered, then disintegrated as he exhaled. He hadn't smoked for years, had never even thought about it until a Chinese officer had extended the cigarette to him. The man spoke no English, so the offer was accompanied by a variety of gestures so amusing to Ben that he accepted the cigarette and a light without a second thought. It tasted awful, but it was a way to pass the time.

They were in a room well under the Defense Ministry in Beijing. It was probably what Washington would have proclaimed a Situation Room. He'd seen movies with setups like this one. In one corner were important-looking older officers clucking to each other at each updated report. Teletypes clicked unceasingly, noisily augmenting the silent, brightly glowing, computerized display. The dull hum of muted voices added to the tension. But in this case, it wasn't Washington, or even Hollywood. The characters were Chinese and Ben was unable to understand a word they said, yet he was very much a part of it. It was a bad dream.

"Coffee, Mr. Goodrich?" It was the first spoken English he'd heard other than from Mr. Li. He looked up into the serious face of a young woman in an ill-fitting PLA uniform. Her pronunciation was thick.

"No, thank you . . . uh, tea please."

"We do have a coffee if you desire," she said hesitantly.

"No, tea, please. I've learned to like tea here . . . I enjoy it."

"As you wish, sir."

Ben's eyes followed her across the room to a makeshift kitchen area, where she poured a cup of tea, adding some tiny cookies on the saucer. On returning, she half bowed, a faint, polite smile on her face. "Please tell me should you require anything else."

It was odd, he thought. First the cigarette, now the tea. Perhaps Mr. Li is correct and these people have accepted the fact that we never were in cahoots with the Russians. Or perhaps they're just being polite. He looked up from the steaming tea to find Mr. Li standing before him.

"We have very good news." The old man was beaming, his tired eyes radiant. "The Japanese have been conducting exercises off Kyushu for the past week. Word has just been received that they are sending a force of destroyers around the southern tip of that island toward Tsushima. Their ambassador has just met with our Prime Minister to explain this. It seems your government called in the Japanese ambassador in Washington to ask for their aid. Admiral Tokuno, the Japanese Commander in Chief, has apparently taken full responsibility and is aboard his flagship, ASAKAZE, a guided missile ship. They will be close to our XIAN this evening."

"Is that why people are a bit more outgoing toward me?" Ben asked, sipping his tea.

"They had to be sure first . . . assure Yeh and some of the doubters that it was in fact your government who had initiated this. But, yes . . . or no, you are not going to end up in a torture chamber."

Mr. Li smiled for the first time that day, a sad
smile, but one that was also reflected in his eyes,
indicating a great load was lifted from his shoulders. "I think it might be good if you contacted
your friend, Mr. Royal, on the EISENHOWER.
I'm sure they are already aware, but it won't hurt
to let them know that your ships have nothing to
fear from ours."

Admiral Pickett crouched slightly to steady his
binoculars on the bridge railing, concentrating on
the masts on the horizon. Jack Royal was beside
him in the same position, his bare fingers stiff and
numb from the cold as he focused on the same
point.

"You talked briefly with Goodrich?"

"Briefly. That commander that runs radio central was touchy as hell . . . mumbling something
about small talk and circuit discipline."

Pickett turned his head to Royal, never moving
the binoculars. "My purpose in sending you down
there was to establish contact, not to plan a reunion. I appreciate your concern for each other.
You'll be welcome to plenty of time after this is
over." His eyes went back to the glasses. "You got
'em on the horizon?" he questioned.

"Yes, sir."

"That's what I'm more concerned with right
now."

"Yes, sir."

"Now, mind you, I don't think they're going to
pull any rough stuff. But I can't take any chances,

you know. If we get caught with our pants down out here, and some investigating officer goes and tells the people in Washington that some character not even attached to ship's company was having a chat on the radio while missiles were zooming around our heads, I'd be in deep shit." It was the first time Royal had heard an off-color word escape from Pickett's mouth, and the Admiral chuckled as he said it. "If anything happens, we're all going to have enough trouble explaining away you and your friends anyway."

Royal's head whipped around. "Who's 'we all'?"

"Ted Magnuson, myself . . . anyone else involved in Seagull." There was no other response from Pickett and it seemed obvious he had no intention of continuing.

An aide's head popped out of the pilot house. "They're in easy missile range, Admiral."

"They've been in range since the sun came up," Pickett snapped.

"Sorry, sir, I mean their own missiles, the ones on those destroyers."

"Any of our pilots up there see them doing anything foolish?" The Admiral gestured at the helicopters on the horizon that had lifted off EISENHOWER half an hour before.

"No, sir."

"Then don't bother me with that crap. I only want to know if they're doing anything I should worry about."

"Yes, sir . . . Captain Knowlton wants to know if you'll be joining him in flag plot, Admiral."

"Not immediately. It's a nice day. He can handle it. I'm going to watch them from right here, 'cause I think they're just going to play cat and mouse."

"Yes, sir. I'll tell him that."

"Don't go away yet," Pickett snapped. "How far's our screen out there to the closest Russian ships?" He gestured at the screening destroyers preceding EISENHOWER.

"I'll check, sir."

"And when you come back, I want to know when they're in gun range or torpedo range. It would be more like them to slow us down by bothering just one or two of our little cans out there." His eyes went back to his binoculars as the aide slipped back inside.

Jack glanced sideways at the Admiral a few moments later and discovered Pickett was looking closely at him, the ships on the horizon seemingly forgotten. "You have a clear picture in your mind of what's going on?" The question allowed too many answers.

"Well, yes, sir . . . in a way. I mean I know where we're headed . . . pretty much what's happening out there." He pointed in the direction of Maslov's fleet. "I don't know where each ship is, or what each one's doing if that's what you mean."

"That's not what I mean at all. That's what I have a staff of junior officers for. I'm not concerned about your understanding of the big picture . . . not tactics or strategy, or anything at all like that. I want you to understand your value to me."

"You need me to contact the Chinese in Peking . . . through Ben Goodrich."

"That's a simplification. Let's be honest with each other. You know the original reason Admiral Magnuson wanted you and your friends out here . . . or at least part of it. And the reason you were sent with me to Vladivostok was simply because you and Miller might get that computer tape—the one that became so unnecessary. We were hoping you might dig up the real facts about Maslov's final plans, sortie time, what he intended to do with us, that sort of thing. Well," Pickett shrugged, "that didn't work. They were on to our undercover people too fast . . . got them all, I guess. And, unfortunately, they were smart enough to play games with you and Mr. Miller, just in case they hadn't gotten all their little turncoats. That's the trouble with the Russians . . . don't even trust their own people."

Pickett leaned casually on the railing. "That, Mr. Royal, was the primary mission we had in mind for you and your friend. It was just something that didn't work out the way we wanted it to. Now, perhaps your secondary contribution will be just as valuable. Since you're here, I plan to make use of you."

Royal could feel the same emotions he remembered from the night before, the rage, the helplessness of someone else pulling his strings. "Just who the hell planned these so-called missions?"

"You know as well as I do. Stupid question."

"I just want to hear someone say it . . . just once. Magnuson's been screwing over us since the day he made this all sound like a lark."

"Wrong. He offered the carrot, the money angle,

and you people loved the idea. And, from what he told me, you guys were ripe. Listen, Royal, each of you fell into this because you were the right people. The Chinese and the Russians have got such a line on our intelligence organization back home that I doubt we had anyone left to go into Russia or China that they wouldn't have pegged before they ever left Washington. The idea was a good one, and to an extent, it's worked. Your buddy, Goodrich, has apparently done wonders in Beijing. He just charmed the hell out of Admiral Magnuson's one ace in the hole, and that contact's going to come back in spades now. Because, Goodrich, knowingly or not, has got himself right in the middle of the big boys in Peking, the Defense Ministry, and that's right where he was supposed to be and that's right where none of our specialists could have gotten. Now, if they keep trusting him and keep him alive, I think we might have a happy ending to this mess."

Royal kept quiet. There was nothing he could say. He felt that vague empty feeling one has after being used. He brought the binoculars back to his eyes again, scanning the horizon, catching sight of EISENHOWER's helicopters in the distance. Finally, he said, "I suppose you've been planning to be right here . . . steaming behind Maslov . . . I suppose all along you and Magnuson had this all figured out."

"Oh, don't be so goddamned self-serving about it all. This is exactly where we belong. Everything has happened the way we'd have liked it to, but there was no way of being sure. Hell, Royal, we even hoped you'd be here. I'm just disappointed your friend, Miller, didn't make it."

"Just disappointed?" Royal spun on his heels, eyes flashing.

"No . . ." Pickett was at a momentary loss for words. "That's not what I meant. We don't plan things like that. But Magnuson couldn't have picked four better people for Seagull.

"I don't know how much Admiral Magnuson told you. But you know as well as I do that the basic idea is always to help ourselves. Either way this turns out, you know, will benefit the U.S. One or the other of these two countries is going to take a hell of a political beating. Maybe not like losing a war, but it will set them back a hell of a long time. And that's the way to keep the peace, Royal, set them back on their heels."

"Admiral!" It was the same aide again. "The Soviet destroyers just barely came into range, then turned south again."

"What speed?"

"I'm sorry, sir, I don't know. I'll find out."

"Forget it. Get back in there to Knowlton and tell him to maintain the same speed as those Russians. Whatever they do, speed up or slow down, adjust force speed accordingly."

"Yes, sir."

"And another thing. Where's their main force . . . KIROV and those heavies?"

"They're pulling away a bit, Admiral. I'd say they were about forty miles distant."

"Thank you, son. Go back and tell Captain Knowlton what I told you. See, Royal?" Pickett

turned back to him. "Cat and mouse. Drag us after
them so it looks like we're joining up with them.
Scare the hell out of the Chinese. Maybe make
them put down their guns before the shooting
starts." Pickett rubbed his hands together, trying
to warm them as he spoke. "But don't let them fool
you. They don't need these destroyers we're following. They're just in front of us to slow us down.
KIROV and the big boys are far enough in front so
they get to play with that sad little Navy the Chinese have when things start to get rough."

"What about the Japanese?"

"That's been Magnuson's hole card for a long
time. We'd look foolish as hell getting into a shooting war unless we had to. He knew the Japanese
wanted to set the Russians back on their ass rather
than let them get any more foothold out here, especially from an economic standpoint." Pickett
chuckled to himself. "That's another thing about
Admiral Magnuson. He knows everyone's soft
spot, and he figured the Japanese would offer
help."

"The Russians have to know the Japanese ships
are out there."

"Oh sure. Of course they do. But they don't
know yet what they're going to do. That's where
intelligence work comes in, Royal. He who saves
his own ass gets someone else to do the dirty work
for him. And the Russians have no idea what the
Japs are going to do."

"So you're going to sit back and watch the fun?"
Jack said caustically.

Pickett responded sharply. "We're going to evaluate the situation as it develops. If necessary, we'll be right in the middle."

Admiral Maslov finally accepted Krulev's suggestion and went below to his sea cabin to rest. It would be another dozen hours before KIROV steamed into the East China Sea. He would want to be on the flag bridge at first light.

There was a knock on the cabin door, a soft tentative one.

Maslov knew by the sound that it was Krulev. "Come."

"I'm sorry to bother you, Valery."

"I wasn't sleeping."

"A few hours would help. You'll be refreshed."

"I don't need to be refreshed. I'm fine . . . perfect. I'm not tired. I'm excited, and that keeps me going. I'll sleep when it's all over." He raised his brows quizzically, chiding the other. "You're not tired I suppose?"

"No." Krulev would never use the reason that he was younger and that he didn't need as much sleep. It would just put Maslov on edge and there was no reason to get the man more excited than he already was. It was the culmination of a brilliant career for the Commander of the Pacific Fleet and Maslov was the type of person who lived for hard work.

"Then we understand each other, Pietr. Tell me," he asked happily, "what did you come here for?"

"I don't think it's anything," Krulev shrugged,

taking a chair at Maslov's gesture. "It's the commander of the squadron of destroyers you sent back to slow down the Americans. He worries me. He's touchy, too touchy. Keeps calling up to report any little thing about them." Krulev took a deep breath. "I'll tell you, Valery, I think he's too nervous. He's the type who could shoot when least expected. If the Americans picked up speed and perhaps closed his ships, he might just shoot and ask questions later."

Maslov grunted.

"That would ruin everything." Krulev spread his hands in distress. "We'd never get to Tsushima. I think we'd end up fighting a force at least as strong as ours . . . and with more airpower. Remember, our carriers are too far south to offer any help."

Maslov stretched his legs in front of him, yawning and folding his arms. "The Americans aren't going to challenge anyone yet. They want to get there just as badly as we do. If we fire to warn them to stay back, they will. Their Admiral Pickett wants to get there as quickly as I do, and he'd give orders to hold fire. I'll tell you what." The Admiral leaned forward, his hands on his knees. He couldn't help but be pleased with himself. "Tell your squadron commander to set his torpedoes extremely deep, deep enough so they'd never hit any ships. And, if one of those American ships gets too close, then fire one of those torpedoes. I'll bet . . . really, I'll bet with you right now . . . that nothing will happen . . . except maybe that American ship will fall back into place."

"If you say so." Krulev couldn't muster confidence to equal Maslov's.

"What I'm more interested in is EISEN-HOWER. Where is she . . . what's Pickett doing with her?"

"He's been keeping his Tomcat and Hornet fighters aloft, but away from us. The carrier is staying well out of missile range for now."

"Yes, Pietr, well out of missile range from us, but in a perfect position to launch reserve aircraft squadrons without any trouble. Now that's the one thing that's been bothering me. But you just helped me to solve it. After midnight, I want you to drop some submarines back. Have them keep close to shore, where they'll blend with the bottom in the shallow water. American sonar won't be able to pick them up there. Just in case we run into more than we expect, those subs can keep EISEN-HOWER busy. And I want aircraft launched from shore bases also. Keep them well astern of that carrier, but still within missile range."

Krulev stood up. He walked over by Maslov's desk, studied the photograph of the Admiral's wife for a moment, then turned, his arms folded, his face firm. "What about the Japanese? You're not worried about them?"

"The Japanese!" Maslov dismissed them with a snort and a wave of his hand. "The Japanese don't bother me. A little self defense force. That's all they are."

"That's what they used to be, Valery." His hand slapped the top of the desk. "Used to be. Those

destroyers you're dismissing so lightly are
equipped by the Americans. They have helicopters,
torpedoes, guided missiles. They're able to fight at
sea. Those are no little gunboats running around
protecting Japanese fishermen. Those are ships
with the same fire power as we have . . . some of
them have even more. I think we ought to be wor-
rying about what they might do."

"Pietr, forget it. They're not going to get themselves involved in any fight that's not their own."
Maslov caught the stubborn look on the other
man's face. "All right, if it will make you happier,
you keep an eye on them. But I'm not going to
bother myself. They've been out on exercises that
have been well publicized. Everyone knows about
it and they're probably headed back into port
now."

"On the contrary, they're not heading back to
port at all. The last message I got said they were
due south of Kyushu and steaming west at thirty
knots. Their exercise area is a hundred miles astern
of them and getting farther behind every hour."

Maslov was becoming irritated. Krulev rarely
argued with him and now wasn't the time to start.
"As I said, keep an eye on them, if you please. If
there's a direct problem with them . . . if you can
show me without a doubt that they plan to interfere, then I'll take action. In the meantime,
perhaps you could use a little sleep, Pietr. You
seem to be getting irritable, just like your destroyer
commander back there, and we can't have that
with so little time left."

The helicopter swayed in the wind, lazily sometimes as if it were swinging at the end of a rope. It
also shook dangerously at other times as far as
Tom Loomis was concerned. He didn't like being
on the helicopter, but there was no choice. Admiral
Chen had explained, quite politely, that not only
was there no choice on Tom's part, but that he was
simply following orders from Mr. Li. And he
added, his friend, Mr. Goodrich, would be glad to
confirm that it was really necessary. Never satisfied, Tom was allowed to speak with Ben, and the
latter explained what was already a foregone conclusion. It seemed to be beautifully planned. They
were actors in a play that only they had not read
beforehand. Everyone else, including the Chinese,
Admiral Pickett, and finally, Admiral Magnuson,
seemed to know exactly what was happening.

Loomis looked out at the sea below. Whitecaps
sparkled, reflecting the reddish glow from the late
afternoon sun behind them. Across the small
cabin, Chen sat peacefully, his back against the
fuselage, arms folded. He smiled pleasantly when
Tom caught his eye. The American squeezed the
bag underneath the bench with his legs, something
he had done at least twenty times since they had
been airborne. It was still there and there was no
reason to believe it would not be when they were
deposited on the stern of XIAN, the guided missile
destroyer Admiral Chen had chosen for his
flagship.

Chen had attempted to talk him out of bringing
his luggage, explaining that they would return di-

rectly to Shanghai, and then he could fly out of China in comfort. Tom politely argued with Chen until the latter, frustrated and tired, agreed that it would really be no problem, and that it was certainly possible to transfer him to an American ship when they joined up with the Seventh Fleet.

The wind outside grew stronger and Tom guessed that his face gave him away. Chen removed his headphones and lurched across the little cabin to sit next to him. "Your face is a picture, Mr. Loomis. I can tell you are most unhappy." The roar of the engines was loud, even in the soundproof cabin, and Chen had to shout into his ear to be heard. "Please, don't worry. We will be aboard XIAN in less than an hour and then you will be more comfortable."

Tom's stomach heaved as the helicopter lifted briefly on a gust, then dropped twice as quickly. "How is a ship down there," he gestured with an index finger toward the ocean, "going to be any more comfortable than this?"

"We will be inside. It will be warmer." The helicopter was cold, very cold, with only a tiny heater struggling against the winter temperature. It had been built for fighting, not to transport passengers, and additional creature comforts had been mostly forgotten. "And we will have something to eat. I am certainly hungry, and I imagine you must be also."

He was right, Tom realized. The man thrived on work, pushing himself constantly, and those around him followed the same pattern. Like it or not, Chen had explained that Mr. Loomis was most important to him and it was necessary they stay close. Tom had done just that and he now realized that he was hungry, just as Chen had said, and he was also very tired.

The hatch to the pilot's cabin opened, and the man gestured to Admiral Chen to put on his headset. Chen did so and Tom saw his face light up. At the same time, the helicopter banked to one side, the angle increasing so they could easily look down. Chen had poked him, pointing out the window to the ocean below. Dusk was coming quickly and it was difficult to pick out anything on the gray, dark water.

And then he saw what Chen was after, at the same time the Admiral did. "Oh, yes," Chen exclaimed as the burning vessel came into view. The helicopter had dropped much lower and they could see a ship burning furiously, men leaping into the icy water. Even as the flames grew, flashes could be seen on the deck from new explosions. And then the cause of the damage came into view, another destroyer, smaller and also burning.

Chen pointed at the blazing wreck. "Russians," he yelled. "A Russian destroyer, torpedoed about an hour ago. She was dead in the water when our frigate down there picked up a message from our submarine. The submarine was out of torpedoes and needed help and luckily that ship happened to be nearby."

The Chinese frigate, which had apparently been hit before the Russian became engulfed in flames was now pouring everything it had into the other ship. No matter where Russian sailors tried to hide, the searing, wind-whipped flames or the Chinese guns would find them.

"You see," Chen shouted above the noise of the engine and rotors, "we are not afraid of the Russians."

Tom said nothing, his eyes riveted on the burning vessel. The reality of people burning together with their ship horrified him.

"We're not afraid of the Russians," Chen repeated, a bit more softly and almost to himself. "We're not afraid," he said again, as the stern of the Soviet ship exploded, tearing itself and its sailors to shreds.

Admiral Magnuson knew he'd have to take the time to use his private bathroom shortly. He'd been going non-stop for almost forty-eight hours and he could smell himself. He could feel it, too, that grimy closeness that came when the same clothes covered the same skin for too long. And, there was no doubt in his mind that the meeting with the President had contributed to his general, unpleasant aroma.

As ready as he was to defend his earlier warning via Benjamin, state his case bluntly, then leave little room for the President beyond the obvious solutions, Magnuson was a bit overwhelmed by the proceedings. The man sitting behind the desk in the Oval Office, regardless of personal feelings, is the single most powerful man on earth. The office and its responsibilities are awesome. The Admiral saw this etched on the President's face as he entered the room. This sensitive and good man radiated profound disappointment, perhaps even bitterness, Magnuson thought. He wanted so badly to trust his enemy. Yet there was also a determination and a perception of power in the man's words and his tone that silenced Magnuson's headstrong intent until he was requested to speak.

Magnuson was comfortable with the Joint Chiefs of Staff. They knew his work. There was mutual respect. The President's staff and cabinet members paid little attention to this Rear Admiral from Naval Intelligence. Their days were spent rubbing elbows with the most powerful military and civilian authorities in the world. They saw only the man who had enraged the President a few months back, and he was nothing, just a junior flag officer.

Magnuson offered his carefully prepared folder to the President before the meeting commenced. The man looked at it briefly, then placed it to one side of his desk. The President conducted the meeting calmly and with barely a hint of concern until he brought up the declaration of war by the People's Republic of China. He was livid and pointedly asked Admiral Magnuson for his thoughts.

"My understanding is that the declaration is provisional in nature, sir . . . that is, it was delivered with the understanding that it would be acted upon depending upon the mission of our Seventh Fleet." Magnuson knew exactly what it meant.

"Nothing is provisional about war with a country that possesses nuclear weapons! It is my opinion this is a subtle form of blackmail, an effort to coerce us into joining the People's Republic in a direct attack on Soviet forces."

"If I may, sir, the Russian Pacific Fleet is right now engaging the Chinese Navy all along her coastline, and Admiral Maslov is himself leading a major strike force south to finish off the remnants of their navy."

"My initial reaction, Admiral, would be to avoid conflict and let the two countries settle their differences if at all possible." The President's eyes narrowed as he searched the room for another opinion.

"That would be ideal, sir." The Chairman of the Joint Chiefs leaned forward. "However, it is our opinion that the Chinese defenses will quickly collapse. You said yourself, yesterday, that we are all agreed we cannot let the country or its resources fall into Soviet hands. While the Japanese have agreed to assist us because of the economic implications if the Russians succeed, their reasons for taking aggressive action for the first time in forty years are even more complex. We are in a position requiring the utmost in diplomacy with each country involved. Our own use of arms must be either limited or totally negligible to avoid conflict with the Soviet Union. As much as you disagree with the methods of Admiral Magnuson here, we do owe him the courtesy of reviewing the situation from his vantage point."

The President grimaced. He had never been disposed toward intelligence types, and was even less so toward this admiral who had apparently acted contrary to his orders. "Admiral Magnuson," he began with a grace he somehow found within, "perhaps your indiscreet methods could prove of some value."

This was the moment then. This was what the last six months had been about. Without explaining how he had created the unique agents he intended to use, Magnuson outlined what he felt was necessary to assist the Chinese, what would have to be done to halt Maslov's fleet yet maintain a very tenuous peace, and what he considered acceptable casualties to units of the Seventh Fleet. "There is one final item I have been unable to press upon anyone in this room with success. The repositioning of Soviet missile subs off our West Coast is closely involved with the action against the Chinese. It may seem illogical to all of you when you see the Russians facing the Chinese and Japanese on one front, with our own Seventh Fleet behind them. Yet their plan all along has been to hold the Seventh Fleet hostage and use the threat of missile attack as a means of bringing us to the bargaining table."

Magnuson looked directly at the President, disappointed that the man's expression hadn't changed. "We must initiate an action that will convince them we have no intention of being held hostage, or boxed into the Sea of Japan, or whatever their final plan may actually be. My belief is that they will station submarines on either side of the Strait of Tsushima, a perfect place to avoid detection and a superb location to bring us up short. If Maslov can accomplish what he intends against the Chinese, his next objective would be to wheel and face us. It's superb strategy from their point of view and we might possibly be sitting there with our pants around our ankles."

"A picture of doom, Admiral." The President may have been a man of peace, but Magnuson found him the most formidable figure he'd ever faced. He remained expressionless and calm, thriving on a crisis he refused to accept until the day before. "Just how are we going to surmount all these obstacles?"

"If you will allow that Admiral Pickett has no intention of being held hostage, and will coordinate his efforts directly with Washington, I believe my three agents can work with the Chinese."

"My understanding was four," remarked the President.

"We lost one in Vladivostok, early this morning."

"A man who had no intention of becoming involved?"

Magnuson nodded. "The incident will be detailed in my report on Seagull, sir." The President studied him unpleasantly for a moment.

The meeting continued for another half hour. Magnuson's only other contribution was to explain how the hotline might have to be used when Pickett came within torpedo range at Tsushima.

"Jim," Magnuson called as he readied himself for the shower, "could you get me a change of uniform, please. I can't stand myself any longer."

MacIntyre smiled. "Imagine how the President felt about you."

CHAPTER TWENTY

The soldiers were dressed in white, padded uniforms. They crouched inside the main entrance of the Palace of Sport. Their dark, oriental features were vaguely illuminated in the night by the flames consuming sections of Khabarovsk. Behind them, a medic tried vainly to stem the life flowing from the chest of one of their comrades. In the flickering light, the red contrasted with his white uniform and the snow drifting through one of the blasted walls.

The People's Liberation Army had captured the V. I. Lenin Sports Stadium in a dawn attack. Now they waited in silence, exhausted, as the artillery to their rear pounded the Soviet city. The temperature was well below zero. A howling Siberian wind, an invisible Russian ally for centuries, compounded their discomfort. The Chinese advance across their own border into the disputed territory left a trail of rigid, frozen bodies to compound the rubble produced by the planes and tanks and artillery.

A Russian veteran of the great sieges of World War Two surveying the ruins of Khabarovsk would have been reminded of the horror of more

than forty years before. The civilian population
that survived the initial bombing was gone, transported up the rail line to the town of Litovko.
Those unable to board the trains on time escaped
eastward into the frozen swamps to survive with
the peasants in the countryside. The less fortunate
froze to death in their carts, cast into lifeless snow-
covered statues.

The orders from Moscow had been clear—no retreat. Remain in position until you are ready to attack. The only direction the Red Army units could
move was forward. The children and grandchildren
of the survivors of Stalingrad and Moscow and
Leningrad now knew exactly what their parents
had faced before them. The enemy was different
but no less determined in their invasion. Mother
Russia must stand fast at any cost until new divisions could be transported over the sabotaged rail
lines.

An eerie whistling sound presaged the Soviet response to the Chinese artillery. The huge Soviet
shells vaulted across the Amur River in a precise,
concentrated barrage, smashing targets before the
invaders could shift their locations.

The Chinese huddling in the Palace of Sport
winced. Ear-shattering explosions bracketed their
hiding place. Frozen earth and shrapnel whipped
through the air above their heads. They saw or
heard other small units destroyed in a single burst
and they scratched frantically into the rock-hard
earth with their bayonets to escape the whistling
death.

Their captain shouted into his radio telephone,

relaying their fear to the command center in the rear, calling for tanks to support their move to another location. In the distance, he could see the line of Soviet T-72 tanks, outlined against the snow and flame, moving in ragged formation in his direction.

"You can't stop them with those shells," he screamed into the mouthpiece. "If you do not use nuclear warheads, they will recapture this position in less than an hour."

Ten minutes, they told him. Ten minutes at least to get permission. Beijing was on the line, but such a decision could only come from the Ministry of Defense. No more than ten minutes. Be ready to counter-attack.

Ten minutes later there was still no answer. The Soviet shelling continued. The meager security of the Lenin Stadium was blown apart. The Chinese had never thought the Russians would be willing to destroy their revered sports complex. It was thought to be the ideal location to regroup. But, building by building, it was demolished by the Red Army itself, just as their fathers and grandfathers before them had been willing to raze their own cities. The shattered glass roof of the giant indoor swimming pool tore an entire company to shreds before they could escape the building. The Arena of Heroes was reduced to rubble in an instant.

And as the captain looked out the door, the progress of the Soviet tanks was interrupted by the concussion of a burst so close that he was tumbled backward across the room. When he rose to his knees, tasting the blood in his nose and mouth, he realized how lucky he had been. The two men who had been next to him now lay dead, their white uniforms torn and stained with dirt, their blood steaming in the cold air.

The captain crawled across to his radio. The command center answered immediately.

"The nuclear shells," he shouted frantically. "They are the only thing that will stop them. Have you heard from Beijing?"

"Yes," came the reply. "They said 'no' . . . absolutely no." The voice at the command post hesitated for a moment, knowing the despair of their comrade at the Palace of Sport. "That comes from General Yeh himself. He said 'no'. He said it would bring more danger to us than it was worth."

The captain clenched his teeth, his hands shaking. "We cannot hold out. We must retreat . . . regroup until we have tank support."

"No," came the answer. "No retreat. You are ordered to attack in five minutes. The support will be right behind you. We must have Khabarovsk."

The Captain's voice became suddenly calm as the barrage halted for a moment. "You cannot have it until you can stop those Soviet tanks," he said succinctly. "They will not let us have it."

"Attack," came the answer.

The commanding officer of the Chinese submarine LUTING raised his periscope for another bearing. His sixth sense was unerring. The Soviet cruiser reappeared in his crosshairs, her big guns outlined against the clear night sky by a three-quarter moon. He wheeled gracefully on his toes, first to the left, then to the right. His initial count had been correct. There were six other ships in company with the cruiser. He stepped back, allowing the periscope to hiss down into its well.

Returning to the chart table, he flicked on the red reading light. The identification book was still open to the same page. There was no doubt in his mind now. That cruiser was ZHDANOV, a command cruiser. She was carrying a senior admiral when she departed Cam Ranh Bay. The sub captain used the message from the intelligence unit at Fleet Headquarters in Zhanjiang to mark the page. That message labelled ZHDANOV a primary target.

LUTING had not moved from her present position in more than an hour. It wasn't easy to maintain keel depth or stability with that current, but she did it with a minimum of machinery noise. All along the Chinese coast, from the Yellow Sea in the north to the sub's location in the South China Sea northwest of Hainan Island, the water is shallow. Often, the five hundred foot depth line is at least a hundred and fifty miles from shore. The fact that a submarine often cannot dive deep to avoid attack in these shallow waters is offset by the fact that they can also hide from surface ships more readily.

The captain of LUTING knew the water between Zhanjiang and Hong Kong as he once knew the countryside around his village. When he received the message about ZHDANOV and her screen, he knew exactly where he would hide. He prepared the crew that evening, explained what he planned to do, how they would make their attack, that the cruiser was the most important target. If they had time, they would try to sink other ships, but they had to be sure the cruiser was sunk. His men smiled sadly and nodded their agreement. It was their duty. This would be the culmination of everything their political officers had taught them the past month. They would sacrifice just as their forefathers had sacrificed at the Bridge of Luting. There was no reason to die unless the country could be saved, and now was their opportunity to contribute unselfishly.

The captain pressed the button and the periscope hissed again as it rose until his face was glued to the eyepiece. The target was exactly where it had been plotted. The Russians were following a simple zig-zag pattern, a predictable one, and his solution had been correct. A few minor maneuvers were all that was needed to place LUTING in position.

"All ahead one third," he called out softly. LUTING's hull shuddered in concert with the muffled sound of the electric motors. The little submarine came to life. "Left standard rudder." He checked off the course in his mind. "Come to course zero nine five."

He gave the orders quietly. His crew knew each step. There was no need for noise. Four torpedoes were fired from the forward tubes, each one targeted for ZHDANOV. There had to be at least three hits to sink the giant cruiser.

There was no purpose in diving since there would be no room to escape the cruiser's escorts. Instead, the captain watched through his periscope. He rotated it to either side to see what the destroyers were doing. Even before he saw their bows turning toward him, the telltale wash at their sterns indicated that LUTING had been detected. He turned back to the cruiser.

The first torpedo struck behind the after stack, a cloud of spray rising into the air followed by a sheet of flame. Hopefully a fuel bunker. A second hit under the bridge, the explosion sending water over the main mast. He thought she might be slowing down and hoped that at least one of the other two torpedoes was successful. As the shock wave from the first hit rolled through the submarine, the captain was rewarded by another explosion near the bow. Then a second explosion came almost on top of that one, right under the forward gun turret. He couldn't be sure if it was the fourth torpedo or a magazine that had exploded. But, as the spray settled, the absence of the forward turret confirmed that the front quarter of ZHDANOV had broken off. She was lost.

"Right Full rudder," he called. "All engines ahead full." He kept his eye on the destroyers bearing down on him. There was little to be gained by diving immediately.

He might be able to hit one more ship.

He positioned LUTING for firing the aft tubes and waited, sure one of the first destroyers would be right in his path. He delayed until there was no doubt. The Russian ship was so close. Then he fired both after tubes.

It was difficult to keep the periscope on his target. Four destroyers were firing their guns and the surface around him had erupted into a froth. He could feel the near hits as the sub bucked and tossed to the exploding shells.

Then he saw what he had been waiting for. The target destroyer literally stopped in the water as both torpedoes struck. For a moment, the Russian ship was engulfed in spray from the explosion. That was quickly replaced with a sheet of flame. The captain's last impression was of the ship breaking into two distinct pieces, all within fifteen or twenty seconds. Then a shell hit the periscope, the concussion knocking the captain backward into the chart table. He never knew that seconds later the first of the torpedoes fired by the destroyers struck LUTING. But he had known before the action began that his crew was as willing as he was to accept their fate. ZHDANOV had been sunk. They knew that before they died and they had radioed that message. The destroyer was a bonus.

Fleet Headquarters had never reserved a space for their return to the Zhanjiang piers. Their assigned mission had been accomplished.

On a chart of the East China Sea, one could draw a line due west from the tip of South Korea to the Chinese mainland, a distance of about three hundred miles. It would touch the Chinese shoreline just below Qingdao, a major shipping port and home of the Navy's East Sea Fleet. Above that line is the Yellow Sea, through which much of China's industrial might must pass. To the northwest, it becomes the Gulf of Pohai, one of the country's newest and richest offshore oil fields. The land to the north, Manchuria, was once Russian.

The Defense Ministry determined that these waters must be protected from Soviet incursion at all costs. Due to the lack of large warships, Admiral Chen recommended that the first step should be mining. In the preceding weeks, the waters along the line had been seeded by air with the limited supply of mines that existed. There were not enough, and it was decided to protect the coastline first, then seed the Yellow Sea, allowing access lanes for merchant shipping. This would also allow the East Sea Fleet to patrol open areas more effectively. Their responsibilities were twofold; control the access lanes and sink any Soviet vessels damaged by mines.

Admiral Chen ensured that as many fast patrol boats as possible were transferred to Qingdao. The Commander of the East Sea Fleet then assigned them to missions according to range and weapon capabilities. He sent the Osa class patrol boats the farthest. They were equipped with both surface missiles and small bore guns.

On the evening before Maslov's fleet was to pass through Tsushima, a division of four Soviet Krivak class destroyers unknowingly headed across the sparsely seeded mine field. Their assignment was to close the port of Qingdao in conjunction with submarines already on station. They had been spotted by a patrol plane at sunset. Before they could bring it down their position had been fixed.

The squadron of eight Osas responsible for that sector raced to intercept at almost forty knots. The sea was reasonably calm and a three-quarter moon improved vision to almost twelve miles. Their radar picked up the Russians at an even greater distance. But before their first missiles were fired, a brilliant orange explosion lit the skies.

One of the destroyers detonated a mine. The Soviet division commander ordered one of his ships to assist the burning vessel while the other two cut off the Chinese boats. His intelligence reports indicated they would likely be Osas and their missiles concerned him. He must maneuver to make it difficult for them to fire. The Osas were old and it was reported their success ratio with missiles was low. His guns had longer range than theirs.

The Chinese commander knew as well as the Russian that it would be foolish to use his missiles early. The odds would be poor. Instead, he extended his formation, spreading the boats away from each other. They zigzagged to make shooting difficult for the Russian gunners. Two boats on each end were to swing around behind the destroyers. The four in the middle would charge straight ahead.

At a range of four miles, the Osas each fired one missile. Within seconds of detecting the missiles, the destroyers opened fire on the little boats. It was too great a distance for the Osas' poorly designed missiles and all but one fell short of their mark. This last dove needlessly into the already burning ship, its heat-seeking nose attracted to the raging fire.

Soviet 76mm shells were the first to meet with success. Aimed by fire control radar, miniature computers kept the guns targeted on the zigzagging boats. Sixty rounds a minute poured from each Russian gun. The first boat was torn apart by a dozen shells, hitting within seconds of each other.

The three Osas fired their second missiles. This time the range was close enough—one direct hit. The Chinese commander ordered the successful boat to fire its last two missiles at the same target, then follow them in.

A third missile hit the Russian ship. The fourth missed. The destroyer was damaged and flames were evident yet she continued firing her after mounts. As the little boat was racing in, trying to get under the larger Soviet guns for the kill, she disappeared in a sheet of flame.

A second boat followed her in. But before her last missile could be fired, Soviet shells bracketed her. The explosion of her remaining missile warhead tore the stern off the little boat. Russian gunners ripped apart the forward section.

The last Osa was more successful. Her third missile silenced the stern mounts on the damaged Russian ship. Three Chinese boats had been sunk. Two destroyers were burning.

But the Russian gunners, with the advantage of their computer-controlled guns, had already engaged the circling boats. Another was blown apart before firing any of her remaining missiles. Another missile, drawn to the heat of the first burning destroyer, hit her forward magazine. With a mighty explosion, the forward section of the Russian ship lifted almost clear of the water. The illumination from the raging flames outlined the bow as it broke away from the hull. Then, as if a hand was pushing from underneath, her stern came up out of the water, her rudder and props showing, and she slid forward under the surface with the remainder of her crew.

A second Chinese boat was found by the Soviet guns. Her two remaining missiles exploded under the Russian shelling. The boat disappeared.

The three remaining Osas charged directly at the destroyers, their final missiles fired blindly and ineffectively as shells ripped into their hulls. The little boats sped in under the Russian guns passing down the sides of the ships spraying their little 25mm guns into the destroyers.

But too soon they were away from the safety of the Russian hulls. Once again they were picked up by the fire control radar. Only one of them was able to make another pass before it, too, was torn apart.

In a few minutes the squadron of Osas had vanished along with more than two hundred Chinese sailors. Of the four Krivak destroyers, one was sunk, and one was burning and unable to proceed. The other two picked up survivors before proceeding toward Qingdao.

The Russians had lost more by far.

Krulev stood politely just inside the door of Maslov's sea cabin. The Admiral studied the messages again and again in disbelief. He ran his fingers over his bald scalp, his busy brows knit in anger.

Maslov, his ill temper controlled, finally looked up at Krulev, gesturing for him to sit down. "These Chinese play rough, eh?" he said, slapping the messages against his other hand. He exhaled slowly through his teeth. "I'm glad their Navy is so small. They could make trouble if they were any bigger."

"They're doing pretty well with what they have," Krulev answered.

"Yes . . . yes. But look at how they're doing it. Suicide tactics. Pretty soon, there won't be any of them left to fight."

"You are correct, Valery . . . to a certain point." Krulev hesitated. He had no intention of angering the Admiral, nor was he ready to start an argument. "But I think we must establish an acceptable loss ratio . . . set a point at which this is no longer worth the sacrifice."

"You think we have that much of a problem?" Maslov asked truculently.

"Not exactly, Valery. The question is one of balance. There's no doubt we can handle the Chinese regardless of their tactics. There's only so many of them. But, even if the Chinese are still uncertain, we know that the Seventh Fleet has no intention of supporting us. As a matter of fact, we don't know whether the U.S. ships might not fire on us at a certain point." He leaned forward. "In my mind that's unacceptable. There's nothing to be gained by fighting with the Americans."

Maslov looked up from the messages he'd been shuffling in his hands. Krulev had stopped. "Go on."

"We must make a decision in the next two hours. At that time, we will be within missile range of Admiral Chen's group. It has been confirmed that he's aboard one of their ships."

"Have the others joined up with them?"

"Three frigates, all small and fast, with guided missiles. But that's still only seven ships. We know there are some submarines hovering off Cheju-Do and the Japanese islands, but our anti-submarine forces are sweeping through there now. We should get most of them before Chen's surface ships can attack. But the fact remains that a squadron of Japanese destroyers are coming up behind Chen. Intelligence indicates they have formally agreed to support China and that makes it a bit more formidable."

Admiral Maslov said nothing. He had not taken his eyes from Krulev's and he knew the man spoke accurately. And the capital ships—ZHDANOV, IVAN ROGOV, more destroyers than he could believe, and the submarines that had not reported back . . . even a nuclear boat! He thought back to the months of planning, the security efforts, the realization that the best approach was a quick, decisive one, a surprise. But he had acknowledged weeks ago that total surprise was lost. He knew that General Yuan's Security Group 8341 had done an excellent job. Even the Americans had taken a different approach by introducing non-professionals. And the Chinese had taken the offensive by attacking first. Krulev was right. It was a matter of balance, perhaps a pinch of desire. He accepted in his own mind that what would happen in the next two hours was critical.

The sky was coloring to the east. It would be another clear day.

Tom Loomis and Admiral Chen had arrived over XIAN in the middle of the night. Chen was the first to be lowered to the stern of the bucking ship, her crewmen easily catching him as he dangled at the end of the helicopter's cable.

Loomis' arrival was slightly different. He had been lowered from a helicopter before, but he'd also been in his early twenties and still fearless. Chen, the one man who spoke English, had immediately been hustled to the bridge. Tom's bag had already been successfully lowered into the arms of a crewman.

XIAN's rear deck was illuminated for the transfer and the helicopter pilot had his spotlight on Loomis as he descended. Looking down at the deck, which would heave up at him then suddenly drop away, he caught sight of the after gun mount, its barrel waving menacingly at him as he drew near the deck. At about six feet, a sailor leaped up and successfully caught his legs. But the man was too short. His own feet left the deck. Now the two of them were swinging and the sling dug sharply into Tom's back and armpits. The sailor was grabbed by another, and for a moment Loomis thought they were secure as the deck came up to meet them. But the first sailor, as his feet touched the deck, let go and once again Tom found himself swinging, this time toward the gun mount, its barrel a formidable club.

Loomis decided this was enough. Somehow he'd take care of himself. He raised his arms straight up, in an attempt to slide from the sling, and began to wiggle free. But as he did, the deck fell off to one side. He was slipping from the sling at the same time the ship was slipping away from him. The helicopter's light reflected green water just to his right. Frantically, he tried to bring his arms back down, but the weight of his own body was too much. One arm slipped free. With the other, he hooked his arm through the sling, reaching for his wrist with the free hand in a death grip. When he looked down again, he was swinging over open water, the deck of the ship a few feet to his left.

The sailors on deck were obviously upset. Some made hand signals to the helicopter while the others shouted instructions to Tom in Chinese. Now the deck began to roll back under him. His best chance was to let go as soon as it was well underneath. The decision made, he loosened his grip in anticipation just at the time the deck dropped away. The two or three foot drop became five or six feet. His hands could no longer hold on. He felt himself falling, waiting for the sharp thud as he hit the metal deck that was now rearing back at him.

But it never happened. A sailor, larger than the others, took matters into his own hands. Deciding that the American might do something else foolish, he timed the heave of the deck perfectly, tackling Loomis in mid-air. For a man unfamiliar with American football, the tackle was perfect. Loomis felt the impact of a shoulder in his midsection. Together they slid across the wet deck, crumpling in a heap by the depth charge rack. The babble of voices was lost in the roar of the helicopter as it lifted into the night. Untangling himself, Tom reached over and shook the sailor's hand while the others cheered. He had been welcomed to the Chinese Navy.

XIAN was half the size of TEXAS. Built more slimly than the American cruiser, she was only a third the weight and her seakeeping ability reminded Loomis of a paper cup. XIAN was racing at high speed toward a point on the chart roughly between the island of Cheju-Do and the Japanese city of Sasebo. A ship of that construction routinely buries its bow riding over ocean swells at high speed. XIAN would also roll fifteen or twenty degrees to one side, hold that angle momentarily, then gradually roll the same amount in the other direction.

Loomis hadn't found the sea a comfortable place to live twenty years before and it was less so now. It brought back memories of his early days as an ensign when the first day at sea of each cruise alternated between a bucket and his bunk. Forcing himself to stand his watches at sea, he would gradually gain his sea legs. By the end of the second day, he would have made an uneasy truce with the ocean, broken only by storms which would send him miserably back to his bunk. It was part of navy life he had not missed from the day he left his ship for the last time.

Loomis attempted to sleep, at the same time convincing himself that there was no time for seasickness. When a messenger pulled back the curtains around his bunk and pointed toward the forward part of the ship, he was mentally ready. Physically, he had his doubts. As he stumbled up the ladder to the bridge, following the messenger, he put out his hand for support. The sharp pain reminded him that he'd landed on his wrist during his arrival aboard ship.

His eyes were still unaccustomed to the darkness as he entered the pilot house. The glow from electronic instruments furnished the only indication of where he was. Being a small ship, XIAN had no space for an Admiral. Chen had positioned himself to one side of the pilot house.

A voice from that corner broke the silence. "Mr. Loomis, I hope you are feeling better."

"I'll get by, Admiral. Just need time to get my bearings."

Chen came across to grasp his arm. "Come over here. You'll do just as well in this corner with me." The Admiral thrust a life jacket at him.

Off the starboard wing of the bridge, Tom could see color on the horizon. He looked at his watch. Six thirty. It must be close to sunrise. He hadn't expected to be left alone for so long.

"That is the sun you are going to see shortly," Chen said. "We are getting close to our destination. Soon we will be within their missile range," he added pleasantly.

"We should be already," Loomis responded.

He felt Chen looking closely at him. "Technically, yes. But we are close enough to land, and the Japanese ships are near enough to us, that I doubt the Russians will fire until they are more sure of their targets. As a matter of fact, they may be waiting for enough light so that their aircraft can spot us correctly. I'm sure Admiral Maslov would hate to hit a friendly vessel. He'd want the Japanese to fire first."

"No doubt." As Loomis' eyes adjusted to the darkness, he became aware of the pilot house and the people in it. In the corner he and Chen occupied, it was obvious the ship's company had made some special preparations. Radio/telephone units were newly installed. A radar scope glowed green in front of them. Looking back out to his right, he saw that the sky was turning pink, clouds now reflecting rays from the sun still below the horizon.

Chen tapped a telephone unit with a large "B" inscribed on it. "That is the frequency connecting you with Beijing. I have even had an English 'B' drawn on it to ensure there is no mistake. Your friend, Mr. Goodrich, is on the other end." Loomis looked at the Admiral curiously. "Go ahead, call him."

Loomis lifted the instrument, studying it. It was no different from those he had used twenty years before. He placed the receiver to his ear. There was static. He keyed the speaking button and the static disappeared instantly.

"Believe me, it works. I've already used it. Try it."

Loomis spoke into the transmitter, calling Goodrich's name. He had forgotten anything he had ever learned about radio/telephone procedure. Immediately Ben's voice came back to him, just as Chen had said.

Admiral Chen raised his hand to attract Tom's attention. "Ask if they have established communications with your Seventh Fleet . . . Admiral Pickett."

Goodrich had. Chen asked for the frequency. It was a low one for long ranges. The only radio capable of that distance aboard XIAN was the same one they were using to Beijing.

"You begin to see your own importance, Mr. Loomis?" Chen smiled.

The sun lifted out of the water, its orange orb brightening until they could no longer look directly at it. Above, the Soviet aircraft that Chen had expected circled at high altitude, relaying tactical data to Maslov. The Chinese planes vectored to intercept them had no chance against the sophisticated MIG fighters.

At approximately the same time the first Soviet ship appeared on XIAN's radar screen, thirty miles distant, the bow of an adjacent destroyer was suddenly and without warning enveloped in a sheet of flame.

"Missiles," hissed Chen as he spouted orders to the men around him. XIAN veered to starboard. The other ships also took evasive action. Another was hit amidships, her after stack completely gone. Just as XIAN swung back in the opposite direction, an explosion close aboard engulfed the ship in spray.

Near miss! Loomis could feel the shock wave followed by the whine of shrapnel. When they emerged into the bright sunlight, XIAN heeling in a tight, high speed turn, all ships were firing missiles as they scurried in separate directions.

But there could be no doubting their purpose. Their base course was still directly in the path of the Russian fleet.

Admiral Magnuson, along with MacIntyre and the entire staff, were transferred to the White House Situation Room. The Admiral disputed the idea when called by the Chairman of the Joint Chiefs. The system at his own office was more than adequate, he explained, and it ran like a well-oiled machine—besides, he was only an instant away, what with modern communications. The request then became an order and within an hour his well-oiled machine occupied a corner of the Situation Room. The President's Chief of Staff explained, "Once the President is convinced about an individual or a concept, he wants access at his fingertips."

There were hourly briefings for the President,

limited to three minutes. He would enter the room quickly, nodding to military people he was familiar with on a day-to-day basis. Occupying the comfortable chair provided specifically for him, he would ask a question or two, then depart. At one point, he strode over to Magnuson, disengaging himself from the advisors hovering at his elbow. "You have more than a passing interest in China, Admiral."

Magnuson came to his feet. "Yes, sir. I am very attached to the country and I've met some fine people there."

"In high places, I understand. Officially?"

"Unofficially, sir."

"On your own?"

"No, sir."

"You were acting under orders?"

"Yes, sir." Magnuson hesitated, then blurted, "From President Kennedy, sir."

"I see. I had the opportunity to read some interesting papers from that administration a few hours ago." He smiled at Magnuson for the first time, almost as if they were discussing old times. "It just about took the Freedom of Information Act even for me to find them. Your name was most apparent. For a young lieutenant, you met some very powerful men there."

"Yes, sir, but it didn't succeed."

"You are still in touch with these people, you say."

"The ones that are still alive. They've assisted me with my agents."

"The man Darby, in Shanghai, how did you find

him? He seems to be the key to your contacts."

"Through British Intelligence. Whitehall understood the necessity early on to recognize the People's Republic, if for no other reason than economics. There were Englishmen then, John Proud, Norman Watts, Jack Darby, who also realized that and made the early efforts. Watts once saved Chou in Shanghai as Chiang Kai-shek's men were closing the trap. British Intelligence put me in touch with Darby. He's the only one still there."

"Could I," the emphasis was on the 'I', "trust these people?"

Should I be honest, Magnuson wondered? "If I told them you and I were working hand-in-hand . . . yes, sir."

"Fine. We're working together, Admiral Magnuson." The President cocked his head to one side, a wry grin wrinkling his face. "It appears I am at your disposal." Again, the emphasis was on 'I' but this time the man's tone was decidedly friendly. "What must I do?"

"Nothing, sir. I hope most of it is already done. The first part depends mostly on the Chinese and Japanese. If, for some reason, they can change Admiral Maslov's mind, then the rest is up to Admiral Pickett and how he handles the Soviet Fleet. Technically, he is no longer hostage in Vladivostok's waters. But as long as Maslov can turn on him, and as long as he steams directly into Tsushima and those Russian subs, he's still hostage . . . so we're still susceptible. That's when you and the Premier will likely want to talk. It is still quite possible to see a deadlock!"

From his flag plot aboard KIROV, Admiral Maslov savored the roar of rocket motors as missiles departed their launchers. Now was the time to see how much the Chinese could take.

"Excuse me, Valery . . ." As Maslov watched the display terminal before him, he felt a tapping on his shoulder. "Admiral . . ." He looked up into Krulev's troubled face.

"The American ships have increased speed. They're closing our destroyers rapidly."

"Well, do what I told you. Start with those torpedoes set for deep running. See if that scares them away . . . and alert the submarines near the coast. Have them ready to fire . . . but don't do it until I give the order!"

Maslov rose from his chair and stretched. He'd never been comfortable in these dark rooms. It was time for a stroll. He went down the ladder to KIROV's pilot house, stepping out on to one of the bridge wings. He was greeted with a glorious sight. The formation was outlined by a brilliant sun, the sky clear in every direction. The sea sparkled around his ships, whitecaps reflecting the sun's rays. Starkly profiled against the horizon, his missile ships were firing toward unseen targets.

Unlike the old days, few sailors could be seen above deck on the large ships. The missile launchers went about their business mechanically, electronically, inhumanly. They fired, the exhaust cloud from the rocket engine sweeping back over the ship. The launcher would return to its original position, the launcher arms automatically repositioned over the magazine. New missiles would slide out, attaching to the launcher rail. The computer's orders would drive the launcher to the proper direction, the arms would elevate, and the missile would ignite, disappearing at tremendous speed.

To Maslov, this was an unromantic way of fighting a war. There was no longer the crash of the big guns, the gut-wrenching joy of the flash of hits on the target, flames erupting from blown magazines or ruptured fuel tanks. He longed to see Chen's ships.

An explosion on one of his cruisers caught his eye. He noticed the flash before he heard the sound, saw the bridge begin to disintegrate before the smoke and flame erupted. His mouth dropped open as the vessel veered off course, out of control, flame spreading astern. It was what he longed to see happening to the enemy. Yet it was one of his own ships. He still had not seen the Chinese.

Perhaps, after all, it was better inside the darkened flag plot, sitting before the three dimensional display that would show him visually what was taking place. As Maslov climbed the ladder from the pilot house, the door to flag plot flew open. Krulev stared down at him.

"I wasn't informed where you'd gone, Admiral."

"To see the sights," Maslov answered matter of factly. "There was little to see."

"Torpedoes were fired, exactly as you ordered."

"Well?"

"The Americans never slowed down. They are closing us. Our squadron commander has asked permission to fire . . . he's also picked up his own speed to maintain proper distance from the Americans."

"The fool. He's just drawing them closer."

"He requested permission to use his missiles, Admiral."

"No!" Maslov's voice exploded from him. "That's what Pickett's waiting for. With the firepower he's got there, that squadron would vanish in minutes." He looked up at Krulev, his foot still resting on the top step of the ladder. "Tell him to cut his own speed. This time, set a torpedo for normal run. They must have known the first ones wouldn't be set to hit. Let's see what Admiral Pickett thinks about that."

Another explosion nearer KIROV told Admiral Maslov that the Chinese were by no means running away.

Admiral Pickett had little patience with the display units in flag plot and he hated pushing buttons even more. They could tell him locations, numbers of ships and aircraft, friendly and unfriendly, distances, missiles, any number of vital facts. But they couldn't answer his questions as fast as he wanted them answered.

"o, goddamn it, they weren't trying to hit us," he corrected one of his aides. "The torpedoes were purposely set to run deep. But it's possible the next ones will be set for hull depth. Now, goddamn it, what are those Russians doing now that our screen's catching up with them?"

"They originally increased speed, Admiral. As a matter of fact, they were matching our own. But my last report indicates they've slowed down. We're going to run right up their backs pretty soon."

"That's pretty unlikely, I'd say," responded Pickett sarcastically. "But they're going to do something to try to slow us down . . . ."

Before he could finish, "Soviet ships firing on our destroyers."

"Missile or torpedo?" Pickett asked.

"A torpedo, Admiral . . . funny, only one ship, one torpedo."

Pickett stood up as if he were in the room with his squadron commander. "Now, I want to make it clear that we're going to do the same thing. Just one ship . . . one torpedo. All we want to do is answer him." He searched the darkened room for Royal. "See, what'd I tell you? Maslov's getting touchy. He still won't try any rough stuff on us. Call Beijing. Tell them what we're doing." Pickett was impatient. "See what's happening down south with their own ships and the Japanese. And, Jack . . . we're in a great place for a submarine attack. Intelligence says the Russians could have some attack subs just huddling on the bottom waiting for this carrier to hit the narrowest passage and that could be it. Have Goodrich ask his friends if they know of any Russian submarines in this area the last twelve hours. They've got to at least have intelligence in South Korea who might have warned them of sub activity."

A few moments later, it was Pickett's aide, Knowlton, calling to Pickett. "Squadron Commander of those destroyers reports a direct hit on one of the Soviet cans, sir. One's on fire now . . . and our frigate MORRISON has taken a torpedo, too . . . a pretty bad hit."

"Okay . . . okay." He whirled to Royal. "Now you get back on that radio, and you tell your friend there just what's happening. We are engaging Soviet destroyers and Americans are getting killed out here defending China! And, damn it, ask them again about those submarines around here."

Royal's instant reply was almost an echo to Pickett. "Beijing replies Korean gunboats have reported unidentified submarine activity around their coastline. But, for some reason, it died out about midnight."

"That's because they've been hovering near the bottom." Pickett called for Knowlton. "Get some of those frigates over near the shoreline superfast. And make sure they have their helicopters in the air, too. Tell them there's absolutely no doubt in my mind there's submarines down there and I won't accept any negative reports. And do the same around the Japanese islands. If they're on one side of the strait, they're probably on the other side, too."

Pickett looked around the dimly lit space. "Royal," he bellowed. "Royal. Where the hell are you?"

"Right here, sir." He'd been looking over

Pickett's shoulder at the displays.

"Find out what's happening down south with Chen's mob."

When the President learned that the frigate SAMUEL ELIOT MORRISON had been torpedoed, he remained in his comfortable chair. He waved a finger at his Chief of Staff. "We're staying. That spook admiral seems to have hit it right on the nose."

Not more than five minutes later, a coded Soviet message was intercepted which stated simply, "Delta minus two." It was easy to determine the addressees—all Soviet guided missile submarines. Within another five minutes, Hawaii reported movement from each of the Soviet missile subs assigned to new stations off the Pacific coast.

As Magnuson approached the President, the man turned in his direction. They were anticipating each other.

"Mr. President, I think that's the final signal concerning Delta, whatever that meant originally. Their firing position was apparently given to the sub captains before they left Petropavlovsk. The new station assignments we intercepted were apparently never the final ones. Delta minus two must mean that they have two hours to reach that final position. It must have been predicated on when Maslov's force anticipated a wheeling movement to halt Pickett."

"What do you recommend, Admiral?"

"It would help if you had access to the hotline to

the Premier from here if possible, sir. A lot depends on the next hour . . . whether or not the Chinese ships are destroyed . . . whether the Russians might decide they've had too much . . . whether Pickett is able to neutralize those Soviet subs on either side of Tsushima. There's a lot of ifs. We'll know when it's time to use that phone."

"Would they fire missiles beforehand?"

"About as much chance of our subs firing Trident missiles without your permission, sir. They have to have us by the balls, if you will, and that means threatening Pickett's force. If they can't control the scene there, the Premier will never give the order for those missiles." Magnuson looked into the President's eyes. "They don't want to fire those missiles, sir. It will be up to you to give them a reason not to."

A thought passed briefly through each man's mind. They were beginning to like each other.

There was no air conditioning in the Situation Room under PLA Headquarters in Beijing. While the chill, dusty winds from the Gobi Desert howled outside, the interior air had become warm and fetid. Too many people and cigarettes contributed to an increasingly unpleasant odor.

After the first cigarette, Ben found himself lighting up again and again, each one tasting worse than the last. The events taking place around him were frightening. Mr. Li was more than willing to explain what was happening, both on land and sea. The battle for Khabarovsk was deadly. Neither side anticipated the staying power of the other.

When Ben realized the use of nuclear artillery shells on the border was under discussion, he became conscious of his heart. He'd never been as aware of its alarm potential. Now, the sound in his chest grew louder and louder. His breathing became shallow as he sensed the intensity of the argument. It couldn't happen like this . . . not a nuclear decision made in a basement in China. It was supposed to come in Washington or Moscow . . . power centers of the world. Ben held his breath.

"We are taking heavy losses at sea . . ." Mr. Li remarked to Ben as he removed himself from the debate, his voice drifting away tentatively. He was trying desperately to select the proper words.

"What is it you want," Ben asked.

"American help . . . of course. Complete help—not that minor shooting between destroyers. I don't think we can stop the Russians. We have always known that. But your Seventh Fleet could. And we've already provided them with intelligence on Soviet submarines," Chen added.

"They won't!"

"They must be in touch with Washington."

"Of course, but the President wouldn't interfere with someone else's war at this point. We've done that once too often. We'll protect ourselves, but we won't step into someone else's problems."

"Please call Admiral Pickett," Li said, his eyes saying more than his words. "I promised the other ministers I would try," he added, gesturing faintly over his shoulder. "If not, I think they'll turn to nuclear weapons out of desperation."

Ben did call Royal and the request was relayed through Admiral Pickett. As expected, the answer was negative, but the effort was enough for Li. Perhaps he could beg a bit more time.

"I have one other plan," Li explained to Ben. "Once again our Security Group has been successful in their own way. We believe they have broken enough of the Soviet code system to send false reports of heavy submarine losses." He shrugged. "It could be enough to tip Admiral Maslov's decision."

"I suppose it's a chance. It would have to be your last one."

"Quite definitely. We will wait until there is nothing left."

From the bridge of XIAN, the Soviet ships had come into view. Only one other Chinese vessel still remained. The Russian ships had suffered a number of hits also. Chen was pleased that they had inflicted as much damage as seemed evident. But there was still one objective he must try for— KIROV.

On their radar screen, he had picked out what he was sure was the giant nuclear cruiser, no longer well behind a double screen. Maslov, motivated by his desire to observe the conflict, had insisted that KIROV increase speed. She was now only a few miles behind her forward screen and vulnerable.

While his other ships had expended their missile load, Admiral Chen saved two of XIAN's on the slim hope that he might encounter Maslov's flagship. Now, maximum speed was ordered from XIAN's engineering plant, one last effort. Her chief engineer said they had already passed the maximum. Chen replied that his concern was not the return trip to Shanghai. It was to engage the enemy. If they were to survive, and speed was the only means of survival, then he wanted everything the little ship could give, and more. It was easier to be towed home than to be sunk. There were no further objections.

Krulev finally decided it was his duty to propose the idea—that they break off . . . that they give the signal for all units to return to base. Krulev came well prepared. He had messages concerning ship losses, and these casualties were impressive considering the relative superiority of the Soviet Pacific Fleet. The battle at Khabarovsk was a standoff, both armies dug into the frozen soil, neither willing to yield.

It was time to face realities, Krulev stated. It was then that the argument became heated.

When KIROV shuddered from the impact of XIAN's first missile, Maslov vaulted angrily from his chair. It was beyond his belief that KIROV could be attacked by any element of the Chinese Navy. Racing down the ladder, he bolted into the pilot house, only to find all but the essential bridge personnel on the port wing staring aft. Calming himself, he stepped outside to join them.

At first, he could see only smoke and flames. A

gust of wind momentarily blew the smoke to the opposite side, revealing heavy wreckage near KIROV's stern. The after gun turret, knocked completely from its mountings, was embedded in the helicopter elevator. Where the turret had once been, a huge hole was now visible, extending to the hull and down below the water line. As KIROV heaved in the gentle swells, water would flow into the hole, then back out again. Another gust drew a curtain of oily, black smoke over the scene.

The Commanding Officer of KIROV appeared at his side. "How could that have happened?" asked an astounded Maslov. "Their missiles are so ancient . . . so undependable."

The Captain pointed to an object off their port bow. Maslov strained, squinting to make it out. Perhaps six miles away, it was masked in smoke. He shook his head in question.

"A Chinese destroyer, Admiral. She came well ahead of the others. For some reason . . . who knows . . . she managed to evade us. No one can say why. But I can assure you that KIROV was her goal. She bypassed better targets."

"She has been destroyed?" Maslov asked.

The Captain brought his binoculars up to study the Chinese ship. "She's been hit a number of times . . . she's listing to starboard . . . can't last." He watched the destroyer closely. "No, she's not gone yet. There's still smoke coming from one of her stacks." He dropped the binoculars to his chest. "I assure you, Admiral, she cannot last. She has been hit very hard."

Maslov knew who was aboard the ship. "Give orders to close and torpedo her. I don't want to wait."

The Captain stepped into his pilot house to relay Maslov's order. If the Admiral wanted to waste torpedoes on a sinking ship, that was his privilege. He wasn't about to argue with him. "The closest destroyer is commencing a torpedo approach now, Admiral . . . just a few minutes."

Maslov stretched out his hands for the Captain's binoculars. "If you please," he said, accepting them and hanging the strap around his neck.

Steadying his elbows on the railing, he peered at the burning ship. He could make out a boat in the water nearby. Men were jumping over the side. Her starboard list was pronounced now and she probably had very little time to go. As he looked more closely, he noticed her bow was turning slowly in KIROV's direction. He dropped the glasses for an instant, then looked back again.

Yes, it was more obvious. The bow angle was less. She was turning. He saw the wash of propellers astern. The ship was using what little power was left to turn. As she did so, the smoke blew back from her hull.

What Maslov saw chilled him. It was a puff of smoke from one of her missile canisters. He couldn't see the missile leave the tube. That was impossible. But he had no doubt the destroyer had fired a missile. Guts, he thought. Guts. That was what the old Navy was like. You could see your enemy and they could see you. They knew they'd managed to hit KIROV. It must have satisfied

Chen. He knew Chen had to be aboard that ship. And now, he would watch the final torpedo sink the Chinese ship.

Maslov returned the binoculars to the Captain and went back into the pilot house to find a pair for himself. He chose the newest pair on the chart table. He set the focus on the nearest ship from the comfort of the pilot house before he went back to the cold bridge wing. Satisfied, he pushed open the hatch and stepped outside.

Maslov never raised the binoculars to his eyes. He sensed the blinding flash and the shock of the explosion.

Admiral Chen's last missile struck just below the pilot house.

When Krulev pried open the door of flag plot, KIROV's entire bridge and everyone that had been there no longer existed.

"Go on, tell them." Admiral Chen would not take his binoculars down. He was still savoring the effects of his last missile on KIROV. He knew the Soviet cruiser would not sink. That was too bad. But he had struck a blow against Maslov's flagship. What could be more indicative of the extremes the People's Republic would go to? Maslov must be assured they would not capitulate.

"Did you tell them?" Chen asked. Loomis shrugged his shoulders. "Why not?"

"The receiver," Loomis shouted above the din. "I can't hear a thing. I don't know whether I've still got them."

"Then keep repeating it. No . . . wait!" The excitement in his voice attracted Tom's attention. The Admiral's smile filled his grimy face, as he peered toward Maslov's flagship. "Just keep repeating that KIROV has turned north and that the other Russian ships have also."

The list had passed twenty degrees. XIAN had little time. There should have been nothing to celebrate. Yet the Russians were turning north. They'd had enough and they were leaving as Chen's last ship was sinking.

"Also," he added with a catch in his throat, "inform them that we are abandoning ship. We will need assistance."

"I already have. I don't know if anyone heard me but I already have." The phone slipped out of his hands, bouncing back and forth noisily against the bulkhead at the end of its cord. "And now, I'm leaving, Admiral. You don't have a hold on me any longer."

Chen didn't answer. He stared expressionlessly at the American, but said nothing. Instead he turned back triumphantly to the sterns of the Soviet ships.

Loomis was having more trouble than anticipated in finding his way back to the compartment that had been his for a few brief hours. He wasn't about to leave without that bag. It would be awkward taking it overboard but he was willing to try anything. It was the magnet that kept him in China and it was the reason he'd agreed to cooperate with Magnuson and ended up on XIAN. It was more than worth the chance.

He found himself walking partially on the outer bulkhead of the ship as he got to the main deck. She was taking on water fast. He had to hurry. Few precious minutes remained. Black smoke gagged him. His eyes were streaming. As he neared one of the engine room hatches where flames licked up hungrily at the open air, the deck became hot, so hot he could feel the heat through his shoes.

It was difficult to identify the hatch he wanted for it had been blown off its hinges. The same blast that had ripped off the door had also wrecked the compartment. If he'd been in what remained of the bunk, he'd be a dead man.

Bending down to search under the bunk, he saw that the metal frame had been hit, twisting it into sharp, jagged edges.

The bag. My God, what if the bag had been hit.

But it hadn't. He saw it, intact, wedged neatly behind a piece of jagged metal. He used a torn piece of blanket to help bend the frame back far enough to extricate the bag. As it came free, XIAN shuddered, then heaved farther to starboard. He both sensed and heard the agonizing sounds of a ship breaking up.

So little time! But it was worth it. It would make everything worth it.

Racing back out on the deck, he peered through the smoke for a boat—anything he might swim to. The life jacket Chen had handed him was still secure. That would keep him afloat. But he would not last for long in the frigid water.

Vaguely he glimpsed an outline of something

through the smoke. Straining his eyes, he unconsciously waved his hand in front of his face, as if that would clear the smoke. There was a boat of some kind out there. He could see people in it. He poised on the edge of the slanting deck, looking down at the oily water. The list had to be more than XIAN could bear. A tough ship!

He couldn't take the chance of hitting the hull as he leaped. Backing up a few steps, he prepared to lunge outward.

But before his feet left the deck, the torpedo that Maslov had ordered punched into XIAN's bow.

Loomis was aware of the blast, and of being lifted bodily and propelled helplessly toward the stern by the shock wave. There was also the faintest memory of his body smashing into something. Unbearable pain flooded his body. He lost consciousness mercifully, but not before he felt the icy softness of the East China Sea.

On the bridge, Admiral Chen stumbled to his feet, pulling himself up by the shredded railing. He realized the blood coloring his uniform was his own. Pain racked his body. Flames now licked higher than the bridge. Intense heat puckered his flesh but he had to see for himself.

He'd been watching Loomis since the American appeared on the main deck. When Loomis came back through the hatch, bag in hand, Chen extracted the pistol from his jacket. The contents of that bag belonged to China. But Chen couldn't leave the bridge. For some reason, he was sure he had to stay up there until the last minute. It was his duty. The Captain was dead. There were still some sailors on board and he would stay until they had left. He was levelling the pistol at Loomis with both hands when the torpedo struck.

Chen knew his own end had come. He was badly wounded and it was too late to try to escape. The rumble of collapsing bulkheads came to his ears. The ship had begun to roll. He searched anxiously for Loomis but saw nothing. Then, more than thirty yards from the ship, he saw the American. His life jacket was keeping him afloat, but he was motionless when he should have been trying to get away from the ship. His head hung limply to one side.

Then, Chen's heart leapt. The bag! It was bobbing about twenty feet away from the American. As Chen watched, it filled with water, gradually at first, then more rapidly, until it disappeared below the surface leaving a wake of oily bubbles. Chou's treasure had completed its long journey. In its own way, it had contributed to the People's cause.

And as Chen smiled peacefully to himself, XIAN, with one last violent death rattle, rolled over.

The President held his index finger out to the light, then turned his head slightly toward Magnuson as if measuring something in the distance. "When I took the oath of office, I swore to myself that my finger would never come near that button." He wet his lips with his tongue. "Now, it seems I may have no choice. I depended on trust . . . on faith . . . whatever values other men may have . . ." He chewed on his lower lip briefly as he gathered his thoughts. "I was even pretty sure I'd fire you. You came this close." He brought his thumb near the index finger still held toward the light. A scant inch separated them.

"I thought it was closer than that, sir. I guess I even felt a couple of times you might be right."

"Ah . . . it's all water over the dam." Shaking his head, the President added, "Considering that the people in Beijing seem to be jumping for joy now, I would have thought that Maslov would leave well enough alone. It doesn't make sense, turning on Pickett like that."

At Delta Minus One, another message, this one unintelligible, had gone out to the Soviet missile submarines. The only assumption that could be made in Washington was that Moscow was continuing with the plan. The initial message had gone out to the American ICBM arsenal, both the underground silos and the Trident subs. There could be no doubt that Soviet intelligence was aware of that fact. Yet the Premier had not rescinded the Delta plan. The President hoped the Premier would be as close to the hotline as he was.

At Delta Minus Thirty, Magnuson's communications officer correctly understood the Seventh Fleet message before any of the others in the room. He was ready for the code words Pickett included and in a short time he was able to shout, "Seventh Fleet units engaging Soviet submarines at Tsushima . . . two sunk!"

The President turned to Magnuson, eyebrows raised in question.

"Let's wait just a second, sir." To the elated officer, Magnuson called, "Reconfirm."

Time appeared to have stopped. It seemed to Magnuson that he could count to a hundred each second. It was so important that Pickett neutralize the Russian submarines. It conceivably could keep the Soviet Pacific Fleet steaming north and away from Pickett's forces.

"Confirmed, Admiral," the officer shouted back. It had taken less than a minute.

"I think you can call him now, sir. Pickett's no hostage. Any action on Maslov's part would endanger their entire Pacific Fleet. The Chinese seem to have embarrassed them enough today. I think you can talk to him. He'll call Maslov off."

The President nodded, his face expressionless. "I'll do that." He had agreed with Magnuson that they should intercede for the Chinese also, and stop the fighting at Khabarovsk.

The Soviet Premier acceded to each request. Word was relayed from Washington to Admiral Pickett and then to Beijing. Three of the men Magnuson so badly wanted to be in the right place at the right time had been there, and he silently congratulated himself.

It was during this exchange that Goodrich confirmed Admiral Chen and XIAN had been lost.

Admiral Pickett could think of nothing else to say in his excitement. "But it's all over, Jack." His voice was sympathetic. "Maslov's heading for the barn. It's all over!"

"Like hell it is. You heard what Ben said . . . just as clearly as I did. It came right through that speaker." Royal jerked his thumb at the radio speaker above their heads. "They were abandoning XIAN . . . not far from the main body of the Russian Fleet. Ben heard Loomis calling them. Even though he couldn't answer, he could hear Tom calling." He knew he was shouting at Pickett but it no longer mattered. "Chen just about took them into the middle of the Russian Fleet before they were sunk. Goddamn it, Admiral . . . they were abandoning ship not too far from here."

"Mr. Royal," answered Pickett, his tone hardening, "there's not a hell of a lot I can do for you, or your friend, right now."

"He's right out there," shouted Jack, pointing in what he knew was the right direction, ". . . maybe freezing to death. Nobody can last for long in that water."

"I'm sorry, I can't just order an aircraft carrier off on a search for a missing person floating around in the middle of the ocean. I'm sure other ships are already searching for survivors."

"Which ones? I want to know." Royal's voice had become shrill. He was exhausted. At this point he couldn't have cared less about Pickett or his aircraft carrier. Royal just knew another one of his friends might be near death out there on that damn ocean. And he, Jack Royal, was the one . . . he was responsible for them all.

"Captain Knowlton." Jack heard Pickett talking to his aide. "Would you see that Mr. Royal gets transported to whichever ship is searching for sur-

vivors. And I don't care what the problems are,"
the Admiral said under his breath, "just get him
the hell down to that flight deck and onto the first
helicopter that lifts off."

Knowlton was as understanding with Royal as
he was patient with Admiral Pickett. Taking Jack
gently by the arm, he led him over to one of the air
officers. Jack heard him explain to the man that
they were going down to the flight deck and that
they wanted a helicopter right away . . . Admiral
Pickett's orders . . . to get Mr. Royal over to TEX-
AS. She'd been closest and was searching for survivors of the Chinese destroyer.

Royal was fully aware he wasn't functioning
properly . . . his mind just wouldn't work as he
wanted it to. All he could think about was Tom
Loomis on that damn Chinese destroyer. And then
Ben had called saying it was going down. Something snapped then. Royal imagined a dozen horrible endings for Tom. He realized he was irrational but that damned Admiral was just as stubborn as ever. Screw Pickett! Screw them all! At
least he'd have a chance to get out there and help.
Anything to keep his mind off what might have
happened to Tom.

And then they stepped into daylight on the cold,
windy flight deck. He'd been inside the immense
steel hull of EISENHOWER since departing
Vladivostok. He realized suddenly how little time
had gone by, that not much more than a day had
passed since they sailed. He squinted in the sunlight. His eyes hurt. The roar of aircraft engines
assaulted his ears.

Then Knowlton had him firmly by the arm, leading him to a helo. He saw the two men up front return Knowlton's wave, the co-pilot jerking his thumb toward the rear door. Someone reached out and grabbed his arm, lifting him up and in. Even before he was strapped in, they were airborne, banking off EISENHOWER's port bow and heading south.

Not more than a few minutes passed before he sensed the helo descending. Glancing out the door, he realized they weren't more than a few hundred feet above the water. As he stared blankly at the ocean below, a ship came into view, growing larger as they settled toward her stern flight deck until he recognized the familiar outline of TEXAS.

Friendly faces greeted him. And, as his feet touched TEXAS' deck, the executive officer appeared at his side. "Captain Haven's on the bridge, Mr. Royal. EISENHOWER radioed that you were coming, and the Captain asked to see you as soon as you arrived."

The pilot house was silent as he entered. Captain Haven reclined in his bridge chair, hat jammed over his eyes, paying little attention to what was going on around him. But when Jack walked over to his side and began, "Captain . . ." Haven bolted upright, then jumped down from the chair.

"We're pleased to have you back aboard, Mr. Royal. You and your friends have done a hell of a job."

"Captain, the reason they sent me over here . . ."

"I know. You're worried about Mr. Loomis."

"Yes, sir. I'd like to go out with your men while

you're searching for survivors."

"We've already found him."

Jack recognized something very wrong with the look on Haven's face.

"What's . . . he's alive, isn't he?"

"Yes, he's alive." Haven stared at Royal, holding his eyes, hesitating as he searched for the right words. "But he's been hurt badly. He was more dead than alive when they brought him back. You know . . . the water . . . damn cold . . . tough for anyone to last long in that stuff."

"Is that it? Just the exposure . . . or is it something else?" Jack felt that empty feeling in his stomach . . . the same one he'd felt in Vladivostok when he'd looked into the back seat at the blood and that faraway stare on Miller's face that he knew would be with him forever.

"No. It's more than the water. He had a life jacket when they found him. That's what kept him alive. It's his leg . . . he only has one. The other was a mess. Part of it was missing when they brought him aboard. The surgeon removed the rest down in sick bay . . . right to the hip."

Haven's words were clear, but somehow they seemed to stretch out, each one clipped off after being expanded for what seemed an eternity . . . "right to the hip." That's what Royal heard. "Right to the hip." A man can't get around very well like that . . . a cripple for the rest of his life.

"Why don't you go down to my cabin." It was Haven speaking again. "Make yourself at home. I'll get you myself as soon as you can go in to see him."

"No! That's not the way I want to do it," Jack replied, suddenly calm. "I want to see him now."

"There's nothing you can do for him now. He's still out. You might as well wait until the doc says he's coming around."

"I'll go down there now . . . sit with him until he comes out of it. For Christ sake, don't you know what you just said . . ." Jack sucked in a deep breath, then shouted, "Right to the hip . . . right to the goddamn hip. You better bet your ass I'll go down there right now and sit with him until he comes out of it. How'd you like to come to . . . wondering where the hell you are . . . nobody you know there . . . and suddenly realize you don't have any goddamned leg." He took another deep breath. "You don't see, do you, Captain? That leg of his might as well be my leg. I'm responsible for that leg and I'm going to be sitting right there when he opens his goddamn eyes . . . I'm going to be holding his hand . . . and before he finds out what happened, I'm going to tell him about that goddamned leg. No one else is!"

Haven nodded grimly. "I understand. The XO will take you down there now." Then he added more softly, "Mr. Royal, please give him my respects."

Jack followed the executive officer down into the bowels of TEXAS to the sickbay. It was one of the few places in the ship he'd never been. He was introduced to the ship's doctor who led him over to a bunk in a corner where Loomis lay. His face was cut and bruised. Jack looked down at the lower end of the bed. A hoop arrangement raised the sheets so that it was impossible to tell anything was missing.

"Mr. Royal," said the doctor. "There's something here you might be interested in. When they brought Mr. Loomis into the sickbay, he was still holding this in his hand." The doctor handed Jack a black handle that looked as if it had been part of a suitcase.

EPILOG

February 1985

Admiral Magnuson's office hadn't changed at all. Nor had the Admiral. Nothing appeared to have changed since Royal's last visit. In deference to his callers, Magnuson wore his uniform rather than civilian clothes, his gold-striped sleeves symbolizing an aura of power and authority.

When they entered his office, Magnuson gave little notice to the wheelchair. He came around from behind the desk brushing his flag as usual, a cordial smile on his slim, athletic face.

"Why don't you move your goddamn flag back a few feet," said Loomis. "Some day you're going to knock the son of a bitch over and that's just going to break your heart to see it lying on the floor." His tone was unpleasant. He'd lost weight in the hospital. His face was drawn and tired. His afro haircut looked out of place, the Pancho Villa mustache too bushy for his gaunt features. It drew attention to the dark circles under his eyes. They no longer contained the sparkle that had been much of his charm.

"I may do that, Tom. You may have a point." Magnuson shook hands with each of them, his pleasure in seeing them apparently sincere. "I've read everything about Seagull, especially the reports prepared for Commander MacIntyre. You might like to know some of the other interesting facts. There were no U.S. ship losses. Personnel casualties on our side were acceptable. And, most important, we have access to Chinese oil, and the Russians don't! It was a fantastic success, absolutely fantastic . . . directly attributable to you! I can't thank you enough."

"You're right . . ." Loomis continued nastily.

Royal interrupted him. "We've talked this over, believe me, and we've decided there's nothing you can do for us, Admiral." He paused, looking to Loomis and Goodrich before turning back to Magnuson. "But there is something you can do for Bob Miller."

Magnuson had been afraid something like this was coming. They wanted to start hammering right away. No small talk. No war stories. He'd hoped they might sit back and relax, relate the details that never get into the written reports. He'd expected flak from Loomis. He didn't know Goodrich that well, but thought Jack might have been more pleasant about it.

Miller's death was unfortunate, something that happens in operations of this type. He remembered telling MacIntyre in December how pleased he was that no one had been hurt up to that time. Perhaps it had been bad luck to bring it up then, like mentioning a no-hitter in the eighth inning. Luck seemed to be with them. After the Vladivostok incident, he told MacIntyre three out of four surviving was pretty damn good in this business.

"Anything I can do within reason for Miller's family will be done with a great deal of personal pleasure. He was a fine man."

"You're still as full of shit as the last time I saw you," said Loomis. "The proverbial Christmas goose . . ."

"I didn't ask you here to be rude," Magnuson snapped. "You've all been through a hell of a lot . . . more than most men . . . I'll forget what you said."

Royal touched Loomis' arm gently. "Take it easy, Tom. Let me finish." Jack looked back at Magnuson. The man's eyes were those of an Admiral instead of his old friend. He remembered last summer how Ted had said that the one thing he wanted to avoid was losing their friendship . . . that once Royal began working for him, he would be working for an Admiral, not an old friend.

Losing friends was sad, Jack thought . . . we have so few of them.

"I don't think we're going to ask for the moon, Admiral. The three of us don't really give a damn one way or the other. But Bob Miller had a wife and family, and right now they're still pretty much in the dark about what did happen. I went up to Vermont a few weeks ago to see Margie and the kids and it was something I wouldn't wish on anybody. They're lost . . . they don't understand." Royal wondered why he was talking so rationally, so matter-of-factly. "Oh, for Christ sake, they still don't really know what he was involved in. Everybody can read the papers or watch the news on television. They all know what happened over there, that the Russians and the Chinese had a big shoot out . . . that the Seventh Fleet was there. But, goddamn it, no one knows how the U.S. was involved."

"That's the difficult part of this business, Jack," Magnuson interjected. "No glory."

"Oh, cut the shit." It was the first time Goodrich had spoken. "No one gives a damn about glory anymore. We're talking about someone who's dead . . . the family of a man who's dead. Don't you understand people? Don't you love anyone?"

Before Magnuson could respond, Jack continued. "Forget it. We're not here to start a fight. Admiral, all we want is recognition of what we did . . . or rather, what Bob did. We can worry about the details later. It's got to be something his family can get hold of, something to be proud of so they can understand why he didn't come home." The words came hard. Royal rose from his chair, pacing over by the file cabinets as Magnuson often did. "Maybe I ought to take you up to Vermont with me to meet those people. They're so empty. But they can recover. Right now there's a big hole there in that beautiful family and it's going to stay that way until they know why it's there. The only person who

can do that is you. Do you see what I mean? . . .
Bob's oldest boy, Billy . . . he just stares back at me
with these haunted eyes. He doesn't say a thing to
me. He used to call me 'Uncle Jack' and now he
just stares at me."

"I'm sorry . . ." Magnuson began.

"That's not it," Jack interrupted. "We don't
want you to be sorry. We want you to do what's
right . . . nothing more. I want Billy to be proud of
his father and be able to tell his children and grandchildren what their grandfather or great grandfather did for his country. None of this crap with
the haunted eyes and the furtive looks for the rest
of his life. Just release the information about what
happened. The news people will pick it up and for
a little while those people up in Vermont will be
part of reality again . . . just long enough to get
their feet back on the ground. That news won't last
forever. You don't have to worry about notoriety.
The three of us plan to disappear and keep our
mouths shut. But I want to make damn sure Bob
Miller's family knows why they have to suffer."

"Well . . ."

"Uh, uh, uh . . ." Royal raised his hand. "I'm
not finished yet. Let me tell you why we're here
right now, rather than just blabbing about it to the
first reporter that comes by. Before Bob died, he
asked me to be sure his family knew why. He said
that there has to be a reason for a man to die like
that, and he was absolutely right. I promised, Admiral. I promised that they'd know what happened
to him and why, and I promise you that's exactly
what I'll do if I have to."

"Jack . . . Tom . . . Ben," Magnuson looked at each of them individually. "First of all, believe me. I know exactly how you feel, and I know why better than you'll ever understand. But," he shook his head from side to side madly, "my hands are tied. This office can't release information of that nature."

"Well this time, baby, is going to be the first time." Loomis would have been on his feet in the past, shaking his fist in Magnuson's face. "I've got nobody who gives a shit about this." He waved an empty pant leg at the Admiral. "And I don't care if anyone ever knows. But what Jack's telling you is straight. We'll blow the whistle on this whole goddamn thing if you don't get off that high horse of yours."

"Gentlemen, I'm limited in what I can and can't do. Releasing classified information to the news media is one of the things I can't and won't do." The kinship for the three men that welled up in him when they came into his office was quickly disappearing. Magnuson got up and walked behind his desk again, very careful to avoid the flag. "Very few people in this country know how early we got onto Seagull or how we might have done it. The fact that we knew one country planned offensive operations against another, six months before the fact, and that we would say nothing about it, wouldn't sit too well. And it doesn't particularly matter what side you're on. If you favor the Chinese, we did them a disservice they should never forget. If you side with the Russians, we should have told them we wouldn't go to Vladivostok, or else we should have supported them in their effort to neutralize the so-called yellow tide. If you look at it from an impartial point of view, we should have gone to the UN or set up some sort of special liaison mission to debate it to avoid loss of life. And if our own people know how close the President was to the button . . ." He shuddered at the thought. "No matter how you look at it, there's no way we can release this and still hold our heads up."

"OK. Release it and hang your goddamn head," Loomis snorted.

"Don't be so sharp, Mr. Loomis. You don't have a hell of a lot to be proud of, do you?" Magnuson's eyes narrowed. His finger was pointing directly at Loomis' chest and his face said a great deal more. "I had a very old, very fine friend in Shanghai who lost his life also. We were in touch a few times before he died. He . . ." Magnuson cut himself off.

Loomis glared back across the desk, trying to gauge what the Admiral was keeping to himself.

Magnuson took a deep breath, expelling it slowly. "I guess I'm stuck. My hands are tied. There's nothing I can say, I suppose, that will make you believe me. I've already arranged for a fat government check for Miller's family. They'll never have to worry again. I know that doesn't satisfy you," he shrugged, "but that's one of the ways we can try to make it up to them. A lot of men have died for their country without the glory that's supposed to be associated with that sort of thing. The silent war's a dirty one. And this country's been at war, silently, since 1945, and we're probably going to be that way when the year 2000 rolls around unless we can take advantage of a situation like we tried with this one." He leaned forward. "You know, if the Chinese had been able to take Khabarovsk, we might just have stuck it out with them . . . we might have been able to cut Russia off at the Urals," he added wistfully.

"That's it?" Jack inquired.

"I'm afraid so. There's nothing else we can say to each other." Magnuson stood up, remaining behind his desk. He pushed a button by his phone. "MacIntyre will show you out."

Ben Goodrich stopped just before he got to the door, half turning toward Magnuson. "Why'd you have four of us out there? You didn't really need four. One in each country would have worked just as well."

The Admiral nodded. "You're right . . . as long as that one person survived. In this business you can't be too careful about the success of the mission. And in this case, I was correct. Miller proved that. When we lost him, we still had one man left—instead of none."

"But you really didn't need them in Vladivostok as it turned out."

"I suppose you're right again. But, then, it created a tremendous diversion for Maslov." Magnuson folded his arms over his chest to show he had nothing more to say.

* * *

Mid-winter in northern Vermont is cold, the arctic wind blustery. The ground has been under a snow cover for a couple of months. Almost every day, westerly winds coming off Lake Champlain bring a dusting of snow to add to the cover of the major storms.

Royal had been painstaking on each of the arrangements. He was able to plan everything but the weather. It was bitterly cold, the temperature hovering just above zero that morning. The sun shone brightly in an ice-blue, crackly-cold sky. Neither Magnuson nor anyone else in Washington would approve of this approach, but Royal didn't give a shit either. They could do what they wanted when it was over.

Jack had friends at the networks. The deal he offered was simple. If they didn't like it after they saw what had been done, forget it. He'd cover expenses. If they understood, put it out on the evening news.

TV crews were there as promised.

The procession wasn't an extravagant one. That wasn't the purpose. It was to honor the man. The local American Legion post paraded the flags at the head of the procession. They were followed by Billy Miller's Boy Scout troop. Next came the Little League team Bob had coached that summer. They were bundled warmly against the weather, but each wore his baseball cap. Local townspeople who called Bob "friend" followed.

Then came the caisson. The horses weren't fancy but they moved slowly, raising their hooves high. Snorting and shaking their heads against the icy wind, they hauled the flag-covered casket down the main street of the little town. The local police chief led the riderless horse, stirrups reversed. Bob Miller's family followed, their heads held high. Only pride could replace their loss.

Behind them, at a respectful distance, came Bob Miller's friends. Jack Royal and Ben Goodrich took turns pushing the wheelchair. The only music came from the bagpipes that Bob had loved so well, and the only piece they played was his favorite, "Amazing Grace." At the grave, there was silence. Then one last lament drifted across the snow-covered hills from a lone piper.

Admiral Magnuson received a call later that morning. It hadn't taken long for the word to get to him. It would be a long night and it would be his responsibility to prepare the necessary reports for the media to explain OPERATION SEAGULL.

MacIntyre had a TV set brought into the office. Magnuson watched the procession on the tiny screen, nodding his head in admiration. They'd gotten him right between the eyes . . . they'd gotten in the last word. Magnuson smiled to himself when he noticed what the TV cameramen had missed. The middle finger Loomis had extended in his lap had been meant for him. He accepted that. He switched off the set as soon as he'd heard the piper. There was so much to do and it rested on his shoulders now.

He should never have gone outside. The pros were more dependable.

Before he began, he unlocked the bottom drawer

of his desk and extracted the picture. He smiled as the memories flooded back. They had been so happy then in that strange, new country so far away. He'd been one of the first Americans to go there and those fine people had treated him like a son. Magnuson had been much younger then. His hair was jet black and his eyes still lively and adventurous. And Darby should have been a professional leprechaun with that mischievous grin. On either side of Magnuson stood Li Zhiang and his wife. She had been crippled even then but she stood proud and tall for the camera. Li Han was in front of them, her hands holding Magnuson's around her neck. She was just a youngster at the time, but he had known what a fine, beautiful girl she would be. She'd called him Uncle Ted. He and Li Zhiang often talked about the world they hoped she'd be able to grow up in.

Perhaps Bob Miller's kids would do better.

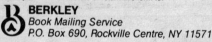

WAR BOOKS FROM JOVE

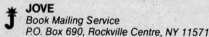